NIGHT OF THE AUTUMNAL EQUINOX

MARY GRAVES

Copyright © 2024 by Mary Graves.

ISBN: 979-8-89465-101-9 (sc)
ISBN: 979-8-89465-102-6 (e)

All rights reserved. No part of this publication may be reproduced, distributed, or transmitted in any form or by any means, including photocopying, recording, or other electronic or mechanical methods, without the prior written permission of the author, except in the case of brief quotations embodied in critical reviews and certain other noncommercial uses permitted by copyright law.

All persons in this book are fictitious and any resemblance to persons living or dead is purely coincidental.

Printed in the United States of America.

Integrity Publishing
39343 Harbor Hills Blvd Lady Lake,
FL 32159

www.integrity-publishing.com

This book is dedicated to love of family,
the greatest of life's treasures.

EPIGRAPH

Ephesians 6:12

For we wrestle not against flesh and blood, but against principalities, against powers, against the rulers of the darkness of this world, against spiritual wickedness in high places.

King James Version of the Bible.

ACKNOWLEDGEMENTS

Thank you, Edit Ink, 1998.

CHAPTER ONE

Slowly the old lady rolled back and forth in the creaky, oak rocker. She listened to the distant howling of her wolf who broke the constant moan of the surf with his eerie sound. So secure she felt with Elkin, her protector, in this desolate place she called home.

High Cliff, as it was known throughout history, was a wild, craggy island off Canada's coast. It was here in New Foundland that Dina Darrendon's grandfather had used his fortune, from sales of his famous artworks, to build the grey, brick castle which stood behind large, black boulders, and elevated high enough to view the ominous North Atlantic. After Grandfather was murdered by art thieves, the estate had become hers, as she was the oldest known surviving relative. Of course the living expenses were horrendous, and up until now she had no trouble paying them with her own money from the sale of her artwork, but time and heartache had dwindled away a large part of her fortune.

The creditors were after her, and refinancing options were becoming slim. Even her wealthy friends offered no more relief. With a quick thrust of her hand, she pushed aside the stack of bills on her table, some dropping to the floor on top of a mildewed pile from last month. Spiders even spun their webs admist the debris.

Leaning forward in her rocker, she turned her head to gaze out the bay window at the low water clouds of dark indian red. *That precious, ocean view, this house, and these lands must stay in the family.* The howl of Elkin once again pierced the June air, and she knew if the estate would fall into others' hands the motion of a future gathering would be destroyed. It would happen during the autumnal equinox on September 23rd, when the sun crosses the equator, and day and night are equal everywhere. In this year 2001, the twenty-first century, the dead and undead Darrendon family members would reunite in the castle corridor. The large vault would be opened after midnight, and they would walk forth into eternity.

Time was running out she knew, and she raised her body from the chair. "Four months. I have only four months," she said loudly. She went toward the winding corridors of the basement to search once more for the letter which could save them all. "I must take light with me," she said. Removing the lantern off the fireplace mantel, she paused to light it with a big wooden matchstick. Its glow lit up the room with a golden hue. Slowly and deliberately she made her way from the front sitting room, down the hallway, and to the basement door. Brushing a tangled sprig of red hair from her face, she grasped the brass doorknob. She opened it slightly, her long, slender hand aching from the strain. Then suddenly she saw it. There were two beady, red, glowing eyes at the bottom of the staircase about eight feet from the ground.

"Elkin," she screamed, the acrid basement smell stabbing her senses. Soon she heard her companion rush through his entryway in the pantry door. His thick, grey fur brushed up against her slender legs. "Elkin, you're here at last. Now get 'em," she ordered. The one hundred and seventy pound wolf bounded down the wooden steps.

I must be more careful she thought, and then she grabbed the rifle from the stairwell wall mount. She set the lantern down and loaded and cocked the gun. Newly armed, she picked up the lantern and proceeded onward until she heard the growls of Elkin and the running footsteps of the big, nocturnal beast. *He must have come in through the underground entrance.* "A new barracade will be made to keep that thing out," she said aloud. Furtively she walked through the winding corridors of moss wallpaper and carpet, the dampness chilling her very bones. Thirteen feet ahead, she knew to take a right at the fork. Then fourteen steps ahead she was forced to climb five stairs into a room measuring twelve by fifteen feet. It was here she would begin to search for the lost letter.

She propped the rifle against the wall nearby. Standing on tiptoes, she raised her five foot and four inch frame to reach and pull forth a large, black brick. The soothsayer gave great directions she thought, feeling its surface for the initials of her grandfather, S. D. for Samuel Darrendon. With all her might, she tugged until the brick toppled down, barely missing her feet. Into the black hole she reached her hand. "Aha," she said when she felt a thin paper in her fingers. She pulled it out, knocked off the dirt, and began to read in the lantern light.

Dear Dina,

I knew this day would come as Seth the soothsayer, the immortal soul, promised to grant my wish to tell you of this secret place. You must only share this revealing poem with one relative with whom you have complete trust. This person must have the courage to fullfill these obligations completely to promote our quest for reunion. Find the items soon, for the soothsayer's premonition told me you would have a future financial difficulty. Sell these stones, and you should have enough money to keep the estate. Follow these steps, and pray nothing serious befalls you. Good luck, and may the power of the stones be with you.

In the hollow of the banyan tree
Fifty feet from Ft. Mariner's pier,
You will find a ten carot ruby
In the shape of a very large tear.

Down to Jamaica
To Grey Grotto Cave
It lies in the lake
Beneath a rock grave.

Saint Lovell's lighthouse
In old Georgia holds
A gem beneath its
Many brick folds.

At Buzzard's Bay
In the oldest Inn
Is a white gem
In a silver tin.

In the graveyard
Of the Atlantic,
You'll find gem five
In a bird's blue beak.

I carefully put these jewels in hidden places only for you. These gems were those of our ancestor, a good pirate, who confiscated them from Mitch the Magnificent. He was an evil pirate who stole the jewels and a woman from a Spanish ship that now haunts the sea. It is because of you, Dina, that the jewels are still in our possession, but you have blanked this tragic moment from your mind. The evil pursuer, Devon, stepson of Mitch, tried to take these stones, and I was in fear of losing them forever. They must remain in familiar hands, for they will bring you wealth to keep the estate. Always remember to take the ocean route through the Atlantic. The good angels I pray to guard you follow those waters but beware. Seth says they too struggle with the evils of the Spanish ghost ship. One last word: the lost Book of Eternity is yours to find.

Love,
Grandfather

Hearing a sudden snarling, she called out, "Elkin, is that you?" Then a fetid odor filled the room, and she felt her hair stand on end and goose pimples protrude on her arms. Scrunching the letter into her skirt pocket, she swung her lantern toward the doorway. Screaming in terror at the red, beady, glaring eyes, she picked up the rifle, aimed it, and stepped back along the wall. Abruptly, the floor beneath her gave away. Falling into open air, she dropped the rifle and lantern. They sank past her as she sailed by trees that extended their arms to cradle her descent. Then, finally, she felt the cool sensation of a pool of water. After plunging deep, she began to fight for submergence. Soon her head bobbed to the surface, she opened her eyes, and much to her surprise, she found herself in a familiar setting behind her own house.

Immediately, she could see what had happened. The basement room she was in grew out of a hill and extended over a lake she called Fern. Two giant pillars supported the basement hideaway. It had been decades since she had been in that end of the house.

Thank goodness the wooden floorboards had given way, or she may have misfired and found herself in the clutches of the mad beast. So often she wondered just where the hideous creature came from, but it, too, was a lost family secret of which one day she would know the truth. Over the years Elkin had usually been successful in chasing him away, but this time it had come too close.

"Elkin," she called. Then she swam for shore. Where could he be? She wondered and pulled a lily pad from her hair.

After squeezing the lake water from her long, purple skirt, she felt for the letter she had plunged into her pocket. She pulled it out to see the inside of it remained dry and the ink unsmeared. Carefully she folded it neatly and stuck it back into her skirt pocket. Then she followed the stone path. It wound through the lush garden that was tended by Dean the live-in gardner. Springtime was here, and flowers were in bloom amid the balsam, fir, black spruce, and yellow, birch trees. A pair of lynx crossed her path on her way up the stone walk. Large, black ravens dotted the trees like sinister dress designs, and she felt the wind stroke her body. It felt like a rain storm was on its way she thought as she rounded the bend. The west side of the castle was coming to an end she knew upon spying the green ivy lacing its way up the fifty-five foot brick wall. One hundred years ago this was only a virgin forest. It had taken one thousand men ten years to build this castle home. It had been her grandfather's dream.

She had vivid recollections of this complicated man with whom she had spent many a summer. He was six feet tall, and he had thick, grey hair ever since she could remember. She had loved him so, for he was her mother's father, and they all had much in common. They were determined, hard working, compassionate people up to a point, and Grandfather had reached that point many times, bringing out his other side. It was a dark, demented, callous side which frightened even the most hardened criminals.

Then, of course, there was the artistic side to Grandfather. It showed his creative ability, for he loved nature and people, especially beautiful, young women, which he included in many of his well-known, still life paintings. It was only through his painting that he felt he could express himself truly. These works were very popular during the 1850s, when Impressionism was in full force. His nudes had their own touch of naturalism and beauty that no one could resist. His paintings were not unlike the professionals whom he had admired at the College Rollin in Paris. He was a master at creating light to give the full effect of nature, yet Grandfather never used elaborate detail. He spent hours in this very garden painting nude women. His days seemed endless and undisturbed.

Spying Elkin's leather chew in the grass, she bounded around the front tower to the entryway only to find him sitting quietly on the soft, braided rug. His grey fur gleamed like silver threads on the dark fabric, and she could see he was fine.

Then she removed Grandfather's letter from her skirt pocket and went into the laundry room to her left. She set the letter atop the clothers dryer, stripped off her wet clothing, and donned a dry, blue skirt and top. Then she slipped the letter into her blue skirt pocket. She exited into the next room and sat down in the rocker by the red brick hearth which spanned eight feet in the twenty foot by twenty foot living area, or greatroom as she called it. There above the mantel she longingly stared at the portrait of her grandmother which was framed in oak. Her auburn hair was pulled back to show off a delicate face and strong green eyes. She had been his favorite nude with skin of ivory, full breasts, and long, firm limbs. Her vibrant eyes and full lips had set his heart on fire. She resembled her own mother she thought, and then suddenly she felt a painful hollowness inside that she could not explain. She rose to check out the pantry.

She loved the way the house was laid out, because it was large and airy with much space for her many hobbies and interests. In the corridor to the castle greatroom, she displayed her Lepidoptera collection which was mounted in its large oak frame on the east wall. She had various assortments, including Ornithoptera Priamus from Australia. As a young women exploring the Outback, she had captured the insect single-handedly. There were five thousand species in all, and each one was carefully mounted and labeled. Many of the butterflies were found on her numerous travels with her grand niece, but after years of netting, she felt guilty of having robbed them of a longer existence. "Life is precious," Grandfather had told her. "Choose carefully what you do with it, and enjoy it to its fullest." This Darrendon attitude reaped many centenarians in the family.

Once in the kitchen, she opened the refrigerator to retrieve the cheese and crackers. In the large hutch near the oak table was her teapot collection. Each one was from a different part of the world she had visited. Carefully she opened the door and took out the blue porcelain one from Paris with the braided handle. Quickly she filled it half full with water from the tap and placed it on the burner. Nothing like a cup of herbal tea to calm the senses she thought, and then she took a seat at the table by the bay window. The sky had darkened considerably since her walk down the path, and she could see lips of rain fall, kissing the grass below. For ten minutes she watched while sipping tea out of her blue cup. Then the sky's hair grew matted and more menacing, and she heard thunder crack like a whip. Suddenly a lightening bolt struck her favorite yellow, birch tree, sizzling and snarling its bark. It also sent a glistening flash through the suncatcher on the window. It was a stained-glass ornament carved in the shape of a beach pail. It was at that time Dina became paralyzed with a gripping fear of a tragic past. So deep was the memory and so terrifying the thought that she drifted off to a time she had forgotten.

"Octopus, come here," she said. Gently she held the red-legged blob in her small hand. The waves of the Atlantic were calm, and the sun was shining down on her, warming the day to seventy-five degrees. She sat playing with her bucket, her shovel, and her newfound friend, building mounds with her large shell and puffin bone.

The eight-year-old knew only how to play where she sat contentedly in front of their castle home. To the west was Ramea Island, and far to the east, outstretched into the North Atlantic like a foot, stood the Grand Banks. She hiked carefully among the small, rocky protrusions with her bucket and shovel, and now and then, she tapped a toe at a meandering crab.

This was summertime, and the beach sand felt warm to her feet, and the wind, coming from the west, carressed her sun-kissed face. Ten feet from where she walked she saw small caplin swimming and scurrying away from large, hungry cod. Off in the distance she noticed large boats filled with fishermen called longliners who hunted patiently with their small lines baited. Near them, some gill netters were preparing their nets weighed on the bottom and held veritcal by floats. She walked faster until she came upon a four foot crevice in the rocks. She climbed in and out. Then, turning toward the beach, she spied something floating in the water. From a distance it looked like a large dolphin, but a closer look proved that vision false when a bloated, pitted face came into view.

Screaming frantically and running toward home, she tripped on a rock. Her bucket flew up in the air and came crashing down into the sand. Suddenly she heard her grandmother and mother shouting her name. "Dina. Dina, are you all right?" Two fleshy arms embraced her, and she smelled her grandmother's sweet perfume amid her breasts. Then, she lay her head between the large mounds.

"The man, mom. The dead man."

"What man?" Mother asked. Dina pointed toward the sea.

"Stay here while we go check," Grandmother said. She released Dina and pushed her down into the sand.

Dina heard the old woman rasp, and then the comforting ray's of the sun disappeared. Wearily they strode toward the figure, a mass that bobbed back and forth with the waves. Gasping readily at the bloated flesh, Grandmother reached down and tugged at a large rope tied to its waist. Then rapidly she motioned her daughter to retrieve their sack on the beach. In a few minutes, Mother donned her wet suit, snorkel, and flippers, and in seconds she was heading into the water holding and using the line as her guide. Soon her head disappeared in the dark sea, but shortly she submerged, gulping for air.

"Shark," Grandmother yelled, pointing to a large fin skimming the water.

Quickly she ran to help her daughter, diving in and swimming until she reached her side. Putting her arms around her neck, she pulled her toward shore along with the waves that helped wash them both inland. Mother's face was blue, and her body was limp with a jagged and bloody bite mark on her thigh. She was dead. Grandmother started weeping as two men appeared from behind a large cliff fifty yards down the beach. Suddenly they started running toward Grandmother with their knives extended. Quietly Dina slipped into the crevice she had discovered earlier that day. In a crouched position, she was completely hidden by the rock.

"Don't kill me! Don't kill me!" she heard Grandmother scream. Then she heard knife blades slashing as if to cut the air itself. Soon it grew quiet, and Dina peaked her head out from her hiding place. The bodies of her mother and Grandmother were gone. Only a streak of red could be seen in the foamy waters. The two men were gone too, or so she had thought.

Hauntingly numb with terror, she stumbled in a daze toward the still bloated figure gliding on the surf. Then without warning, a large wave broke, cascading the human being onto dry land. Casting it suddenly upon a sharp rock, its stomach split open. A gold sack spilled out which she looked upon with disgust. Quickly and without forethought, she ran up, grabbed the bag, and raced back to the crevice. Once there, she opened the bag which was held fast by a string and carefully dumped its contents onto the floor. Five sparkling gems lay at her feet. Suddenly feeling dazed, she nervously stuffed the gems into the secret pouch in her leather belt. Then Dina blacked out just as the sun peaked its head from behind a cloud.

When she awakened, she was no longer in the tight crevice but on a bed in a room lit only with a small lantern on a corner table. Crisp sheets like a protective coat had been pulled around her clothed body, and the pajamas she wore she had never seen before. Carefully emerging from the linens, she crept to the door. Outside she could hear the voices of men, maybe two or three. Afraid for her life, she dared not open the door, just yet, so she only listened.

"The bodies. What did you do with them, gravedigger?" a gravelly-voiced male spoke.

"We put them in a bag and buried them six feet under out by the old graveyard on Boarder Road. Lars too, I'm afraid. Another dead comrade, but no one'll ever find them there, Devon," the gravedigger answered.

"And the gems?"

"What gems?" a third man asked.

"You mean Lars, the tub of lard, wasn't carrying the powerful gems?"

"Not that we could tell. He'd been in quite a mess when we came back to retrieve the girl. His body had been split open on the rocks," the gravedigger said.

"And the girl didn't have them either?"

"No. We searched her too, and then we even followed the rope that was tied to Lar's body out to a sunken ship. But we couldn't find them there either," spoke the third man in an irritated tone.

"That shark took care of that snooping woman though," the gravedigger said.

"They must be somewhere. I must have those stones," the gravelly-voiced man called Devon said. Dina opened the door just enough to see the long-haired, blond male with brilliant green eyes. A black-haired scorpion climbed his arm and settled on his shoulder. "I'll find them if it takes a hundred years. I will use their power, and then I will be the one to turn the gems in to the high masters." His eyes grew large like sand dollars as he slammed his fist into the table.

"We'll have to do another more thorough search, but what about the girl?" the gravedigger said.

Soon Dina noticed a purple haze appear in the far corner of the room, and then a man appeared. A deep scar rode over his left eyebrow, hardening his soft hazel eyes, and above his thick lips stood a dark moustache.

"I will pick the flesh off the red-haired child's bones first before you kill her, my brother Devon."

"Damn you, Oliver. We will not torture the girl. Instant death is all I want for her. Then you can bury her with the others," Devon said. The gravedigger nodded.

"You can't stop me." Oliver's hazel eyes looked hard and cold as frozen tundra. He held out his arm, which had a a strip of flesh missing, and pointed at Devon.

"Stop it now," Devon called out. Then he stood and pointed back at the creature. "I banish you back into your statue of stone." Soon Oliver disappeared, and Dina tried hard not to gasp.

Slowly and quietly Dina pulled the door shut, tore off the pajamas, and quickly donned the clothes she found on the red, velvet chair. The gems had not been discovered in the belt's secret pouch she knew, and then she notched the leather tighter about her thin waist. The belt's inside slot was so well concealed that sometimes she had a hard time finding it. Rapidly she tied the bed sheets together in strong knots, securing one end of its length to the bed post. Then she walked over to the one window in the room and gazed down three stories to a stone driveway. The window opened easily, and then she lowered the sheet rope to the ground below. Gently she began to slide herself to freedom's open gate.

Halfway down she lost her grip and fell with a thud to the ground. In an instant, she heard dogs barking. Quickly she stood upright. She must get over the fence she knew, and then she ran toward the wooden barrier which stretched ten feet into the air. Climbing a large birch tree, she clammored over the top just as two dobbermans savagely lunged at her feet.

This time, the drop to the other side left her bruised and with a swollen ankle. Limping, she headed across the road into the bog. Less then ten feet in front of her was a river docking area with a canoe, two paddles, a cushion, a rain jacket, a sack of dried fruit and nuts, and a two-gallon jug of water. What luck, she thought, and then she pushed the craft from the bank, jumped in, and paddled rapidly. The river was wide and cold with a strong current that pushed her along. Quietly she passed many stunted trees, the smell of their rot permeating the air. Lichens, mosses, and ivies covered every limb visible, dressing them in velvet clothing. The night was dark, but the pale moon, a waning crescent, had a halo around it. In the shadows, a family of black bears ambled through the forest, and an otter splashed about in front of her canoe.

Soon the wind began to pick up speed, and she donned the oversized raincoat she found partially tucked away beneath the seat. Then the rain began to come, and she tucked her red hair inside the hood. When a cloud completely covered the moon, the forest around her grew black and thick as ink, the sound of an owl echoing in the distance. She tried hard, through the blinding rain, to look for shelter. Then the tiny slice of moon slipped out and shone a hazy light, and up ahead in the midst of a large sprawling tree, she saw the outline of a cabin.

Edging her canoe toward the shore, she stepped out, sinking into thick, sticky muck. Each time she tried to pull herself free, she seemed to sink deeper. Sensing the quagmire would overtake her, she screamed for help.

"Save me. Somebody save me," she hollered through the steady rainfall.

Right before the muck crept up the back of her neck, her feet seemed to hit solid ground. Feeling helpless as a wingless bird, she began to cry tears for her mother and grandmother. Why had such a horrible fate become them? What was happening to her young life? Blurry-eyed, she gazed ahead at a hulking figure approaching from behind the sprawling tree. It looked twenty feet tall from her position, and as it came closer, she believed it to be a beast she had read about in a book once.

Bending down on its knees, it began to scoop the mire from her shoulders. Its breath blew the putrid stench of rotted teeth, and its tongue stuck out of the left corner of its mouth as if lodged there indefinitely. Atop its pointed head, it had no hair. The sallow complexion, riddled with deep pits, held three eyes of a deep, dark shade, and its nose was large and furry inside. Grunting and groaning, it reached its three-fingered hands beneath her armpits and began to pull. In fear, she closed her eyes and heard the sucking sound of muck and felt the creature bring her up, leaving her shoes behind.

Laying on the hard, wet, cold ground, she finally opened her eyes. A horrifying scream from the depths of her soul she emitted upon beholding the beast with clear vision.

Then the howl of a wolf broke the night, and she saw the beast jump up and run into the forest. Gently she felt the sandy tongue of a large animal lick her face. Quietly it wimpered, and then it lay next to her, attempting to keep her warm. Gathering strength, she raised herself from the ground. Then the wolf tugged her coat sleeve, pulling her toward the distant cabin. Suddenly she saw a golden glow coming from one of the windows. She approached the door and saw a figure of a man standing tall, and then she collapsed.

She came to on her back and clothed in an oversized t-shirt. She was sprawled on a mattress in what looked like an attic. Four wooden beams lay at a sloping, vertical angle only two feet from her head. To the right was a small, glass window which looked out over the treetops, and stretched out next to her in a soft, warm heap was a large, grey wolf with a bushy tail. His familiar smell told her it was the animal who had chased off the beast. Propping up her head, she saw a beautiful, antlered elk walking through the undergrowth of the woodland home.

"You, too, came from the undergrowth," she said to the animal beside her. "So I will call you Elkin."

Then she spied a tall, bearded man, as skinny as a bean pole, holding out a piece of salt to the seemingly shy but tame elk. On top of his head, which was cocked at an angle, he had an old, blue cap. His hands looked as knotted as old, tree roots, and his long legs were not youthful as he walked with a slight limp. His holey, blue jeans were held up with suspenders, and a long-sleeved, red, plaid shirt covered his bony arms. He looked about as tall as Grandfather at six feet, but his beard was more stringy and pure white, unlike Grandfather's grey one.

In need of nourishment, she removed the t-shirt and donned her dry clothes that stood in a pile near her pillow. Then she made her way to the ladder at the foot of the mattress. Elkin, her new friend, quickly jumped down. Once on the first floor, she found herself standing behind a worn, rose-colored chair.

Next to it was a pot-bellied stove, sooty and black with dirt. Straight ahead on an old wooden counter, she found a plate of food consisting of eggs and bread. Shaking, she gulped the food down and slowly felt herself regaining strength. Burping uncontrollably after hastily slugging down the cow's milk, she came face to face with the hermit.

"You're lucky to be alive," he muttered through yellow, stained stubbs of teeth. "My wolf dragged you up to the cabin door two nights ago. I found you hunched over all mops and brooms," he said. Then Dina remembered, running her hands through her greasy hair. Two days, she thought, was an extended sleep from what she wished was just a horrible nightmare.

"Who are you, and where are you from?" the old man asked. He slapped his hat on the counter, exposing a bald head.

"I am Dina Darrendon from High Cliff," she said. Then she told him of her castle home. She failed to tell him of the murderous tragedy and shark attack because she herself could not believe it, and she did not trust this old man yet.

"I found this too," he said while pulling a leather belt from the top cabinet. Dina grabbed the belt quickly and then recalled what she had placed in its secret pouch. Feeling the hidden area with her fingers, she knew her gems were still safe. The gems the gravediggers were after were hers and hers alone. The man Devon, with the green eyes, would never find them. Sucking in her stomach, she put the leather belt through her pant loops and drew it tight.

"Where am I?" she asked. "I live on an island on the beach not far from Ramea Island. Is this place far away?"

"Yes child, it is. You've journeyed farther than you thought. I live about five hundred miles inland. There isn't a town for miles. I suspect your family will be looking for you. Did they know which way you were headed?"

"No. Actually I was being chased by some very evil men who had taken me captive. I traveled down the river by canoe, and it seemed like hours on end before I spotted your cabin. Then there was the beast," she said, her voice beginning to quiver.

"Oh, you mean Big Barney. He's quite frightening to look at, but he would do you no harm. He doesn't have much of a mind, but he's usually gentle. I found him a couple of years ago stumbling about naked and nearly starved. He lives in a cave over yonder. I guess he was banned over at the nearest settlement for stealing sheep and chickens. A man's got to eat." He chuckled.

"In the meantime, don't be in a hobble about it. I'm sure your family will come looking for you," he said. Then Dina felt tears making a trail down her cheek. "Wolf has taken' a liking to you. Why don't you two get to know each other a little better while I chop wood for tonight's fire. Just make yourself at home. And this weekend, if your family hasn't shown up yet, I'll make a trek down river and see what I can do." She saw him take an old, beaten ax off the wall. "The spiders are working their webs, Dina, so should be a fair morning."

Spiders or not, she did not care much about the weather. She was just happy to be safe for now, but would that evil man Devon and his lot come here and kill her. She wondered, and then she stroked her belt.

Upon stepping outside with Elkin, she spotted a chicken carcass in a heap on the ground. Suddenly she felt a sickening feeling overwhelm her. That bloated man's body on the beach was so grotesque, yet those jewels so beautiful. She thought he had eaten them to hide them. To whose sunken ship did the rope from the corpse lead?

They started walking down a wooded path, and then they heard Knotty call. "The toads are out. Rain is coming soon." He motioned them back toward the cabin.

Soon they were seated around the kitchen table. "What does that mean about the toads?" she asked him. What do they have to do with weather she wondered.

"They soak up the moisture, my girl. After living in nature as long as I have," he said, "you get to make observations about your environment. I've been able to forecast the weather pretty good by watching the skies, birds, insects, trees, flowers, and by tasting the air, feeling the dampness of the ground, and even by the aching of my bones. Mind you, I'm not schooled, but I've noticed a pattern of sorts. For instance, this morning I looked at the sky and at the red sun, and I recalled this poem.

If red the sun begin his race, be sure the rain will fall apace. In fiery red the sun doth rise, then wades through clouds to mount the skies. Remember last night when the moon had a circle around it?"

"Yes."

"The moon with a circle brings water in her beak."

"Oh, I like that one too," Dina said, laughing for the first time since the tragedy.

Soon Knotty leaned over and grabbed some bread off the counter. "Have a piece, my child. It's so nice to have company out here. I've been alone for most of my life. My wife died in the city when we were just in our early twenties, and I decided to live out my days as a loner, making and meeting my needs from nature. I've done very well for myself so far. I guess I'm just a healthy critter." He poured her some tea into a chipped mug made of hardwood.

"What do you do with all of your time?"

"Time? I don't have any time. I fish and hunt for my food almost every day. I chop wood for my fires. I build, and I tend to my foul, cow, and garden. Time? I haven't any."

Dina spent the rest of the week waiting for help to arrive and absorbing Knotty's weather tips. On Friday, Grandfather came galloping on top his golden horse.

"I knew you would save me, Grandfather." She jumped for joy, and then she and Elkin dashed into the meadow to meet him.

"Mother and Grandmother are dead. You're the only one I have left."

"Dead, you say?"

"Yes, a shark killed mother, and two men killed Grandmother back at the beach days ago."

"Justice must be served. But thank God you're alright," Grandfather said. Then he lept from the saddle. "I've searched endless hours to find you." They wept hard and hugged in relief feeling secure in the safety of love.

"The hermit, Knotty, took me in. He found me on his doorstep one week ago after this wolf here saved me from a beast. Come with me." She ran toward the cabin motioning to him with her hand. After tying his gelding to a nearby tree, he followed close behind.

"So you're my Granddaughter's savior," Grandfather said, reaching out a hand to the thin, straggly figure that stood inside the kitchen. "My soothsayer pointed me to this area. Then, about twenty miles back, the townsfolk told me about your cabin, and I thought I might find my Dina here. You have a reputation for taking care of wounded and stray animals."

"Yes, sir. This was one scared rabbit when I found her." Knotty pointed a bony finger at Dina. "What's this all about anyway, Grandfather? Pull up a chair, fill me in, and maybe I can help." Grandfather sat down, and the story began to unfold.

After selling many artworks, Grandfather bought a large boat and set sail looking for a treasure on board a ship that had sunk hundreds of years ago in the North Atlantic. Its captain, an ancestor pirate whose sunken ship had once held these gems, had confiscated them from Mitch the Magnificent, an evil man who had stolen the gems and a woman from a Spanish vessel. Grandfather found the ship and the treasure consisting of five perfect stones but soon he realized that a crew of sailors had followed him to the booty. He paid them well, but they were greedier than most men. This wicked crew admitted being led by an evil man named Devon. He was Mitch's stepson and child of the abducted woman. The sailors wanted the goods all for themselves. So Grandfather hid the jewels in a golden sack inside one of the men whom he had killed in a mad rage upon discovering their evil plan to steal his booty. The other two men had escaped his blade by jumping overboard. He did not know whether they were dead or alive, but apparently they swam for shore and survived the cruel ocean. Then during rough seas, the dead man with the bag in his innards washed overboard. Attempts to lasso him were futile when the rope encircled the body but pulled loose from Grandfather's hands. It had been Lar's body Dina saw washed ashore being trailed by Grandfather's rope. And those men who had killed Grandmother were the two escaped, callous crew members.

"I believe it was Devon's men, the ones who tried to steal your booty, who murdered Grandmother as she held onto my dear mother's body. They thought you hid the jewels days later in the sunken ship near shore. They never thought to search the insides of that corpse," Dina said.

"What do you mean?" he asked between sobs. He hung his head low and began to weep tears of deep sorrow for his dead wife and daughter.

When Dina explained that it was she who confiscated the jewels from the dead man's innards, Grandfather stopped crying and gave a sigh of relief. Quickly she unbuckled her belt and dumped its contents from the secret pouch onto the table. The five rocks gleamed and sparkled in the sun's rays shinning through the window. A ruby, emerald, star sapphire, diamond, and topaz all of perfection lay before them.

Knotty leaned back in his chair and spoke in a serious tone. "Of such wealth I have never yearned. Why are these so important to you?"

"It is important for the name and future of the Darrendon family. In years to come, you shall understand completely, Dina," Grandfather said. He carressed her face with a fingertip.

Quickly Dina explained to Grandfather about the men who had taken her prisoner and about the great escape. "Maybe they followed you here," Grandfather spoke in a worried tone.

"I even saw the evil leader, Devon, you spoke of earlier. He wants these stones for their power," Dina said. "He also has a brother, Oliver, a ghost, who is crueler then most men. Devon sent him to be imprisoned back into his stone statue."

"An Oliver statue. I wish I knew his Spanish mother's married name so I could place it geographically. It's probably near one of Devon's meeting places. We must not let these gems fall into the hands of evil. Come. We must go now," Grandfather said. Then he stuffed the stones into his front pocket.

Dina gave Knotty a very long hug and kissed him gently on the cheek. He had taken care of her as if she was his own. He squeezed her hard, and his eyes teared at the corners. Then she jumped up high onto the gelding with Grandfather.

"Take Elkin. He's yours now. I'll get another pup this summer," Knotty said. Then the wolf howled a good-bye. "The locusts are singing. Should be dry weather for your trip." He smiled and waved and ordered Elkin to go. Then Dina took a last look, held tight to Grrandfather, and they raced off through the field.

"I've got a noggin to scrape with those men," Grandfather said. Then they rounded the bend with Elkin, toward their castle home. "Only days ago, when I went to Seth, my soothsayer, to help me find you, he also advised me what to do when I reconfiscated the gems."

"And what might that be?" she asked.

"I must take a journey, for it is the one I promised to take Grandmother on before she died. I will take these jewels and hide them for safekeeping as the need will arise for their use someday. This trip will be for the memory of the dead ones, Grandmother and Mother. Someday you shall find the gems again, and we shall all be reunited in the great vaulted room. Don't worry, my little one," he said. She sighed and hugged him tighter.

"I do love you so."

"And I love you, too. And you're safe now, Dina, but always beware the evil Devon, a centenarian. He may walk the earth with you for many years to come." He squeezed her small hand. "Seth says Devon will receive hints from his own prophet about the whereabouts of the gems, but only we must know the exact location of the stones. My Dina, he's out there somewhere, and he and his lot will congregate in the areas of the world where these valuables will be hidden and waiting only for you. You see, Devon has split loyalties. One is for Mitch the Magnificent who spared his mother's life and the lives of his brother and himself. The possibility is great, however, that Devon's own father was horribly murdered by Mitch. His second loyalty is with the crew of the Spanish ghost ship, his true family."

"Then both Mitch the Magnificent and the Spanish ghost ship and its offspring band against us," Dina said aloud. Grandfather agreed.

Jolted back to the present by the telephone, Dina regained her senses. After three rings, it stopped, but soon it started again, so she picked up the receiver. "Hello. Hello," she said. But no one answered back. She slammed down the receiver and feared a night prowler was approaching. With Elkin by her side, she made her rounds and then went upstairs to her room. Quietly she lay in bed reading over repeatedly the letter she had found that morning.

By early evening, she lay exhausted. Even small signs of hunger had abandoned her. The past memory, just relived, was making her future clear to her now she knew, and she drifted off to sleep.

The alarm awakened her at six a.m., and she arose feeling as fresh as a budding leaf. The letter was still there under her pillow. She kept going over in her mind about the part demanding a courageous individual. She needed someone young who possessed bravery, strength, smarts, and a good knowledge of sailing and diving. She knew only one person who would be capable of completing the difficult chore ahead. Sentra, her companion on those butterfly expeditions, was her grand niece. Sentra was the eventual offspring of a dear sister whom had passed into spirit. She was a meteorologist, and she could sail anywhere. Dina called her. She answered on the third ring.

"My precious one. So good to hear your voice. Please come to New Foundland at once. I have some important business to discuss with you."

"Yes, I would love to see you again. I have an accrued four month vacation in two weeks. I'll make arrangements to fly in to High Cliff."

"That will be fine, Sentra. I give you my love," Dina said.

Standing in front of the bedroom mirror encased in a black lace camisole and slip shorts she studied her wrinkle-free face and body. She felt beautiful at age seventy and hoped small signs of arthritis would not damage her long, thin fingers. Her breasts, still firm, rose in two plump mounds, and her thin waist and hips accentuated two long legs. Her slender arms were attached to two broad shoulders, and she felt fit from her daily workouts with her beloved Elkin. She would run a mile, and then perform muscle firming exercises which included weight lifting. Oh, how she longed for a romantic encounter. It made her feel revived and refreshed, and she needed that boost now to regain strength.

It was nearly seven o'clock, and he would be there soon. Waiting patiently by the window, she saw him ride up on his black bike. Her lover was a retired art dealer from down the lane. She had met him by the seafood market last week and invited him over for a viewing of her best work. They had a sizzling attraction from the start, and Dina longed for this moment. Upon opening the large window, she saw him look upward.

"Come through the side door to the left of the front tower. I'll meet you at the top of the steps," she said. Then she slid her tongue over her freshly brushed teeth. There was a small amount of time for love, she knew, and an even lesser amount to make arrangements for Sentra's visit.

Hearing a tap at the back entrance to her bedroom, she rushed over to greet her guest. Dressed in small, tight, blue shorts and a tank top of yellow, he looked younger than his years. His muscles glistened, moistened with sweat. A bouquet of yellow flowers he handed to her, and then he brushed back her red curls and kissed her passionately on the lips, igniting their fire.

"Oh, how I have waited for this moment, my red-haired beauty. From the first time I saw you, I wanted you," he said, gazing at her loveliness.

After sending him on his way into the noonday sun, she began to prepare a room for Sentra's arrival. Choosing the suite adjacent to her own, she changed the black bed linens to lavender. It was Sentra's favorite color she remembered, and then she thought back to the time they had fought over the lavender-colored Grenitz butterfly they had found in Nova Scotia. Of course, Sentra had let her have it for her collection but only for exchange for frequent viewings. She had visited often coming from Fort Mariner, Florida, sailing in on the Empress, her magnificent craft. Her grand niece would be perfect for the difficult chore, and the young woman's trustworthiness and desire to help others less fortunate were other qualifying characteristics.

Dina knew her front and back for they had traveled extensively in search of new sensations. They spent Sentra's teenage years traveling and sharing a kindred spirit. Dina could barely wait to see her.

Almost two weeks had passed during which she cleaned and prepared. Now, she had time to tend to Elkin who was due for a bath and a trim. They walked to the outdoor shower in the backyard by the pool where she placed her supplies on the concrete table. "Elkin, stand beneath the showerhead," she ordered. The old, yet lively, wolf obeyed. She held his six foot long body steady and washed him with a gentle moisturizing soap, the froth running like tails down the silver drain. Then she smelled something odd, and when she looked up, something in the distance caught her eye. Smoke was pouring like grey frothy water from the open castle window at the front tower.

Jumping to her feet, Dina ran to the fire with a running hose in hand. Elkin followed, barking frantically. Before she could come within ten feet of the blaze, she spied the beast hobbling down the front drive. He was crying out something which she could barely understand. "I lit it up," he said. Then he ran into the woods.

"Stay, Elkin," Dina said. Then carefully she aimed the hose at the open window. Within twenty minutes the blaze was extinguished, leaving only some ash and smoldering carpet in the empty tower room. It was only a small space at the top of a flight of steps that led to a bedroom further upstairs. Had the beast become jealous of her amorous encounter weeks ago with the art dealer?

Relieved at the quick control of the blaze, she turned off the hose and hurried maid-like to clean the space. She stripped out the carpet and found a small door underneath the far right corner. Lifting it, she came upon a tiny room which must have been behind the closet wall below. Lighting a lantern, she lowered herself into the opening with Elkin right behind her. It was a strange arrangement with a small table and chair pushed into a little corner. Upon the table was a leather-bound book which was engraved with the family name of Darrendon. Although the book was bolted down to the wooden funiture, she brushed the dirt off the chair and sat down to read by the lantern light. In amazement, she looked at the words engraved in gold. "The Book of Eternity," she read aloud. She soon found it contained a history of the family, recorded in the year 1816.

Apparently one of the family members was burned at the stake for dabbling in witchcraft. She had been a truly good witch but was twisted before death and now possessed an evil spirit. Her name had been Sazran she read. Before she died, she vowed to be changed in spirit and reunited with her family in the year 2001, on September 23rd. The book went on to explain what Grandfather had told her.

She also found out there was a spell cast on the directions and map to the great vault not allowing the information to be revealed until the autumnal equinox. But before she was able to turn the page, the door above slammed shut, blowing out the lantern and casting Elkin and her in pitch darkness. She felt around the room for any openings but found none until she saw part of the outside wall open up and a head peak in.

"What are you doing in here?" a voice boomed out. She could see the outline of a face through beams of light. The opening obviously led outside she saw and rushed to the entrance behind Elkin. "I heard a strange sound coming from the castle near my maintenance shed, Dina."

"It's so good to see you, Dean," she said. Elkin playfully bit the man's calf. Pushing back his greasy cap, the ancient man smiled, showing a toothless mouth. "Were you upstairs? Were you the one who shut the door above?" she asked.

"No. It was the beast. He started the fire, and then he circled back after you went inside and shut you in there. I doubt he knew about the other entrance. He must want you as his prisoner." He chuckled and stuck a blade of grass between his lips. "I'll warn him of his eminent extinction if he does it again. By the way, Dina, I've grown just the right plants for Sentra. Come to the garden with me, and I'll show you what I have this time."

The all-knowing man motioned them down the path where she spied the colorful plants like an artist's palate ahead through the trees. He was a master gardner, among other talents, she knew as she feasted on the varieties of flowers that were difficult to grow in this soil. Tons of New Foundland tulips in red, yellow, and white outlined the circular plan. The next row consisted of sweet peas, gardenias, and delicate pink roses. It was magnificent, and she could pick a big, beautiful bouquet for Sentra in a few days.

Thanking the gardner for releasing them from their cell, she and Elkin padded back to the front of the castle to check out the door in the burned out room. It was the one that had so mysteriously closed. When they arrived, the place smelled strongly of soot. In the corner on a tall, wooden table was The Book of Eternity encased in glass. The beast must have moved it up here she thought upon gazing at the open trap door below. The case was fastened tightly, and she searched for something to break it. She soon left the room to find a tool while Elkin remained behind. She raced down the tower stairs and turned the corner. Then, she felt something strong grab her from the rear and lift her off the ground. Was her life about to end in this one petrifying moment?

CHAPTER TWO

"Surprise," Sentra said. Then she laughed.

"Let me down, you." Dina's feet touched the ground and she turned and hugged Sentra. Then Elkin came bounding down the steps to greet the guest.

"You look well," Dina said. Intently she studied the young woman. Sentra's long, blond hair hung straight around her oval face. Within it, two green, almond-shaped eyes stared at her lovingly, and her full mouth turned into a smile, exposing a decorated incisor. It showed a carving of a rose filled in with gold. Dina remembered her having it carved once in the Caribbean while on a butterfly expedition.

"I called earlier to let you know my flight had arrived, but no one answered."

"Very thoughtful of you, Sentra. I'm just so glad you're here. And I've found something about our family history," Dina said. She grabbed one of Dean's discarded sprinkler pipes from the ground. "Come with me."

The two turned and walked up the steps behind Elkin. Easily Dina retrieved the book from the case with a crushing blow from the pipe. Carefully she scraped the broken glass of tiny and sharp prisms into a corner with her shoe. Then quickly they took the book to Dina's bedroom for a private reading. Together they devoured its contents explaining the history of the family dating back hundreds of years.

"A witch in the family," Sentra mused. Carefully she read the letter written by Samuel Darrendon and quickly agreed to carry out the mission she found too exciting to turn down. "This is a journey that I look forward to with pleasure. It will be fulfilling to restore the destiny of our family, Great Aunt. Those gems are as good as ours."

Before Dina tucked The Book of Eternity into her suitcase, she saw the back pages were empty. The route map to the vault remained a mystery. As for Grandfather's poetic map route, Sentra and Dina both memorized its contents and burned the paper in candlelight.

"No one shall read this poem again," Dina said. They watched the last corner of paper turned to ash, mesmerized by the flames.

Sentra had acquired over time a four month vacation from her job as a chief meteorologist at the local television station in Ft. Mariner. The weather would be warm, and although they would be in the early hurricane season of June, she assured Dina that she would not let her nasty experience with previous tropical weather intimidate her. Using her meteorology skills and the common sense forecasting she had taught her, Dina knew she would be able to overcome the great dangers that lie ahead. One week of preparation was in order, and Dina felt good about accompanying Sentra as she still felt spry as a grey squirrel.

Sentra adored Elkin, and they were often found next to the fireplace in her room where she read and mentally mapped her route. Would the gems still be in their hiding places? Would the weather be accommodating? What did the future hold Dina wondered.

After seven days, locking up the castle had been easier then she had imagined. She also wondered how long her money would last. Of course, Sentra offered to pitch in, too. The flight to Fort Mariner, Florida was smooth, and the walk to the boat dock refreshing. Once on the Empress, Dina helped Sentra check off items required by the Coast Guard. After all, they needed a safe adventure she thought to herself, and she made sure the craft was properly registered with the state. The boat already held personal flotation devices for rough seas and calm water, throwable devices in the shape of a ring, red flares, orange distress flags, an electric distress light, handheld air horns, and fire extinguishers. Other gear included oars, an anchor, with five times as much rope as some of the depth sailing in, a first-aid kit, a tool kit, a rigging knife, a horsehoe buoy, a Dan buoy, a personal harness, docklines and fenders, and a local chart.

A duffel bag filled with clothing and personal items included sea boots, hats, visors, suntan lotion, and seasick remedies. Sentra was well aware of the instruments she would need, and she checked each one to make sure it was working properly. The compass, depthsounder, VHF radio transceiver, knotmeter, hand-bearing compass, windspeed, Loran-c for geographical location of the boat for long-range navigation, single sideband and ham radios were all in good condition.

Her forty-foot vessel, the Empress, was in shipshape too. Carefully she swabbed the deck for dirt and oil spills from her last venture at sea. In the cabin below, Dina decided to wait for Sentra to review the route with her. In ten minutes, Sentra appeared wet and dirty from her cleaning duties. While taking a seat on the vinyl couch next to Elkin, she took a folded unmarked map from her pocket.

"First, we'll locate and collect the gem near the pier," Sentra said. She pointed at her paper. "Then we'll set sail for Jamaica's north coast to Grey Grotto Cave. It's located on the other side of the island of Cuba. From there we'll turn back and head up the coast of Florida, following the Gulf Stream, to Saint Lovell's Island to the little lighthouse in Georgia."

"I hear it's haunted," Dina said. She felt an icy chill.

"Then on to Buzzard's Bay, Massachussets to the Oldest Inn on the coast. That place was built in the sixteen hundreds if I recall my history correctly. I believe Steven visited that area once while preparing for a sailing competition."

"Steven? How is he?" Dina asked.

"You're grand nephew is fine, but he hasn't won a sailing race yet. He came in fourth in the Annapolis, Maryland to Newport, Rhode Island race last year, and he's gearing up for the Newport to Bermuda race held this summer. He wants so much to be a success."

"He competes with you since your victory at the Southern Ocean Racing Conference Series."

"He has a healthy, competitive spirit, but I believe it's good for our relationship with no jealousy involved. It's only a feeling of admiration and love. I know my brother would die for me."

Smiling, Dina knew Sentra was the more competent sailor, for Steven was not as intelligent or experienced as her grand niece. She hoped her decision to offer Sentra the task would not falter the relationship with Steven. Although Dina did not see him more than once a year, he would write often and send her gifts on the holidays. Still she could picture his strong shoulders, bulging biceps, and the bold tattoo of the naked woman on his arm. He was a sensitive man, maybe too much so for his own good.

"Have you run into Amanda recently?" Dina asked.

"No. Last I heard she was waitressing once again trying to refrain from alcohol. She and I disagree about everything under the sun, although I feel she argues for the sake of arguing. If only she would move away from that run-down neighborhood over on the east side of Fort Mariner. The crack heads practically run the entire area with their drug sales and prostitution. Amanda's even sold herself for some drug money."

"I haven't heard from or seen her in over ten years. I sent her a package last Christmas, but I never got a response. Sometimes she is so rude, but maybe the alcohol's causing memory loss. I find it difficult to believe she's your sister."

"Yes. Such opposites we are."

"I wonder if she's still dating that sailor she met in Georgia? He was an alcoholic, too. He would guzzle a fifth of rum a day and chain smoke those nasty nonfilter cigarettes."

"You can't help those who don't want to help themselves," Sentra said. Then she gazed back at her map. "From Buzzard's Bay we sail to Cape June and dart out past Jeffrey's Ledge. And then to the 'Graveyard of the Atlantic.'"

"Ah, yes. That would be Sable Island off the coast of Nova Scotia. It might be tricky to find it due to the shifting sands that slowly move eastward, and the fog can get as thick as soup out there, especially during the summer months."

"Let's just hope for good weather. We'll still run into the fog where the gulf stream meets the Labrador current. This is due to the fact that the air streams blowing over the warm gulf stream water take with them a large amount of moisture. When this wet air is cooled by passing over the cold Labrador current, the moisture condenses into fine droplets called fog. This interaction of air, water, and heat, exchange in sea and air and form the New Foundland fog."

"Aren't there important shipping lines there?" Dina asked.

"Yes. The ships from northern Europe and North America come to this same point, so the navigation in this fog will be hazardous indeed. Hopefully we won't run into any ships or icebergs."

"Then once we get home to High Cliff," Dina said, "our efforts will be nearly over. We shall be quick to cash in our booty and pay those creditors before the autumnal equinox. We must then have the lien taken off the property."

"When did the bank take such action?" Sentra asked.

"I just received notice this week," Dina sighed. "Grandfather's soothsayer forewarned him of future financial woes. The ancient one's vision was accurate."

"I'm hungry. Let's go to Crabby Christopher's for lunch," Sentra said. Then she started munching on a fingernail.

Rising from their cushioned seats aboard the Empress, they made their way to the bike rack. "Go back to the ship, Elkin, and wait for us there," Dina ordered. The animal wagged its tail and then ran off into the distance. Poised on bicycles, they rode slowly through the traffic to Gull Lane. The sun was shining brightly, and the gulf breeze was zapping their damp skin.

Once inside the dimly lit restaurant, they took a booth near the window overlooking the water. Maroon placements and tall, golden glasses decorated the round, wooden table. A bearded, piano player hummed old sea ballads and occasionally sang a few bars. A small, vanilla candle glowed from the center of the table, and within minutes, a rugged-looking waitress ambled over.

"What shall it be mates?" she asked. Dina looked up in surprise.

Immediately she recognized her other grand niece Amanda. Although the last ten years had etched a road map in her face there was no mistaking that deep voice and those steely grey eyes. Shoving her glass forward, she spoke hesitantly at first.

"I would like a lobster, steamed and served with drawn butter. Add to the order a slice of key lime pie, please."

"Great Aunt Dina," the waitress said. Her face broke into a skipped - tooth grin. "After all these years, that's still your favorite fixings." Dina saw her stare intently at Sentra who began to speak.

"Just a friendly visit, my sister, and you are looking none the worse for wear."

"Life's been tough, but I get by. Seeing how you're in town, we'll have to get together soon. I get tomorrow off. Why don't we meet at my place at seven a.m.?"

"Sounds fine with me," Sentra said. She strained to sound friendly.

Winking at Sentra, Dina agreed to the meeting knowing it would be a short one. Discretion would also be used because she did not trust this wayward family member. After all, was she not hard up for drug money? The summer adventure would remain a secret as long as she could help it.

Amanda quickly scribbled her address on a napkin. Dina kindly accepted the invitation, and Sentra nodded and sipped on her iced water.

"Gotta go fill the order," Amanda said while pushing the pen into her apron pocket.

"Glad to see her still waitressing. We'll have to make our visit limited, Dina. Time is wasting. We plan to set sail tomorrow at eleven o'clock sharp," Sentra said. They watched Amanda disappear behind the kitchen door.

After eating the meal, they rode home to finish with their preparations and continue their plans. First, they dropped off Elkin for a flea dip and rabies shot. Unfortunately the vet would keep him overnight. He was booked and would not get to him until late in the evening. Dina hated to be without her bodyguard, but it would be convenient just to leave him there and stop back in the next day.

It was six o'clock in the evening, and a cooling breeze blew off the gulf. "I don't want to walk down the pier. Let's just search Banyan Forest for our prize," Sentra said. Then they spotted from their car Amanda sitting with a fishing pole propped between her legs. Amanda glanced their way and took a hard look. The slurred voice of her drunken companion could be heard thirty feet away. Hoping not to run into her again that day, they zoomed down the dirt road to the forest entrance. The massive, Indian fig trees stood like wooden centipedes reaching toward heaven. Fifty trees crammed the thirty acre park which was woven with dirt paths. Admission was free, and they parked Sentra's car near a green tractor that was sitting out front near some rakes and hoes hanging precariously off the inside of a barn door. A handsome, velvety-skinned Puerto Rican blew a big wad of chewing tobacco from his mouth.

"Adios," he said, a park attendant badge standing out proudly on his chest. Then Dina and Sentra walked by.

"I wonder if he's the only one on the grounds," Sentra said. "It seems pretty desolate this evening, but then this is not tourist season. Let's start over here." Pulling the visor down on her forehead, Dina followed close behind, carefully walking among the giant trees. "Well here we are fifty feet from the pier, but how are we supposed to know which tree it's hidden in," Sentra questioned, recalling the first poetic phrase of Grandfather's letter.

Tripping on a root, Dina fell forward, bopping her head on a large knot. Looking up, she saw a circular, rotted hole in the trunk of one of the trees. "Sentra. Look at this," she said. The opening was so big she could actually crawl in on her hands and knee, but suddenly something furry bit her on the tip of her nose. She ran out screaming in pain, and then the Puerto Rican walked over.

"Raccoons live here. No go inside. You lucky my pets have rabies shots," he said laughing.

Further down the path, they came to an old sign explaining the history of one of the largest trees in the park. It had stood for hundreds of years, and its aerial roots had become secondary trunks for two acres. It was one hundred feet high, and its dense, twisted stems resembled a thicket. Dina felt a sense of forboding, and then she witnessed a small snake slither into its recesses.

"That was a pygmy rattler. Watch your step," Sentra warned.

Carefully they climbed into the mass of wood, and after walking two hundred and fifty feet, they spied the immense trunk approximately ten feet in diameter. A large, green vine with elephant ear-shaped leaves wound its way up and down the tree clinging to it with hundreds of toe-clenched feet. Brushing aside one of the giant leaves, Sentra spied a large carving in the shape of a tear which stood ten feet up.

"This must be our tree," she said. Then Dina approached, carefully stepping over a root.

"You get on my shoulders, Great Aunt, and see what you can find," Sentra said. Then she kneeled down.

She found a rock two feet high which led to another rock in stair-step fashion. Standing upon the third rock put Dina straight in front of the carving's center. Placing her palm on the trunk, she pushed and pushed again. The carving suddenly caved in and fell with a thud on the floor of the large tree. Taking a small flashlight from her hiking belt, she peered inside.

"Who goes there?" she asked. Then she spied a person gazing into her very own eyes.

Grasping the outer edges of the opening, she pulled herself inside lighting upon small steps. Walking straight ahead, she approached the figure who seemed to be approaching her, too, and at the same speed. It also had a flashlight.

"Ouch," Dina said, smacking herself into a large mirror. Suddenly Sentra was by her side.

"Are you okay?" she said, upon helping Dina to her feet. Carefully she placed her sharp climbing knife, which she used to scale the tree, into its sheath. "You must have jarred it open," Sentra said. In amazement they stared ahead into the room behind the mirror. It was small and musty and held something gleaming in its side. Dina walked in and plucked the sparkling gem from its place in the wall. Looking at the stone with her instrument and using the general skill to determine authenticity and gem size, Sentra told Dina she was satisfied that this probably was the original ruby with its shade of red and weight of approximately ten carots. Dina was joyed to know she had found the place where Grandfather had secretly placed it. Sentra slipped it into her front pocket.

"So glad you dated that gemologist. You can apply that general skill to the rest of Samuel Darrendon's gems when we find them." They both laughed with relief and the satisfaction of accomplishment. "My flashlight batteries are growing dim. We'd better get out of here," Dina said. But when they had entered, the mirrored door had closed behind them, and now it would not budge.

"Someone followed us. See the extra set of footprints." Sentra pointed near the door, and then Dina stooped down for a closer look.

"You're right. Perhaps someone discovered our reason for this visit. We must exit quickly," Dina stood up slowly, carefully looking for anymore clues of a stranger.

Claustrophobia began to make Dina feel uncomfortable, the more aware she became of their close quarters. Maybe there was another entrance Dina hoped while pressing the walls and floors for possible openings. None could be found. Then sitting down, Sentra pulled a small bag of fruit from her backpack, and they started to munch on their only food.

"These are Banyan Days for us, hey Great Aunt," she said. Quietly she explained about the sacredness of the banyan trees to the Hindus of Asia. The Royal Navy excluded meat from the men's diets twice a week due to the vegetarian diet of the Hindu merchants. Dina hoped they would somehow be rescued before they starved to death, but time passed slowly, and repeated efforts to open the door failed. Finally, they decided to dig their way out. Taking some tools from their supplies, they carved and poked until they had a hole wide enough for passage. They each crawled through and then dropped ten feet to the ground below.

"Out so soon. I had hoped you would suffocate or better yet starve to death." They heard the familiar voice of Amanda.

"You were right behind us, weren't you? Dina said.

"Of course. You don't actually believe I thought you were sight-seeing. Now hand over the stone, or you still won't be leaving the park alive. Tie them, George, while I search their belongings." Carelessly Amanda ripped open the backpack, spilling its contents onto the ground. Furiously disappointed, she held a switchblade to Dina's throat.

"Is this what you're looking for?" Sentra asked. Then she looked down at her breast pocket. George thrust a hand in and roughly pulled out the gem.

"Excluding the black sheep from the family fortune?" Amanda said angrily.

"You have it all wrong, dear. It has to do with destination for the entire Darrendon family. I can explain it to you if you would only give me a chance," Dina said.

"Destination or no destination," Amanda said angrily, "this stone is mine, and you two will have to suffer the consequences of your greed."

Amanda and George laughed and walked away leaving Dina and Sentra bound and gagged to the thick fig tree, its massive structure towering above. Within minutes, Dina dislodged the tape from her mouth. "Help! Help!" she screamed, hoping the Puerto Rican would hear her. Sentra squirmed upon seeing the little pygmy rattlesnake come by for another visit, slowly approaching the vicinity of her pant leg. Then in the distance, they could hear the foreign mumblings of the park attendant.

"Permitame," he said. Then he untied the women. "Someone does not like you, no?"

"That's right," Sentra said.

"Did you see a man and a women leave the park in a hurry?" Dina said.

"Si."

"Which way did they go?" Sentra asked.

"El rio, senorita," he said, pointing to the river Loosahatchee.

"Gracias," Dina said. Then she and Sentra quickly grabbed their belongings and ran after the two theives.

From the bank, she could see them paddling a canoe toward the gulf entrance. Sentra quickly flipped off her shoes and swam like Tarzan towards the couple.

"Alligators!" Dina shouted. "This river is full of them."

But Sentra kept swimming, being intent on retrieving the gem. Going under water, Sentra slowly approached the canoe and quickly tipped it over. In her childhood, Amanda had always kept items hidden in her shoe, and Dina knew Sentra would know just where to look. George and Amanda were not very good swimmers, and while they were frantically hurling their arms in the water, she quickly slipped off her sister's right shoe being careful not to upturn it. There in the toe, Dina could see her pull out the stone.

In the meantime, George and Amanda had grabbed the life vests and were floating and screaming obscenities. With the stone in her clenched fist, Dina could see Sentra swim for shore as an alligator skimmed the water close behind. She picked up speed, outswam it, and safely crawled like a sea snail onto the beach. They drove Sentra's car back to the Empress.

"It is good to be home. We had quit a day." Sentra pulled the covers over her head and instantly dozed off to sleep in her cabin while hugging her stuffed, grey cat. Dina thought it was so sweet how brave Sentra was in the face of danger and yet how her childlike nature always seemed to prevent her from becoming hardened by the cruelness of life.

"Pleasant dreams," Dina said sweetly. Then she went to her own cabin and flung open her old suitcase and pulled out the gem and The Book of Eternity. The gem was in the leather belt, and she encassed the cover of a cookbook around The Book of Eternity. Carefully she placed them in the safe behind a faux wooden partition in the kitchen cabinet of the Empress.

Back in Sentra's cabin, suddenly Dina had an idea as she gazed at the stuffed animal. It would be so nice to take another pet on board. Elkin would not mind, and surely Sentra would adore it. Easily she could remember a grey cat when she sailed with Sentra to Australia. It had fallen overboard in a storm after surviving numerous sailing adventures. Sentra had grieved for a long time and had felt guilty buying another one, but Dina knew this was the right time. She would find a cat, show it to Sentra and Elkin for approval, and then accustom it to the Empress before the morning, sailing trip.

After a good night's sleep, Dina arose at eight o'clock and quietly slipped out the back entrance to her bicycle. She peddled across town to a humane shelter and bought a cat like the one she saw in her dream last night Then she retrieved Elkin from the veterinarian's office.

Dina arrived back at the Empress at ten thirty. Elkin sniffed curiously at the charcoal grey cat. The feline stared at him with its lime green eyes and moaned an eerie sound. She then saw a note Sentra had left behind. Her friend went across the street to buy some more food for the trip to Jamaica, and they would set sail in thirty minutes.

Glad to have time to rest before the journey, Dina sat down on her firm mattress on the boat. The craft was forty feet long, and it was built for speed and comfort. The cruising sailboat was small enough to be handled by a crew of one or two but capable of sailing great distances. The masts were low and strong making the sail area smaller to allow less strain on the hull and rigging. It did not possess difficult spinnakers and flying jibs. The canvas rigging and construction was heavy making the boat well-built to weather viscious storms and bear the crushing blows of breaking waves. Although the port and cockpit were not very large, Dina and Sentra had their own little cabins in which to retreat. In fact, there were two more bedrooms and a roomy kitchen. The rigs could be balanced so the crew could sleep or eat while the boat could sail itself with the wheel lashed. She felt they would be safe on the Empress.

The two animals provided her with security, too. At first, the cat was wary of Elkin who sniffed at its soft fur. "I shall name you Feather." Dina reached her hand out, and the cat pulled from her fingers a tuna snack. Then it lept into Elkin's water bowl and lapped up the cool contents.

"Well it's good you like water, because there will be lots of it around us for the voyage." Suddenly she heard Sentra with an armload of crunchy paper bags. Then Dina saw the cat slip in snakelike silence beneath the cabinet. She would let Feather make her entrance on her own time she knew while they stocked away canned foods including vegetables, meats, and peanut butter. Soon the animal bravely slinked out from its hiding place.

"Where did you get this beautiful animal?" Sentra squeeled. Then Feather rubbed up against her leg.

"It's your new seacat, Feather." Dina said. Sentra picked it up. "She loves the water, and she's fond of fish-shaped tuna treats." Sentra gazed into its lime green eyes, and the animal seemed to look right through her. Then it began to moan the eerie sound Dina had heard it emit at the humane shelter, its past home.

"Such a strange noise coming from a cat," Sentra said. She set the animal upon the counter. Suddenly Elkin began to howl, too, and soon everyone was laughing. Then out from beneath the cabinet strolled a little grey mouse. Quickly Feather pounced on it and grasped it about the neck. Elkin pulled on its head until it ripped apart from its body. Then they both munched on their morning snack.

"They are good for something after all," Dina chuckled.

Soon they were sailing into the Gulf of Mexico, heading south to Cuba. Then they would turn west, travel around Cuba, sail down by the Cayman Islands, then southeast to Jamaica.

It was obvious how much Sentra loved to sail. She was at harmony with the elements, for she could feel the tempo of the wind and water. It was a good rhythm, for she never rushed but took it gently, anticipating the balance and sense of her boat. She was such an expert at finding the correct sail angle that rarely did these sheets of cloth flap in the wind. Of course, her meteorology skills helped her understand weather conditions, predict possible problems, and handle the sails in a storm. She had been in various sailing races around the world and had actually sailed hundreds of nautical miles.

Sailing, after all, had been in her blood since she was twelve years old when she learned about boats, and she often sailed up and down the Gulf of Mexico. Dina had taught Sentra weather wisdom that she had learned from Knotty, the old hermit, and this she knew had strengthened the girl's interest in meteorology. She had graduated Magna Cum Laude from the University of Florida and had practiced meteorology for four years. Her current employment as chief meteorologist with WZZD news was her most rewarding job as she loved the responsibility of forecasting. She held a ninety-five percent accuracy rating of which she was very proud. She took kindly to the weather wisdom she had taught her understanding it fully due to her scientific knowledge. Sigmund, her pet frog, served as a secondary barometer, and she kept him in a small, plastic jar with a rock inside. When the air is dry he stays in the water, but when the humidity rises before a storm, the frog comes out of the water to enjoy the moist air. It was common sense.

The days passed swiftly, and the calm seas provided an easy trip for all. Elkin would dive into the waters with Dina and Sentra to swim and play while Feather stood on the deck watching. Fresh fish were caught everyday, and they lavished in fruits, nuts, and cheeses. Cool water and juice helped them from becoming dehydrated, and sunscreen saved their skin from the ravages of the penetrating rays.

Dina tried to imagine Grandfather traveling through these waters without Grandmother by his side. How lonely he must have been. She knew he had felt responsible for their deaths, because the gems brought those greedy criminals and murders to the shores of New Foundland in the first place. With knowledge of the soothsayer's vision, to preserve the family destiny, he had to provide a monetary means to keep possession of the castle, for it held the secret and the entrance to eternity. One gem she had found in Ft. Mariner, and there were four more to locate. Then all would be saved.

She knew Sentra could come through for them, and Dina was glad she had joined her, because she felt twenty years younger despite some encroaching arthritis in her fingers. She ran her hand over her inner thigh and felt a warmth of romance.

In the distance of the Florida Straits, they spied another sailboat heading their way. Two dark figures could be seen, and Elkin began to bark while they sailed portside. What had looked like two men was actually five men, and they were fit and handsome. One blond one with his long hair in a ponytail resembled Devon who was the evil one Grandfather had warned her about and the kidnapper in her childhood. She could not yet be sure it was him, because they were too far away. She grabbed the binoculars from the cabin door, and just as she was focusing, they whistled at the two women and threw the anchor overboard. Sentra looked frightened, and Dina saw her grab her gun from underneath the cockpit.

"How about a little party," the one with the red bandana said in a Spanish accent. Then he held up a bottle of tequila. Suddenly he tore off his clothes, exposing his dark, hairy chest, and dove into the warm waters.

"Let's hope we can sail far enough away from those beasts," Sentra hollered. They watched the man swim rapidly and disappear underwater.

"It's too late," Dina cried. "He's already next to our craft." Then a dark, weather-logged hand slipped over the side of the boat near the stern. Suddenly they could hear a clunk and saw the man's rope with a metal bar on board. Elkin was on him in an instant, gnawing at the knuckles until they were bloody and bone barren. Howling in agony, the man let loose and sank into the blue sea. Sentra and Dina were terrified upon seeing the boat sailing their way again. Only this time Dina could see they, too, were brandishing guns.

"How about a little fun ladies," a tanned one yelled.

"He's just trying to distract us," Dina warned. "Look over there, Sentra."

Soon a red-haired man with a rope and hook climbed on board so quietly that Elkin did not even hear him before he saw him. Sentra shot at him, but he darted out of target. Then, within seconds, the intruder grabbed Sentra by the arm, pulled her to the deck, and lay on top of her. Next, Elkin lunged at his throat and tore it out, leaving a bloody pool beneath Sentra's golden hair. Dina pulled him off of Sentra and threw him overboard. Sharks tore at his flesh, and the evil crew looked on.

"You've had it now," the tanned one hollered from the enemy craft.

Sailing was slow on this calm day, and they traveled at two knots through a sea that appeared in small ripples like fish scales. Her Empress had no motor in use, and it was cruising, and hopefully the other craft had no motor at all. Being horribly bold in their pursuit, two more men had jumped overboard. Soon the first man climbed up on deck. The tanned intruder hit Elkin hard in the head with a small wooden club that knocked the wolf unconscious.

"Elkin, you okay?" Dina hollered.

"Stay back," Sentra ordered. Then she shot at the tanned man, only grazing his shoulder.

Then, instantly, he was on Dina. She bit and screamed with all her fury. His throbbing manhood pressed against her, stabbing upward on her belly. Then she bit him harder until he bled profusely and clutched at his face in agony. Next, Sentra shot at him again, nipping off his index finger. He rolled off Dina in horrible pain.

"Look out behind you," Dina screamed. Suddenly, the second intruder, a bald stout man, climbed on deck. Sentra shot at him, piercing his cheek. He grabbed her gun, and she fired aimlessly into the air.

"I'll return," Dina said. She disappeared below deck. Soon Sentra was being attacked too, but she stayed calm on her abdomen, for the bald man held a knife to her throat. Then he pressed the blade deeper into her neck until she was still and unbreathing. Arising from her damp, limp body, he sighed in relief. Then, without warning, she came back to life, pulled an eight-inch bowie knife from the deck, and thrust it into his skull right between the eyes. Blood spurted out, his blue eyes rolled, and he fell backwards into the sea. Next, the injured, tanned one dazedly lunged at Sentra with a small switchblade, cutting her on the left breast. Blood oozed out onto her lavender shirt, and then she spied Elkin getting to his feet. Soon Dina appeared from the cockpit with a savage-looking speargun. Taking aim, she pulled the trigger, shooting the tanned man through the heart.

"There's one more to go," Sentra said, throwing the dead man into the bloodied waters. Firing flares into the air, they soon saw the less menacing, lone man sail away toward the coast. For a second, Dina caught the glow of his bright green eyes in the sunlight. She grabbed the binoculars again, and this time she was able to focus clearly.

"Its's Devon, Sentra. The battle is over for now, but maybe we should radio for help. You can transmit messages on the VHF radio within a twenty mile limit, but in this circumstance being at least one hundred miles out to sea, the single-sideband radio at 8mhz ought to be more sufficient."

"No. They may find out about our mission and confiscate our booty. We have fended off the evil Devon, the lone survivor, and the sharks have taken care of the other men. I'm sure he'll have a good story to cover up for himself. We must be on our way and hope he doesn't return anytime soon."

"Yes. We were only protecting ourselves." Dina reviewed her memory once again. Devon's golden hair and bright green eyes could not be forgotten. "That man who sailed off wants the gems badly for their power you know." Sentra listened intently to her tale of their enemy. "Pray to God we can fend him off next time, too, but for now we need medical treatment."

"You're right," Sentra agreed. Then Dina opened the young woman's blouse to gaze at the wound.

"Let's stop at Grand Cayman. It's on our way," she said. Sentra nodded approvingly.

Dina knew the girl was losing too much blood from the knife wound, and she decided it needed immediate attention. She fetched the first aid kit from the kitchen cabinet and removed the antiseptic. She applied it generously. Then she threaded a sterile needle and stitched up the gapping hole. Sentra only winced a bit at first when the sharp point penetrated her skin. Dina then bandaged it carefully and offered her grand niece immediate doses of antibiotics to ward off possible infection.

It was a gruesome, humiliating experience which would go with them to the grave. Those brutal thugs only got what they deserved.

"Survival of the fittest," Dina said. "Our gem is safe, and now we must look for the other stones." Sentra nodded in agreement, and Dina led her to her own cabin.

Then Dina went to the kitchen to place the first-aid kit back into the cabinet. Upon opening the cabinet door, Feather jumped out. She seemed happy to see her and purred loudly for a can of sardines. Elkin lay sleeping, with his fur coat stained and bloodied, on the cabin rug. Soon Feather darted off and jumped into bed with Sentra. Dina watched them doze off together, and knew all was well for now.

The next morning the sky filled with whispy clouds. "There could be an approaching warm front. If the winds keep picking up speed, we could have rain in the near future," Sentra said.

"Yes. The sky looks like a painter's brushes," Dina said. She began to sketch the surrounding waters from her place on the boat. Suddenly she jumped up. "Look out there." Dina pointed to a red sailboat coming up from the rear. "Quick, Sentra. Hand me the binoculars." She pulled the leather strap from its hook on the cabin door and handed them to Dina. "Oh no. It's Amanda and George." Sentra grabbed the binoculars to see for herself.

"A very nasty pair, indeed. Let's hope they keep their distance. Maybe we'll lose them in town and make a secret escape back out to sea."

"Are we on course?"

"Yes, Dina. This Loran-c is a wonder. It has pulsed signals sent out by two pairs of radio stations. It keeps a constant position fix on latitude and longitude, provides courses to steer, and adjusts them by keeping record of current and wind. All I had to do was input nautical signposts on our track, and it signals which one tells me the time to destination. It is actually guiding the Empress from waypoint to waypoint."

Crossing the Florida Straits and the Tropic of Cancer at twenty-three and one-half degrees south of the equator, they sailed southwest around Cuba. They could easily see the coast of the largest and most populous island in the West Indies. Its long, narrow shape stretched out seven hundred and forty-six miles, along an east-west axis, from Cape Maisi to Cape San Antonio. Its gentle slopes and rolling hills were accented with broad mountains. Rounding the tip of the island, they changed direction and headed southeast toward the Grand Cayman Islands. Amanda and George kept in pursuit, and their red sales like stark warnings shone brightly against the blue sky.

Soon they could spot the broad lagoons and dense mangrove swamps. Seagrapes, coconut palms, and almond trees shaded the shores. Exotic flowering bushes could be seen such as poinciana and oleander, and fruit hung ripe with passion from the mango and breadfruit trees. Slowly they approached the west side of Grand Cayman at George Town, the colony's capital and international banking center.

Using her awareness of wind, current direction, velocity, and how her boat handles in small spaces, Sentra docked starboard with wind on the bow in George Town Harbor. Having grown weary of the ocean ride, they were glad to step on land for the first time in days. Feather remained locked in the cabin, and Elkin was chained to the rail. The ruby and The Book of Eternity were both stored in the kitchen's metal safe hidden on board. It had a pickproof lock with an alarm if anyone, like Amanda, George, or Devon, would attempt to rob them. Of course, Elkin guarded the entrance to the cabin.

"We shall take care of our medical needs here and restock our fresh fruit supply. We're approximately one hundred and eighty miles north-west of Jamaica. We should be on our way by tomorrow," Sentra said. Then Dina secured their craft.

"We need citizenship proof and an ongoing status to stay here up to six months," Dina said. She pulled her birth certificate from a file folder where Sentra's was intact too.

Gladly walking along the streets, they felt good stretching their sealegs. They passed a dark-skinned woman wearing tangerine-colored clothing, and a tall man in green trunks smiled and waved when they walked by. A pleasant sounding English accent could be heard with its own flavor of West Indian, Irish, and Scottish sounds. The small, clean city seemed to have a seaview from every direction, because there were no immense barriers to be found. The tiny stucco houses, which looked like scenes from a painting, were tidy and brightened with flowers.

On Edward Street they stopped at the post office for stamps. Dina knew Sentra needed to write a letter to her brother Steven. He wanted them to keep in contact throughout their journey. They never actually told him the exact purpose of their trip, only that the mission was vital to the family future. He was their loyal friend, unlike Amanda who would do anything to confiscate those gems for her personal greed.

Quickly Sentra filled in the back of a postcard of the Grand Cayman sunset. Dina knew there was a good chance that they might run into Steven while traveling up the Gulf stream on their journey up the east coast toward New Foundland. His sailing race was coming up soon. She heard Sentra plop the post card into the mail receptacle.

Four buildings down from the town center, they found the office of Dr. Simon Joba. The dark-eyed receptionist greeted them warmly and seated them in the dimly lit waiting room. The smell of anitiseptic filled the air, and they felt the breeze of the overhead fan. Within an hour, they found themselves in the examining room. The rotund doctor was very kind and gentle while he proceeded with the examination. Following a two-hour wait, the test results were in.

"Despite some lacerations, you have no infections of any kind," the doctor said.

"Your blood looks good," Dr. Joba continued. Dina sighed in relief. "You are one lucky lady. Where did this assault occur?"

"We were attacked while sailing through the Florida Straits," Dina said. "The Coast Guard will be notified at once."

She pushed a red sprig of hair out of her face and looked at the doctor suspiciously. Then quckly she handed him a wad of money before they walked out into the sunstreaked streets. Feeling relieved there was no permanent physical damage, they prayed they would never run into the evil Devon and his kind again.

Turning onto West Bay Road, they walked one-half mile until they came to a small hotel called the Beachcomber. They chose a two bedroom apartment with a kitchenette overlooking the water. First, Dina turned on the air conditioning, and then she sprawled across the bed. Sentra sat down in the recliner.

After an hours rest, they went to the Wreck of the Ten Sails Lounge and found comfort in tall glasses of rum. The Barechest Man was entertaining with his own brand of calypso, and country and western music. Later that evening they would return to the boat and bring Elkin and Feather and the contents of the safe back to the hotel. Tucked away in a small booth, they looked out upon the partrons of the bar and a familiar face appeared across from them. It was Amanda, and the tall stranger she was serving was none other than George. Dina knew they were being followed, and she wondered if they saw them enter the lounge. Carefully they put on their sunglasses to remain inconspicuous, but the couple spotted them and walked over to their table.

"Visiting Grand Cayman I see," the gravely-voiced woman said, sending a chill. Dina rubbed the skin on her arms.

"We saw you out at sea with your red sails," Sentra said.

"Yes, we've been right behind you all along," Amanda said.

"Oh. And sorry about the incident in Banyan Forest. But you practically drowned us in the river," George said chuckling.

"Hey, you guys have a nice boat," Amanda said. Then she held up a leather collar.

"Give me that," Sentra ordered. She grabbed at the grey, furry neck-piece. "What have you done to my cat?"

"What have you done with the gem?" Amanda said.

Excusing themselves to go the ladies room, Dina could feel the eyes of their two evil stalkers on them. The single entrance to the bathroom was in full view of their table, but once inside, Sentra spied a small window above the sink. She opened it quietly, and Dina quickly locked the door. Then they slithered out into the alley below.

"We must go to the Empress and bring Elkin, the ruby, and The Book of Eternity back to our hotel. Our safety system has failed us. Hope Feather is still alive. There's no telling what they did to her," Sentra said with a tear in her eye. Dina flagged down a bus, and soon they were at the harbor.

Elkin was glad to see them, jumping and whining at the sight of the two bedraggled women. Apparently someone had passed by the animal, because an attempt to distract him, a t-bone steak, lay gnarled. "However, they did not get by without a struggle from our wolf's jaws," Dina said, picking up a piece of torn denim with hairy human flesh stuck to it.

"The burglars must of picked the door lock," Sentra said upon stumbling into the open cabin door. Beneath the kitchen cabinet behind a faux wooden partition they noticed the safe had not been tampered with. Opening it, Dina removed the belt with the gem inside, and Sentra put it on her waist. Dina recalled having a belt just like that one years ago. The storage slot was so cleverly concealed it was even hard for her to find. Carefully Dina checked The Book of Eternity in the safe, still disguised as a cookbook. She left it inside and closed up the safe and cabinet. They searched thoroughly for Feather, but she could not be found. They unchained Elkin and put him on a leash and hopped on a bus back to West Bay Road. They retuned to their room, placed the belt with the ruby in the room safe, and slipped off to sleep.

The next morning after a dip in the sparkling pool, they decided to tour the island despite the appearance of the fiendish couple. The winds were strong, and they did not feel like battling a possible storm at sea. Sentra shared with Dina that the morning sky of Indian red altocumulus clouds usually brings rain often accompanied by winds and thunderstorms.

"Evening grey and morning red will bring down rain upon our heads," said Dina, pointing to the heavens. Never would she forget the wisdom of the old hermit, and so glad she was to be able to pass it on to Sentra. Now her grand niece was a meteorologist, an expert sailor, and saviour of the family destiny. It was all falling into place. They would cautiously enjoy the day and then be on to Grey Grotto Cave for gem number two in Jamaica. Perhaps a beautiful emerald awaited them she thought. Sentra pulled the belt from the room's safe and cinched it tightly to her waist, securing the safety of the ruby.

Deciding it would be safer and easier to flee if necessary, they rented a small car at Coconut Car Rental Incorporated. Dina drove, and Sentra sat next to her. Elkin hopped into the back seat.

The first stop was the turtle farm, where green, sea turtles, were grown commercially. Turtle eggs, hatchlings, and adults were seen throughout the tourist attraction.

"Don't buy any tortoise shell jewelry," Sentra warned Dina. "Those turtles are on the endangered species list."

"And so are we," Dina said. Then she recalled how the fiends had so quickly ended her Grandmother's life and how the shark had killed her mother. She ran her fingers over the leather belt around Sentra's waist. The gems would aid them on their quest for eternal life. The Darrendons would all meet again one day.

A blue jeep with two men inside pulled up next to them while they steered out of the turtle farm. Elkin stared at them curiously. "Next stop, Hades," Sentra said. Then they drove up to coral rock formations and exited the vehicle. They strolled along the ramp, looked out over the limestone fields, and then walked to a small wooden structure.

"Hell, Grand Cayman," the post mistress said. Then she stamped and mailed another letter Sentra wrote to Steven. Dina knew it was best to inform him of Amanda's pursuit.

They drove down Seven Mile Beach Road and turned onto South Sound Road. The pine-lined street was interrupted by quaint, wooden, Caymanian houses. One older home attracted Dina's attention. It was painted in colorful abstract designs. A large, dark woman smiled and waved, and then they turned into the gravel driveway. Instantly Dina saw a beautiful painting of a phoenix. She asked the woman about her festive art and told her about her own artistic talents. She felt a kindred spirit. Then the dark lady led them into her home and pointed at one of Dina's paintings on her kitchen wall titled "Beach Bucket." It was one of her works that was well-known, and it was even one of Dina's own favorite, still life paintings.

Happily, the Caymanian woman presented Dina with a carving of a dragon on a gold chain. "A good luck charm," the black lady whispered in her ear. Dina put it on her neck and vowed not to take it off until their journey ended. Sentra sat back in a rattan chair, and the woman began to tell them of her life in Jamaica. Many a day she had spent exploring Grey Grotto Cave with her sister and many lovers. When Dina recalled the secret lake she had to explore to find the gem, she asked the lady about its existance.

"It's one mile north on the first fork and then down fifty stone steps." She smiled and served them fresh breadfruit. "You can't miss it. And if you meet my sister over there, she'll have some very helpful information for you, too." Dina wondered exactly where the sibling might be located, but suddenly the woman rushed them off. "Now go, and happy hunting."

Waving farewell and feeling grateful for the meeting, Dina, Sentra, and Elkin drove on.

"Looks like stratus clouds above," Sentra said. "Let's go to Bat Cave," she continued, reading a lopsided roadside sign. "It will be a good shelter when rain comes." Dina nodded in agreement.

They took the dirt road off the main drag to Bodden Town heading east all the way to the end. Soon a brown pick-up truck sped around them almost grazing their car. "Look out, you," Sentra shouted. Dina honked two times.

Soon they stopped and proceeded on foot. They turned left at the sea and walked along the cliff for ten yards until they stood above a sandy beach. Elkin panted in the morning humidity. Then they climbed down the ten-foot cliff to the mouth of Bat Cave. It was not a bat that appeared from within but a dark figure with a gun pointed at their heads.

"Look out," Dina cautioned. "There's the brown pick-up truck that nearly hit us." She pointed past the cave to the beach. Then they turned and ran for their lives.

CHAPTER THREE

Retracing their steps, the three adventurers raced from the sea to the spot where they parked the rented car, but it was gone. In a dusty haze, they saw a jeep approaching from the north, but behind them the dark figure still loomed, gun in hand. Two men in the blue jeep skidded to a stop, and Dina, Sentra, and Elkin jumped in the back. They ducked down when shots rang out. Heaving a sigh of relief, Sentra clutched at her leather belt with the gem inside.

"I'm Jackson, and this here's my friend Olgilvee. We've been following you two ladies all morning."

"Yes. Come to think of it, the both of you were at the turtle farm," Sentra said.

"What interest do you have in us?" Dina asked.

"Steven sent us," Jackson answered. He smiled, and Sentra noticed two large dimples in his cheeks. A black moustache decorated a thick top lip, and he gazed at her with lust in his eyes. Dina could tell her grand niece felt an immediate attraction to this tall, firm stranger.

"Where are you taking us?" Sentra pressed.

"Peyton's Castle. We own the bar and restaurant. It will be a haven for you two until your pursuers grow weary of the search and back off."

"Just think of us as your bodyguards," Olgilvee said. Dina found his silver hair attractive, because it gleamed like tinsel. His dull green eyes lowered, sizing her up. Reaching out a large hand, he brushed a red sprig of hair from her face, uncovering a dirt smeared cheek.

In the back of the rustic restaurant was a three-bedroom apartment with a convenient rear entrance. Refusing to go in at first, Sentra felt uneasy until Jackson pulled out a photograph of her brother Steven on his boat the Sea Serpent. Jackson had his arm around him, and they were grinning widely.

"We nearly won that Bermuda race. If he hadn't stopped to save my life, we probably would've done much better. He told me about your trophies, Sentra, including the win of the Southern Ocean Race."

"Where did you two meet?" Sentra asked.

"We went to school together, and we gradually became close friends. We share two of the same interests: woman and sailing." Sentra grinned. Then he brushed a thick finger across her parched lips. "Steven heard you two were attacked near the Florida Straits, and he asked for our help. I didn't mind seeing how I owed him one. Besides, you're worthy women."

Leaning up from her place in the back of the jeep, Sentra planted a kiss upon his lips while holding a crop of his jet black hair in one hand. Menacing clouds were pushing across the sky, dimming the light of day. Then eagerly Dina and Sentra left the jeep, waved good-bye, and entered the strange apartment. Elkin stretched out on the kitchen rug as the noonday sun, for only a second, squinted in from the window over the sink.

"I don't think they know about the gem and our search for more," Sentra said to Dina once inside the solitude of their room. "I believe they think we're just traveling and were attacked by present-day pirates."

Two double beds filled half of the large, rectangular space. A dresser and two lamps lined one wall, and a picture window opened out across the sea. A spacious bathroom with a giant, shower stall and whirlpool bath extended from the walk-in closet area, and the low hum of the ceiling fan could be heard overhead. Although there were no phones, a thirteen-inch television set was perched upon a wooden table and parquet floors glowed as if freshly polished.

Soon someone knocked at the apartment door, and Elkin stood at attention. Upon opening it, Sentra and Dina beheld a standing tray filled with fresh fruits and seafood. A large pitcher of apple cider sparkled and beckoned to them. Attached to the crystal vase was a note stuck amidst the purple and white hibiscus: "Be ready for dinner tonight at seven. See you at the raw bar. J. and O.," Sentra read. Then Elkin retreated to his rug.

"That gives us four hours," Dina said, looking at her watch. Feeling salt singed and longing for some soothing relief, she filled the whirlpool bath. Lavender oil beads scented the air and water. She sank into its depths where jets sprayed her aching muscles with relief. She was glad the gem was safe and hoped their pursuers were gone.

Beyond the partition, Dina could see Sentra strip naked, stash the leather belt and gem under the mattress, and then search the room carefully. The top dresser drawers were filled with underclothes and satin lingerie, another drawer held bottles of exotic perfumes, and a third drawer was the home of a canister of bath powder. Tropical print shorts, tops, and sundresses were folded neatly in the closet along with colorful socks and silk hosiery. Sentra opened the bottom, center drawer of the closet dresser and gasped. Out popped hundreds of small packaged objects of various colors.

"Condoms," she said to Dina who splashed in the hot, oily water. Wondering if these items were placed there for their benefit, or if they were there for use by other women as well remained a mystery. Dina knew Sentra, and she would not allow these men to intimidate and use them. They would do what felt right and satisfying.

Dina let a jet of water run along her thighs. Feeling romantic sensations in minutes, she sank under, wetting her red, dry hair in the oils. Secretly, she fantasized about Olgilvee. Together they danced slowly, touching cheek to cheek with hands entwined. In the romantic candlelight, they sat and stared into the depths of each other's souls. Bits of shrimp and lobster they plunged into each other's mouths. His tongue, coated in dripping butter, longingly licked her fingertips. Then his hand slipped upon her thighs. Inching up until almost there, his fingers rested impatiently. Then they walked hand in hand to this very bath.

Suddenly, when she heard the mournful howl of Elkin coming from the kitchen, she bolted upright. A dark sky let loose buckets of rain, and thunder crackled and lightning flashed. "It's okay, boy. Sentra?" she called out. Her grand niece did not reply. She realized that she was alone in the apartment. She stepped from the tub and grabbed a towel, wrapping it tightly around her body. Then she noticed Sentra's sandals were still where she had left them inside the bedroom door along with her keychain. She perused the apartment and looked at the hallway wall clock. Two hours had passed since she slipped into the whirlpool bath, and Sentra and the gem were nowhere to be found. Where could she be?

Was that a dark figure in the kitchen window she wondered while gazing out at the rain?

Someone was peering in at her. Then she heard a continuous tapping sound at the door. Quickly she dried off and donned an orange dress from the bedroom. "Who is it?" she said. Then the tapping hardened to a rap. Elkin growled.

"It's Olgilvee. I know our date is not until seven, but I became anxious. May I come in?"

The familiar voice comforted her, and her heart quit pounding quite so hard. He entered soon as she let up the metal latch. In a wet, yellow parka he stood smiling, exposing white teeth. The strong smell of aftershave permeated the air, and she greeted him with an outstretched hand.

"Those clothes fit nicely," he said. "Are you enjoying the accomadations?"

"I'm worried. Where is Sentra?"

"Jackson took her for a walk in the rain. Don't worry. She went obligingly," he said. He grabbed Dina by the waist and glided across the floor. She willingly danced with him. To the bedroom they strolled to retrieve a condom. Then tenderly he kissed her lips and pulled her to the couch, where they undressed and made love.

"Olgilvee, I feel so free and easy with you." Dina nibbled on his fingers. "You are unjudgemental." Olgilvee brushed the red hair from her face.

"I'm seventy-five, my angel, and I feel as spry and healthy as you look. I work out with weights and eat a healthy diet of fruits, nuts, cheeses, and seafood."

"I share a similar regime," she said. She stretched a firm leg into the air. "You're so wonderful though. You seem well educated."

"Yes. I spent fifty years as an oceanographer studying the sea's structure and movement. I measured various aspects such as salinity, depth, density, and temperature. Many dynamic properties interested me like waves, tides, curents, humidity, winds, geology of the bottom, and chemical properties. Did you know there are now instruments of thirty-four generic types which are used to test samples of the ocean?"

Dina shook her head no. She was completely enthralled with him, partly because she loved the sea, too. Being an accomplished artist, seascapes were her favorite subjects of still life. Many a day she had spent combing the shores for interesting places to paint. To know someone who deeply understood the ocean's mysteries was intriguing.

"My specialty is biological oceanography," he said. "I've studied ocean organisms and how these forms of life interact with the evironmment and each other. I've learned behavior evolution and the life processes of the sea. Botony and zoology were also studied in depth."

"I'm from New Foundland, and I've always wondered why the Grand Bank's area is such a good fishing ground," Dina said.

"Because the phytoplankton from the bottom are stirred up by ocean currents. There's lots of food for marine life."

"Have you ever seen a sea monster?" Dina asked. She drew pictures in her mind of fantastic marine life.

"Yes. I saw one while diving in the North Atlantic. I spotted a fifteen foot squid that weighed over a ton. He wrapped a tentacle around my leg, and I thought I would perish, but luckily my partner cut me free. It took him ten minutes to saw through his thick arm. He was by far the largest sea monster I ever laid eyes on."

Dina felt herself being drawn in by Olgilvee, because he fascinated her like no other man had ever done. Maybe her feelings for men was changing she knew, while gazing longingly at her new lover. For the first time in years she did not want to move on. Perhaps this stop with a man would be her final resting place.

Standing up, he pulled on his pants and looked out the window at the rain. Dina, too, put her dress back on. Soon Sentra and Jackson entered soaked to the tendon. Dina could see Sentra's leather belt cinched tightly to her waist. They became well acquainted in the hour they were together. A fisherman all his life, Jackson was amazed at Sentra's meteorology skills, as she confided that fact to Dina.

Eagerly they talked about Steven, and they shared the same feelings about his qualities of loyalty, patience, and kindness as Steven would never hurt anyone. Of course, his caring for Dina and Sentra came forth, because he sent his two friends to be their bodyguards. Amanda and George, however, were showing their two tough character sides. In this desperate time of their lives they were brutal in their dealings, not only with animals, but with people too. Without Jackson and Olgilvee, Dina knew Sentra and she may have perished in the hands of the gunman at Bat Cave. Did Amanda send the killer she wondered? For now the gem was safe, secretly hidden in Sentra's belt, but would their two new male comrades get greedy too? Did they know about the expensive, powerful stones that would bring them wealth to keep the castle, gate to eternity? Could she preserve the destiny of the Darrendon family? Only time would tell, and she would keep her guard. For now, the map and gem hunting details would remain the secret of Grandfather, Sentra, and herself. What a pity Amanda knew of their pursuits Dina thought, and then she bit into her lip.

"Where are you two ladies headed?" Jackson asked.

"We thought we'd cruise the islands, then travel to Newport, Rhode Island to see Steven off in the Bermuda race," Sentra said.

"You aren't going anywhere for awhile. You need to lay low until you're pursuers grow weary of the chase," Olgilvee said.

"But we must stay ahead of the evil one, and our savings are very low," Dina said.

"A week won't do you in," Olgilvee assured her, "and by the way, we don't know exactly what everyone is after. Would you two ladies mind explaining?"

"Oh, no. It's six thirty," Sentra said. "We must get ready for dinner." She turned on the hair dryer.

Suddenly Dina stood up, adjusted her dress, and led the two men to the door. "See you tonight at seven," she said while latching the lock. She did not trust the two men enough yet to reveal their plans.

Within thirty minutes, the women were dressed. Dina wore blue and Sentra wore green. Seated at the Peyton's Castle raw bar, they waited patiently for their suitors. The gem was still hidden in the leather compartment of the belt Sentra wore cinched at the waist. She could hear her grand niece tap her high-heeled shoe anxiously on the bar stool. In her hand, Sentra held a rum and coke upon which she occasionally sipped. It was now seven thirty, and Dina was working on her ginger ale when in walked a tall, familiar gentleman. It was the silver-haired Olgilvee, and Jackson followed close behind.

"Sorry to keep you ladies waiting, but we found two prowlers out back," Olgilvee said. Dina noticed a small bruise on his left cheek and a slice upon his neck. "We caught them by surprise sneaking into the back door of the restaurant. They got away in an old, brown pick-up."

"Maybe the same people that nearly hit us and threatened to shoot us at Bat Cave," Dina said.

"But I was able to get ahold of this," Jackson said. He held up a silver pin of the letter A.

"Amanda," Sentra said. She instantly recognized the initial pin she had given her sister a few years ago. Amanda had told her she wore it often, and now their presence was known.

They all dined in silence. Then they walked back to the apartment. Dina felt a shiver crawl up her spine when she heard the howl of Elkin by the front door. She saw Sentra look up at the moon which hung motionless in the clear, rained-out sky.

"June 22nd. A waxing crescent moon," Dina said. "Time is slipping by."

The next morning was bright and sunny. Jackson and Olgilvee arranged a deep-sea fishing expedition, not only for fun and pleasure during the week long wait, but for something far more important, money. Dina knew the Caymanian waters were abundant with tuna, yellow tail, dolphin, bonefish, and of course, the fantastic blue marlin. A chartered fishing boat, led by Captain Smithers, would leave at ten a.m.

Feeling rested and still full from last night's dinner, Dina and Sentra put on their swimwear, hats, and sunblock. Carefully Sentra stashed her leather belt in their beach bag and then drove them two miles to the Aqua Delights Dock. The thirty-four foot boat had two fighting chairs, tackle, bait, snacks, juice, dog bones, and ice for the five of them. The clear blue sky beckoned them into the sea, and Dina was glad Olgilvee had thought of the fishing excursion.

Maybe her interest in his oceanography skills had spurred him to show off a bit. She knew they both felt young again, as love can have that effect.

"This is the month of June, and the Million Dollar Month Sport Fishing Tournament is in progress," Olgilvee shouted.

He was exceedingly determined to win the enormous cash prize for catching the largest Atlantic blue marlin, money Dina needed to complete their journey.

White-tailed, tropic birds called out to them on their walk down the wooden dock. They were greeted by Captain Smithers, a stocky man who carried a full, grey beard with dignity. The ruggedness of sea life was etched deeply into his tanned face. A large, Roman nose was topped with two small, beady, brown eyes, and a stogie hung out of the corner of his mouth. He talked and swatted gnats from his sweaty flesh. "All on board the Salty Alitha," he called. Then he motored them to the south side of the island range to Cayman Trench.

"Its depth reaches twenty-four thousand seven hundred and twenty feet," Olgilvee explained. "We're in the deepest part of the Caribbean."

"There must be quite an array of sea life here," Sentra said, her feet propped up on a bait bucket. "While fishing off New England for a sailfish, I caught a beauty using a whole squid for bait. It weighed sixty pounds, and it had a high, wide dorsal fin. I was trolling in deep water when I hooked it. It lept, twisted, and tail walked on the water for two and one-half hours. My hands were aching from the strain." Dina was awed at her grand niece's stamina.

"Those big blue marlins are more common here than in the Atlantic Gulf stream, because of the warmer tropical waters," Captain Smithers said. He expertly cruised the Salty Alitha. "Best to go slow as fast trolling tears up the good bait."

Dina sat back in her chair watching Sentra scan the sky. White, fluffy cumulus clouds appeared like cotton strewn across a blue blanket. "We're doomed to have more good weather," Sentra said, adjusting her visor and applying more sunblock to her bronzed skin. Her thick mass of blond hair was braided tightly in a french style. Her biceps bulged upon lifting the heavy bait bucket which she placed closer to her chair.

Mentally and physically sturdy, Dina knew Sentra could weather the storms of adventure. With the brutal assault set deep in her mind, so easily she could remember Sentra's bravery and protective measures during the attack. The band of cutthroats had met death on the high seas because they did not deserve life. Dina was well-pleased with her selection of Sentra, and their destiny would be fulfulled she knew. Feeling strong herself, Dina did some deep knee bends on the deck as Olgilvee looked on.

"You're a tough chickadee, my beauty," Olgilvee said.

Prepared to take on any evilness that may befall the crew, Dina hoped Amanda, George, and that fifth surviving cutthroat, Devon, would not discover them on the beautiful day. If she did see Devon again, she knew she would recognize him immediately.

"Yowee," Jackson said loudly. He pointed portside where Dina could see the sharp, triangular dorsal fin of a cruising blue indulging in surface feeding.

"What will you use for bait?" Sentra asked.

"Just some strip bait and a sewn mackeral with the backbone removed to give it added life," he said. Then he cast his line over the side and drew it past the blue. At the same time, Olgilvee cast in a fair-sized bonefish. Suddenly the fish rapped Olgilvee's bait with its bill. "Free spool it," Jackson yelled.

Giving the reel the familiar drop back, the enormous fish was hooked. It heaved its powerful body out of the sea, and then it dove to the depths with a hearty tug. "With that heavy tackle you ought to be able to pump that fish to the surface," Jackson assured him. "It must weigh three thousand pounds." The blue giant slapped through the ocean's surface as it rose.

"Look at the size of that pike," Sentra said. It flashed its extended upper jaw into the air.

Olgilvee battled the fish for three hours. Exhausted, he sat down and let his fresh partner try to bring it in. They were all hoping it would not dive to the bottom and die from exhaustion many fathoms beneath the boat. Positioned in the fighting seat, Jackson was able to turn at any angle. In his hand he held fast to the laminated wooden rod, its butt fitting into the socket in the chair, allowing him to exert maximum pressure on his victim. He was also in Olgilvee's harness which was connected to the center pin reel. After two hours of Jackson struggling, Olgilvee got back into his harness and attempted to bring the weakening brute in. He released the throw-out lever to allow the fish to run free, and the drag regulated the tension.

Sentra watched enthusiastically, proudly looking over her catch of the day: bonitos, a moonfish, a black grouper, and a fifteen pound wahoo. Munching on a sweet, ripe peach, she playfully spit the pit out at a weary Jackson.

Elkin jumped as an anguished cry rang out. Suddenly Olgilvee screamed again in agony and bent sideways, grabbing his arm, The ulna, the long bone in his right forearm, had twisted, nearly breaking in two. So excruciating was the pain that he blacked-out for an instant in Dina's arms. Soothing her wounded friend, Captain Smithers applied first aid. Olgilvee sucked down a double shot of whiskey making his brain slowly forgot about the pain torturing his once supple form. Jackson still lay exhausted, and Sentra slipped on the vest and took control, but the fish had regained strength and was on its second wind. After three more hours passed, she finally began to reel in the monster.

At nine p.m., the sun had completely sunk, and the weary crew made their way back to shore with a prize marlin. Weighing three thousand five hundred pounds, it was the largest fish ever entered in the Million Dollar Contest. If during the week no one topped it, they would be thigh-high in money. They all smiled brightly for Captain Smithers who took their photo with the giant fish. Olgilvee, his one arm in a sling, was holding Dina by the waist. Her face was slightly sunburned, and dry, salty, sprigs of red hair covered one eye. Sentra was on the other side of the marlin atop Jackson's shoulders. Her arms reached up the side of the fish, pointing to the heavens. Dina knew if they won the money they would split it four ways. Sentra and her cut of five hundred thousand dollars would help them finish their journey.

Soon they stumbled into their apartment at Peyton's Castle. Elkin gulped down a dish of dog food, and Dina and Sentra bathed. The two men retreated to their own rooms after a warm goodnight. Carefully Sentra took her leather belt from her beach bag and stashed it under her mattress, where she could easily retrieve it for the next day.

Dina awoke to the sound of the doorbell. Elkin paced nervously while she dressed and slipped out into the foyer. Who would be calling at five a.m. she wondered, and then she opened the door as much as the safety chain would allow. A small box lay on the pavement, and no human beings were in sight. Cautiously she poked the box with a yardstick. Then she dislodged the safety chain, stooped down, and carefully untied the string around it. Opening the lid of the shoe box, she found a pile of grey cat hair and a picture of their long lost seacat Feather. Her bald body looked emaciated, and her once bright eyes looked dull and unseeing.

"Damn you, Amanda," Dina shouted, standing in the doorway. Suddenly Jackson, Olgilvee, and Sentra were by her side with mouths agape.

"What's the commotion about?" Sentra asked. Elkin wimpered and sniffed at the box.

"Look for yourselves," Dina said, pointing to the box. Anger swelled in Sentra when she saw the picture of her beloved pet and fingered the fur.

"How dare they abuse that poor creature," Sentra said sadly. She cinched her leather belt to her waist.

Dina explained to the bewildered Jackson and Olgilvee about their special love for Feather. The cat was replacing the first seacat Sentra had lost during a storm. It had fulfilled the empty spot that was in her after its death.

Sentra was not about to lose another pet, especially to animal torturers. "We must find those two and settle this completely. They may again resort to confining one of us next."

The restaurant was ringing with the sound of clanking dishes, and the morning hour was crowded with locals and tourists. Many of the customers ate avocados mashed with cream cheese, filled with saltfish gundy, in a seafood salad, or stuffed with crabmeat. Callaloo, however, was Dina and Sentra's favorite dish. It was a potpourri of fat pork, crab, salt meat, and fresh fish stewed with okra and spinach. The callaloo greens were garnished with floating fungi and served with a Caribbean lobster. They ate fast.

Questioning neighbors and hotel personnel, Dina discovered that two people fitting Amanda and George's descriptions were spotted leaving the parking lot in a dirty, brown truck. The witnesses said they were headed back toward Bodden Town. Having only a few days to find their cat, they took the bait with great caution. At one time hiding from their enemies, they would now hunt them down for their personal property. Elkin, Sentra, and Dina sat in the back seat while Olgilvee sat in the front passenger's seat. Jackson got behind the wheel of the blue jeep and drove down the road.

Royal terns and magnificent frigate birds dotted the shoreline where they drove along the sandy beach. Finally, they spotted the small, seafaring village of Bodden Town. The day was bright, and the sun glowed like a yellow flame upon the small crowd that meandered into the Eastern Wreck, a cozy surf shop. A dark, obese man wearing a white cap welcomed them at the door, his massive fingers sunburnt and showing days of sand beneath the nails. Elkin quietly waited and stared.

Sentra quickly described the couple to him. "Seen them anywhere?"

"Yes," He answered. He immediately recognized the description of the two. "To your right down at Pirates's Cave. They entertain at the music club," he said, pointing with a swollen finger.

The pulsating rhythm filled the air, and they pulled into the parking lot next to an old, brown truck. Behind large, flowering gardenia bushes, they spotted a steel band and numerous calypso dancers. A crowd of fifteen people stood nearby swaying to the music and sipping rum coolers. The natives were dancing seductively to the sensuous beats. The drummer, known as Mighty Windsong, was none other than George, and the sexy dancer in the magenta scarf was, of course, Amanda. A beautiful turban adorned her head, and she twisted snake-like to the drum beat.

While band members played electric guitars, string basses, and maracas, Sentra and Dina tried to remain inconspicuous by hiding behind a breadfruit tree near the back of the crowd. George was playing a sawed-off drum with its top hammered to produce scale notes and various voices. Wriggling in a version of the limbo, Amanda moved her way toward freedom beneath a sugarcane pole. Soon upright, she was greeted by Sentra.

"I've found you, now," Sentra yelled. Seething, she grabbed the long end of Amanda's bandana. While running the opposite direction, the cloth unraveled to expose brown shoulders and mid-length hair tied in a ponytail. George jumped off his stool and raced toward his woman.

"Run, darling, run," he screamed at Amanda. Jackson, Olgilvee, and Dina followed quickly. Elkin ran ahead of the group and pounced on George, bringing him down. Then he took off for Amanda.

Heading toward the ocean, Dina could see her go to a beach house. Amanda ran past the edge of a small swimming pool where Dina saw Elkin lunge at her, knocking her into the deep end. Before long, Jackson, Olgilvee, and Dina were in the pool surrounding Amanda. She screamed and lashed at them with pointed fingernails.

Grasping both wrists behind her, Olgilvee dragged her to the pool steps with his one good arm.

Amanda admitted the cottage was their rental. George and she were ushered inside followed by one hour of questioning by Dina. Neither would speak. Quietly their two captives fell asleep under Jackson's watchful eyes.

Dina took a can of lemonade from the refrigerator and perused her surroundings. The beach front cottage was cool and comfortable, and large windows of tinted glass covered every wall to the outside. Huge ceiling fans hummed to the rhythm of the wind, and the Caribbean breeze rustled in the royal palm fronds. Dina was intent on developing an understanding with her grand niece Amanda. Hardened by the cruelties of life and aged by drug addiction, Dina wondered if she would be willing to open up and hear her story. Then a grandfather clock chimed, and the sun disappeared behind dark clouds which stood out against the background of emersing and glaring white sunlight.

"In twenty hours we'll have rain," Sentra said. She observed the alto cumulus clouds shrouding the sky with their gloved hands. Then suddenly Dina saw Sentra jump, and she looked down at her niece's legs. Feather was purring and rubbing its bristly body on her golden calves. Sentra quickly grabbed up the cat, holding her tightly to her chest.

"My beautiful friend, you're alive," she said, snuggling her nose into its neck.

Soon Amanda and George were rested from their nap. In securing their pet and capturing the enemy, Olgilvee and Jackson had proved loyalty to Dina. With them Sentra agreed they would now share their plans. A hearty, late night snack of shrimp and crab helped them all regain strength, but Amanda complained of naseau, and her grey eyes looked slightly glazed. Dina felt extreme pity for her. Gathered together in the large family room overlooking the sea, Dina decided to include ailing Amanda and George in the secret, too. She spoke most intently to Amanda about their great adventure and the destiny of the Darrendon family. The grand niece needed to hear the whole story, not just the bits and pieces she had overheard at the Banyan Forest. "The castle must remain in our hands. The creditors must be paid soon, as the entrance to eternity will open on September 23rd, 2001 during the autumnal equinox. We shall be there, Amanda, the living and the departed souls of the truly undead."

Amanda began to weep as if trying to wash away the lines of resentment that had been etched into her brow.

"You must not alter our plans," Sentra said. "Great Grandfather has sent us on a mission, and it must be fulfilled. The sale of the gems will give us money which must not be used for frivolous purpose but only for our family debts. Now are you for or against the family?"

Unbelieving at first of the future of eternity, Amanda remained silent. Dina knew she would not be easily swayed. Olgilvee and Jackson were astonished and remained speechless.

"If you continue to harass us and threaten our lives, we shall have no other choice but to turn you into the authorities. Then perhaps they would discover our plans and halt our hunt, or maybe you or I would perish without ever fulfilling the plan," Sentra persisted.

Amanda leaned her head against George's shoulder, and silent Jackson and Olgilvee looked on. Soon her expression softened, and she asked to return to her room for the night.

"Sleep on it," Dina said. The woman stood and gasped, and then she grabbed the right upper quadrant of her abdomen. Vomit spewed from her mouth, and she covered it and ran for the bathroom. Suspicious of possible food poisoning, George helped his friend to bed for the night while Elkin sat poised by their bedroom door, guarding against their departure. Olgilvee and Jackson retired to the two hammocks outside Amanda's bedroom window to make sure they did not escape the premises through that route. Dina knew they would all still be there in the morning. She could see the hope in Sentra's face for rekindled friendship and renewed family ties.

The next day, Amanda had a fever of one hundred and two degrees, and the pain in her abdomen had not subsided. She remained in bed while Olgilvee and Jackson searched for a doctor in Bodden Town. Within two hours, Dina noticed a small, thin, white physician dressed in shorts and a white shirt enter the dwelling. Dr. Ravender was kind and gentle during his examination of Amanda. He spoke distinctly and with an air of experitise while peering over his thick spectacles.

"The liver is tender and enlarged, and she looks jaundiced," he said, pointing to her yellowish flesh. "The symptoms she states were abrupt and accompanied with nausea, fever, and malaise. Her urine contains bile, and she also has itchy skin and diarrhea. We shall do some further laboratory tests, but at this point, I would say she suffers from acute hepatitis, Virus A. She may have picked it up from contaminated food or infected water."

Putting his medical supplies back into his black bag, he left a phone number where to reach him if an emergency should arise. Sentra slipped the doctor three one hundred dollar bills with an understanding that the illness would remain untold to anyone else. He accepted and asked no questions as if he had done this before.

"What can we expect?" George asked the doctor.

"She won't have much of an appetite, and when she does, nausea will follow. Headaches, chills, and fever are not uncommon, and jaundice, a yellowish discoloring of the skin due to bile, may occur now and again."

"Can we catch it?" Sentra asked.

"Generally, she could be noninfectious about one month after the onset of illness, although she could be a carrier. Anyone who has been in contact with her can be given gamma globulin as a prophylactic measure. It proves quite effective against hepatitis A."

"Where do we get gamma globulin?" George asked.

"George Town Caribbean Hospital."

"What type of care can we give her?" Dina asked sympathetically.

"First of all, she must be put into strict isolation while the disease is active. Bedrest is very important during this acute phase, especially while she is jaundiced, in abdominal pain, and having abnormal liver tests. You may allow her to use the bathroom; however, she should be aided while walking."

"What about food?" Dina asked.

Dr. Ravender pushed his glasses up his nose and leaned against the kitchen wall. "High protein and high carbohydrate foods can be eaten, although she'll probably be revolted by the food. Be sure to serve it in small quantities, and make it look as attractive as possible. Force fluids, especially while she is jaundiced. The main treatment is building up resistance. I have no drug to affect the virus directly." He ambled toward the door as sprinkles of rain hit the tile roof like small toothpicks. "Be sure to wash your hands before and after doing anything for the patient. We don't need any more infections." He quickly washed his hands at the kitchen sink and then jogged to the waiting pick-up truck. Jackson and Olgilvee sped off into the watery eyes of the new morning.

Dina allowed Sentra to be her assistant as primary caregiver. However, they needed to get their gamma globulin, because this blood protein was essential for protection. Catching this infection would only prolong their journey for six, maybe eight more weeks. As soon as the two men returned from Bodden Town, they could all go to George Town to the hospital.

Amanda slept quietly, and George waited by her side. Two hours passed when Olgilvee and Jackson returned with a housekeeper to sit with Amanda for a day or two while they all made their trek across the island. This housekeeper's husband had been cured of the same illness, and she had been treated with gamma globulin. She never caught it. Dina knew everyone was anxious for treatment, and at the same time, she knew they were all hoping for Amanda's quick recovery. Show love to the weakling, the ignorant, but beware a backlash. A complete trustworthiness of Amanda and George had yet to be earned.

They traveled easily in the blue jeep while keeping George securely handcuffed. Past Savannah and Prospect Olgilvee drove, traveling until they reached George Town. The hospital was small and friendly, and service was quick. They all felt a sense of relief, and even George seemed to throw aside his anger and greed. While having his freedom returned, he never attempted to escape. Maybe he was beginning to see the more important reason to their lives. Perhaps he was beginning to feel that he, too, had a vital part to play in the destiny of the Darrendons, but Dina would still be cautious. However, she remained confident that the gem was safely hidden on Sentra's waist, and Elkin would protect her from wicked ones.

It was a good idea to check on the Empress while they were so near George Town Harbor. Although the ruby was hidden with Sentra in her belt, The Book of Eternity was in the boat's safe. At the dock, the two women searched the boat for any missing items.

"This your craft?" A tall, skinny man stood on the deck. He right arm was in a cast, and the left eye was blackened and swollen.

"Yes it is," Sentra answered. Dina noticed the old guy become angry as Jackson and Olgilvee looked on.

"I was attacked by an intruder last night. Found him on your boat trying his darndest to pick the lock on the safe below deck. He really let me have it, but I didn't let him get too far."

"What did he look like?" Dina asked.

"He had long, golden hair and bright green eyes like a cat. A scar crossed his right cheek. He said ' voodoo will get them,'" the injured man said. Then he scurried off.

"We'll keep a look out for him," Jackson said.

Dina groaned upon recognizing the description of the nasty Devon, the evil one from her childhood and the sole survivior of the band of cutthroats they had encountered on their way toward Cuba. He searched hard for the gems she knew. Carefully she checked the boat's safe and found The Book of Eternity inside. Dina shivered at the thought of running into him again. Grandfather was right. "Always beware the evil Devon," he had told her. "A centenarian, he may walk the earth with you for many years to come," she said aloud.

Quietly they drove back to the beach house.

It was half past six, and Amanda refused her second meal of the day. The doctor said the pre-existing liver damage was from alcohol abuse. Her jaundice had deepened, she became mentally confused, and the vomiting continued. Sentra remained by her side almost twenty-four hours a day. She would hold her hand and soothe her with stories of their childhood, but at times Amanda did not recognize her. Sometimes she would mumble nonsense of which Sentra could only make out a few scattering of words.

"Father, Father," she said repeatedly. "No, no. Don't leave."

Dina looked on and knew the sad story. Their father had abandoned her, Sentra, and Steven, when they were very small, and their mother had died of cancer not long after. They had been raised with three different sets of foster parents. Sentra's and Steven's separate foster parents had loved them so much that they eventually adopted both of them. Then when Sentra became a teen, Dina took her in. Amanda, however, was passed from family to family making for a very unstable home life. Feeling unwanted, she had turned to drugs and alcohol. Her friends were con men and hardened criminals, and later drug addiction nearly killed her on several occasions. The years passed by, and Amanda's bitterness and resentment grew, some of it toward Sentra who lived in a life of easier times.

Now the past horror of being abandoned had emerged, and Amanda's tortured mind could no longer hold back the pain. Dina could see tears of helplessness drip down Sentra's face, and then Amanda spoke. "Sister, Sister, love me, hold me tight."

Days slipped by during which her condition worsened. Refusing most foods, she became emaciated. Although Dr. Ravender was summoned, he was unable to provide a fast cure. "It is up to God," he said encouragingly.

"Sit tight," Olgilvee said. Then he and Jackson took the doctor back to town. The housekeeper decided to stay.

George remained near, but he grew restless and bored. He spent most free time fishing off the beach and carving animals from the fallen coconuts. The next few days were long and dark, and shallow and unknowning, but Dina hoped they all held onto their future goals.

"What is all the racket?" Sentra asked. Dina could hear a truck engine revving loudly and men howling and laughing with great pleasure.

"We did it," Olgilvee and Jackson cried out. They joyously deposited buckets of bills on the living room floor.

"Thank, God," Dina shouted. She knew a week since the fishing contest had elapsed, and no one had topped their prize marlin. Silently she had prayed for the winning to be in their favor. The journey must continue for time is of the essence. The short, necessary delay was not in vain. Soon Olgilvee and Jackson took some cash and decided to return to town for supplies.

Dina knew the winnings from the Million Dollar Month Contest would help them complete their voyage. "We don't need jobs now," she said. She remembered the last dollar spent from the sale of her artworks. Chiding Sentra, she knew her savings from her meteorology position would not last the entire journey either. The money was a godsend, and she wondered if the fantastic three thousand five hundred pound Atlantic blue marlin they caught was put there by the God of the Sea.

Dina saw Sentra slip into Amanda's room and decided to make preparations for the next morning.

It was in the middle of the night when Amanda's fever broke, and in the morning she was ready to take down some eggs, toast, and fruit. George, completely free of thoughts of escape, would be left to help out the housekeeper in tending to Amanda's needs.

"Be back soon, my sweet." Sentra kisssed Amanda's face and promised to return with supplies and many gifts for her sister. For the first time in years, Dina knew Amanda felt an awakening of good old feelings.

Leaving Elkin to guard Amanda, George, and the housekeeper, Dina and Sentra, in a rented car, headed for George Town. It was July 1st, and Dina knew the fun trip would break the stress of the past days and the long, arduous search for the gems. They figured Olgilvee and Jackson would be back from their buying trip by the time they returned. The spectrum for aquirables was expansive in the capital where they would choose select gifts for Amanda. The winnings would be placed in a bank, because most duty free shops accepted traveler's checks. It is never good to carry cash Dina knew for crime is worldwide. Quickly she pointed out to Sentra a photograph of a wanted thief that was posted on a palm tree.

On Cardinal Avenue they parked the car and strolled along the paved street past the brilliant yellow elder and the fragrant, red and white striped trumpet blossom. The window of Kirk Freeport was filled with sparkling crystals. Once inside, Sentra chose a large, crystal bowl, a set of exquisite china, earthenware, and baking dishes. Dina was quite impressed. She knew Amanda would especially like the hand-painted china. They also chose an elegant, gold Swiss watch, a movie camera, jewelry made of shells and semi-precious stones, French perfume, cosmetics, cashmere sweaters, and a lovely, crystal paper weight. It was a joyous experience they knew as they loaded up the car.

Stashing the goods in their trunk, Dina felt hunger. "Let's find a place to eat, Sentra." she said. Sentra nodded. On South Church Street they entered Chef Bell's Grand Old Coconut Inn. The picturesque place stood smiling on the seashore, and after they entered Brown Bar, they enjoyed a rum and coke. Sentra called the beach house in Bodden Town to check on Amanda. She talked softly as Sentra told Dina, but there was more strength in her voice. She too was eating some lunch that George made for her. Of course, she was speechless after they reminded her of all the presents they would bring home to her in just a few hours. Then a tearful but happy good-bye was heard before they hung up the receiver at the bar.

In the veranda they served a meal of Cayman lobsters and shrimp cocktail. The sea breeze carassed her red hair, and the view of the playful seagulls delighted Dina.

"Key lime pie?" Sentra questioned suspiciously. "We didn't order this, yet."

"But ma'am. It is compliments of the gentleman, Devon, seated to your left," the waiter said.

Glancing over at a small table, Dina saw a tall, tanned man with long, golden hair which hung down from the menu he held over his face. Suddenly the menu was lowered, and they noticed two bright green eyes gazing over the top. Then still lower the menu dropped until it uncovered even more of his features. Dina could clearly see a deep scar riding over his right cheek.

"Why, that murderous fiend. He's stalking us," Dina said fearfully. She rose from her chair and walked toward the man.

"So we meet again," Dina," Devon said. He stood up and extended his large hand. A diamond ring glistened from his index finger. The gem caught her stare. "Ah, you like jewels do you." Dina looked into his brilliant green eyes, and then he drew back his hand.

"What do you want with us?" Dina asked. Devon sat down and ogled Dina.

"Just looking over posssible companions for my plantations. Which do you prefer, bananas in Jamaica or peaches in South Carolina? Or perhaps my undersea city, historic inn, or your choice of a fantasy isle would amuse you." Dina thought the offer odd. "You're still nice enough for the duties I would have for you." He reached out and stroked her firm thigh.

"Stop it," Sentra yelled. Suddenly she raced to Dina's side and swiftly grabbed a cream pie off a waiter's tray. Dina took it and smeared it atop Devon's head. A blob of whipped cream dripped down the center of his scar, and onlookers gasped.

"Take those wildcats out of here, now," Devon ordered. Soon two large waiters grabbed Dina and Sentra from behind and led them to the door.

Toward Bodden Town they drove off in their car, but they were not alone. In the distance, a black car with tinted windows was following their every move. On a desolate part of the road, their pursuers side-swipped them, almost pitching them over the embankment into the sea. Then they heard pop sounds and saw a masked man shoot at them from the passenger's side. Dina ducked and swerved their car, losing control and crashing into a large palm tree.

With legs in the front seat and body in the back seat, Dina opened her eyes. Sentra lay unconscious in the passenger's seat with her head lodged in the open window of her door.

"Get the bitches out of there."

Dina felt someone tugging at her arm. She took a deep breath and prayed, and then she felt herself drifting off.

CHAPTER FOUR

Dina awoke to the sound of low moving water and sun gleaming on her face. Her jeans felt damp, and her shirt was buttoned one button too high. They had been searched. Sentra lay next to her on a mattress on a dirt floor, the belt still cinched loosely to her grand niece's waist. "So good they did not find the secret pouch," Sentra said while slipping it off and quickly checking that its contents were safe.

"Thank God," Dina said with relief. She sat up and pulled twigs from her red hair. Although neither of them had been bound or gagged, she noticed ropes and handcuffs sitting on a woven chair near their bed. The small, wooden hut was barely big enough for the two of them, and the one tiny, open window allowed for poor circulation. Pushing open a small thatched door, Dina could see a muddy river flowing just eight feet before her. The atmosphere was serene, sweet smelling, tropical, and desolate. Across the river was a large banana grove, and to her right was a small sugarcane field. A larger house was nestled in a patch of lush tropical growth behind her, and the sun's position in the sky told her it was early morning.

"Where are we, and what time is it anyway?" Sentra asked. Past Dina she walked, readjusted her belt, and stuck a toe into the slow current. "I don't know about you, but I could go for a bath."

She removed her belt, placed it under a rock, and quickly perused the river for any predators. Then she stripped off her top and jeans. Baring firm, large breasts and tight buttocks, she dove into the water in naked splendor. Within minutes, Dina joined her, and the two women splashed and played and soothed their aching bodies. Fortunately the car accident had not done any permanent damage. But Dina did notice a large, shallow gash on Sentra's forehead and a small scratch across her chin. It was good they were both wearing seatbelts.

Seeing no one, they emerged from their swim and laid out to dry upon two large banana leaves that Dina had pulled from the water. Sentra retrieved her belt from beneath the rock where a jungle spider the size of an orange spun its web. Dina felt morning hunger pangs drive splinters into her stomach as they dressed and planned to visit the partially hidden house. Up ahead they could see a thickly forested mountainside with a stream rushing down over rocky precipes. Walking past a hedge of pine and purple bougainvillea, Dina spotted the front door to a large, red brick house. Preferring to sneak in a side entrance, they walked along the pathway amid hummingbirds flitting back and forth in the lavender-blue trumpet vines.

"A Jamaican swallow," Sentra said. Dina watched a giant, bright yellow and black butterfly with a six-inch wing span dart among the flowering gardenia bushes. "This species is found in the Millbank area near the Brown River. I wonder if those could be the John Crow Mountains," Sentra pondered.

"Yes," Dina said, pointing to the large, yellow fruits across the river. "And this is probably Devon's banana plantation, but how in the world did we get here in the northeastern end of Jamaica?" Dina said.

"By plane, ladies."

Dina saw Sentra jump, startled by the familiar baratone voice that rang out. His long, golden hair was tied into a ponytail, and his bright green eyes watched them closely, even while he hacked his machete at a ripe guava. "Care for some fruit?" Pointing the machete at their necks, he urged them onto the back patio. "I'm glad to see you two have recuperated from your accident. How tragic it would have been had you been killed." He grinned showing off sparkling, white teeth and a glowing, gold incisor.

"What do you want with us?" Sentra asked. She stood tall and proud staring directly at the enemy. "Why have you brought us here?"

"We'll have time to talk later. First, you must eat. Then I will tell you of your surroundings. Edwin," he called.

A tall, thin, blue-eyed, black man entered with a tray of drinks in hand. Dina and Sentra each took a wine sangria, and then they walked toward a table arrangement of luscious treats. While hungrily eating, they listened to their captor describe their whereabouts. Then Edwin returned inside.

"This is the John Crow Mountain Range at the northeast tip of Jamaica. Over there is my banana plantation," he said, pointing across the river. "It provides a tidy income. Here where we stand is very rugged terrain, so don't try to escape. Crevasses and small ravines lie at all angles and can be as deep as twenty feet. There are only two ways out of here. One, you can go by river which is loaded with crocodiles."

Dina saw him ogle Sentra as if he was looking upon a naked lady. He must have seen them down by the river she realized as he continued.

"Two, you can climb across the top of this tangled vegetation where one bad step may be the end of you. This is undisturbed native forest, ladies, so take heed."

"And we're in the path of the prevailing northeast trade winds. If I'm right, we'll be due for one of your daily rainstorms this afternoon," Sentra added.

"Yes. We'll get plenty of showers that keep this lush vegetation green and abundant. Please ladies, try some more of Edwin's special

Jamaican concoction." Dina and Sentra each drank another full glass of the sweet nectar. "Wilderness wine," Devon said.

"So how long will you keep us here?" Dina asked.

"Until I get what I want."

"Which is?" Sentra asked boldly. Grabbing one of the wooden stools, she stood and pointed its legs at the blond-haired man. Dina saw Edwin come from the kitchen and grab Sentra from behind before she had a chance to warn her. He pinched her shoulder with two large fingers. Then she let loose of the stool and dropped to her knees.

"I can see you two cannot be trusted. Edwin, take the women back to their cabin by the river. They could use a nap."

Dina could feel Edwin jab her in the back while he herded them away from the house. She felt suddenly sleepy which was unusual at eleven a.m., the patio clock's time. Soon the trees started to spin, and she saw Sentra collapse in front of her.

Dina turned over on the mattress feeling a bit groggy, and she listened to a night bird. Edwin must have carried them here she knew, because she remembered blacking out on the garden path.

"That was some sangria," she said loudly. She felt beneath the sheets for Sentra while listening to her soft breathing and intermittent mumbling. Her fingers soon latched upon the belt and its contents. No one ever discovered the gem hidden inside its fine leather. The secret compartment was so well concealed. She knew their bodies were always searched thoroughly as thought by their captors. They were very careful now not to hide their precious goods in a pant's pocket, bra, or even a body cavity. The belt, so far, had been the perfect spot.

Feeling nature call, she rose and kicked a foot at the thatched door. It did not budge, and she assumed it was bolted from the outside. Dina decided to squeeze through the small opening of the window into the night. Whoever was responsible for their confinement was not too worried about any immediate escapes, for they all knew the secluded, dense forest and river were their barriers. Once outside, she picked up a distant sound of drum beats reverberating through the trees behind the big house.

"Dina," Sentra summoned. Suddenly her partner was by her side in the balmy, night air. "Remember not to drink any more of that special concoction," she said while rubbing the sleep from her eyes. "And listen to the intricate rhythms of those drums. What an eerie sound. There's only one reason to play drums this late at night."

"The Cumina Cult must be having a voodoo ritual," Dina said. Then she felt her hair stand on end as a painful shriek echoed through the mountains. "Let's hope it's not the Obeah. Their practices are filled with cannibalism, orgies, and sorcery. Very dangerous."

"Let's check it out," Sentra said.

"I wish Elkin was here," Dina said. She could remember the obedient wolf standing guard next to Amanda. He must miss her terribly she knew. Then she squeezed the good luck dragon around her neck and recalled the black artist she had the pleasure of meeting. Soon she hoped they could find out if her directions to the underground lake in Grey Grotto Cave were accurate. And greatly she hoped they would meet her sister for another tip. Would they live to find gem number two?

"Look," Sentra said pointing upward. Behind the big house, flames shot up into the air, and howls echoed softly. Quietly they crept and hid behind giant banyans and smaller breadfruit trees. Then they crawled on hands and knees through the undergrowth where twigs and stones cut into their flesh. Soon sticky blood oozed forth, and the full, summer moon cast a spooky glow from the heavens. They snuck into a small, cool stream which ran forth from a large rock tower that rose twenty feet into the air. The ritual was taking place behind the rock formation. The steel drums continued their song, and they kept crawling and shivering in fear.

"Yow!" Sentra yelled. A baby crocodile had clamped onto her right foot, and it was tugging fiercely. Quickly Dina wedged a stick into its jaw moving it down toward the croc's throat. Sentra pulled her foot free, watching small teeth holes drip blood into the cool stream.

Standing up, she leaned on a banyan tree for support. Its bark was carved with strange designs, and Dina recalled the symbol's meaning from the artwork the bountiful black lady of Grand Cayman had produced. "This bird carving, called the phoenix, is representative of death and rebirth. Surrounding the bird is a pentacle or symbol of magical regeneration. These three circled crosses represent the dangerous, important area of the crossroads, and the loa is guardian of the crossroad."

"What else did she tell you about the loa?" Sentra asked. The drum beats continued, and the wind blew the scent of roasting coals in their direction. Dina seated Sentra on the large, flat, dry root of the tree and applied aloe juice to the stinging wound.

"Loa are chiefly divine creatures of African pantheon. They can be angry relatives who have been defied, but some loa are identified with saints of the Catholic religion. Each one has a ceremonial color, song, day of the week, sacred emblem, and possession behavior."

"That feels better," Sentra said reassuringly. She slipped on her leather sandal, and Dina saw her motion to go forward to the rock tower that was only a few feet away. Soon dark figures could be seen with their heads like apples bobbing up and down in the moonlight. Finding a deep crevice, they ducked into its recesses just as a dark cloud covered the moon.

"It's a voodoo ritual," Dina whispered to Sentra. They saw the white-clothed natives dancing around a black pot which spewed grey smoke and flames from its mouth. To the far left, a pen stood filled with chickens, goats, and bulls, their fearful squeals ringing out. And up high, a tall man in a white turban was seated on top of a wooden platform, watching the natives dance before him in a circle. Soon he began to drink from a goblet which dripped the red liquid of blood down his chin. Creeping a bit closer, in the moonlight that slipped out from a darkened cloud, Dina caught a glimpse of his bright green eyes. They glowed lustfully at a young, native girl who was brought before him. The drum beats grew louder, and she began shrieking, twisting, and groaning.

"Devon. I'm yours," the young woman said in submission.

Then Dina could see chickens brought forth onto a pedestal where one by one they were beheaded and their blood squeezed forth into an urn.

Suddenly a small bull broke his way through the gate and trotted nervously toward Sentra. One of the natives followed carrying a gleaming machete. Dina crouched down into the plush vegetation securing her hold on a large, fallen tree limb. When the bull trotted past, she yanked up a vine and tripped the unsuspecting native. He cut his own throat on the blade of his machete which was partially buried in his neck.

"Let's hit the road," Sentra said.

Upon hearing one more native come their way, Dina followed Sentra through the dense brush. Vines and roots reached out to grab them, tripping them on their stumble through the forest. Quickly reaching their hut, they ducked inside and latched the door. Sentra held a large club she found in the woods, and Dina was equipped with a homemade, wooden pick. They waited, and Dina could feel her heart beating hard and fast. Then they heard shouting outside their cabin and leaves rustling nearby. Soon the noise stopped, and Dina was sure they were alone again.

"We must make an escape, for they may use us in one of their rituals. Devon is such a cruel man. He'd kill for the jewels," Sentra said. Carefully she checked out the cinch in her leather belt to be sure it was clasped tightly shut.

"You're right," Dina agreed. "We must make a raft. That river could take us to safety as long as the crocodiles don't tip us over."

"They'll usually leave you alone if you stay out of their way," Sentra said in pain while massaging her right foot.

Feeling there were no pursuers about, Dina crept behind Sentra, and they headed for the big house. Cutting supplies, ropes, and food needed to be confiscated for their river journey. Since the side door to the pantry was locked, they crawled in an open window. Into huge kitchen basins they stepped in the glow from the corner lanterns. Copper pans and pots hung from hooks above an oak island in the center of the room looking as if they had just been polished. Cabinets were filled with various spices, and the gigantic refrigerator freezer was stuffed with seafood, chicken, and veal. Large loaves of homemade breads filled the bread box, and vegetables were piled high in a large tin basin.

"Whoa," Sentra said with fear in her voice.

Dina turned around and saw a three foot, grey rat scamper across the tile floor to a hiding spot beneath a large cabinet filled with canned goods. Another guest, a hairy, brown spider, spun his web inside the strands of a low-hanging basket lamp. Then Dina noticed upon the wall an old, khaki-colored backpack on a wooden peg.

"Perfect," she said. Soon it was packed with vegies, bread, and canned goods. Pulling open a drawer, Dina yanked forth a spool of hearty twine and sharp shears. "We have what we need."

Suddenly they heard voices from behind the side door, and as a key jingled, the doorknob began to turn. Dina barrelled after Sentra with backpack in hand and quickly climbed the stairs at the front of the kitchen. The wooden steps creaked beneath their weight as they bounded upward. They entered a large bedroom and quietly shut the door. There were two wooden chests at the end of a king-sized canopy bed. Dina hid Sentra beneath the blankets in one. Then she hid herself in the other one. At the exact moment she let down the lid to the trunk, the bedroom door opened.

"Devon, my love. Why do you want these two women so badly?" a female voice said.

"Those gems are rightly mine. I must have them back. They will give me power to reach a source, and of course, there is the matter of eternity."

"But I don't understand. Please explain it to me."

Dina heard the sweet sound of harp music as a whiff of Jamaican ginger darted into the trunk's cracks. Who was the woman, Dina wondered.

"During the Tudor period from 1485 to 1603, my ancestor, grandfather, was a notorious Spanish pirate. He had taken more than five hundred ships in his heyday while sailing the great oceans. In the Caribbean and New England coast, he headed a mutiny and was elected Captain San Chez.

Mitch the Magnificent, an enemy pirate, was known for beheading captains of other ships and propping their heads on his canons. Once he seized my grandfather's Spanish vessel off New Foundland which had two hundred thousand pieces of eight aboard and my beautiful, red-haired mother, the captain's daughter. Mitch beheaded my grandfather because he thought him to be an evil leader. After killing my father, Juan, too, Mitch spared my brother, Oliver, and my life, and married my mother, Gretchen. Then he sailed around the world along with my mother's jewels to keep his love content.

Pirates, you know, were described as enemies to the human race who acted with predatory intent for personal gain and without political purpose. Although Mitch murdered the older men in my family, he at least spared my mother's life and the lives of her two children. He felt all was fair in love and war. He even thought himself to be a brave and daring man, a fighter for nature's gifts, and a destroyer of those who were weak. But he was known for treating his family and crew like they were kings and queens."

"Yes, go on. I'm listening," the woman said.

"Anyway, most states had laws punishing pirates by death or life imprisonment. When Mitch was captured and convicted by the London Admirality Sessions, he was sentenced to death. His wife, who was my mother, my full brother Oliver, and myself, were taken away to start a new life with one of the admirals. She died a year later. The five beautiful gems her father had given her were laid before Mitch as he hung on the gallows between ebb and flow tides.

Sazran, his favorite sorceress whom he had met at a witch burning, put a spell on the holder of all five gems to possess the key to wealth and power and eternity. That night, at the stroke of midnight, her spell was to be complete. Mitch would rise from the dead and take full control of the gems."

"He must be talking of our Sazran, my reincarnated ancestor who was twisted in death by the evil entity," whispered Dina to herself in the cramped trunk.

"All for the family, step and otherwise, of Mitch the Magnificent, these good thing were to come. But late that night, a second before the stroke of midnight, while he was hanging on the gallows, Captain Darrendon, Mitch's arch enemy, stole the jewels that lay at the swinging man's feet. The power now belonged to him. Mitch would not regain his right on earth. When Sazran the witch lashed out at Captain Darrendon with her powers, he burned her physical form on that desolate shore. Once a Darrendon, but enlightened before death, she is my helper now. At night, through black magic, I try to summon her, for only she knows where the grand gates to eternal life are located."

At this point, Dina knew he was not aware of The Book of Eternity which contained the map to the vault, although presently blank, where the gates stood. Hopefully it was still safe on the Empress in Grand Cayman.

"Soon I will see her. I only need those five jewels so I can take possession of all the surprises ahead."

So our ancestor burned the witch and robbed the evil enemy. She knew Devon's story was slanted, for they were truly the evil ones Dina thought, and she began to feel as if she were suffocating. Soon the horrific vision of that bloated, dead man on the beach returned from her childhood memories. Fate had it that she found the gems then, and she was sure fate would have it that she would find them all again. The terrific loss of lives haunted her like the darkest hell, but they would be together soon.

She hoped Sentra could hold out a little longer. The gem was still safe in her grand niece's leather belt, but for how much more time could they remain hidden? Sooner or later, someone would find them.

Following lovemaking, the music was turned off, and the room became quiet except for the hum of the fan. Dina's backpack was beginning to dig into her side where she lay scrunched up in the chest, but soon she saw the lid open and felt hands tear at the blankets.

"Dina, it's me," Sentra spoke in a low murmur. "They're fast asleep, but we must be very quiet." Carefully they crept out of the room and fled into the night.

"We know he's after our gems, and he'll take our lives to get them," Sentra said.

"I wouldn't doubt it," Dina said. Then carefully she hid the back pack of supplies beneath a banana leaf eight feet from the cabin. They gathered the logs and twigs for the raft, but it took a long time to cut the materials, and daybreak was fast approaching. They were just about finished when Dina heard early morning sounds coming from the big house. Hiding the completed raft in the crevice of a large root, they made their way back to their cabin to get the rest of their belongings.

Dina pushed open the door and saw an armed guard perusing the inside of their room. "You ladies done with your morning walk?"

"Stay calm. We'll get a chance to flee later," Dina whispered to Sentra.

"Come with me," the two hundred pound, black guard pressed the gun into Dina's back. He quickly took them to the main house backyard. They were held captive seated by the shell-shaped, swimming pool. It was neatly adjoined to the big house by a brick sidewalk which was covered with a tapestry of shiny, green vines that hung from a white, wooden archway. Brilliant yellow butterflies flitted among the lavender trumpet vines as a scarlet tanager darted in and out of the greenery. The sun was bright in the clear, blue sky, and a balmy breeze blew by.

"Let's go ladies. And no questions," Devon said. Quickly Dina and Sentra rose, their blue jeans clinging tightly to their sweaty legs. The guard held a gun on them and forced them to climb into the cramped back seat of the brown pick-up truck. Dina felt for a seat belt buckle.

"Ouch," she screamed. Then she pulled her hand out with a throbbing finger bleeding, the red liquid oozing from a tiny hole in her pinkie. She sucked on it and spit the blood to the floor.

"No seat belts back there, woman, but don't worry," Devon reassured them. "That old syringe has been there for awhile. You'll be okay," he continued. Then he reached back and handcuffed Dina. He also handcuffed Sentra but blindfolded her, too, with a dirty rag by her feet. Tightly he had pulled his long, golden hair into a ponytail. His brilliant green eyes were hidden behind dark sunglasses, and the scar on his right cheek made him look evil. His words were of no comfort Dina knew, because there were many drug addicts in the area. She only hoped whoever had used the needle did not have a nasty infection or worse, AIDS. She would be sure to douse it with alcohol when she got the chance.

"Bye, guard," Devon said. Then he hit the gas.

"Where are you taking us?" Sentra asked Devon. Dina saw the young woman's belt dig into her stomach. She was cramped and hot and sweat dripped like saltwater from her brow into the cloth blindfold.

"Didn't I say no questions," Devon scolded. Sentra groaned. "If you must know, we're going to Blue Mountain Peak to pick up supplies. So glad you could join me," he said.

"What are the supplies for?" Dina asked.

"Our little party tonight. And guess what? You are both invited." As he reached under the seat, he cried out. "Great. Another bandana and just in time." He stopped the truck and quickly blindfolded Dina, too. Then he pulled a cage across the back of the seat to separate himself from the prisoners. Dina remained silent, but her mind was lit up like a candle in the darkness.

Enough time slipped by to allow Sentra to pick the lock of Dina's handcuffs with a bobby pin in her teeth that she had taken from Dina's hair. She poked it into the slot until the cuffs cracked open. Then Dina carefully slipped the blindfold over one eye and peeked out. They were traveling up a mountain on a dirt path bordered with rocks and heather, and soon they passed by coffee and sugarcane plantations. She could see many native Jamaicans working in the fields in the hot sun that glazed their foreheads with glistening beads of sweat. A large banana plantation rose up to the north as they drove farther up the steep mountain.

Carefully Dina slipped down Sentra's blindfold and picked her handcuff lock until she too was free. Unfortunately the cage that separated them from Devon was locked, and the doors had no handles. Dina knew that soon they would have to make a run for it, or they may be murdered. The sound of reggae music eased out from the back speakers, and they could also hear the faint humming of Devon. He was truly out for revenge she knew, and he would probably stop at nothing to get his hands on the five gems. Sentra still had the ruby in the secret pouch of her leather belt. It was best that way. Although many had given Sentra's belt a good once over, no one had ever thought to search it more carefully. Dina fiigured Devon may torture them to make them tell, and they did not want to be at his mercy. They would have to escape soon for time was of the essence. They slipped their blindfolds back on and pretended to be handcuffed.

They drove onward up the increasingly steep road. Soon Devon parked and exited the truck. For a second, Dina peeked out from her blindfold and saw Devon fill his water jug outside of a vacated forestry cabin. Only a worn pair of hiking boots stood on the front steps. Soon they were driving through a canopied forest where Dina snuck a look again and spotted a Jamaican woodpecker, a rufous-tailed flycatcher, yellow-bellied sapsuckers, and a warbler.

Despite the uncertainty of their journey and the danger involved, she found the nature to be relaxing, and the sway of the truck lulled her to sleep along with Sentra.

Upon feeling the truck swerve violently, Dina awoke suddenly and peeked out. Crossing their path was a grey wolf that looked like Elkin.

"Get the hell out of the way," Devon yelled. Then he lost control and crashed into a boulder.

"Ouch," Sentra cried. She had thumped her face into the grate before them.

"You okay?" Dina asked. She saw her swipe blood from an inch-sized cut on her high cheekbone.

"Watch where you're going," Sentra screamed at Devon. But Devon only moaned like death itself. Although he was wearing a shoulder harness and a seat belt, he had twisted his right foot under the gas pedal. He held it in his hand and groaned for a second.

"Damned animal," he said, looking over his wrecked heap of metal. "Should of hit and killed it."

A feeling of sadness swept over Dina, and she longed to pet Elkin again. Although her pet was ancient by wolf standards, he was still good and loyal. She remembered the first time she saw Elkin by the river when he had saved her from the beast. He was just a year old then, when she was eight. That made him sixty-three years old today she knew. How unusual he was she thought and remembered where she had last seen him. Lying on a soft blanket, he was poised by Amanda's bed intent on guarding her until she grew well.

Suddenly the grey beast appeared in front of the truck again. "Stand still so I can kill you," Devon commanded. He took his rifle from the front seat and aimed steadily.

"Put that down," Jackson ordered. Elkin snarled and growled at Devon.

"You're here to rescue us," Sentra hollered. Their friends stood in the forest road with guns aimed and cocked.

"Elkin," Dina said. "Come to me."

The wolf wagged its tail furiously, and he ran toward her. Dina saw Devon place his rifle back on the seat and pull out a huge conch shell. Placing the small end to his lips, he blew repeatedly, and the sound echoed like a yodel through the mountains. Soon the forest was filled with Jamaicans behind every tree. Two snuck up on their friends, foiling the rescue. Then Devon's machete-carrying natives herded them all within minutes. Where did they come from? There must be a village nearby. She also wondered if they were voodoo worshipers when Devon stared at their freed hands and wide eyes with hate.

Closely she looked at the trees for any unusual carvings of symbols, but she could see none. The natives spoke in Creole, and they dressed in khaki-colored, loose-fitting clothing. They all wore bandanas upon their heads, and their jet black eyes seemed cold and empty. They huddled together with Elkin, and soon the natives herded them into a dry, brown riverbed.

Within minutes, they were on a trail that was steep and treacherous, and upon rising higher, the island's tall peaks came into view. The city of Kingston was on the South, and the city of Port Antonio was on the north. Olgilvee pointed each one out to Dina.

"We're in the Blue Mountains," he confirmed.

"How did you find us?" Dina asked.

"After the police found your abandoned wrecked vehicle on Grand Cayman, we immediately expected foul play. The island people were circulating rumors that you had been taken to Jamaica, to Devon's banana plantation. First, we informed Amanda and George of the danger you were in. Then, leaving the Empress where you docked it, we came here to Jamaica by plane. When we arrived at Port Antonio Airport, some natives gave us tips as to your whereabouts as they had seen you two. Then we put Elkin like a detective on your trail."

"And he picked up our scent and brought you here?"

"That's right, my wife," Olgilvee said. He leaned close to her until his lips brushed her cheek. "We've traveled long and hard to find you."

"God bless you," Dina said sweetly. Then she patted the wolf's soft fur.

Soon they arrived at the summit which consisted of a rough plateau covered with scrubby trees and bushes. A large, thatched hut stood at one end near wooden houses built on a slope where the natives lived. Dung-filled pens were packed with chickens, pigs, and young bulls. A few mules and goats wandered aimlessly throughout the compound where they munched on piles of hay and corn. Then Elkin bounded off after a fat rat that barreled out from the corn pile.

"Come back, boy," Dina called. But he disappeared into the forest. Then a burly native man appeared and took Dina and Sentra away from the group.

"We'll get out of here," Olgilvee said. Then Jackson pulled at Sentra's arm when they parted. Once inside the large hut, the native man tied Dina's hands tightly behind her and laid her upon the rough ground. Then she saw Sentra drinking water from a gourd, and Devon running his fingers through her golden hair. Carelessly he knocked the gourd from her hand, spilling it on her shirt and jeans.

"You shall have a change of clothing," he said. "Take those wet ones off now. I'll have one of the native women bring you a sarong." Dina could see Sentra's look of disgust when Devon firmly stroked her swollen breasts. Slowly he uncinched her leather belt and pulled her jeans to her ankles and off each foot. Standing naked from the waist down, he stared at her coldly. "You won't be needing this anymore," he said. Then he cinched the belt around his own waist. Kicking her pants into the dirt, he marched off into the sunlight. A tall, dark native tied Sentra's hands behind her and laid her down next to Dina. Then he tied their feet together with a long, thick rope.

"Take a nap," he said.

Dina felt a lumpy pillow placed beneath her head, and a soft, blue, cotton sheet was draped over them.

"I have no intention of sleeping," Dina said. "And what did they do with Jackson and Olgilvee?"

"I hope nothing too horrible," Sentra said, moaning uncomfortably.

Soon a willowy native girl came into the hut, but she did not have any clothes for Sentra. Quickly she untied Dina and spoke and pointed to Dina's necklace, which was the good luck charm the black artist on Grand Cayman had given to her.

"You have symbol of dragon. Go. Go," she said, speaking sincerely behind beautiful dark eyes.

Dina stared in amazement. Then the native girl scurried out of the hut. She wondered if the Grand Cayman woman's sister with an important secret lived nearby. Quickly she untied Sentra and offered her a burlap bag to hide her nakedness. She ripped a small opening in the bottom and slipped it on like a skirt. Then Dina peered out the door into the compound. Tied to two splintering wooden posts were Jackson and Olgilvee. They were weary and wretched, and a beady-eyed vulture sat menacingly on the low branches of a fig tree. The men each had a white piece of cloth stuck into their mouths, and their faces were bright red from the sun. The vulture flapped its wings twice and stared at the meal sitting before him.

"The John Crow waits for you," a Jamaican said.

Then Dina recalled the tale of the fiendish, black-robed minister of Port Royal, Jamaica for whom the vultures and the John Crow Mountains in the northeast were named. Where was Elkin, too, she wondered.

Spying a small, wooden structure at the edge of the compound, the two crawled cat-like on their hands and knees, keeping low beneath the hedges that grew nearby. A few Jamaicans could be seen tending the herds of animals, but most of them were on the side of the mountain in their village. Devon was nowhere to be seen.

"We must find that belt," Sentra bossed. "I really don't think he knew the gem is in the belt. The compartment is so carefully concealed inside. He just likes the leather."

"Yes. Hopefully we'll be able to get it back before he makes the discovery. First we must help our men. They look so vulnerable."

Suddenly Dina felt something wet and rough upon her arm. "Elkin," she whispered. Happily she embraced the furry grey wolf, and Sentra patted him lovingly on the back. Dina saw Sentra point to their two comrades forty feet in front of them.

"Chew up their ropes," Sentra bossed. "Set them free."

A tall native woman carrying a basket containing live chickens upon her head walked slowly past the men. Another Jamaican was toting long bamboo poles, and he walked past too, as if they were invisible. Soon the area was clear, and Dina urged the wolf on. He went to the men, first gnawing through Olgilvee's ropes and then freeing Jackson. They were joined with the two women.

"Thank you, ladies," Olgilvee said, wiping sweat from his brow. "We were almost vulture snacks today, Jackson."

Jackson smiled warmly and wrapped his firm, young body around Sentra.

"Can't you lovers wait? We have to get out of here, or we may end up as a voodoo sacrifice," Olgilvee said.

"The belt. We must find it soon," Sentra said anxiously.

"Let us in on it. What does all this have to do with a belt?" Jackson asked.

"I hear Devon," Dina said. She shuddered upon hearing the gravelly voice of their enemy echo throughout the forest. Soon they heard the familiar sound of the conch horn as the madman summoned the natives.

"This place will be crawling with soldiers. Let's head down the Blue Mountain," Dina said to guide them.

After stepping through the dense foilage, they came upon a dirt trail, and suddenly Elkin started barking and heading for a large banyan tree. A native girl stepped into the path, and Elkin walked up and sniffed her. He did not seem to be threatened, and Dina knew why. It was the girl who untied her in the hut.

"She thinks I bring good luck," Dina said, running her fingers over the gold dragon necklace the black woman had given her. "Perhaps she'll lead us to the sister of the Grand Cayman woman. She has a tip for us concerning gem number two."

"Come with me," the native girl said.

Her two, large, bare feet slapped the earth as she led them through the thick forest. After twenty minutes when they came to a fork in the trail, they turned left. The pace grew slower, but soon they neared the safety of her village. A large dog resembling an anteater greeted them upon their entry to a path to a small collection of houses built from bamboo. The high-peaked roofs had small cupolas on top, and some were painted with brilliant colors of red and yellow. An outdoor market place was decorated with bouganvilla and flame vines, and thick, green grass grew around wooden pens filled with pigs, chickens, and calves. Elkin quickly ran up to acquaint himself with the other animals.

Within minutes, the natives gathered around them and offered baskets of fruit. One tall, thin woman started braiding Dina's red hair into corn rows, and Sentra munched on a ripe avocado. The sweet aroma of hash from small smoking pipes fogged the air from females who puffed and bartered with merchants. In one section, bleating goats were tethered, and on the other small side, donkeys carrying beautifully carved, wooden statues, stared off into the mountains.

Many of the merchants stood arranging the fruits, vegetables, and charcoal they sold in their stands, and men were gathered at a hut in the fat end for the weekly cock fight.

"Come with me," the native girl said. Dina followed along with the others down a crooked, narrow path until they came to a weathered hut. A large, black woman in a faded, white dress sat on a hanging chair which swayed back and forth to the rhythm of the breeze that was passing through her home.

"You have carving of dragon on gold chain. Where you get?" she said, pointing. Elkin sniffed her meaty hand. Then Dina took the necklace off and gave it to the old woman. Carefully she examined it. "JVK. Those are the intials of my sister in Grand Cayman. She gives you good luck."

"Yes," Dina urged. "We met and talked about our art work. I felt a kindred spirit. Then before we left, she presented me with this gift."

"Well, gift saved your life. You stay here safe from evil Devon, witch hunter."

"My friends, too?" Dina asked.

"Yes. Friends, too." Elkin barked a short and quick sound.

"Do you know of Grey Grotto Cave? I was told you may have some information to aide us in our search for a family heirloom."

"Ah, yes. Some thinks only one way out of cave lake. But me knows second way out."

"Yes. Go on," Dina urged.

"Give me dragon charm." Dina hesitated. Then she took it off. The woman held it closely and kissed it gently.

"You look for rock with fish head carving. Channel to the outside right there." She handed back the dragon charm. "Now its magic pass into me through my lips. Put back on, woman. Come see me later. We talk more. Neeta, show them to their hut."

Dina slipped the charm back around her neck, and then the young native girl led them to a hut one-half mile down the path. It had two bedrooms, a bathroom, and a kitchen.

"Go to lake for bath," Neeta said. Gently she handed them four sets of towels and bars of gardenia-scented soaps.

"Where might the lake be?" Jackson asked. But the girl had scampered out into the sunlight. Dina looked out the back window, unbelieving of the serenity of the crystal liquid. The large, beautiful, blue water hole stood nestled amid hilly mountain tops, and a few man-made boats floated freely with natives casting bamboo fishing poles into its depths.

They walked out to the water where Dina made lunch from the food left on a gritty table. It was time to relax and regain strength. She hoped Devon would not find them here in this haven. She prayed he had not discovered the contents of the belt. They would have to find it, but how and where she was uncertain. She quickly stripped down and dove off a massive grey rock.

The cool water felt refreshing, and it immediately soaked into her salty, sweaty skin. Being naked felt great, too. Olgilvee soon joined her, diving below her and then racing her toward shore. Clearly she could see Sentra and Jackson diving off the giant rock. Elkin lounged by the water's edge, occasionally lapping at it with his long, pink tongue. Soon Dina curled up next to Olgilvee on their towel. Then quietly they rolled beneath a gardenia bush and made love.

Three days had passed since they escaped from their captor whom Dina knew was probably on their trail at this very moment. Even if he had found the gem in the belt, the exact directions to the whereabout of the other jewels were locked in their memories, and he would come for that information she was certain. Sentra kept busy weaving baskets while Jackson and Olgilvee fished all day. Dina enjoyed the native people, and she spent hours talking with the black sister of her Grand Cayman friend. She was known in the village as "Mother" because she practiced healing and sold bush medicine. Many of the superstitious ones visited her hut for treament of sickness, both mental and physical. The villagers practiced the religion of Pocomania, a combination of old-fashioned Protestant revival and African Obeah magic which was a type of African witchcraft.

"You come to service tonight," The old, black woman said soulfully.

Dina could almost see her reflection in the large woman's shining white teeth. Her jet black hair was braided in corn rows, and her large, brown eyes held depth of unknown measures. Five copper bands jangled from her left wrist, and large, gold stars dangled from her ears. She was quite a festive vision in her purple tent dress, which covered the mass of woman underneath. Dina willingly obliged, as to turn her down would be a grave insult.

At eight thirty p.m., the sun was setting behind a Blue Mountain peak. The rich sound of vibrant, black voices filled the air, scented with hyacinth, and a warm July breeze blew across the lake. Dina joined in with the group who sang hymns and prayed. Sentra kept Elkin still, but he began to howl when the "shepherd" started his speech condeming Satan. He was dressed in a yellow, green, and blue robe, and he held a staff. A brilliant headress covered with bird feathers stood proudly atop his shaven head. Then a black woman appeared dressed in a flowing white gown trimmed in gold lace. When the sky grew dark, the last quarter moon cast an eerie glow on the group, and frenzied members begged for possession. People got down on their knees and shouted and sang out to the heavens.

Suddenly they began making loud roaring sounds like leopards. Then the shepherd began leaping high into the air. Soon the entire congregation began growling and jumping with the shepherd. Dina heard Jackson and Olgilvee laughing at one native who jumped into the pot of warm stew they prepared. Soon the smell of ganga scented the air from people's burning pipes. Within minutes natives fell to the ground writhing and flailing, and some like crazed Baptists even spoke in tongues.

Where is Elkin, Dina wondered. She carefully looked about the camp. "Elkin," she called out.

Jackson and Olgilvee began searching the woods, and Dina followed Sentra into the cluster of houses. Dina heard Sentra scream when two men grabbed them from behind. One held a fourteen-inch bowie knife to Sentra's throat while the other one pointed a machete at Dina's head.

Then the sudden rush of branches was heard when a grey flash of fur ran by. Quickly Elkin chewed out the knife-wielding man's throat, killing him. Then the other one with the machete tried to hack Elkin to death. Twice the razor sharp blade cut into his side. Dina and Sentra ran into a nearby house for a weapon, but it was not necessary. They heard the other man groan and saw blood spurt like lava into the air. Wounded and whining, the wolf stumbled to the ground, but no one heard him over the loud service. Quickly Sentra dragged the two men into the brush, and Dina tended to Elkin. The wounds were only surface ones, and soon he was regaining strength.

"Look what I found on the second dead native." Sentra appeared with her leather belt cinched to her waist.

"The gem still there?" Dina gasped.

"Yes. You were right. They only wanted it for the leather to hold up their pants. The hunters must have traded Devon for this fine belt."

"Yes," Dina said. She saw the moon's glow touch up the young woman's hair. Then Sentra grinned widely exposing the rose-carved tooth.

"They may have been Devon's men, too," Sentra said. "There's probably more coming. Let's find Olgilvee and Jackson and get out of here." Dina knew she was right, and she trusted Sentra's instinct. Elkin recovered and limped along back to the roaring service.

The river felt refreshing to Dina, and she waded in to soothe her hot, sweaty feet. "Those mules came in handy," Jackson said. "Someone is probably missing them by now."

"We must have traveled fifteen miles over that rough terrain," Olgilvee said.

"Yes, heading due east, this must be the Brown River. Thank God for that waning crescent moon, or we'd be in pitch darkness. I wish we had that bamboo raft we made up in the John Crow Mountains. Why we could drift right into the Caribbean near San Antonio," Sentra said.

"I'm great at raft building," Jackson said.

Dina stretched out on a rock to dry where she could see Jackson and Olgilvee gather bamboo and vines from the water's edge. Jackson was so strong, and he possessed a never-give-up attitude. He was good for Sentra, because they had much in common. They were both adventurous and enjoyed physical exertion. Jackson loved to hear Sentra predict weather forecasts, and she delighted in hearing his brave fishing tales.

Dina still had a wad of travelers checks stuffed in her pocket from the Million Dollar Fishing Contest they had won. The money would get them through the rest of the trip, she was certain. Four more gems needed to be found. Once back at New Foundland, she could sell them and pay off the creditors and keep the castle estate. Then, during the autumnal equinox on September 23rd, in the year two thousand and one, they would enter the gate to eternity and be reunited. It was all so fantastic she realized. Silently she watched Sentra bind the bamboo poles together with vines. Soon they would be navigating their raft to freedom. Grasping her good luck charm, she hoped it would come in handy again if Devon ever caught up with them. He was relentless in his pursuit.

"I haven't had a minute to ask, but what was Amanda's condition when you left Grand Cayman?" Dina asked.

"Actually, she seemed to be improving," Olgilvee answered. "George assured us he could keep her in good spirits until we returned."

"Great. Hopefully with her improved health she'll also have a new outlook and a change of heart. Only time will tell."

"All aboard," Jackson said. He pushed the raft into the Brown River where he was determined to be captain, standing tall with rafting pole in hand.

Slowly the raft wound down stream through quiet fields. Soon the waterway became very narrow, and shadows of yellow and orange bamboo groves appeared on either side. A huge nut like a small canon clunked onto the raft barely missing Olgilvee's silver head as they passed by coconut trees. Long Iliana vines hung three hundred feet from tall branches, their snake like coils weaving a tight web around the river. Many tamarind trees gently brushed their bodies upon gliding underneath them. They rode wearily, quenching their thirst with coconut milk and filling their stomachs with the meat of the fruit.

"Look ahead," Jackson said. Dina could see rapids just twenty feet from their raft.

"Hold on, ladies," Olgilvee warned. In seconds, the raft bumped into rocks in the narrow channel.

Suddenly the swirling waters overcame them, and the raft tipped over. Dina gulped for air when water entered her open mouth, and soon she was choking and gasping. She screamed when the rapid's teeth tore her body over sharp rocks. Finally, she grabbed onto a large tree root and pulled herself to shore. Then she could see Olgilvee floating on top, his eyes glazed. She crawled out on the tree root and grabbed him as he rushed past. Mouth to mouth resuscitation quickly revived him. Soon Sentra, Jackson, and Elkin tumbled onto shore at a sharp curve in the river.

"Hold it right there." Standing above them on a rock was Devon, and he had a rifle pointed directly at them. He held up a large conch and blew into it. Soon the area was filled with natives.

"Dupies, dupies," one native said fearfully.

"They think we're ghosts," Dina shouted. One grabbed her and tightly bound her hands behind her back. Then she was forced to sit atop a donkey along with the others who were also tied securely.

Away from the Blue Ridge Mountains and back toward Devon's banana plantation they rode into the early morning hours along a dusty trail. Mosquitoes continuously bit in their relentless search for blood causing welts like buttons to protrude on Dina's arms. They were nearing the John Crow Mountains. Dina said a prayer and closed her eyes. The lovely sound of a Jamaican owl called in the distance.

Drum beats frightened Dina, and she felt her body being dragged off the donkey. She was seated next to her comrades inside a mud hut. They were at the top of John Crow Mountain she knew by the familiar setting. The music continued, and she heard the howl of Elkin in the distance.

"You are all invited to a grand party," Devon said. Dina could see his tall stature fill the doorway, the moon glowing down on his golden hair. "By the time the night is over there will be no more secrets among us. Is that understood?"

Dina saw Jackson and Olgilvee wince when Devon drew his machete gently across their throats. "Ah. Blood to fill our gourds," the madman uttered. Then Dina saw trickles of red liquid slowly ooze from two small cuts on each man's neck.

"You're a demon," Olgilvee shouted. Jackson spat on Devon. Then swiftly Devon drew his blade across Sentra's thigh. She arched in agony.

"Here," Devon said. He cut loose Dina's ropes. "Fill this gourd with her blood, or you will meet a quick death." The gourd decorated with colored beads and snake vertebrae, filled quickly from Sentra's surface wound that readily leaked forth. She bandaged the grand niece's cut with strips of cloth she tore from Sentra's shirt.

"I wonder what symbolic meaning the gourd has," Dina said.

"Perhaps it's a symbol of the position of high priest or priestess," Sentra said.

"Its use seems customary in voodoo rituals practiced in Haiti. I used to fish with a Haitian man who told me some pretty weird tales of those religious ceremonies," Jackson elaborated. "These natives speak Creole, the unofficial language of Haiti. They must be a type of Jamaican-Haiti mix."

"Whatever they are, we don't want to be at their mercy," Olgilvee said. Suddenly the smell of smoke from a nearby campfire drifted into the hut. Then the drum beat began in a long, steady rhythm.

"Tell us more about this voodoo, Jackson," Dina said.

"It's a cult that originated from Africa, where it was the religion of the Dahomey Negroes. In Haiti it was transformed to either Rada or Petro, the more violent form. Listen to the drums and notice the three distinct sounds. The biggest one is called maman, the middle one is called seconde, and the smallest one is known as boula."

"What's the purpose of these drums?" Olgilvee asked.

"Well they set the rhythm of the ceremony and guide the high priest, or Houngan, and his people through the ritual."

"And they draw symbols on trees to invite the spirits," Dina said. She recalled the carvings of the phoenix and the three circled crosses whose meaning was told to her by the black lady artist of Grand Cayman.

"They also draw these symbols in the earth, sing chants, and dance to invite tie Laos, or spirits. The Laos have human strengths and weaknesses and control Haitian life elements," Jackson continued.

"Do the spirits have names?" Sentra asked.

"Yes. Wind, air, water, trees, fire, jungle, old age, and death release their subjects into earth by possessing the body of a human," Jackson said.

"Gourd, gourd," the native said. Dina handed the tall, black man the carved bowl filled with Sentra's blood. He smiled pumpkin-like, showing his scattered, sparkling, white teeth. A freshly severed chicken neck hung from his waist. Then he turned to leave the hut. Soon the drum beat grew louder, and she could hear Elkin howl in the distance.

"Wanga," Jackson said. "They're practicing the black magic of spells, potions, and evil charms."

Dina could see Jackson roll over to the door to peek out. Dina followed, and through a veil of grey smoke, she could see a man wearing a black top hat, a black frock coat, and dark glasses. A huge cigar hung from the corner of his mouth, and he held a goblet in one hand.

"Who is he?" she asked.

Jackson spoke quietly, then he flicked a large, black beetle off his hairy arm. "My Haitian friend told me of such a character. He is invoking the god of death, Baron Samedi, who is of the Petro form of voodoo."

To the far side of the compound, Dina could see a large, open-sided, palm-roofed shed with a tall pole in the center.

"That must serve as an entry and exit for the spirits," she said.

"To your feet," a voice rang out. Dina felt someone dig fingernails into her bicep, and she was roughly pulled to a standing position. The smell of perspiration and blood drifted past with the warm breeze that blew into the shack. He led her to the other hut along with the rest of the group. They walked through the back door where the fire burned furiously, and red coals glowed like devil's eyes. Dina stood in front of the altar, which was decorated with jars, calabashes, and voodoo symbols. She could see the natives encircle them where they stood helpless and shivering from fear. She clutched the gold dragon charm beneath her shirt and prayed to God for protection.

Suddenly Devon appeared dressed in a colorful robe made of beads, yellow scarves, and bird feathers. His eyes seemed flourescent, and they glowed and stared right through her. He began the service with an invocation of the spirits. Then the drums called forth in a rhythmic manner, and the followers chanted ancient groupings of words. Suddenly a tall, black man with hair the color of milk and ink stiffened and then thrashed about the ground uncontrollably. He began speaking in an odd way, and then he stood and walked with a limp while hunched over.

"Papa Legba," Jackson said. "He is a spirit in the form of an old man."

"We will bring forth many Loa tonight. Drink up," the native said. Then he placed a gourd to Dina's lips. She sipped the rum. Everyone was drinking, and she could see small, brown pipes being passed around. The group swayed, chanted, and lost themselves to the rhythm of the night.

Dina could feel Sentra catch her while she sank to the ground. The rum was more potent then she realized. Then they saw a tall beauty dressed in a purple robe grab Olgilvee. His eyes were red and glazed, and he walked with uneven steps to the altar. The woman towered over him at six foot three inches. She announced she was twenty-one and untouched as a black rose bud. Gently she laid him back on the wooden platform which rose to her waist. Silently she stood back and watched another woman appear, strip him bare, and slowly massage a sweet smelling oil of hyacinth and musk into the palm of her hands. She drew it across his forehead, down his neck and shoulders, and across his erect nipples. The grey hair on his chest glistened, and he stopped shaking and began to moan softly. She drew her hands down his waist, and then she started at the tip of his toes and came forward to his groin, massaging more vigorously.

The crowd looked on dazedly, and they continued chanting, smoking, and swaying. Then lightning struck a nearby Banyan tree, drowning out the sounds of ravishment amid sudden screams of terror.

Next they sacrificed chickens and pigs, and the night crept on. Some of the natives walked, like Gods, painlessly across coals, and others ran their hands through the flames of the fire. Gourds filled with animal blood were passed around, and people sipped and ate fried cockroaches and lizards.

Dina was placed facedown on a mat. Then someone pulled her jeans off and covered her with warm blood that smelled goatlike.

"Dambella. Come forth," Devon said.

Dina could see the man with the golden hair draw an intricate symbolic sign in the soil. In the center he etched a snake climbing a pole. It reminded her of the medical caduceus with one reptile instead of two. He moved his hand rapidly about while a fine, yellow grain fell through his fingers. The meal formed patterns on the dark dirt floor that were soon brushed away under the shuffling feet of the worshippers. The drumming and dancing became increasingly hypnotic, and Dina saw the natives take Sentra to the altar, but this time they did not just lay her down. They stripped her naked and tied her hands and feet to the platform. Fear rose in Dina's heart when she saw Olgilvee and Jackson passed out cold on the lawn. Then she heard the howl of Elkin in the distance and the fire crackle. She saw grey smoke curl up into the air in pigtails.

"Elkin, Elkin," she called. Then she heard the sound of screeching metal and saw Devon sharpening his blade.

"No! No!," Sentra shrieked. Clearly she could see Devon carving lightly into her chest. Then blood oozed forth onto the knife.

"Sazran, the sorceress, come forth. Open these woman's lips to release the secret whereabouts of the jewels. I must have them. We shall go on to eternity. I shall have the power of the gems."

A vast flash of light pierced the sky, and Devon began chanting louder while Sentra squirmed and snarled. Then Dina saw Sentra's leather belt next to a pile of coconut shells at her own feet. Elkin stood before her, his large eyes beckoning. The wolf had retrieved it when it had fallen to the ground after the natives disrobed her. She quickly checked that the gem was safe, pulled her jeans back on, and then slipped the belt on her own waist.

"Now save Sentra," Dina said.

CHAPTER FIVE

Dina took cover behind a rock to avoid spears the natives threw in her direction. Then the pained shouts of Devon echoed in the night. "Damned wolf! Let me go."

She peeked out and saw Elkin biting into his flesh, gnawing on his arms that covered his head.

"Chew through my ropes," she heard Sentra call out to the wolf. Quickly he obeyed, leaving his snack bloodied. Then suddenly Sentra rose to her knees and drove a knife into the top shoulder of Devon, deterring him from spearing Elkin. Blood spurted out down his chest, he stiffened, and tumbled to the ground writhing in agony. Dina watched Sentra continue to battle the natives.

Amid all the commotion, Dina ran out and dragged Jackson and Olgilvee behind the rock, but a gaping wound smeared Dina's body blood red. She turned Jackson on his stomach and saw a three inch knife gouge directly over his heart. Blood drained out at a furious rate, his breathing stopped, and his eyes stared empty and glazed. Olgilvee held his friend tightly in his arms one last time. "Good-bye, pal," he said. Then Elkin howled like sorrow's voice at the stars.

Soon Dina heard voices from behind her. "Stay, Elkin," she ordered. The wolf stood at her side. Slowly she turned and saw the outline of Amanda and George standing in front of a thicket.

"So you want me dead." Devon stood leaning on a tree, staring at Amanda who held a gun on him. "No way. But I will get what I want. You," he said, pointing to Amanda. "I imagine you have your weaknesses, too. I'll make your mind do my bidding one day." She fired a last bullet, just missing Devon. He sank to the ground, his bloody shoulder painting the bark from which he slid. Quickly she tossed the gun, and she and George searched for another weapon.

How did they find us here Dina wondered. Then she saw a blue jeep parked near a tall banyan. Dina knew it would be their only means of escape, but poor Sentra. She could see her still battling off numerous natives who tried to kill her with their spears.

Then a gun sounded from an unknown location. Dina saw a tall one drop, allowing Sentra, still naked, to make her way toward the jeep. Looking up, Dina saw Amanda standing eight feet up on a thick tree limb shooting the murderous tribesmen one by one.

The ride was hell on them all, jerking them like loose twine over rough terrain on their race down the rugged John Crow mountain road. Sentra donned a long jacket from the jeep to keep her warm on their way to Port Antonio. They drove to the dock where Amanda pointed out the Empress bobbing up and down in the sea. Dina did not know whether Devon was dead or alive, but it did not matter now. They could make an escape on their vessel to find gem number two Dina knew. She ran her hand across her leather belt.

Sentra got out a first aid kit, and Dina tended to her wounds. Luckily none of them went very deep and only a few stitches were needed. As for Olgilvee, he just wanted some coffee to overcome the grogginess from the ganga and rum hangover, but poor Jackson was gone forever. They had left his body shoved underneath the big rock. The grief was evident in everyone, creating a lead veil under which Sentra sailed the Empress to Discovery Bay to Grey Grotto.

That night, Dina heard Sentra weeping into the sea, for the young woman had never loved and lost so greatly.

"Amanda, how did you and George find us?" Sentra asked. Elkin licked her salty, wet hand that hung at her side.

"Olgilvee and Jackson sent us a telegram telling us that Elkin picked up your scent at Port Antonio, and that they would search the John Crow and Blue Mountains for you. I had almost made a complete recovery from the infectious hepatitis at the time. In Georgetown Harbor, we checked out the dock, found the Empress, and sailed to Port Antonio. The town was abuzz with gossip of a sacrificial offering to Sazran, the sorceress. So we hauled ass up here in the blue jeep, and sort of snuck up on you all."

Dina gave Amanda a hug, and she saw George embrace Sentra. The day was clear, and the wind was strong making it good weather for sailing as careful as an angel driven wind to their destination.

"Down to Jamaica to Grey Grotto Cave. It lies in the lake beneath a rock grave," Sentra said. She sat on deck stuffing her backpack with food, water, flashlights, swimsuits, snorkel gear, and an orange portable float.

"Good morning, my dear," Dina said. She watched and listened to Sentra recite the poem Grandfather wrote. The first jewel was safe in the leather belt now, and the second jewel would soon be in their possession. Dina slinked off into her bedroom below deck to study the beautiful ruby. It should bring many dollars, perhaps a million or more. She stretched out on the bed and gazed at the gem. Slipping it back into the secret compartment, she cinched the belt to her waist and slipped off to sleep.

Something soft and furry brushed her cheek, and a sandy tongue scrapped her face. "Feather," Dina said. Elkin nuzzled the sea cat.

She held the cat close to her and recalled the days of her youth. There were many happy times spent with Grandfather at the garden and in the fields. He had been so kind to her after Mother and Grandmother had died, but his life, too, had ended brutally. Perhaps Devon had been responsible for his death. She never knew for sure. No one did. They only knew that foul play was involved. The art business, as prosperous as it had been, had brought him many enemies. This combined with the confiscation of the five jewels of the evil pirate, his greatest and bravest feat of all, may have eventually led to his traumatic death.

The legacy lives on in his poem she knew, and she tried to understand the true meaning and power in her hands. Time was running out. The large sum to pay off creditors would be theirs once they cashed in the jewels. Their future would then be secure, for on the night of the autumnal equinox, September 23rd, in the year two thousand and one, they could enter the castle gate to be reunited in eternity. The thought and magnitude of such an event happening sent shivers up her spine. She placed Feather back on the floor and sat up. She looked at the calendar.

Surprised, she read aloud, "July 20th."

"All on deck," Olgilvee said. Dina felt Elkin pull on her shirt sleeve in the daylight that streamed into her cabin. The night journey to Discovery Bay had helped her rest, and she felt new and vibrant.

"Happy birthday," everyone said joyfully. Dina felt her face turn red, and she saw her companions blow horns and thrust gifts and cake her way. A small table was set up filled with fresh fruits, seafood, and punch. The crew sat on deck chairs and watched Dina open her presents. From silk nightgowns to a new compass, Dina felt all her needs were met. She especially loved the gold ring Olgilvee gave her to be an engagement band.

"You're never to old to get married," he said.

Dina kissed him softly, and he slipped the band on her finger.

"That arthritis in my hands is the only old age complaint I have," she said. She sat down on his lap, and they hugged passionately. At seventy-one she felt ready to wed, but it would be her first and last time. She only felt for Sentra because losing Jackson left a void in her life.

The rented car had a bad exhaust system but at least it ran. Sentra drove carefully, remembering to stay left and to watch out for wandering goats, and Dina wore the leather belt with the gem tightly around her waist. They drove through small towns and a large marketplace. Then at the top of a hill they spotted a large, metal sign that read "Grey Grotto".

"That's it," Olgilvee shouted. They pulled into the driveway and hopped out.

The day was hot, dry, and cloudless, and the late morning hours slipped by like a slow current. The forest surrounding the cave system was a dense and tropical maze. Giant banyan, fig, and spruce trees hung heavy with lleani vines along the stone path they followed. Then a blue-eyed, black native handed them a brochure and took their money. Not a sole was in sight when they entered the ominous cave where a society of fruit bats hung in clumps from the high ceilings. They squeaked and dove at their heads, gliding across them as if on skis. Olgilvee scraped a blob of bat doo off the top of his head and another string of it dripped from his left ear. With flashlights on, they strolled into its depths. Elkin sniffed curiously at the thousands of insects on the cave floor.

"One mile north on the first fork, then down fifty stone steps," Dina said.

"What?" Amanda said dumbfounded.

"The gem is found there in the bottom of the lake. The black woman on Grand Cayman gave me directions to the water hole." Dina clutched the good luck charm around her neck "And knowing another way out is comforting, too, no?"

"Yes, Aunt Dina. Let's hope Mother, her Jamaican sister was right about the exit point. So far the gold dragon has done its job," Sentra said.

They walked across mounds of dirt and some crushed, empty beer cans. At one point the only opening was a small hole about four feet in diameter. Dina squeezed through along with the others. The new room rose forty feet and spread one hundred and forty feet.

The remains of a bonfire stood near an old rock table. Roaches and roach clips were piled high amidst a mass of brown beer bottles.

"People party here," Olgilvee said. He sniffed at one of the marijuana butts. Elkin stuck his nose into a brown bag and drug out a fish head and then abandoned the bare, bony object.

"Look at those stalagmites," Sentra said. Her small flashlight lit up a corner of the cave where large spikes poked up from the floor. "These are common in limestone areas due to the high rainfall and temperatures."

"But what are these white crystals?" Dina asked.

"Boxwork. I remember seeing those crystal fins and formations at Wind Cave in South Dakota. The honeycomb pattern is so interesting," answered Sentra.

"They sparkle almost as much as diamonds," said Dina. The laughter echoed through the dark corridors where Dina walked with her large flashlight on blink.

"You are quite a spelunker," Olgilvee said to Sentra.

"Well, I've traveled extensively with my ex-boyfriend, the gemologist. The Gouffre Buger near Grenoble, France was one of the longest caves I've explored. This, too, is a much more suitable climate than the weather in the Eisriesenwelt caves in Australia. The five thousand four hundred foot ice caves sent shivers down my spine. Then there was the—""

"Sentra! Look out," Amanda warned.

George huddled to the ground and covered his head beneath an angry fruit bat that zoomed past. It dove and turned and scurried between Sentra's open legs.

"Ouch," Amanda squeeled. A small puncture wound oozed blood from her neck, and the attack bat screeched and sored to his roost in the cave ceiling. Quickly George doused the wound with alcohol. Then Amanda shouted, "Bat from hell!"

"Where is this first fork anyway?" George asked. The corridor wound sharply from left to right, and they seemed to be walking at an incline. One chamber held large rocks which resembled coffins, and yet another one held a stone altar where small candles and religious symbols decorated its surface. Dina walked around the room shining her flashlight upon every corner, thinking maybe they had reached a fork or a new entryway.

Suddenly everything grew dark, and Dina felt herself slipping down into a sandy hole. Then her feet fell flat upon a rocky ledge, and she fell back against a wall. Sandy, small rocks from above rained on her, and she covered her face. But stone curlers hung in every part of her hair.

"Dina, are you alright?" Sentra asked.

"Yes, but get me out of here."

Soon the dust cleared away, and she could see six feet below her a pack of large, evil-looking, mongrel dogs in the faint light. They were odd looking and resembled pigs, rabbits, and anteaters all in one animal. They were hideous and anemic with ribs poking out, and glazed, reddened eyes glared at her hungrily. Carcasses of bats and other dogs lay scattered in the small chamber. A large rock nearly covered what looked like a small opening on the other side. She winced when a sharp piece jabbed into her back like a dull knife blade. The wild dogs began leaping and growling at the intruder. An especially ugly one with a large, crocked snout jumped up on the ledge on the far side. Its small feet held fast to the ledge, and it slowly made its way toward her. Above her head, she pulled out a rock the size of a coconut. Then she hurled it at the beast clinking it on the skull. It fell six feet to the rocky floor, howling, but it quickly stood up. Dina began to feel faint, and she hoped she would not lose her foothold.

"Help! Help!" she hollered.

"Grab onto this rope, and we'll pull you up," Olgilvee shouted.

Dina could see a bright light shining down from above, and she knew she fell at least fifteen feet. She held tight, and they slowly pulled her upward. Then five feet from the top, she felt her hands become clammy. Soon she lost her grip and tumbled back down to the ledge. Only this time one of the mad dogs was waiting for her.

It grabbed at her waist with sharp teeth and a clamp like jaw. She poked its eyes out with her fingers, causing it to howl and retreat for an instant. Then it clenched onto her arm, and she tried to beat if off. She could hear Elkin barking in the background. "God, help me!" she yelled in pain.

Then the gun sounded loudly, and the beast fell to its death. Dina rubbed the small indentations on her not so injured arm.

"Amanda. Thank God you're here," Dina shouted. Five more shots rang out, slaughtering all the dogs.

"It's safe now, Auntie. Walk over this way, and I'll help you out." She walked along the ledge to the small partially hidden opening on the other side. Then they climbed through to a decline where Amanda grabbed her arm and hoisted her up over a rock. After climbing a narrow stairway, they were back into the altar room. "Lucky for you Amanda found the secret passage," Sentra said.

"Thank you, grand niece. You saved my life." Then Amanda patted Dina on the back. Soon Olgilvee embraced Dina, smashing his crusty lips upon her bare and gritty cheek.

"Haven't we all worked up quite a hunger?" Dina said as her stomach growled. She spread a tablecloth across the altar. Neatly she arranged sandwiches, cakes, and fruits upon a foldout platter, and everyone gathered around. They ate the food and sipped on warm beers. "So what do you think about limestone caves? How were these created?" Dina asked Sentra, who chomped on a peanut buttered celery stick.

"Years ago by the solvent action of circulating ground water. This is an underground water course; its length is more than its height or width, similar to a pipeline. It's like a roofed valley where once it had a river on its floor."

"Look at these strange symbols. They look so ancient," Amanda noted.

"Yes," Sentra said. "I suppose primitive man used these caves as shelters. Tools, weapons, ornaments, bones, and pictographs such as these prove their early existence."

"Pirates, perhaps," Dina said. "They probably hid their gold and jewels here because many of the tunnels must lead off into the Caribbean Sea. Maybe Mitch the Magnificent docked his treacherous crew here."

"Must be our own Samuel Darrendon was quite familiar with this cave system. We must keep searching for the fork. That lake can't be far from here," Sentra said.

They wound down the corridor for hours until exhaustion overcame them. Dina called a halt for the day, and they all clammered into a small chamber with a convenient loft. The area immediately above the loft was batless, and they managed to slip in among the stalagtites. Elkin curled up to Dina where they fell asleep in the pitch darknesss of the subterranean home.

"Who goes there?" Olgilvee asked.

Dina was just waking up to the snarls of Elkin. She glanced at her watch. Three a.m. it read in the glow of her small flashlight.

"Who goes there?" he repeated firmly. Dina could see tall, dark figures standing below the entryway to the chamber.

"This is our home. You're sleeping on our bed," the man said. Sentra put on her big flashlight and lit up three Jamaican men standing before them. The smell of body odor and beer hung heavy in the damp room, and they carried some large, palm fronds, probably for bedding. A brown paper sack overflowed with fruits, beers, and raw fish heads, and they smiled, exposing toothless grins. Dried braided locks of hair hung in sticks jutting out into their faces.

"Who are you?" Olgilvee asked. He had his gun cocked and pointed at their heads.

"We're Maroons banished from the Land of Look Behind. We no harm you. Don't worry."

Amanda and George sat up looking surprised. Dina offered the men some bread which they accepted. Then the Jamaicans took some coals and sticks from their backpack and built a small fire.

"Why are you tourists here? This is no place for nighttime adventures," the youngest one said. He giggled.

"We are on a journey of discovery, my man. Perhaps you can widen our knowledge of the area. Tell us about Maroons?" George asked. Dina noticed they were barefoot, and their nails were so long they curled around the ends of their toes. They all climbed out of the loft and sat in a circle around the fire like prehistoric campers.

"We are from a group of slaves who fought the Spanish for freedom from slavery. We didn't want to be owned by the Spanish or by anyone. Years ago an Admiral Penns of the British army landed here, overwhelmed the Spanish, and set the black slaves free. Our brothers settled west of here in the Cockpit Country," the eldest explained.

Suddenly the cave echoed with belches, and then the men continued their stories. The old one kept staring at Dina's dragon charm as he continued. "Then the British, of all peoples, tried to make us Maroons move out of Cockpit, but the ex-slaves whipped 'em. Then a treaty was signed with the British promising our freedom."

"Were there any more wars afterwards?" Sentra asked. The middle-aged, blue-eyed Jamaican handed Dina a fish head which she accepted graciously from his clutches in the dark cave.

"Yes. The British broke the promise and released sixty pairs of manhunting hounds called Maroon Hounds to hunt and kill our brothers. They captured many of our men unawares and shipped them to Nova Scotia for slavery. We fought back and luckily many of our family members escaped the slavery and murder, and here we are today," the eldest finished.

"Many of our loved ones are buried in these caves," the young one said. He reached over and carressed Dina's gold charm. "Banished from the Land of Look Behind."

"But why did the British break the promise?" Dina asked.

"Enough said." The old one pulled out a joint and lit it up. Dina saw him rise and go to the loft. The others followed. "My favorite spot," he said. He pushed over Dina's belongings and crawled in against a jutting stalactite.

"A new bedfellow," Olgilvee said.

Dina grinned and decided on an early course of action.

"We've slept nearly six hours. We'll be on our way," she said. Then everyone quicky gathered their supplies and began their trip down the long corridor.

"No problem," the Jamaicans said in unison.

"Is there a fork nearby?" Sentra asked.

"Ya. Five miles ahead, but be careful. Some place no space to pass," the middle-aged one said.

They could see the glow of the fire die out behind them, but they kept trudging along the corridor. Dina munched on a fish head and noticed a feeling of desolation enshrouding the cave. Then it happened.

"No! No!" George screamed. The tumbling rocks could be heard a quarter mile behind them where George and Amanda were bringing up the rear.

"Sentra! Dina!" Amanda hollered.

The flashlight's beam was clouded by dust from the fallen ceiling of the cave, but Dina could see George's arm sticking up from the center of the pile. His fingers were bloodied and bruised, and his nails were chipped or broken. The rest of his body was hidden under the chunks of limestone. At first, moans were heard from where Elkin sniffed and licked at his hand, but soon the sounds stopped. Then Dina and the three tried to dig him out. They freed his head and upper torso and checked for a pulse, but there was none. His chest had been crushed, and blood poured out like red paint from a tipped can.

"George. Come back to me," Amanda pleaded.

Dina tried to comfort her grand niece who held the dead man's head in her palms. The last large rock was heaved off his legs, which were crushed and torn as well.

"What'll we do with him?" Dina asked.

"Bury him there," Olgilvee answered, pointing to a sandy area. The task was soon accomplished and the eulogy read. Amanda wept for her lost love.

Standing on an edge of a cliff, Dina, in deep sorrow, threw a rock. It took several minutes before they heard it hit bottom. It made a plunk sound when it did, and Dina yelled. "Water! The lake must be below."

They made their way on a decline, and Dina flowed with memories. Amanda and George had spent years struggling to make ends meet. Their drug and alcohol addiction was shared Dina knew. But it seemed Amanda's near tragic bout with hepatitus had made them all aware of the preciousness of life. The young woman's feelings of hatred toward life itself seemed to vanish as she recovered. Life took on a new meaning after George and she abandoned their drug habits. "We truly wanted to help the family," Amanda told her. "I'll take over George's part in this hunt. We'll find those jewels and end this quest. Eternity for the Darrendons." Dina grabbed her hand and squeezed it softly.

"We need to find the way to the lake. The fork must be up here somewhere," Sentra said. She wrapped her long, golden hair into a braid and mopped the dirt from her face with a bandana. Dina could see Olgilvee rush ahead and squeeze past Sentra in the narrow corridor.

"The fork is here," he shouted. "Now we go north and travel one mile."

"Great," Dina said. "Be careful."

"Be our good scout," Sentra hollered.

Dina took the rear, following behind Amanda. Elkin stayed by Dina's side, occasionally sniffing out a cave cricket or dead bat. The excitement mounted during the half hour hike.

"Eureka! The stairway," Olgilvee explained.

A thick mass of slime covered each stone step that led down to the water. The enormous cavern was one hundred and eighty feet high. The eeriness of the enclosure captivated the silent group who gazed into its recesses. The underground lake spread out a quarter mile before them, and every so often bat droppings, like muddy darts, would fall into the water from the ceiling. Thousands of the beady-eyed creatures roosted in their nursery colony, and sharp, audible sounds echoed through the cave in which many bats wove their way to their destinations.

"Guiding system," Sentra said. "Those echoes are reflected from obstacles giving the bat its safe traveling path." Olgilvee stuck his hand in the cool, lake water.

"Anyone care for a swim?" he asked.

"No, but this raft should come in handy." Sentra quickly inflated the orange portable float she carried in her backpack. It was large enough for three people, and it would glide easily across the lake.

Suddenly several bats dove past Elkin. He sneared and growled at the beasts. "Don't worry. I believe those are just fruit bats," Olgilvee said reassuringly.

Sentra flashed her large light up to the ceiling for a closer observation. "Look how they stand on their hind legs, prop themselves with their folded wings, and jump fast."

"Oh no," Olgilvee warned. "Those are blood thirsty vampire bats."

"We'd better hope they don't take a chunk out of our necks," Amanda said.

Quickly she pulled her collar up around her throat during the continuous screeching.

"Their bite is so slight that even a sleeping man may not be awakened," Sentra said.

"But rabies," Dina said. "Those mammals transmit that deadly virus."

"And it's common in the tropics," Sentra continued.

"Well let's hope for the best," Dina said. Then she, Olgilvee, and Sentra stripped, donned the swimsuits, and climbed into the float. Dina checked to make sure the belt was clasped tightly to her waist. "Can't even trust the bats," she said. She knew the gem was safe in its secret compartment. Soon crickets, the size of palmetto bugs, jumped into the raft from the cave floor.

"Ever eat raw cricket? It's quite good, and crunchy too," Olgilvee said. Dina could hear Amanda laugh for the first time since George's tragic death. She had rarely spoken a word since the incident, but grief must take its course.

"Down to Jamaica to Grey Grotto Cave. It lies in the lake beneath a rock grave." Dina recited the passage and then waved to Amanda and Elkin on shore. The water, except for descending stripes of bat feces, was crystal clear and at least forty feet deep. Quickly, Dina tried on her mask and snorkel set. Blind, colorless crayfish darted beneath the raft, and sawfish swam in between the rocks.

"Eyes aren't needed here. Darkness is constant," Olgilvee said. "Through the long evolutionary process they have completely lost the use of their vision." Under the boat, five-inch fish swam back and forth surrounding Dina who lowered herself into the water. She could see clearly with her light, and she flashed at all angles from the center of the lake. Many colorless sealife swam into the beam, and she gazed with amazement at the creatures. Near the back wall, piles of skeletons lay motionless, their empty eye sockets knowing only of death. She rose to the surface and swam up to her friends.

"Olgilvee, I'm going to explore the back wall where dead men lie."

"Be careful," Sentra warned. "I'll man the raft."

Soon he joined Dina, and they swam toward unknown territory. She admired the gold rings and bracelets on the cold bones in which small fish swam in and out of the intricate mass. Olgilvee pushed aside one of the skeletons, revealing a handle.

It looked like a chest Dina knew. Then Olgilvee motioned her to surface with him. Gently she felt for their safety rope that lead to the raft.

They both resurfaced for air, but only Sentra returned with Dina while Olgilvee manned the raft. "He saw crossbones on the wall and got spooked," Dina said before submerging. She also knew Olgilvee did not have the lung capacity she possessed.

Tugging on Sentra's shoulder, they headed for the chest. Pulling on the skeleton, she gently moved it away to reveal a massive metal box near which a large crowbar leaned on its lid. Dina and Sentra pushed the metal finger under the slightly open lid and hung onto the part that grew out from the chest. Soon they felt the top move. While Dina held the lid up, Sentra dove into the five foot deep rectangle. There in the bottom was a small box. Dina tried to open it, but it was sealed too tightly. Holding it firmly, they swam for the surface. In the raft, Olgilvee opened the box easily with his big, strong hands.

"I've never seen such a deep green emerald completely unflawed as so it would seem," Sentra said. "Perhaps this one is from a deposit in Columbia? Many pirates robbed the keepers of these stones, the Peruvian Indians, during the Spanish conquest of South America. There seem to be no flaws hidden in this specific cut. How beautiful." Sentra held it up for all to see as the constant screech of bats left no room for silent admiration.

"Look there," Dina said grimly. She hand rowed to shore, bumping into skeletons that had floated to the surface, looking eerie with their stiff arms and legs pointed peculiarly at the onlookers.

"You mess with our dead," the old Jamaican said angrily. Then Elkin snarled. Quickly Dina grabbed the emerald from Sentra and thrust it into her leather belt pouch. The three men who had nearly been their bedfellows stood staring from shore only ten feet from Amanda and the wolf. They held machetes in hand, the steel blades shimmering in the flashlight beam.

"Hold up the gem, quickly," Sentra said. "It's believed emeralds drive away evil spirits. Old folklore says that those who harm its protector will suddenly be burned to death. Let's hope this gem shows the power of which Grandfather spoke."

Dina pulled it out fast. The gem shone its green color beneath the light Sentra shone upon it. On shore, Amanda tried to calm Elkin, but he began to bark and pace back and forth toward the intruders. Upon seeing the emerald in its brilliance, they backed off, then lept up the flight of stairs, soon returning with palm fronds shielding their faces.

"You disturbed the sleep of our dead. You stole from them. Curses to you," the Moroons shouted.

Suddenly one of them hurled a rock at the thousands of bats roosting above. In a few minutes, the screeching grew in intensity, and thousands of the winged creatures darted and dove in the cavern, the faint ticking sound of their orientation system echoing. Dina screamed at five of the fuzzy, mouth-foaming beasts that dipped down to the raft swooping past her arms and legs. On shore, Elkin lept and clawed at the mammals screeching past.

"Rabies! Rabies!" Amanda cried.

"Quick, everyone. To the cave exit," Sentra ordered.

"Find the rock with the fish head carving!" Dina yelled. She remembered the words of Mother, the Grand Cayman women's sister.

"Yes. This island cave must have an underground tunnel to the Caribbean sea. The water has to go somewhere" Amanda said. She rushed from the shore into the lake. "If there is one, it may be our only way out."

"We'll get you," the Jamaicans shouted. Quickly Olgilvee and Sentra dove off the raft.

Then, Dina carefully sealed the emerald back into her belt and lept off the raft, too. Elkin swam in behind her. Sure enough a large rock with a fish head carving led to a hidden passageway. Taking deep breaths, she and Elkin entered completely submerged. Sentra squeezed through the small opening, too, and Olgilvee and Amanda swam side by side through the increasingly deep and narrow corridor. Sunlight lit the waters ahead, signaling safety in sight. Dina was glad the ordeal was over, and she hoped no one would destroy the conclusion by springing on them once they were outside. She checked the cinch in her belt. The gems were still safe.

Once on land, they jogged one-half mile to a small grocery store. Olgilvee called a rental car company to pick up the vehicle they had left at Grey Grotto. Then he phoned a local cab company. Dina noticed a tear seep slowly from his eye.

"God it's good to be alive and with my beloved." Olgilvee squeezed Dina's hand as they rode quietly in the rickety car, its windows open, dust clouding in. "Stop at this church, cabbie" Olgilvee gave him twenty dollars and ordered everyone out. "Dina, it's time we were married."

"God bless you," Sentra said. Amanda smiled.

A small wedding ceremony was just ending at the white, wooden building, and Olgilvee took charge. "Minister. We're next," he said. He pulled Dina from the cab and displayed a tin, pop can ring for the wedding band. "Try this on for size."

"Oh, Olgilvee, I adore you," Dina held out her trembling hand, and he slipped the silver ring above the gold engagement band.

The old, bald man married them at the altar in everyone's eyes. "Now do it right with the courts," the minister said. Then suddenly the church doors burst open behind them.

"Give us the gem," the young one demanded. Elkin growled.

"Oh no. The Jamaicans from the cave," Sentra alerted. They raced out a side entrance and back to the cab.

"To Discovery Bay," Olgilvee ordered. The cabbie hit the gas.

"Those Jamaicans aren't giving up," Amanda said. The three men raced behind them on dirt bikes, their dreadlocks flying in the breeze.

The cab approached town, slowing to a stop at a parade in progress. "Let's filter through the crowd," Olgilvee said. He could see the Jamaicans stopped down the road. "Hey. Looks like they're out of gas. Hopefully we'll lose them," he surmised. He looked up at giant, silver crayfish marching by on silver legs. Then they ran out and hid amid the costumes made with thin, grey sheets of cotton held together by silver threads.

"There in the crowd by the marketplace, I see the Jamaicans again," Dina said. She gazed up at the crayfish and into its large, bulbous eyes. They were made of black balloons stuck out on its face, and silver aluminum antennas pointed forth from its cheeks. Coral threads decorated the leg joints, and blue threads emphasized the hinges in the tail sections. Sentra and Amanda crouched low near a beautiful, tropical parrot that walked by decorated in purple, green, and yellow feathers. Next, Dina and Elkin found shelter within the red ibis group which turned heads to the audience taking pictures and moving in closer to get a better view. The creativity was drawing Dina into it, into her past.

"I think they see us," Olgilvee said. He approached Dina who was enthralled by her surroundings.

The Jamaicans bore down on them, Dina could see, and she cleared into reality and gathered Sentra and Amanda. They crouched down among two thousand butterflies, and stepped to the beat of their rhythmic band. Then Dina noticed the artistic process of design for many of the costumes included fiberglass poles, beads, animal bones, styrofoam, rubber fish, beach balls, shells, and fish skeletons. Some costumes had mirrors attached to them to emphasize reflection. Texture was evident in the hard and soft, smooth and rough surfaces that were combined in one costume. It was a gala affair of creative expression, and Dina hated to cause disruption. Soon they made it safely to the end of the procession and jumped on a bus.

"Hey. Give us our gem," shouted the old Jamaican. Olgilvee waved out the window.

"Finders keepers, losers go away," Dina said.

Soon they were back on the Empress where Dina put the emerald into the safe along with the ruby, both enclosed in the leather belt pouch. Then she wrote a letter to Steven explaining their current whereabouts, Jackson's death, the cave adventure, and the wedding. Along with a coconut gift, quickly Dina gave the letter to a local woman, near the Empress, to mail it ASAP. The tall thin woman obliged smiling at her gracious gift. In moments they set sail.

That night she decided to put her feelings on canvas. Maybe creativity would tell her something. The parade had definitely revived her spark.

Quickly she began. The water color palate was simple, and she blended freely, creating new shades of her own. She understood the vocabulary of color, and she used it to create unforgettable paintings. She had a trained eye that could see light and shade, color, and the intricacies of design in the world around her. Her paintings brought to one's attention a new insight on nature's creations. She took the world of French impressionism that stated that the basis for all design was the triangle, the circle, and the square. A Japanese friend had once told her that these shapes were symbolic in language. The triangle stands for heaven, the circle signifies man, and the square symbolizes earth.

With shapes, and the light and shade technique, she brought the vivid colors to life smiling, frowning, laughing, or crying on her canvas. She could take a hue, or color straight out of the tube and add white to create a tint. Adding black to hue would create a shade, and to get tone she would add grey.

Carefully she began to paint an empty beach. She used the value of a color by surrounding the light area of sea form with a darker shade. Its whiteness glistened with intensity. A blue beach bucket appeared on its side in the sand where small footprints led away to a cluster of grey rocks. The painting was truly taking on a life-like quality based on her observation, intuition, and deep memory. The memory of a tragic childhood pulled her into the painting. She could not stop drawing, and what she created began to frighten her.

She used various geometric shapes to create the rocks. She emphasized the texture on the light side of the rock, and then turned it into shadow, slowly getting darker until reflected light brought back its brightness. Was that a spray of red paint dripping off the rock onto the sand? Was not the granite round and smooth from being battered and pounded by the sea? Next, two figures developed. An old woman lay on the beach with deep gashes in her head. The eyes were glazed and staring. Next to her lay the red-haired woman. Dina could paint the coarse sprigs of hair perfectly, because they were just like her own. This person, too, had big gashes in her body, and the blood, from her punctured thigh, drained into pools on the sand. Inside the rocks, she began to see the head of a small girl. Red sprigs of hair stood up on her brow which was furrowed from looking on the gruesome scene. She painted the eyes light and they, too, were staring and horrified. From each one two tears dropped down the smooth cheek.

The sea was easy to paint. The distant ocean she made much darker than the rest; the middle water was true color. The beach water, however, was warmer in colors of yellow and orange as influenced by the rocks and sand. Texture was apparent in the forewater that appeared to break up in places.

Suddenly the sea broke up greatly, and her brush developed a mind of its own. The huge, grey blob began to appear. It seemed to float on the surface. Its gruesome, bloated face was emphasized in shades of blue, and rotted teeth were stressed in yellow. Scattered directly in front of the grey mass of man was a burlap sack. Jewels glittered in the sand. A ruby, emerald, sapphire, diamond and topaz reached out to her. These gems were painted expertly on the canvas. Then she painted a large, gold key next to the sapphire, and she wondered what it meant. A skeleton key to open a lock of which she did not now its location. Dina was puzzled, and she lay her brush down feeling exhausted.

A lightning storm was blowing in from the north. Olgilvee awakened from his place on the bed, and she slipped into the sheets.

"Why up so late, my bride?" he asked.

She told him of the painting, and he wept for her past sorrows.

"So that's where you first discovered the gems."

They made love, and soon a storm rocked the boat, passionately gliding them into numerous waves. Afterwards, Olgilvee dropped off to sleep, and once again she felt herself drawn to the canvas. She rose from their bed.

At her easel, she stood painting her castle home. The mortar was smoothed sloppily around each grey brick, and the windows were painted large and white with thick, black tar between each pane. Then a hulking, grotesque figure, with three eyes, began painting itself in the center of the front yard. Her brush painted the beast high and wide. A big head stood atop a short, stubby neck. The face cast a yellow tone, and deep pits stood out like small caverns. The nose was prominent and covered with thick, dark fur inside, but atop its pointed head it had no hair. She painted in the brown, rotted teeth, and a thick tongue protruding out of the left corner of his stench hole. Three long, thick fingers stood root-like on each hand, and mud covered every inch of its lower body. Upon the ground in front of it, Dina drew a small, broken child. The red hair rose in curly sprigs across its head, and the clothes were muddied and torn. The little girl's eyes were open, and fear emanated from within.

She sat down on her stool and thought of the beast in that dark swamp. Had he truly come to rescue her that night from the quicksand, or had he only pulled her free to drag her off and kill her? She never really knew, but he had followed her to the castle. For years he hid in the deepest recesses of the surrounding forest where no one dared trek. The few who did were found torn to pieces, their internal organs leaving a trail of gore where they had been dragged into the underbrush. Through the years, no one had been able to catch a killer. It was even thought a crazed bear with bad teeth had murdered the humans so savagely.

The beast seemed to be ageless, like herself growing old in years alone, except for a few minor frailties. In the background the brush drew an old man. He was tall, and his face wore a mask of sadness and despair. The night closed on picture number two, and she turned over a new page.

A torso of a male appeared on the canvas, its thick, grey hair smeared with blood. The man's limbs were scattered everywhere, arms hanging from the oak tree and legs dangling over the birdbath. Vultures were gathered in a bare, birch tree, and the sky looked dark and menacing. In the corner sat the beast, and she painted in its blood-red eyes. In its hand was a heart with a mouth-sized chunk bitten out of the center. Dina began to weep upon realizing the intensity of what she painted.

Quickly she turned to a fourth page. Olgilvee mumbled in his sleep, and Feather curled up beside him. Dina felt dazed and increasingly unaware of her surroundings. Once again the paint brush took over. This time it drew in a close-up of the castle's kitchen window which overlooked the large birch tree. A small face appeared in the pane. It was her child-like face framed with sprigs of curly, red hair. The eyes, wide and unbelieving, were looking upon something horrific, but the face soon became clouded in a mass of blood which she painted in splattered strokes across the large window.

"Dina. Dina," Olgilvee said sharply. "Snap out of it, my wife."

Dina began to cry hysterically. "No, no. Not Grandfather," she said woefully. "Don't hurt my grandfather, too."

Olgilvee threw a blanket around her and laid her on the bed. "You're not a child anymore. It's okay. No one's going to hurt you or Grandfather."

Dina felt herself calm down and her heart stop racing, but Olgilvee's tenderness brought sobs from deep within her being. "It was the beast who only wanted to brutalize Grandfather in his mind. It was the goat's heart he was holding. He had reached into the very chest of my pet and ripped out its still beating heart. Grandfather had been furious, and he had scolded the beast. It cried and ran off in shame."

"How awful, my wife, but let go of the past and cling to our future hope to fulfill your grandfather's last wish. The family future depends on it."

Dina lay in Olgilvee's arms and heaved with deep sobs. Hours passed until at three a.m. she slipped into a dream. She was at her canvas drawing a woman with raven hair and deep, green eyes which were curved upward at the far corners. The pupils were elongated in serpent-like style. Upon her head she wore a purple crown embedded with glistening jewels, and a dark, plum-colored gown covered her long, lean figure. Around her thin fingers rose rocks of many carrots, and sharp, plum-colored fingernails pointed out from her hands at the ends of upstretched arms. Engraved on her upper chest was the word Sazran, and after she smiled, gold saliva dripped from her lips.

Dina saw her walk toward her, and she suddenly woke up. Her body was drenched with sweat, and the bed sheet was tangled up in her legs. Olgilvee still lay asleep, but his head rested flat on the mattress, for she had taken his pillow. Could the dream of Sazran, their distant relative turned bad, be some kind of warning?

CHAPTER SIX

They headed northwest past Grand Cayman Island, and then around the tip of Cuba. Dina was clearly focused on the future. The void, however, had left everyone with mixed emotions, for they were leaving without George and Jackson. In the Florida Straits, they held a memorial service for the two brave men, and Amanda read a passage from Psalms. "Do thou, O Lord, protect us, guard us ever from this generation. On every side the wicked prowl, as vileness is exalted among the sons of men."

Then she threw a garland of gardenias into the sea. "George and I had wild times in our reckless lives. At least he died a good man," Amanda said.

"We're all grateful to George for bringing you back to health and saving us from the clutches of Devon," Dina said. She put an arm around Amanda while Sentra quoted another verse from Psalms in memory of Jackson.

"Guard our lives, and deliver us."

Sentra then threw a wreath of roses into the sea. "The love of Jackson is lost. So much grief," Sentra said. Dina clutched at her leather belt with the gems to help them to eternity's door.

"The sorrows on this quest are so unfair," Dina touched Sentra's arm and shed a tear. "But we shall find our glory. Peace be with your friend."

The weather was clear and the wind brisk enough to keep them sailing at a steady pace toward St Lovell's lighthouse in Georgia for gem number three. They sailed up the east coast of the pennisula and into the Gulf stream about two hundred miles from Florida. This current, fed by waters from the Gulf of Mexico and the Florida Current, was dark blue and salty. Its ten degree warmer temperature distinguished it from the surrounding waters. The river in the sea was narrow and deep, running three miles to the bottom, and the area suffered from some unique weather conditions. But Sentra's meteorology skills and the wisdom of the hermit would help them through the roughest and most unpredictable weather. Dina had confidence they would make it to the lighthouse, and if the instruments failed, they could count on Sigmund, their frog barometer. Sentra kept him in a large, glass container above deck where Dina could see the tiny, beige and green amphibian from the stairway. He was sitting in the water next to a small, ceramic mermaid. The air was dry as sunbaked sand, and the barometer was accurate. Frog was doing a great job.

They sailed deeper into the Gulf Stream where the precipitation was low, evaporation was high, and the winds light. "How about a swim," Olgilvee shouted.

Dina dove into the warm, clear waters, and Olgilvee threw the anchor overboard. She swam into a mass of gulfweed and played in the brown algae, plucking off the berry-like bladders. "Did you know the Carthaginians reached this area as early as 530 B.C," Olgilvee said.

Dina watched Sentra dive naked, her firm, round breasts smacking the crystal clear water.

"Mighty salty," she said, bobbing up for air.

Dina thought she looked like a sea monster with the floating sargassum bed atop her head. They played and splashed in the ocean until finally Olgilvee and Amanda joined them. Dina felt comfortable knowing they were out of the Caribbean and on their way toward Georgia. Elkin stood on deck watching carefully, guarding the leather belt and The Book of Eternity Dina had locked up in the safe. The water felt good against her naked flesh. She felt so bouyant, floating freely on her back.

"Who did that?" she asked. Dina could feel two hard sticks poke her in the spine. "Ouch! Stop it Olgilvee."

"I'm over here, wife. What's the matter?"

Dina turned over on her stomach and saw an immense, dark shadow appear beneath her. She was suddenly gripped with fear when it swam a distance of ten feet and then circled back toward their boat.

"Everyone out of the water," Dina ordered.

Olgilvee was the first on deck, followed by Sentra, but Amanda was a slow swimmer.

"Help. It's got my leg!" Amanda screamed.

Quickly Dina dove under water to get a closer look. What she saw horrified her and left her heart racing. It was none other than the giant goosefish. She had heard about them in legend but had never actually seen one. Olgilvee had told her about them while reading a book on the subject. It was a member of the deep-sea anglers, a group of fish that usually lives up to six hundred fathoms below the sea. He had never even seen one up close before.

It finally let go of Amanda's leg leaving hundreds of small holes. By then, Sentra had dove in and was dragging her poor sister on board.

"It's over here!" Dina hollered. "A goosefish."

"By golly, you're right, Dina," Olgilvee said.

She could see him aiming his spear gun at the mass that glided atop the water. The brown fish had small gill openings behind its armlike pectoral fins. Its first dorsal spine looked like a large rod. That was the part that poked her in the back she realized, still feeling a tingling sensation.

At the end of the rod dangled a bait with which it attracted other fish by flashing it back and forth like a worm or shrimp. Its mouth was as wide as its entire face, and luring a sargassum fish, it opened its big hole and sucked it down into its gullet. It measured twenty feet long and weighed at least a ton. It was now between her and the boat, and Dina's heart was in her throat. Suddenly an Orca Whale, almost as large as the goosefish, swam by. The monster goosefish gobbled it up in an instant. Dina took in a deep breath and dove beneath the fish and the boat.

"Sentra, help!" she said from the other side of the boat. Her grand niece lowered the ladder into the sea, and Dina climbed aboard.

Suddenly their craft was jolted by the fish who slammed its broad head into the hull.

"Oh, no. It's still hungry," Dina said.

"Hold on, everyone." Sentra pulled in the anchor and set sail once again. The winds were so light the craft barely moved. Then the fish slammed the boat again, tossing Amanda overboard.

"Help! Help!" she screamed.

Olgilvee aimed and shot a spear, hitting the fish's tail section. "Go away, flesh eater," he yelled. Quickly it dove into the depths. Then it resurfaced with Amanda's leg sticking out of its mouth. Blood drenched its thick lips as it munched and swallowed.

"That does it. I'm going in after her," Sentra said. She dove in, wrapped an arm around Amanda, and swam for the ladder. The fish circled and came two feet from her silken body and then darted below the boat. After Sentra hauled Amanda on board, the boat jolted upwards. The fish had lifted them atop its head, and they were hovering above the sea. Olgilvee reached over the edge with a machete and hacked into its tail fin. The boat came crashing down, and all hands hit the deck with a thud. The mass of mutilated fish sank to the bottom where sharks gathered for a feeding frenzy.

"We must stop Amanda's bleeding," Sentra said in a serious tone. She tied a tourniquet above the amputation site and elevated the stump.

"We have two primary dangers: hemorrhage and infection," Olgilvee said.

"I didn't know you were such an expert," Dina said. She held Amanda's head and massaged her brow until she momentarily regained consciousness.

"Ah, awake at last. And don't fret, Amanda," Olgilvee assured her. "I must confess that I was once a medical student in Australia before I switched majors to oceanography. The medical profession didn't offer me enough freedom. Anyway, hopefully the initial flow of blood from the site has washed most of the infectious material out. Ah, a tooth," he said. A large, pointed object stuck out from her flesh.

"Keep it for a souvenir, Amanda" Dina said. "It'll make a fine necklace piece."

Amanda's mouth curved up at the corners almost resembling a smile. "So sorry I've caused a delay," she mumbled in agony. Dina softly caressed her cheek.

Olgilvee gently cleansed the area with soap, water, alcohol, and ether. Then, a copious irrigation of the wound with saline solution he performed as Dina looked on. Sentra handed Olgilvee the needle and thread, and he began to talk and suture the gap. "Hemorrhage wouldn't be so severe if these vessels were torn and uneven. That fish had some large teeth, like razor blades. Poor Amanda."

Dressings were appled and the stump was elevated. Olgilvee looked exhausted. Dina carefully watched the dressing for signs of bleeding. She kept the limb elevated for twenty-four hours and then took the pillow out for fear of causing a hip contracture. They sailed up the Gulf stream heading for Georgia. The climate was perfect, and the ocean water was warm as a spa bath and rapid in its journey. They traveled at seven knots in the river, and none of the bad weather associated with the Gulf stream had appeared yet. They were all keeping their fingers crossed.

Dina carefully used aseptic techniques in changing the dressing. Soon Amanda's depression was alienated by the soothing and comforting care of Sentra. Months ago Sentra had completely forgiven her sister for past dirty deeds. The Banyan Forest incident, when Amanda and George had placed their lives in danger, was soon forgotten. Here was a person she had gotten to know again for the good side everyone had within them. Amanda just had trouble showing her goodness, because for years it had been buried in resentment and jealousy. One turning point came after Amanda's bout with hepatitis. She began to appreciate life and her family, but why had life taken her leg? Would resentment breed again? Only time would tell, she knew.

Every so often Elkin would nuzzle her stump with his wet nose. Dina helped her grand niece exercise to maintain muscle tone and prevent contractures. Olgilvee had done a great job cleaning the wound as no infection was evident. The incision was healed and elastic bandages were applied to shrink the stump of her thigh. Dina helped her change these four or five times a day because Amanda perspired freely in the summer heat. Soon she was able to change her own dressings.

"Look at this as a challenge," Sentra said.

The days passed by in virtual silence, the crew trying to heal from so many losses. The quiet in itself was soothing, and the Empress sailed on to the lighthouse. Gem number three was waiting just for them.

Deep in the night, when silence reigned, an agonizing moan echoed through the cabin. "Oh, God," Amanda said. "My leg. It hurts so badly down by my foot." Dina rose quickly from her sleep and went to her side.

"But you have no foot. You don't have an ankle, calf, or knee." Dina turned on the night light and lay down next to her grand niece. "It's phantom pain. It's caused by the nerves in the stump. It'll gradually disappear."

Dina heard footsteps, and then Olgilvee entered the room with a syringe. "This will eliminate the pain temporarily," he said groggily. He shot into the nerves with alcohol.

"So much has been lost in pursuit of these gems, but we must go on," Dina said sadly. "Keep being brave."

Soon Amanda's pain subsided, and she dropped off to sleep. Dina gently brushed her dark hair out of her deeply etched forehead. Then the young woman began to snore lightly.

A day passed when Sentra and Amanda decided to cook. Dina was the one who suggested they put their chef skills to work. "We have so much talent," she said. They propped Amanda up on the kitchen chair, and she and Sentra mixed, cooked, and baked. This was therapeutic Dina knew, because the business and reward of the work brought Amanda obvious pleasure. She was beginning to put less emphasis on her lost leg.

Olgilvee, armed with a carving knife, was now on deck making her a prosthesis out of one of the wide oak table legs. The lopsided table was propped up on a crate.

"Hey, Dina. Look what I have here," he shouted. She quickly ran up on deck and beheld the wooden leg he held up. It had an artificial knee that actually bent on a hinge he had taken from the wooden chest. "We'll have to explain to Amanda how to care for this prostheses," he said, "and show her how to put it on as soon as possible."

"I know this is an emotionally trying time for Amanda, and we should get her to talk about her feelings," Dina said. "Hopefully she'll accept this with greater ease as time goes by."

"Her skirts or trousers will hide this artificial limb, and I've even made the foot to fit the same size shoe as her own leg." Olgilvee proudly pointed to the foot which he had expertly carved. Even the toenails were polished in a pale pink hue.

"She's preparing a wonderful dinner for you to show her appreciation," Dina said.

They ate heartily, praising Amanda, and Dina could see them all admire the beautifully carved, hollow prosthesis. It was propped up on the high stool, its toes displayed like artwork.

"Not only a limb, but a perfect place to hide the jewels," Sentra said while sticking her fist into its center.

"Why yes," Dina agreed.

Amanda's eyes sparkled like grey crystals. "I would be happy to tote our gems," she said, realizing her new purpose. "Hand me my new leg."

"Olgilvee stood up, and while munching a pecan, he helped Amanda try on her new limb. She walked across the deck, carefully balancing on both feet. Then everyone applauded.

"It's great," she said joyfully. "The knee even bends." Olgilvee sat back for seconds on the maple nut cream cake. Dina knew he felt proud by the way he gleamed while watching Amanda run her fingers over the expertly polished nails.

"Where did you learn to color a woman's toes?" Dina asked. Olgilvee blushed, and Dina ran her fingers through his thick, grey hair.

Dina removed the ruby and emerald from her belt that was locked up in the boat safe. Amanda took off her leg, and Sentra dropped the jewels inside. They fell to the bottom of the foot and were corked shut. Now, Dina knew the trust in Amanda was complete. Elkin rubbed up against the leg as if accepting her too.

It was August now, and Sentra closed in on Georgia. "We'll stay in the center of this narrow river. That seven and one-half miles per hour current will move us along flowing north. We'll travel until we're across from St. Lovell's Island lighthouse. Then with Godspeed, we'll travel west," Sentra said. "It will get chillier the further up the coast we travel. The winds sometime blow from land to sea not allowing the warmer Atlantic waters to provide heat."

"Look at those fins." Olgilvee pointed.

A school of eight dolphins began playing around the boat, and Dina noted they were all from six to eight feet in length. The back fins were ten inches, and their foreheads descended quickly to the base of their flattened beaks. One gulped down a fish, its two hundred sharp teeth glistening in the salty waters. Then Dina could see a black body contrasted against the white underside of one dolphin that lept into the air and squawked, parrot-like, at her. He swam rapidly around the boat and moved ten feet ahead of them. Soon he flew into the air again, splashing all aboard.

"I think he wants to be our friend," Amanda said.

"We must be careful," Olgilvee warned. "They are intelligent and playful but wild animals, none the less." Dina cringed at the thought of being bitten or walloped by one of them, and she hoped the goosefish had no brother.

Hours passed on their travels toward gem number three. Amanda went below deck to rest.

"The sky is changing," Olgilvee said, looking to the heavens.

"Mares tails and mackeral scales make tall ships take in their sails," Dina said to him. She recalled the wisdom of the old hermit and saw the high, small puffs of clouds that resembled fish scales. Clear weather had ended, and a front was on its way. Sigmund, the frog, was sitting atop his rock enjoying the high humidity. Soon he began ribetting because the barometric pressure was falling. The low frequency sound waves of the approaching storm sent Elkin wimpering. Feather began sneezing and carrying on like a kitten, running and jumping around the boat. She finally curled up into a ball and fell asleep, drained of all energy.

"When the cat lies on its brain then it's going to rain," Sentra said.

An hour passed in which they stayed on course.

"Stratus clouds," Sentra said, pointing upward. Dina saw the leaden sky begin to fill with flat, grey clouds. "The rains will move in slowly and last a long time," she warned. Olgilvee sighed.

Sentra tuned into the national oceanic and atmospheric administration, a weather wire service that provided direct links to the national weather service. "Rain tonight and all day tomorrow," the reporter said.

It began with skinny sprinkles, and then the drops became heavier, sloshing the crew. The seas became steeper making the Empress glide up and down on the wave's roller coaster ride. Soon water broke over the lee deck and swept aft in buckets. Small bursts of seafoam sprayed forth, and blasts of wind swept in.

"Shorten the sail," Sentra ordered. Olgilvee followed the command while Sentra went below deck and returned with her raincoat. Dina went below to sit with Amanda, Feather, and Elkin, but the boat kept rocking steadily conjuring up images of motion sickness. Dina served ginger ale to combat nausea. Through the night, Sentra and Olgilvee took turns sailing while Amanda and Dina slept. By morning, the seas had calmed some, but the rain continued its steady downpour.

"Tell me of our destination, Dina?" Amanda asked, munching on her morning toast at the kitchen table. Dina, seated next to her, could hear the gentle breathing sounds of Olgilvee napping from the night's stress. Sentra sailed on.

"Gem number three is on St. Lovell's Island on the grounds of the old lighthouse," she answered. Dina and Amanda peered out the porthole toward land on the borders of Florida and Georgia.

"Just think, Great, Great Grandfather sailed these very waters stopping off to dispense his jewels at desired locations," Amanda said. "I guess he figured they'd be safer from thieves if they were all split up. I wonder if he felt as fascinated by lighthouses as I do."

Dina pointed out the porthole toward the distant shore. "See the blinking light in the fading night sky. That's Manon lighthouse, a place I visited as a child. It was moved to its present island from Cumberland, Georgia in the late 1830s. The island was once crowded with pirates, slave traders, and drug smugglers. A ring of smugglers called the Leather Boys brought the naked slaves from Africa. They were packed in small boats where many died from infection and disease. They'd transport them to Manon Island, then smuggle the live ones up the St. Mary's River to sell. People used to tell us young ones ghost stories about the dead slaves walking the island."

"Those poor Africans. How long did these horrible deeds last?" Amanda asked.

"Oh, until the 1850s when the business was replaced by illegal smuggling of lumber and military supplies. Eventually railroads were put in making the area quite populated."

"Tell me what the lighthouse looks like up close, Dina."

"Manon's has a tapering, white-washed stone tower and a crown made of a lantern room. All lighthouses have a keeper. That one lived in a two-story house with canopies, galleries, and the necessity of mosquito netting. The focal plane of the light is about one hundred and five feet above mean water. The closest town of Mernandino is at least three miles away."

"What about the controls for the light itself?" Amanda said. She sipped a lemonade, sucking in her cheeks at its tartness. "I believe they're automated."

"Yes. Manon's was orginally powered by an oil lamp rotated by a clock work mechanism which was rewound every four hours. It's now electrified and automated, and is visible from twenty-three miles. Lighthouses are quite useful in guiding tankers on the open Atlantic. Perhaps, St. Lovell's lighthouse is similar in looks and automation."

"We shall see," Amanda said through the sound of rain. "Maybe the dead walk there, too."

The boat rocked and swayed and filled with water, but the crew kept afloat by bailing off and on for a day. Amanda stayed safe below deck with Feather and Elkin. Sentra had changed course and was heading west toward St. Lovell's Island. Their sea legs were weary, and Olgilvee warned they needed food supplies. Then he returned below with Dina for the night, leaving Sentra at the helm.

As the full moon cast an eerie glow on the boat, Dina awoke and walked up to the deck. "How long until we reach shore?" she called out to Sentra. But the figure at the helm made not a sound. Then slowly it turned toward Dina. "Dear, God. What are you?" Dina shrieked like a banshee upon beholding the creature before her.

CHAPTER SEVEN

It was a skeleton with oozing eyeballs of purple. Its mouth hung open exposing rotted, yellow teeth, and a foul odor filled the air. The name Sazran was etched into the bones of its chest. Dina grabbed the rifle, aimed, and fired. The creature vanished, and soon Olgilvee was by her side.

"What on earth are you doing?"

"It was a beastie I saw with my own eyes. Before it turned, I thought it was Sentra."

"I'm right here, Great Auntie." Dina soon felt a warm arm around her shoulders. "It has been a stressful journey," Sentra said, squeezing her aunt. "Maybe you should go below deck and get some sleep. We'll soon be docked on St. Lovell's Island." Dina looked intently out into the white light of the sailor's landmark.

"Maybe you're right."

She felt bewildered, and then Olgilvee led her below. Amanda was snoring loudly, her wooden leg chained securely to the bed post. Elkin sniffed at Dina while she lay down on the bed, but Feather's fur was standing on end, and she erected her tail and arched her back. Could she have seen it too? Dina felt goose pimples on her arm, and she lay shivering. Olgilvee served her some camomile tea, which she sipped slowly.

"I know what I saw was real," she said. "These waters must be haunted."

She quickly remembered The Book of Eternity's mention of Sazran, their distant relative turned evil. Then she recalled the sorceress Sazran who was present when Grandfather had stolen the jewels. Her dream, days ago, of this witch with the tattoo of the name Sazran on her chest, could have been a premonition of this appearance. Was her grand niece Sentra being used for possession by the spirit of Sazran, their distant relative?

Suddenly the Empress calmly stopped sailing. "Why have you dropped anchor?" Olgilvee shouted to Sentra. He stood at the bottom of the steps and called up to her.

"I haven't dropped anchor. I don't know what it is. The winds are blowing, but my boat is still."

Dina and Elkin rose from the cabin and followed Olgilvee up the steps. Dina leaned over the railing and extended an oar over the side. "We're on top of a rock." Dina set the oar down. "It didn't even jolt the boat. It's as if it stabbed forth from the depths of the sea."

"I've sailed these waters before on two different occasions. There aren't any rocks here." Sentra looked at her depth finder, and it read six fathoms. "How strange."

"Look there," Amanda said, pointing toward land. Dina could see her rubbing sleep from her eyes in the full moon's glow that shone upon a rock pathway. It led up to the lighthouse. Then suddenly a figure appeared.

"That's the creature I saw on the boat," Dina said. The skeleton, with oozing eyeballs, lept towards them across the rocks, its purple cape trailing behind it. The clattering of its bones, like clacking teeth, echoed through the night.

"Welcome to St. Lovell's Island," it said in a baratone voice so spooky sounding that the night air seemed to quiver in fear. Olgilvee shot his speargun and hit right on target. The arrow pierced its chest, and the creature arched and laughed horrifically. Then it vanished into thin air.

"Let's find that gem and be off. This place is haunted," Dina said.

"Just maybe," Olgilvee said, "someone is playing a cruel joke. I'm going to find out." Armed with his rifle, he started down the rocky path. Dina locked Feather in her cabin and secured The Book of Eternity in the safe. The gems were in Amanda's leg. Then Dina, Sentra, and Amanda followed close behind. Olgilvee, and Elkin darted ahead to lead the way.

Soon they spotted the brick home of the lighthouse keeper. "Closed for renovations," Olgilvee said.

"What is that smell?" Dina said. She and Olgilvee followed the purtrid odor to a trash bin at the side of the building.

"A homeless couple," he said, pointing at two bedraggled people. The man and a woman crawled out of the metal dumpster. Rotten meat clung to their clothing in sticky and foul-smelling strips.

"Just lookin' for a place to get some shut eye. Spare change, man," the male uttered hoarsely.

"Off with you both," Olgilvee said sternly. The two quickly ran off into the woods. "Go find a soup kitchen in town. This here is danger zone."

Suddenly, in the opposite direction, a rustle was heard in the bushes, and Elkin began to growl. "To the safety of the house," Olgilvee said. He raised his gun trying to take careful aim while his body trembled.

Sentra heaved herself into the wooden door and then fell to the floor with a thud upon its splintered remains. She sat up and picked dried mouse droppings like small pebbles from the indentations in her legs. Dina grabbed her and pulled her to her feet, and Amanda brushed the thick cobwebs from her golden hair. A large, furry spider, as big, yellow, and juicy as a grapefruit, crawled slowly under the kitchen table.

Suddenly a gunshot echoed through the night. Amanda pulled back the dirty white curtain from the kitchen window. "The creature has a hold on Olgilvee," she said. "We must defend him."

Grabbing butcher knives, pots, and pans from the cabinet, they raced out the door to aid their comrade. In seconds the skeleton ghost had disappeared, and Olgilvee was walking into the woods near the lighthouse. His arms were outstretched, and Elkin walked by his side nipping at his heels.

"Olgilvee. Olgilvee. Stop. Please stop!" Sentra said. But he continued to walk, his eyes glazed and unseeing. Then a rain cloud covered the moon, and they were plunged into complete darkness. Dina reached out to grab Olgilvee, but the image she sensed in front of her was only a tree.

"Elkin. Elkin. Come here," she ordered.

The wolf howled and then quickly answered her call, lapping at her hands and sniffing her weary feet. Amanda ran back to the house and returned with a small lighted candle. Its glow lit up an area in which Olgilvee did not exist. Where did he go? Was he lost forever? Had the creature put a spell on him? Dina wiped tears from her eyes and pondered these questions.

"St. Lovells' lighthouse in Georgia holds a gem beneath its many brick folds. I must find the gem," Dina said. Then they returned to the kitchen of the house, locked themselves inside, and plotted their next move.

"Why don't we...," Sentra stopped cold upon hearing the rusty doorknob screeching from someone outside turning it. Then a horrific laugh echoed throughout the kitchen, and a skeleton stuck his head through the glass window of the door.

"Go to hell," Amanda shouted. She flung a metal pot clinking it on the skull. Suddenly the creature vanished, and they barrelled upstairs.

At the top of the steps in the small bedroom the air hung heavy reeking of agedness. A water color painting of the lighthouse hung crooked over a dresser, the only wall ornament. A nightstand, covered three inches thick with dust, stood between two twin beds.

"Doesn't look like anyone's been in here any time soon," Sentra said. Quickly, she shut the door.

"Yes. And we don't want to get trapped up here," Dina sounded alarmed.

"Look. A window," Amanda said. She pulled back a mildewed curtain and gagged at the odor.

Suddenly Elkin raised his head, and his ears stood at attention.

"What in the world is it?" Sentra asked tensely. Footsteps could be heard slowly ascending the staircase. They were weighted sounds, like the sounds of wet, water-filled boots.

"Could it be Olgilvee?" Dina asked.

"He doesn't wear boots," Amanda sighed.

"I don't know, but I'm not taking any chances. Barricade the door," Dina ordered. She pushed the large dresser in front of the thick, wooden entry, the sound of footsteps drawing nearer.

Then when they reached just outside the bedroom door, the walking stopped. Elkin jumped atop the dresser and sniffed at the door hinges while snarling.

"That's not Olgilvee," Sentra said.

Amanda gasped when the creature hit the door with a bang.

"This way," Dina said. She opened the window and shoved the two women toward it, their only escape route.

"Dina Darrendon. I know you're in there. Open up. I want those gems," the creature yelled. It continued to pound on the door making the dresser shake.

"We'd better get out now," Dina shouted.

Dina jumped first from the second story window, hitting the ground with a thud. Amanda jumped, too, nearly twisting her good ankle. Next, Elkin and Sentra descended, and they all headed for the lighthouse. Suddenly they heard the sound of splintering wood.

"I'll get you," it said in a deep evil tone.

Dina turned and looked back at the house. "Now skeleton is climbing out the window." Its eyes glowed purple, and Dina could not draw her own frozen stare from it.

"Auntie, look away. It's mesmerizing you. No one look directly into its eyes," Sentra warned.

Sentra smacked Dina roughly with the palm of her hand. "Ouch," Dina cried from the stinging sensation. Then the lighthouse door creaked open, and they entered it. Quickly they secured the three bolts and headed up the spiral steps.

"The gem must be up there," Dina said. "We'll get it before the creature does. Let's not waste any time."

The door at the top of the steps was locked, and no pressure would break it down. "The key in the dream must have been meant to open this door."

"You're right. The keyhole is shaped for a skeleton key," Olgilvee said. "We must find it."

"Olgilvee, you're back," Dina turned and looked in fear and disbelief at his eyes. His trance state was gone. "I came to in back of the house by the ocean. I followed sounds to the lighthouse and snuck in behind you," Olgilvee explained.

"Thank God you're safe." Dina hugged him. Then they could hear the creature burst open the door below and ascend the steps with increasing speed, the sounds of its boots hitting the steel below.

"We're practically cornered," Amanda said fearfully. Carefully she checked to see if her wooden leg was attached properly. The two gems were pushed into its toe secured with a piece of cork, and Dina knew Amanda was proud of her role as protector and hider of the valuable stones.

"We'll have to get out here," Olgilvee said. He led the way, ordering them all to squeeze through a small open window. Soon they were standing on a railed balcony which circled the top of the tower. A long rope lay coiled and ready to be used for their escape. Quickly he knotted one end to the sturdy railing. Placing Elkin in a large bin, he lowered the wolf first. Then they each rode the seventy foot rope to the ground below. The creature was nowhere to be seen, but the tower's peak glowed an eerie purple. Soon the rain fell upon them, soaking them on their route down the rocky path to their boat, the Empress.

A glow from a candle sent a cloud of light up the cabin's steps. "Who goes there?" Dina asked gruffly. No one answered. "Who goes there?" she said again. Elkin snarled.

"Come, my friends. Join me for a seance," the stranger replied. They cautiously descended, and Dina first spotted a dark-skinned woman wearing a rhinestone-studded bandana seated at their kitchen table. Her eyes were golden with long, cat-like slits for pupils. A fired up, red candle scented the room in cinnamon where she sat staring into a crystal ball.

"You're on private property," Dina scolded. "I'll have your hide. Who are you anyway? Where did you come from?" Elkin went to the corner and stared intently at the stranger.

"My name is Mizelda. I'm from New Foundland, sister of Seth, soothsayer. Word is out among the spiritualists that you are hunters of the five gems confiscated from Mitch the Magnificent. This pirate burned at the stake killed many of my family in the olden days due to fear and prejudice of the power they possessed over his sorceress, Sazran."

"Ah, yes. One of our own twisted before death and now possessed by an evil entity," Dina said.

"True, but my people, of good intent, only used their power to help humanity."

"Perhaps, our Sazran will return to good someday," Sentra said. "And it is she, the creature that is chasing us."

"Yes," spoke Mizelda. "It is the being of the evil sorceress Sazran."

"Our distant male relative, Captain Darrendon burned the sorceress, our betrayer, who was desperately trying to manipulate who would be the new owner of the gems. He confiscated the gems from the evil pirate, Mitch," Dina said.

"Only Fred knows the whereabouts of the golden skeleton key," Mizelda changed the subject. The prophetess was quick to proceed with her revenge, thought Dina.

"Who's Fred?" Olgilvee asked. He grabbed the rifle that hung on the wall.

"Fred's dead. He haunts the lighthouse. You see, many years ago, he was keeper of the place. He shared his job with an assistant named Svensen who lived here with his wife and their dog Hex. On a Sunday morning in March, Fred O'Dornne was killed by the assistant lightkeeper."

"Why was he murdered?" Dina asked.

"It seems Fred fell in love with Svensen's wife and had locked her up in the lighthouse tower. Fred enjoyed binding Mrs. Svensen to the railing outside of the room and nearly ravishing her. Mr. Svensen wanted the golden skeleton key so he could release his beloved, battered wife from imprisonment.

"Did Svensen ever find the key?" Amanda asked.

"No. Fred was the only one who knew where this key was located."

"Then how did Mr. Svenson save Mrs. Svensen?" Amanda said.

"He climbed out the window and waited on the balcony in the shadows. After Fred brought her out and bound her, he went back inside. Then Mr. Svenson snuck out of the darkness and released his wife. As the two climbed down the rope," continued Mizelda, "Fred walked out naked, ready to go, and Mr. Svensen shot him."

"So that's why the rope was neatly coiled up there. It saved our lives, too," Sentra said. "Svensen's reminder of a dangerous spot."

"Yes, and Fred has since walked the grounds searching for Mrs. Svenson. Now, I want you all to sit down around the table at which time we shall clasp hands," the channeler said. "Would the spirit of Fred O'Dornne come to us now? We know where Mrs. Svensen is, and we need the golden skeleton key. Come to us now, Fred O'Dornne."

Silence filled the room for only a few seconds. Although the cabin door was closed, a wind swept through, blowing out the candle. Then Elkin began to wimper. Quickly Olgilvee relit the candle, burning his finger on the wooden matchstick.

"Fred. Come to us now," the medium said again.

Suddenly Amanda rose to the ceiling on the chair she was sitting in, spinning uncontrollably. Then as quickly as it went up, the seat settled back down on the floor. Dina could see Amanda's pale face quiver in fear.

"Come to us, Fred. We know where Mrs. Svensen is. Show us where the key is located, and we'll help you find her."

Soon Dina could see a dark shadow of a man appear in front of the cabin door. "Stay, Elkin," she said. He only growled at the figure that was six feet tall and slightly bent over. Two, long, hairy arms hung at his sides framing a bare chest that exposed an emaciated rib section. A large, gaping hole was where his heart should be. A constant flow of blood appeared to gush out of the wound, where fragments of bone protruded.

"My sweetheart. Where is my sweetheart?" he asked. His voice was clear, but it sounded as if it was coming from a very long distance. His head was bald, and his cheeks sunk in. His teeth were as brown as roach wings, and his chin was covered with white whiskers like a large and bristly brush.

"Show us the key, and we'll show you to your sweetheart. Show us the key now," the medium said.

Suddenly the table began to rise, and another gust of wind blew out the candle, but the room did not grow dim. Dina could see Mizelda's eyes glow brilliant green, shading everything with their color. The medium's stare was intense and unblinking, and she focused on Fred, the spirit. "You will show us where you have hidden the key. No more intimidating jokes, Fred. We only want to help you."

"Then come with me." The ghostly form walked through the cabin door. Olgilvee grabbed his rifle and opened the door, and the rest of the group followed. They waded down the beach where Elkin tried to nip at the ghost yet catching nothing in its teeth.

"Spirits aren't edible," Olgilvee said.

Soon they stopped near an area where the sea flowed into a small cove. Fred hovered for several minutes above the water.

"Show us. Tell us," the medium said. Although the clouded sky rendered the night moonless, Mizelda's eyes glowed like internal flashlights across the vast liquid. Then without warning, a large tentacle jutted from the water and splashed down violently, spraying Dina and the group. Amanda shrieked when it encircled her wooden leg only to let go a second later. Dina could still see the beastly arm lounging on top of the water.

"The key, Fred, where's the key?" Mizelda asked again.

After a moment of silence, Fred's voice boomed and echoed through the night. "Octopus is keeper of the key. And I will return for Mrs. Svenson soon." Suddenly Fred vanished in thin air, and the tentacle disappeared beneath the ocean depths.

"So be it," Mizelda called out.

"Anyone feel like going diving?" Olgilvee asked. But Dina and Sentra were already headed to the boat. They soon returned with the gear, and Olgilvee, Sentra, and Dina quickly donned the equipment.

"What are our chances of getting past the giant octopus?" Sentra said to Olgilvee.

"Large octopods have a reputation for being ferocious, but they're actually shy. It will probably be tucked away in its burrow barely visible. Those large underwater lights will probably annoy it, but if it gets too brave, the spear guns will be beneficial. Crustaceans, not human flesh, by the way, are their idea of a good meal. They feed on plankton too. They flush and fade, blanch and darken rapidly, so beware. These intelligent creatures are masters of disguise."

"It looked enormous by the size of the tentacle," Dina said.

"Wish us luck," Sentra said to the medium and Amanda.

"Elkin, stay," Dina said. "We'll return soon."

"And we'll be waiting for you," Mizelda assured them.

Dina could still see the faint, green glow of the old woman's eyes before she slipped beneath the water. She dove down fifteen feet to the bottom where she hid behind a giant rock. Her light lit up a large area where she could see many small fish darting back and forth seemingly safe in their schools. Olgilvee and Sentra glided down next to her where they peeked over the top of the rock. Soon Dina felt a nudge on her shoulder, and she turned to look at Olgilvee's outstretched arm. The long finger pointed to a large hole only twenty feet from where they were hiding.

Dina felt her heart pound fast and hard when a big octopus appeared. It had a secular body with a slightly separated head. Two large, complex eyes glared in their direction from where it crawled along the bottom, with its light, contractile arms spread over thirty feet. Two rows of fleshy, deeply set suckers lined each tentacle. Quickly, with one front arm, it drew a fat crab to its mouth. A pair of sharp, horny beaks bit into the meal, and a file like organ drilled the shell and sorted out the tissue. Suddenly it shot swiftly backward from a jet of water through its funnel upon seeing a menacing looking hammerhead shark swim by. The water filled with purple ink when the octopus squirted its defense juice, behind which it made its escape.

Dina could see Olgilvee motion to her with his speargun to get a closer look from the next bulky rock positioned only eight feet from the cave entrance. They swam through the purple fading ink to get a clearer view. Sentra had her speargun aimed, knowing the danger of being attacked increased. Dina knew none of them were prepared for what they saw in the lair of the octopus. Giant, two inch, clusters of two hundred thousand eggs hung from the top of the cave. Carefully the beast was cleaning them with her suckers and agitating them with salt water from her funnel. Dina hoped she was unaware of their presence, yet every few minutes, the octopus would look directly at them and hold her gaze for several seconds.

"The key! The key!" Sentra mouthed behind her diving mask.

Dina felt a chill upon beholding the magnificent, gold skeleton key housed in a clear, glass case and wedged into the rocks amid the thousands of egg clusters. How in the world are we to get that key out of there without being strangled by the creature, Dina wondered. It is our only means for opening the three foot thick, metal door in the lighthouse where gem number three awaits us. How do we divert the octopus she thought.

Suddenly Dina lost her grip on Olgilvee's underwater light, and it came crashing down into the rocky bottom. Immediately the octopus stopped brooding over her eggs, but Dina slowly retrieved the light anyway. The octopus, however, scanned the surrounding waters with her large, bulbous eyes and settled upon Dina and her two friends peeking out from the bulky rock by her cave. It seemed to study them for a few tense minutes, then it looked away and resumed cleaning her eggs. A meaty crab ambled past the lair only to be snatched up by a long arm. The octopus quickly ate the small meal and then discarded the unedible remains, but soon another crab caught its eye. This one Dina could see was a ten pounder at least, and it was walking toward their hiding place. Olgilvee was aiming his speargun at the octopus, and Dina knew he would have to hit a vital part on the first shot if it attempted to endanger them. They could easily become its victims, she thought.

Soon the octopus came toward them, hunting down the crab. It reached out an arm to grab its prey, and then another arm unexpectedly fastened onto Olgilvee's waist. He dropped his speargun, and it pulled him toward its mouth. Then it grasped his air tank in its sharp, horny beaks. It dropped him quickly, realizing he was not snack material. Dina could see his look of terror, and then he swam toward the cave, his only direction permissible. The beast stood between him and the hiding place.

Sentra swam around the octopus toward Olgilvee. Dina could see the creature shoot backward through the water toward its lair, sending Olgilvee deep into the cave. Now Dina attempted to distract it by banging rocks together, but it paid her no attention.

The octopus cornered Olgilvee in the cave. He crawled into a small tunnel hidden behind a body-sized rock, and Dina could see it try to reach its tentacles in the opening. Soon Sentra came up from behind. Carefully she aimed her speargun, and after she fired, the creature turned. The spear was embedded at the top of one arm. Irritated, the creature filled the cave with its protective purple ink, behind which it made an escape.

Dina could not see anything, and she prayed for her friends who were in extreme danger. Soon she saw the creature in front of the rock she hid behind, but there was a gigantic shadow coming upon them from the left.

Once the ink faded, Dina could see enormous cods attack the octopus. It wrapped its tentacles around one fish, but it bit clean through it. They struggled and thrashed while Dina disappeared toward the cave. She waved to Olgilvee, and he swam out of the tunnel. Sentra was swimming under the egg cases trying to get to the key, and Dina joined her and helped her pry the case loose. Then Sentra cracked it open on the rocks and took the gold skeleton key out. Unfortunately, numerous egg sacks were knocked down. Ogilvee tapped Dina on the shoulder while the octopus with four less tentacles jetted toward them. Dina knew they had to surface.

Sentra led the way, and the creature followed close behind. Dina and Olgilvee surfaced after Sentra, pulling themselves onto shore in the greenish glow.

Suddenly the octopus bobbed its head above water reaching its four arms out toward the group. "Mizelda! Mizelda. Look out!" Dina warned. She could see two long tentacles wrap around the shrieking woman, dragging her into the sea.

"Help! Help!" she screamed. It squeezed so hard the top part of her body dropped off and remained floating on the surface. Then it too disappeared in the grips of another tentacle. Elkin howled an eerie sound that pierced the night.

The dryness and warmth of the cabin on the Empress felt good to Dina. She knew they were all exhausted from the adventure, and she allowed Amanda to run the show. Dina placed the key in the safe while Amanda served the weary divers some hot tea, cheese, and bread. After eating, Dina then placed the key back in her leather belt, and they made their way through the dark to the lighthouse. Elkin, in the glow of the flashlight, sniffed and howled as if some invisible being was in their midst. Olgilvee comforted him.

"Poor Mizelda," Sentra said. "I wonder if Fred, the ghost, had persuaded the octopus to kill her. When the beast reached for her, she seemed frozen. It was as if something or someone was holding her there for octopus prey."

"I know what you mean. Fred could be one dangerous spirit," Dina said. "You have that right," Olgilvee agreed.

They all decided Amanda would wait outside for them to return. The two gems were stashed securely in her wooden leg. Then they commenced to climb the lighthouse's spiral staircase when suddenly Elkin rose in the air and plummeted downward, falling six feet to the concrete floor below.

"Elkin! You okay," Dina hollered. She ran down to help her pet to its feet. "He's only a little dazed," she said to the others.

Soon the air grew thick with the scent of mildew, and beads of perspiration covered their flesh.

"Olgilvee. What do you make of this?" Sentra asked.

Olgilvee turned around from his place on the staircase. Dina flashed her light upon his face and shivered at the sight of the stranger. His thick, grey hair stood up on end above a high, deeply furrowed forehead. Two pointed ears covered with tufts of hair stood out on either side of his heart-shaped face. Thick lips drooled a green fluid over yellow, pointed teeth, and droplets of blood trickled from his exquisitely carved nose.

"My lady, now you can be mine all over again," he said to Dina. Then Sentra sank to the floor behind him.

Dina felt rigid and could not move a muscle. Elkin, too, just stood still, his eyes closed, and then the creature grabbed Dina. She screamed, hissed and bit at the creature.

"I want you now, redhead," he moaned.

Clearly Dina could see Sentra at her feet in a motionless state as if in a deep sleep.

She could feel his hot breath like fire upon her body moments before her mind entered blankness.

When Dina awakened, she found herself laying across the steps. Her body ached. The key was gone from her belt.

"Sentra. Where are you? Elkin, come here," she called. No one answered. Darkness was upon her, but she still searched the stairway for her flashlight.

Suddenly she heard a screech and saw light beam down upon her from the door seventy feet above. Slowly and cautiously, she ascended the spiral staircase, every nerve in her body trembling. Her knees, still wobbly from fear, were barely able to hold her weight on the stairway climb that grew increasingly difficult. She rounded the last curve and saw Olgilvee and Sentra seated in the small room where a fire glowed in a brick fireplace. They all seemed to be in a trance, staring only at the flames. Elkin was lying still on a bear skin rug. Then she heard the eerie moan of Fred.

"Welcome, Dina," Fred said. "We've been waiting for you." She entered the room and saw a skeleton sitting in a rocker. It had long, golden hair braided neatly to one side. Fred was sitting next to her and they were holding hands. "You've made my dream come true. Now you may have what you came for," Fred said creepily.

Suddenly the fire shot sparks at Dina, and the room heated up. "St. Lovell's lighthouse in old Georgia holds a gem beneath its many brick folds," Dina chanted. Then the bricks of the fireplace began to fall forward.

Soon she saw a star sapphire of many carots embedded deep in the wall. The fire dimmed suddenly, and Dina walked up, pulled the jewel out with her bare hands, and tucked it in her leather belt.

Such trouble Grandfather had to go through to place this here. It had stood safe all these years she thought. Then Mrs. Svensen and Fred disappeared, their rockers still creaking back and forth.

"Sentra, Elkin, Olgilvee," Dina called. But her friends stood still. She hoped the spirit of the sorceress would not be inside Olgilvee. She decided to leave with the gem and come back for them later.

Quickly she descended the steps and leaped out the lighthouse door into Amanda's arms. "What took you so long?" she asked. Surprised, Dina could see the figures of Sentra and Olgilvee rush past them racing toward the boat.

"They're in some kind of trance, Amanda. They must not be trusted."

"Do you have the goods?"

"Of course," Dina said. She pulled the large stone out from her belt. It looked dim and grungy but would polish into a star sapphire of recognition. "This will bring us hundreds of thousands of dollars, only a portion of what we'll need to pay the creditors who threaten to take our castle. We must keep searching for the other stones. For now, let's get back to the boat, Amanda." Dina stuck the sapphire back into the pouch in her leather belt.

"Thank God, the other jewels are still safe in my wooden leg," Amanda said, knocking on it with her fist.

"Good," Dina said. She felt secure knowing Amanda guarded the other two stones in her false toes. Soon Elkin joined them after sniffing around the lighthouse. Dina knew he was now unaffected by any trance like the others.

"He's following those two," Amanda said.

Fifty feet from the boat the figures of Olgilvee and Sentra disappeared into thin air. Soon Dina stiffened and felt a shiver creep up her spine. Then she heard the sounds of chains and the moans of tortured souls. "Do you hear it, too?" she asked.

Amanda's eyes were as big and round as silver dollars, and her hands were trembling. "Yes. I hear it."

"This island must have been a slave station at one time." Dina said. "Yes," said Amanda, "and like Manon island, maybe those are the spirits of the dead slaves."

"This place is haunted, too," Dina said, her voice quacking. "Those childhood ghost stories are true!"

The moon peeked out from a cloud, shining upon the Empress, but Olgilvee and Sentra were nowhere to be found. The moon's halo, however, warned of a coming rain. Dina kneeled and said a prayer while gazing at the moon. Then suddenly a terrific gust of wind blew them into the rocks, pounding their skulls.

"Wake up," Sentra ordered. Dina felt a pillow beneath her hair and Sentra dabbing her throbbing head with a cold cloth. Carefully her grand niece plopped an ice pack on it. Then Olgilvee massaged her shoulders.

"What happened?" Dina asked. She slowly ran a finger across the inch long, draining gash on her forehead.

"The wind blew you into the rocks, Auntie," Amanda answered. "I, too, was dashed into the boulders but not rendered unconscious like you. I brought you to the Empress." Dina could see only a blur of faces upon opening her eyes.

"You'll be fine, my love," Olgilvee said. He kissed her softly on the lips and then continued to rub her body.

"And the gem. Where is it?" she asked.

"It's in the safe with the other two stones. What a rock," Amanda said.

"So tell me, Sentra," Dina asked, "when did you come out of your trance?"

"What trance?" Sentra said. "We only recall a blackout. Right, Olgilvee?"

"Well, there were many hours of which we are, unfortunately, unaware. We only woke up a short time ago in front of the Empress. But our boat was ransacked of what little food and water we had left. We caught the thieves leaving just as we approached the boat.

It was the couple from the dumpster who took our supplies. We'll have to stop up the coast and restock. And then, of course, Amanda clued us in on what happened after she met you and Elkin on the bottom of the lighthouse stairs," Olgilvee said.

"Perhaps it was all just a horrible dream," Sentra said. She hoped the sorceress would not take possession again. Dina knew it frightened them all.

"Let's get out of here," Sentra said

Soon the rain came in torrents. Dina looked out the porthole of the rocking boat and watched their departure from St. Lovell's Island toward Massachusetts for the white gem. Dina fell asleep and dreamed.

The beach was hot and sandy. The wind blew her curly, red locks across her face. The shovel she held was full of sand, and her blue bucket was half full. She touched toes with her mother and grandmother and played and laughed. They ate popsicles, and her orange flavored one melted and dripped off her chin, making wet dots on the sand. Footprints led away toward the water, and she waved at Grandfather. He waved back. All were safe and sound. The day was a happy one.

Dina awoke alone in bed the next afternoon after suffering the concussion. She looked out the porthole and saw they were anchored. She knew the crew must have gone inland to restock the food and water supply.

She sat down on the chair and thought of Steven. He was surely on his craft leaving on the east coast race she realized while she looked upon her calendar. It was August 5th. He would win, she thought, and she whispered a prayer. The sailors would be headed down to Bermuda traveling against the Gulf stream current in their pursuit for victory. Perhaps their paths would cross, however it was highly unlikely because the racers would eventually sail farther out to sea. If he wins, she knew he would be willing to forfeit the five hundred thousand dollar prize to pay the creditors. The eight million dollar debt would be paid in full if she had to die for it.

After all, the Darrendon clan would then be reunited with departed loved ones.

The castle and its secret must not fall into the wrong hands. Only the Darrendons should meet at the vault to inherit the gift of eternity and travel into the new world. What little evil they had inside themselves would forever be released here on earth. They would have no need for the likes of Mitch the Magnificent, for they would take with them only good for the new world. The Devons of society would be cast away forever. She clutched at her chest and hoped that wicked man had died from his injury on the island of Jamaica. She herself had seen blood gush from the stab wound in his shoulder, although he was still writhing when they left.

She still held high hopes of retrieving gem number four on Buzzard's Bay. She dressed and went on deck with Elkin and saw the Empress anchored on a coastline that resembled South Carolina. Could Devon's peach plantation be nearby, close to seaside, or do peaches have to be grown further inland? She would be cautious.

We must be here for supplies she knew, and then she observed the South Carolina's Cape Paradise Wilderness Refuge sign. She gazed across a brown, flat, coastal plain where thousands of pelicans lumbered into the air from their nesting place. They brushed past palmetto trees that lined the small, sandy beach, and in the distance, she could see the eerie swampy area introduced by gum, bay, and cypress trees.

"When I see such beauty, I must capture it on canvas," she said aloud. Elkin lapped at her outstretched arm. She checked the safe for the gems but found a note from Amanda instead. She had stashed the three gems in her leg and gone into town with Sentra and Olgilvee for supplies. "Good idea," Dina said aloud.

She put on a cotton knit, taupe-colored dress with a brown bandana at her neck. Then she gathered her survival and art supplies, and Elkin, and waved good-bye to Feather. She left the boat with anchor dropped, masts locked down, and the front end tethered to a tree. No one was in sight. How risky, she thought. Surely Sentra remembered Devon had a home in South Carolina. Dina worried, and she needed room time to think. Her time was precious indeed, so she prayed they would be leaving for gem number four soon.

She and Elkin trudged carefully along the beach, finally resting beneath an unusually tall palmetto tree. She set up her easel and began painting two large, brown pelicans before her. They were clowning with deadpan expressions at their fish catch that flipped and flopped on the beach. She began sketching the scene, carefully filling in details with the sharp point of her pencil. Then she painted in small, yellow eyes, outlining them in pink. The gold feathers surrounding foreheads gave the birds dignity. The long beaks she colored beige, the necks she shaded chocolate brown, and the other feathers she colored a misty grey. She found the nearly black pouch to be intimidating but as necessary to life as were the two black webbed feet.

Soon, in the distance, a flock of them flew in an orderly line. Each pelican mimicked the behavior of the one in front of it as they sailed close to the water. Six of the birds perched themselves atop old, rotting posts that stuck out of the water like petrified tongues. The largest bird had a wingspan of six and a half feet. It soon swooped down and plucked a channel bass from the inlet. In her mind, Dina could fly freely with them, and at times she would put her arms out like wings and run up and down the beach.

"We shall free the earthbound souls of the Darrendons. We, like the pelicans, will all fly into the new world."

Soon a fat raccoon scampered down the beach to an awaiting dead fish. It washed its little hands, gobbled up the fish, and then wet its paws again. Elkin stood still, staring in amazement at the small, fuzzy creature, but when a wild turkey darted out from behind a bay tree, Elkin ran after it. In seconds he had bitten through its neck, and soon Dina found it laying at her feet. "Good boy. This will make a fine feast today," she said. She threw it into her knapsack as a pair of long billed curlews crawled out from a thick clump of tall grass. She crept up slowly to get a closer look.

After parting the long blades, she could see a plantation in the distance. She gasped. "Dear God. Could this be Devon's place?" The large red brick home had a two-story piazza with four large pillars on each story. The balanced placement of the windows and the squareness of it all made it seem so predictable and solid. It was reminiscent of the Georgian architecture she had studied in college.

She crept toward a mass of swamp grass and suddenly spied a male cone grouse spreading his tail feathers and inflating its yellow throat. He was obviously courting a female, but where was she? Carefully Dina parted the grass to see not only another grouse but a sturdy hardwood canoe. Elkin jumped in and sniffed the insides. Suddenly a rat jumped out and swam across the water toward a colorful array of flowers on the distant shore.

Slowly and cautiously paddling toward the garden, she realized curiosity was getting the best of her. She only hoped she would return when her crewmates did for their departure to Buzzard Bay. She did not want to be out too long luring them into danger in their search for her. However, she felt safe with Elkin by her side. And, of course, she had her compass, knife, and some snacks with her should she get lost.

The still water of the inlet mirrored the live oaks and pink azaleas that lined its shore. Brilliant yellow daffodils dotted the grassy clearing five feet inland from where she docked the canoe. She and Elkin walked among the flowers toward the large, brick plantation house. The green draping wisteria vines covered almost every oak in the center of the small forest. Dina felt invigorated in the scent of lilac blossoms filling the air, and soon small trickling sounds of a nearby waterfall lured her to its cool, refreshing taste. Her parched lips sucked up the moisture, and she lay down and drank from the stream. Soon a red-tailed fox darted through a blueberry thicket to her left.

"Elkin, no," she said. But the wolf was intent and bounded after its prey.

Dina knew she was not prepared to make her self visible to the plantationers and maybe Devon. She had to retrieve Elkin, and so she darkened her skin with mud and tied her hair up under her brown bandana.

She walked closer to the house and saw four black women wearing large straw hats. The morning sun was growing hot, and she gently dabbed the perspiration from her brow. She stooped down and picked up a basket filled with peaches and carried it atop her head. Elkin was still running, but now a tall man on horseback was following him with a lasso.

"Oh no! Faster, Elkin, faster!" she said, trying hard not to holler. Then the wolf started howling, and the man pulled the rope around its neck. He jumped off his quarter horse, the hat fell off, and long, golden locks fell about his shoulders. When he turned to gaze in her direction, there was no mistaking the bright green eyes. He stared hard at her, and she trembled.

"Oh no. It's Devon," she gasped. Soon one of the black woman approached her.

"Let me take those for you. I'm on my way to the kitchen anyway," she said with a heavy southern drawl. "Okay sugar?"

"Thank you much," Dina said, faking the twang. "I'm new here, and I'm wonderin' where you keep the ole livestock. I'm supposed to water them."

Dina, head down, could feel the tall, slim, black woman eye her. She hesitated and then pointed toward a barn to the right of the brick mansion as Dina glanced upward.

"Be careful now. The pigs are right nasty in this heat."

"Sure enough," Dina replied. She walked carefully to the barn where she saw Devon disappear with her wolf.

Once inside the pig pen she could hear commotion coming from inside the barn. She stooped down next to a pregnant sow and stared into the dark, dung-smelling adobe. The large room was filled with cells that ran from the floor to the ceiling. Padlocks securely locked whatever was inside, but she could not see into the darkness of the small rooms.

"Get in there," Devon commanded. "Next, we need to go after your precious owner."

She could hear Elkin whimper and the sounds of a whip slash the air. They soon disappeared beneath a screechy trap door in the floor. A basement lies beneath, she knew, and she feared for the safety of her companion and herself.

Suddenly the pig swung its hip into her, crushing her against the barn siding. She tried to suppress the painful moan, but it was too late.

"Who goes there?"

CHAPTER EIGHT

"I's just watering down the pigs. Their mud dried out, and they need to cool off or they'll die." Dina kept her head down and dumped a sitting bucket of water on the swine's backs and into the dirt of the pen.

"Good idea, but you better keep out of the way of those beasts, or they may kill ya, honey. But no matter. We'd just reprocess ya and get a new gal. There's lots where you came from." Dina felt herself shudder and heard the sounds of his boots become distant thuds on the other side of the barn. She did not know what the gruff man looked like, because she dared not look up. Her light-colored eyes could possibly have given her away. And if discovered to be an outsider, and she fled, who knows what kind of men he would send after her.

She decided to explore the barn later for Elkin for fear the man would return. Desperately the wolf and she needed to get back to the Empress and the crew to sail for gem number four up the coast. She hoped she could find Elkin soon and return without the aid of her comrades. She headed for the gate out and heard a weak cry for help. "Come here, please. Over here."

She walked to the barn entrance once again and entered when she saw no sign of Devon.

"Over here," the voice called.

Armed with a pitchfork she had found stuck in a bale of hay, she cautiously moved toward the cell.

"Water. Give me some water."

She peeked inside and saw the creature light a small lantern with a matchstick in its teeth. It looked almost human except for its stumps where appendages should have been. It had short, black hair as thick as a horse's tail, a smooth, flawless complexion, and orange-colored eyes. It must be a male she thought when she saw a small growth of hair growing on its top lip. She dipped the ladle into the bucket at her feet and then stuck it through the bars and poured. The liquid hit exactly into the creature's open mouth where he lay on a bed of golden straw. He smiled with pleasure, and the cool water dropped down its chin and onto its black, furry chest. His teeth were pure gold, and above them two more sets of teeth could be seen through the white gums. Its ears were small and contained triple lobes from which hung silver hoops.

"My name is Joddar. I'm being reprocessed for more work duty. They just brought in a new shipment of laborers from Galaxy Four."

"Who is they?" Dina asked. She jumped upon hearing the trap door screech open. Running as fast as her legs could go, she fled for the thick peach orchard. She climbed high into one extraordinarily large tree and hid among the twisted branches. She felt herself tremble, knocking fruits to the ground below, pounding the earth with small thuds. She waited fearful moments, but saw no one. Her lips were chapped, and her throat was dry. She reached for a peach and sunk her teeth into it. The sweet, sticky juice ran down her neck and dropped onto her breasts.

"Ouch," she cried. She felt fingers pinch her on the bottom.

"I've got me a nice piece of fruit right here, Moe," a man said. Dina felt two arms grab her by the waist and pull her from the tree. "If you utter a sound, I'll slit your throat," the man said, forcing her to the ground.

Dina could see the blade of the machete glisten like his bald head when he waved it in front of her. He set the blade down.

"You are one good piece," the bald man said.

"Bossman was right nice to point her out," Moe said. "We broke her just like he asked."

"Ya, she wasn't so hard to find. Now tie her to that tree. We'll send the slave guard to retrieve her."

Dina lay on the ground with her eyes closed. A thick rope, squeezing her like a boa, wound around and bound her tightly to the tree by the neck, waist, and legs. She heard the two men disappear quickly into the orchard and felt grimy sweat drip from her brow. She hoped she had not caught a disease. She was lucky to be alive, and she knew Devon was their bossman who had sent them to humiliate her and capture her. He had not offered the protection he had given to her as a child as she recalled him fending off Oliver from torturing her by picking the meat off her bones. Adults do play dirtier she knew.

She had to get the ropes loose and escape. She struggled continuously until she squeezed her hands out of the knots. Her dress, tattered and torn, was useless, so she made a bandeau dress out of a piece of burlap cloth she found on the ground. She hurried back toward the plantation house. If she was not careful, it would not be long before more locals would point her out as an intruder, for all the laborers were dark people. Quickly Dina stooped down to smear more mud on her face, neck, and legs. I've got to find out what evil Devon is up to. The cruel bondage here reminded her of the pitiful slaves on St. Lovell's Island. Then she recalled the battle on the island of Jamaica where she had once hoped Devon had died. Blood had squirted forth from the gaping wound in his upper shoulder. But he still lives, she knew. Maybe he too, like his slaves, had been brought back to life by "reprocessing." Perhaps she could get some more information out of Joddar. In the meantime, she needed to free Elkin, get back to the Empress, and sail to Massachusetts for gem number four.

She sat down in a hidden spot beneath a lilac bush at the edge of the plantation house. She wondered about Sentra, Olgilvee, and Amanda. They must be searching for us by now, she knew, for they would not leave for Buzzard'a Bay without them. Devon would do anything to get the three gems already confiscated, but Dina knew the whereabouts of the next two by memory. Surely he would try to catch and break her to get the vital information.

Sitting alone, she began to cry helpless, sobbing tears. Then she felt it. The presence of something very wicked. So wicked, in fact, her hair stood on end, and the lovely lilacs wilted in seconds. She felt frozen in place and saw a dark shadow pass by in a whisp of purple smoke. Could it be the spirit of the sorceress Sazran? She felt herself get sweaty and cold. She felt so overwhelmed with fear that she did not notice the tall, tanned, woman with a bandana until she was standing only two feet away. When their eyes met, Dina could sense a kindred spirit.

"It's me under all this mud," Sentra said.

"I feel so relieved for a wicked force preceded your arrival. Its gone now you're here, Sentra."

"Let's hope it was not Sazran, our evil ancestor. Anyway, I knew I would find you soon. You taught me to be a good tracker, Aunt. I'm glad you're okay, and glad the bad feeling is gone. And don't fret. Amanda still guards the three gems in her wooden leg. They were all worried, too. They'll wait for a reasonable time and then come looking for us. We must be on our way."

"And how, but too bad we've stopped here in Devon's plantation." Sentra gasped. Then Dina squeezed her arm. He has Elkin, and he sent men to humiliate me and tie me up for the slave guard."

"Oh no," Sentra hugged Dina hard.

"I'm alive though, thank God."

"Shsh," Sentra warned "Someone is approaching."

Suddenly the man who had found Dina in the pig pen appeared from around the water shed. "You two get back to work," he growled. His three-day growth of whiskers made his double chin have a porcupine appearance. His large belly popped the last button on his sweaty, wet shirt when he leaned over to steal a kiss from Sentra's bronzed cheek. Dina nearly gagged from his stale odor as he stomped past them, sloshing in his soggy boots.

"You gals be sure to get yourselves nice and pretty for tonight's shindig." He winked at them, and Dina forced a smile.

Sentra's face tensed up when Dina stood up and pulled her onward. "Danger for sure," Sentra said.

"It was not such a good idea to stop here you know," Dina scolded.

"Of course I remembered South Carolina housed another of Devon's lairs, but our needs were grave as you know."

"You're right. We must keep hydrated and fed. It's not your fault, Sentra. So glad you found me. Now let's find Elkin."

Sentra pulled back the length of her skirt revealing a large dagger strapped to her thigh.

"Good thinking, Grand Niece. Let's get out of here."

The day was coming to a close, and the slaves were putting away the machinery and garden tools. All the ready fruit had been taken into the big house, and empty baskets were piled high at the end of the orchard. Then Dina noticed the women lined up outside a small building behind the four-car garage. They were stripping off their clothes and throwing them into a large bin.

"Let's get a closer look," Sentra said.

"Perhaps we could join them," Dina said, while wiping a mud steak off her arm. Dina could hear Sentra giggle as they crept up to the thicket near a window.

Inside was a big open concrete floor with shower spigots protruding from the walls at six feet high every four feet. The naked, dark women were lathering each other from head to toe. They laughed and played, tussled, and fell tumbling to the slippery floor below. One small woman was seated in the center of the room braiding the long, wet, dark tresses of the clean women. After thirty minutes, all the spigots shut off. Then five large ceiling fans began whirling, and the wet women held out their arms to dry. They got into single file and paraded naked down the path to the stairway at the back of the house. One by one they climbed to the third floor. When the last one entered, the thick, metal door shut with a bang, and a bolt was secured.

"They all look so strong and healthy," Sentra said. Then Dina told her about the creature in the barn named Joddar.

"This is some type of slave labor camp. They use them until they are useless. Then they're reprocessed or replaced by new slaves."

"But where do they come from?" Sentra asked.

"That's what we are going to find out."

The morning sun woke Dina before the rooster's crowing could be heard ringing throughout the damp air. She slept soundly in the burrow she had dug in a pile of yellow straw. Sentra woke moments later, yawning and stretching while pulling the blades from her golden hair.

"Hunger is overwhelming me," Dina said weakly.

"Stay here while I get us some food," Sentra said. Her bandana was in place covering her blond head above her muddied face, and she cautiously walked toward the big house.

Dina crawled deeper into the warm burrow and wondered about Olgilvee. Soon she knew he would become impatient and worried and come to save them. Amanda, for certain, must still be back on ship guarding othe gems, but Elkin, she thought. Where was her wolf companion?

"Scrambled or poached?" Sentra asked.

Dina jutted her head out of the burrow and saw Sentra spreading a red, checkered tablecloth on the ground. From a bag she pulled a jug of orange juice, a bowl full of cooked eggs, five pieces of toast, butter, and a jar of strawberry preserves. "How in the world did you confiscate all this food?"

"The hand is quicker than the eye," Sentra said.

Dina saw her take out the blade on her thigh. Quickly she wiped off the fresh blood with a corner of the tablecloth.

"And whose blood did you shed, may I ask?"

"It's pit bulls' blood. Three of them guard the pantry entrance during mealtime. Now three of them lay dead at the bottom of the pond."

"No one saw you?"

"They were all too busy feeding their faces at the long tables in the dining hall."

"And what will become of us when they discover the missing dogs?"

"We aren't going to be around to find out," Sentra said. "Besides, if we don't show up back at the boat soon, I'm sure Olgilvee will come after us before sundown. He's probably very worried."

"Let's get Elkin and leave the mystery of the slaves to the gods for now."

Once again Dina scanned the familiar surroundings of the pigpen. The old sow looked at her seemingly uninterested, her piglets clinging to her elastic-like nipples. The trap door stood open, and no one was in sight. Even Joddar was gone from his cell.

Carefully they crept down the creaky, wooden steps to a large pipe below. Armed with a dagger and a flashlight, Dina led the way through the darkened tunnel. Small mouse-like creatures with brilliant yellow fur scampered past their feet. Then five yards in front of them was a ramp leading into a golden craft. She listened carefully to strange men talking.

"Captain, we've reprocessed these slaves, but we need more of them. Galaxy Four will unload two dozen parts in a few minutes. Have your carts ready."

"Oh, we'll be ready. The deal is set, Brontus. You supply alien body parts for superslaves, and we'll retrieve the super petro."

A special fuel for what purpose, Dina wondered. She and Sentra turned off the flashlight, and Dina leaned back into the wall. Suddenly, for a second, the barrier became transparent, and she alone fell down into salty water.

"Who goes there?"

Dina heard Sentra scream from the other side of the barrier. The sounds of her capture were evident, and Dina knew Sentra was being dragged back through the tunnel from which they had just traveled.

The water felt warm and soothing, but its depths were frightening. Luckily Dina had held onto her flashlight during the fall. She turned it on and heard wimpering, and then she saw Elkin. "My friend, you're safe and sound." Dina pulled herself up onto the ledge of the underground cave. Elkin lapped at her face, and she saw he was thin and blood-stained but still in one piece. "We need to swim through that flooded opening to freedom, boy. We can do it."

Gulping in air, she dove into the water with Elkin by her side. It took nearly two minutes to swim free into the bright sunlight of a small bay where colossal rock formations separated them from the plantation. They perched on a rock to dry off and saw a dark form emerge from the water. "Whales. We've come upon a pod of whales."

She could see the beasts, more massive than elephants, rise above the water, slapping their flippers on the surface. "They're feeding, Elkin. They must be trying to stun schools of fish."

Soon one of the humpback whales opened its mouth wide to scoop up hundreds of gallons of water. Its colander-like baleen caught thousands of sandlance fish and other food particles. Then it swam slowly away to rejoin its friends. A pod of five calves swam closer to shore and breached to Dina's amazement. After four jumps, they turned and swam back to the others. Amidst all the excitement of the magnificent creatures, Dina dared not forget about the danger of the slave camp and the strange craft.

Suddenly Elkin's ears stood on end, and he scampered toward a large boulder. Following close behind, Dina spotted a black and white mass laying partly on the beach. A large gillnet was caught in its tail, and entangled in it were lobsters, fish, and crabs.

The young whale was still alive, and Dina noticed no boat strike injuries anywhere on its grey body, Quickly she disentangled the sealife in the net and set them free. "We need to get this whale back in the water, too" she called to Elkin.

She hacked away at the gillnet until it pulled loose. The whale moaned in frustration, and Dina felt very sad. "It's okay. We'll help you."

She patted the great beast and stroked it beneath its eye. Although he was still in the water, its head was slightly submerged in the sand. She dug beneath it until it began to drift back into the sea, but she had to be careful not to become trapped or squished beneath its bulk. Soon he was in deep enough water where he could swim away. Dina waved, and he breached and swam toward the pod. It raised its fluke, and she saw the distinct pattern of a circular object like a planet.

"Neptune. I shall name you after the God of the sea. Swim free, my friend. Swim free." Dina felt tears drop down her still mudstreaked cheek, and she felt as one with the whale, for she knew what it felt like to be stranded here in this camp and in grave danger. "Come Elkin. We must rescue Sentra and get back to the boat. Gem number four awaits us."

They hiked over the tall rocks until they could inconspicuously peek over the top. Many armed guards were combing the area with more pit bulls. Dina cringed at the thought of being torn limb from limb. They stalked through some dense brush until they came to the barn.

"She must be in there. Let's get her out, now."

"Halt woman, or I'll sik me dog on you."

Dina turned to stare into the eyes of Olgilvee who was being nuzzled by Elkin. He quickly placed a hand over her mouth when more guards walked by. "Be quiet, or we'll be discovered. Amanda waits on the Empress with the three gems," he said. Then he took his hand off her mouth.

"Thank God. And I may know where Sentra is for I saw her being taken away. I'll need your help, Olgilvee. This is Devon's plantation," Dina told him. Then she saw him cringe.

Together they entered the barn with Elkin by their sides. Olgilvee slipped up behind the guard near the trap door. Soon blood squirted onto Dina, spewing out from the man's slit throat. The body lay in a crumpled heap at their feet, its eyes staring silently at the cells.

"Joddar. Maybe he can help us." Dina said. She told Olgilvee of the creature. Then she heard a sound from his cell. Quickly she introduced them and explained to Joddar about their search for the five jewels and the evil enemies in pursuit.

"It's my pleasure to assist you and your friend," Joddar said. "Your comrade, Sentra, is in the reprocessing chamber. It's below the trapdoor, but don't take the tunnel. Simply walk through the wall before you get to that large pipe. This back entrance may save you from being discovered so quickly. And beware the white-horned wolf, for he'll eat you alive. Take my sword. It should be right outside on the shelf above the door where the guards keep prisoners' personal items. At the press of the button, it ejects up to fifteen feet. Right now, I have no appendages, so I have no use for it. Good luck to you both."

Dina grasped the copper handle of the blade above the cell door. It was only eight inches long, and it fit neatly in her hand. Next Olgilvee led the way down the creaky wooden steps. They slipped through the wall into an underground chamber. "Look out. Over there by the barrel," he whispered.

Dina could see a seven foot tall, long legged, wolf with a sharp, pointed horn above its nose. Elkin cowered at the sight of it.

"Quick. Throw me the sword," Olgilvee ordered. He grabbed it in midair and pressed the lever to eject it six feet. The blade glistened like silver in the darkness, and he slashed it through the air, slicing thicknesses of space between them and the beast. Drool, the color of blue sky, dripped from its white fangs, and it snarled and pointed its horn at Olgilvee. Then he slashed into the end of it, slicing it off with precision while green goop oozed from the stub. It splashed downwards until the beast shook its head, splattering Dina with the juice.

"It burns!" she screamed. She rolled on the ground trying to wipe the caustic matter into the floor. It left small pok marks where it touched her skin, but Elkin licked them with his long, pink tongue. The dehorned wolf was very angry now, and it darted after Olgilvee. He slashed off one of its front legs, narrowly missing being bitten in its open jaws.

"Go for it," Dina hollered. Olgilvee lunged for it again.

Quickly he pressed the button extending the sword nine more feet, piercing the creature's belly. It howled in agony, and green goop poured from the wound. Suddenly Dina felt Olgilvee grab her arm and yank her onward through the chamber. Elkin zoomed ahead. Soon they came to the back entrance to the craft, and carefully they crept behind a row of metal barrels. Then she saw her inside the opening. Sentra, still baring her arms and legs, was shackled to a wall mount. Guards were feeding her and brushing her golden hair, and she stood helpless.

"Oh my God. Look what they've done to her," Dina said. "Maybe she's going to be reprocessed like Joddar."

"We need to distract those guards and get her away from danger." Olgilvee shared his plans with Dina, and she began trembling. He wanted to use Elkin as a decoy. "Go boy," he ordered. He darted up the ramp into the craft much to the amazement of the guards.

"Get that stray animal outta here," a tall, skinny guard yelled. But Elkin jumped on the computer board pushing the keys with his paws, causing the room's lights to blink on and off. Carefully Dina snuck in behind Olgilvee into the danger zone of the alien ship. Then suddenly the door shut behind them.

Elkin jumped at the guards and ran down the hall, the guards chasing him closely. Olgilvee slashed off Sentra's shackles with his mighty sword, and she collapsed into his arms. He flung her over his shoulder, and then Elkin appeared behind him. They all ran into a strange, silver-colored corridor. Quickly they locked the door behind them and walked up the winding stairs for twenty feet. Its walls became filled with windows into rooms like small factory centers.

"We're in the reprocessing plant," Dina said. She gasped upon seeing tables filled with different heads, arms, and legs. Human organs of hearts and lungs were placed in large glass jars in clear, thick liquid. One tank held countless numbers of eyeballs, swirling in a gooey madness. Human trunks, pale and drained of blood, lay in stacks in the corner piled as high as the ceiling. Elkin snarled when a guard entered the room into which they looked. The man stood eight feet tall, and he had orange, curly hair and two sets of arms. He was attempting to assemble one of the trunks when Sentra's foot kicked the window. His eyes darted over, and he yelled.

"Guard. The intruders are on spiral four."

Dina slapped Sentra to help her regain complete consciousness so she could escape on her own. Elkin lapped at her hand, and then they scurried up the remaining space. At the top of the corridor they could see a five hundred square foot launch pad where small ships were taking off. The oddly-shaped, cylindrical objects would lift up, descend rapidly, and disappear instantly.

"Some type of slave labor force," Olgilvee said.

They soon came to a bin with a four foot high wall, and inside extended a fifty foot slide to the water below. A large sign read "Waste Departure Zone."

"Oh no. This is a pile of human remnants to be discarded," Sentra said. "They dump them down the slide into the sea where they're gobbled up by sharks and the like."

"Get back, woman," a tall guard said sternly. He carried a long gun and stood across the bin. "We like to reprocess intruders," he said. He spit out small bones from his large, grotesque mouth. "You all come with me, and I promise I won't blow off your heads."

Without warning, Elkin lunged at his throat, tearing out a piece of flesh. He hollered, and soon two more guards arrived. Then a siren began to reverberate. Dina could see all exits were barracaded except for one.

"Oh God. Here come the pit bulls." Twelve of the ferocious maneaters were let loose from their leashes, and Dina motioned her friends toward the slide. "It's our only chance."

They climbed into the bin amid the foul smelling debris. Sentra went down first, followed by Olgilvee, Elkin, and Dina. The slide was slimy, and some human eyeballs and fingers were stuck to the sides. They could hear the shrill barks of dogs and gunfire just as they picked up momentum. One of the guards shot off half of Olgilvee's right ear with a bullet.

"Beware the sharks," Dina hollered. Then Sentra's toes hit the salty sea.

They plunged deep into the clear, blue water, hitting the rocky bottom. In minutes sharks appeared swimming menacingly for them, but Olgilvee bopped one in the nose as it wandered too close. They all pushed off and jetted for the surface, but the terrors of the deep circled the group. Then Dina saw a dark mass fill the water.

"Must be a great white," Sentra cried.

Quickly the mass descended upon them while they floated helplessly in their environment. When it was ten feet away, it submerged and swam beneath them. The smaller sharks scattered rapidly, and Dina could see their fins head toward the deep Atlantic waters.

"Wow!" Olgilvee screamed. The beast came up underneath and lifted them above the water. In the distance they still could hear the gunfire of their enemies.

"Neptune. Neptune!" Dina yelled. Tears dripped from her eyes, and she patted the back of the whale Elkin and she had rescued earlier.

"Its got a name?" Olgilvee chuckled. Sentra casually stretched out on its broad back.

"To the Empress at the Florida/Georgia border," Sentra ordered. She pointed out to sea with her long leg.

The waning gibbous moon, of August 7th, hung in the midnight sky. Amanda lay sleeping, exhausted after listening to hours of their adventures. The three gems were safe in Amanda's leg, and Dina knew a good night's slumber was needed. She could not help but wonder what Devon, plantation owner, would be up to next. He was involved in a modern slave market, but exactly how could the gems be connected with his selfish needs.

"A power source," she said aloud. She felt Olgilvee press his manhood into the curve of her back.

"Sleep soundly, my dear. Sentra is at the helm."

"At Buzzard's Bay in the oldest inn is a white gem in silver tin," Dina whispered.

"Sleep, my wife. We'll need our strength."

Dina could hear the small craft warnings on the radio before she dozed off.

The dream took her high into the sky. Past moons and planets she flew with silver-tipped wings. Behind her, thousands of others followed in a thick band across the galaxy. She was one with the universe and God, and his chamber was beyond the black hole, through the event horizon where no one dared travel. Not just yet.

The jolt of the boat woke Dina, and she crashed to the floor. She felt her forehead where a pea-sized knot began to swell forth. Olgilvee must be on deck, she knew, noticing his absence. Then Feather rubbed up against her leg and lapped up milk from her broken cup. Dina picked herself up and ascended the cabin steps. She pushed fiercely on the hatch the wind's hand held down. Once open, a jet of salt water splashed her face awakening her completely. The sky was black like lead, and the wind howled. Elkin, too, joined in. Sentra was barely visible in her yellow raincoat, but she was at the helm, and Olgilvee was reefing the main sail.

"Need a hand setting the storm jib?" Dina hollered from the hole. Another squall struck the Empress, and Dina was hurled down the steps to the floor once again.

"You all right?" Olgilvee hollered. "We're blowing half a gale. The barometer's fallen at thirty millibars in the past three hours. You better stay put as the seas are mighty rough and high."

Soon Dina heard a whooshing sound and then a sizzling, crackling noise of thunder. The Empress shook and swayed, pitched and rolled, but Dina fought her way back up the steps. "It's okay boy," she said to Elkin. He wimpered.

Then Amanda came up from her room, visibly shaken. "What is going on?" she asked. She adjusted her wooden leg.

"The nasty north wind is blowing against our current making the surface water winds even stronger. This accounts for the steepness and height of the devasting wave masses," Sentra said. "Stay below deck," she continued. Amanda returned to her cabin.

"Then the Empress has never weathered such difficult conditions, Sentra," Dina said. "Am I right?"

"Yes. This is worse than the storm I sailed through five years ago in the wave trains of the Pacific Ocean, but that one I knew was coming on from the radio broadcast. Not even the National Weather Service made mention of this one. Don't worry. I'll handle it."

"While you're up here, Dina, check the instrument on the hull," Olgilvee said from his position by the mainsail. She felt even more uneasy, but was able to translate the visual signals. The electrical device was doing its job sending and receiving its signal to and from the bottom of the sea. The multiple flashes and fuzzy, shapeless marks indicated rock formations on a soft, mud bottom.

Then suddenly an especially cruel wind slapped water into her eyes, and the depth dropped one thousand fathoms.

"Everyone, except Sentra, below deck," Olgilvee shouted. Dina clung to the side of the boat as if it were a rocking and swaying carnival ride. She fell down and then felt a strong arm pull her to safety.

She felt better knowing Amanda, Olgilvee, and Elkin were in the warm cabin with Feather and her. "We're traveling over very deep and viscious seas. These squalls are going to take on hurricane force in these warm waters. I hope Sentra has herself strapped in somehow," Dina said, disappearing back up to the deck to check.

They were moving at seven knots, she knew. The jib had been packed down, and Sentra was traveling only on mainsail. The boom amidship and the mainsail were tied so securely no wind could rip them out, or so she thought.

Dina stood wrapped around the railing where she felt as if she were on top of a mountain. The Empress rode high on the wave, and in the distance she could see the blur of an enormous tanker. She hoped the ship was far enough away to avoid a collision. Steering was almost impossible on the sea's roller coaster ride. Down again into the valley of the pool of water and then up again they rose on the liquid hilltop where Dina could see a small group of islands. Buzzard's Bay must be nearby, she knew.

"Land ho," she heard Sentra holler, her bright yellow raincoat glistening with saltwater. Barely she could see her grand niece standing at the starboard side. Sentra stood erect against the strong winds that bashed into her, never wavering for a moment. Dina wondered if the statue-like figure standing with her back toward her was indeed the women she knew so well. Then, through the howl of the wind, she heard the distinct and mournful wail of Elkin, her wolf.

Soon, a strange, golden glow outlined the stone person. It turned, and Dina felt herself shiver and shriek in terror, for beneath the hood was a mere skeleton of chalky white, with two evil glowing, purple eyes protuding from its sockets. Distinctly, she could see the sorceress's name Sazran engraved on the bony chest of the inhuman beast. Could this be the will of Devon? Or perhaps Mitch the Magnificent summoned the sorceress. These were surely once the waters traveled by that murderous band of pirates. Could they be near the undersea city Devon told them about? Were they in his power zone?

Dina could not stop shaking. She knew the three valuable gems were down below with Amanda, but the rest of the information as to the whereabouts of the two left was engraved in her memory. Devon would not actually try to possess her very mind, would he?

Deep in thought and rigid in terror, she barely noticed the bony hand upon her shoulder until she felt the pain from its pinching fingers. Her eyes were so tightly shut she could not even pry them open with words of confidence. "This isn't real. You are not real," she called out. But the fingers kept pinching, and the smell of putrid, rotted flesh entered her nostrils. The sorceress leaned hard on her.

Then suddenly the Empress seemed to shift its position, turning rapidly. She felt herself spiraling and gasped at the thought that they were entering the vortex of a giant whirlpool. The rotary flow of ocean currents had positioned themselves around a depressed area, and it soon changed to a spiraling motion with a downward draft into a deep center. They were in some sort of narrow passsage, but she could not recall one at this specific location. Perhaps the fury of the sea had taken them farther off course, away from Buzzard's Bay, she realized. This passageway certainly had the necessary depth for such an occurance. Apparently tidal inflow was meeting the tidal outflow.

She opened her eyes and looked up from the cone. She could see a waning gibbous moon glowing even through the leaden sky with clouds of hard, tufted, sharp bands. The position of the moon, sun, and earth played ruler of the tides. And Dina knew the lack of wind would make it impossible to steer out of the vortex, but maybe it was best for fear of being driven into a rocky shore. Rapidly they were descending into the shaft, and increasingly painful was the bony pincer.

She would not dare to look the sorceress in the eyes for fear the gaze of the creature would mean possession, but firmly she attempted to pry off its fingers. One crunched under the pressure and slid down her breast, falling to the deck. Another one broke off and became entangled in her hair, still moving and trying to cling to her ear. She looked above her and saw fifty feet of dark ocean wall encircling the vessel, pulling it into its basement door. Then suddenly they hit bottom, and the ship began to glide through a pitch black passageway in the sea. Through a hatch they slid which enclosed them in an underground city, completely encircled by a clear wall and by the sea itself.

When the Empress settled next to a walkway, Dina felt herself collapse with exhaustion.

Amanda awakened her, but she was not in her cabin on the Empress. She sat up on a firm mattress in a circular room. Olgilvee and Sentra were still sound asleep on their beds situated across from her own. She tried to speak, but she could not utter a word.

"Come with me, Great Auntie," Amanda said.

Soon they were in the large office of a not-so-strange man. She could see the familiar long, golden braid running from the rear of his head down the back of the chair. When he swiveled himself around, their eyes locked. The brilliant green of Devon's eyes pierced her very soul.

"Now I've got you right where I want you, Dina Darrendon. Welcome to my undersea city. As you know, I have offices all over this world. Ha! I hope you and your friends will make yourselves at home here, for the few remaining days of your existence. Of course, count yourselves out one friend. Amanda is mine now. I told you I would possess you someday," he said pointing to Amanda.

"So sorry I am as I never meant to shoot at you on the island of Jamaica," Amanda said. She winked at Devon, and he smiled her way.

Dina again attempted to speak, but words would not form. Then she saw her three gems sitting in a large, glass vase on his mantle. Amanda looked at her, glouting and staring as if in a trance.

"I see you've spotted my goodies. Amanda, take the jewels you gave me and put them in the power chamber, now." Carefully she took them from the vase and went into a back room.

"Mitch had intended these for the power and eternity of our clan, for you and yours are too kind and weak to survive the battles that will one day take place in the universe. Look at you. You can't even speak."

Dina saw him break up into laughter until his eyes streamed with tears.

"Take her to the isolated slave quarters. Just wait until I get my super petro. Guard."

CHAPTER NINE

Amanda grabbed Dina roughly, tugging on her arm. They walked down a ramp which gradually descended into the very floor of the ocean. The tunnels were coated with crystal formations of blue, green, and gold. Carvings of unfamiliar faces were etched carefully into the reef-like wall. Past the crystals, on the outside of the clear partition which separated Dina from the ocean waters, she could see tiny, colorful fish swimming in and out of the coral. Every so often, when at eye level with the sea floor, a flounder would emerge in a blur of mud and sand. The tunnel grew black as ebony, and they began the descent toward the slave quarters.

"Are you taking me to a sea dungeon?" Dina could speak again. Amanda only tightened her grip, but Dina made no attempt to fight her grand niece. She could not run, and she felt weak. She was certain she had been drugged.

Although the environment was much more sophisticated, the slave quarters were not unlike the ones at Devon's camp in South Carolina. The stalls ran along both walls and were barred from the walkway. In the center of the room was a person-sized tube filled with salt water and sea life. Perhaps it was an exit or entryway to the world above. It glowed as if lit by a giant golden moon. At the end of the room was a door with an armed guard poised and staring suspiciously in all directions. She noticed his laser gun was like the kind they used at Devon's peach plantation. Dina wondered what dreadful damage the ray could do to a human body.

"Move it," Amanda said gruffly, pulling Dina forward.

The guard watched Dina walk closer, and she noticed his cold stare turn to lustful desire. Then she heard him whistle, and two more guards appeared. They were all dressed in black body-fitting shirts and pants. Black, shiny boots rose halfway up each leg. The man she had first seen was dark-haired with black and red eyes, but these other two had brilliant red hair and light eyes like herself.

Dina was a youthful seventy years old, her body was fit and trim, and she possessed a sensuality. She began to shake, fearing what the guards might do to her.

"Amanda," Dina said. "Why the change of heart?"

"Shut up, Auntie. Greedy Auntie. You know you had no intention of including me in the family fortune of eternity. Come now. Do you really think me so stupid?"

Dina knew someone, probably Devon or the sorceress, had gotten to her. Perhaps, in time, Amanda would change back to good again.

Dina cringed at the straw floor in the dank, dark cell in which she was thrown. The door slammed shut and the bolt clunked into place, securing her in the grips of the prison. Black moss clung to the stone walls, and yellow flourescent beetles climbed upon the slimy surface. Liquid dripped from a crack in the ceiling forming a small pool of water in an indentation in the floor. Then suddenly something startled her. What could those two orange glowing eyes belong to? Quickly she huddled into the corner by the door. Then a face moved out from under the straw.

"Shh. Shh," it said. "It is only me."

"Joddar," Dina shouted. She instantly recognized the half man, half alien creature, its complexion as flawless and creamy as snowy white paint. He smiled his golden grin, and his teeth sparkled and glimmered like stars. Dina could see one of his silver hoop earrings had disappeared. Perhaps it was lost.

"I was brought here today to run a slave group. I snuck into this one empty cell after I overheard a guard talk of your arrival. My friend, who moistened my parched tongue, it is my turn to do you another favor."

"Oh, Joddar. I must get out of here. Olgilvee and Sentra are being held prisoner in this sea city, and Devon has somehow possessed Amanda to do his bidding. She's even handed over the gems of eternity."

"Yes, red-haired one. I know of the gems and of her possession, for I secretly witnessed the entire ordeal."

"You know of Sazran the sorceress?" Dina asked.

"Yes. She does Devon's bidding, too, and it is she who now possesses Amanda. They want the memory portion of your brain. Then when they torture you to get the whereabouts of the two remaining gems, they will murder you and your clan. It was Mitch the Magnificent who appeared in a fog when Sazran possessed Amanda. The evil ceremony lasted no more than an hour, but it was so dreadfully heavy with fiendish power. Even I grew a grey streak of hair."

He turned his face, and Dina could see the skunk stripe driving up the back of his head.

"And what about super petro. Why does he need it now?"

"Come," he said. "We must go before they bring in the new slave shipment from Galaxy Four."

He shook the straw from himself, and Dina noted his stubs had been replaced with long legs and arms. "They've given me the energized appendages of the aliens, but they can't have my mind," he said. Carefully Joddar took out a small, penlike instrument from his shirt pocket. He aimed the black, slim object at the door and drew a perfect square. Quickly he stood and walked over to peek through the bars.

After pushing out the piece he etched in the door, they entered the open room. Joddar crept up and quickly disposed of the unaware guard who stood near another door. Dina watched his heart plop out of his chest and onto the floor from the neat opening her friend's instrument had carved. She ran over, grabbed his laser gun, and cracked open the now unsecured door. Quietly she peeked inside.

"Oh, no. The new shipment just arrived," she said. Joddar looked, too, at the large, golden craft with green blinking lights. It sat still with its engine running.

"Yes," Joddar said. "Fifty pound sacks of body parts are being brought in for use on large groups of mindless humans. Their thoughts are gone, but they'll soon belong to a race with unusual physical strengths," he continued. "Their body systems are adjusted for work in the underground canals."

"What canals?" Dina asked. She was just beginning to piece together part of what motivated Devon. Could the super petro be found in the center of the earth?

"Sh. I hear men approaching," Joddar said, shutting the door quickly.

"Good ears," Dina said. "Now we must find Elkin and free Olgilvee and Sentra. Last time I saw them, before I was brought to the slave quarters, they were sleeping soundly. Let's get out of here, Joddar, and continue our quest for the gems."

"Yes, Dina. I saw another small exit to the left of our cell. Let's check it out."

Soon they were standing at the entrance no bigger than four feet by four feet. Dina crawled into the dark passageway. Then for several yards they crawled upward until they came to a hard, clear floor where light shown in. Dina put her face down on the surface, and there below she could see Devon lounging naked in a hot tub. The jets were shooting steaming water from eight openings in the basin built for three. Soon a naked woman of small stature emerged with a crystal vase filled with lavender-colored oil. She poured it into his bath, dripping some upon his shoulders. Her long, auburn braid swung seductively down her back, brushing her plump buttocks as she knelt to massage Devon's shoulders.

Then another small, nude woman with short, yellow furry hair appeared with a dish of seaweed, shrimp, and scallops piled high. Carefully she fed him the tender morsels which were drenched in an oily beige sauce. Soon a black-haired, tanned leggy dancer appeared, swirling in her nakedness and then undulating to music Dina began to hear faintly. When the rhythm stopped, the dark woman bent down on all fours. Then she completely melted away into a small puddle of red goo.

"Those women are not human," Joddar said. "They are only his temporary play things. I'm sure that one will be mopped up and taken to the reprocessing plant."

"He is a very evil character," Dina said. Then she saw a grey wolf on a leash enter the room. "Oh my God. That's Elkin," she said surprised. Suddenly a one foot portion of the hard clear floor beneath them popped out and crashed downwards.

"Intruders," Devon shouted. He rushed to cover his naked body, and his two women scattered. Dina aimed carefully through the small opening and shot down at Devon, just below the shoulder scar. The shot missed Devon who dove behind the metal table. Then she jumped down, and Joddar followed behind. Elkin tugged and pulled on his chain, and soon a purple mist began to fill the room. In the faint vision, Dina aimed her laser and severed the sturdy leash.

"Suddenly they're gone," Joddar hollered. "Devon and Elkin vanished in the haze."

The air cleared, and they stood silent in the large room filled with fish tanks of all sizes. One tank housed green-spotted moray eels that smiled menacing grins filled with sharp teeth. They were six feet long and preying on small silvery fish.

"My God. What kind is this?" Dina asked. She peered into another four hundred gallon tank which housed a bizarre fish with a large, spiny head. It swam up to greet her.

"A sculpin. Used for lobster bait where I'm from," Joddar said. Then it turned to swim away, and Dina could see a glistening jewel embedded in its back. It was a red gemstone, reminding Dina of their own ruby and the quest for eternity. "Watch this," Joddar said.

He hopped up the ladder at the end of the tank, aimed his laser, and severed off the sculpin's head.

"It's still swimming," Dina shouted. Soon, in her amazement, a new head emerged from inside its body, and the gem blinked erratically. "Regeneration from a gemstone power source," she said.

Suddenly Dina sensed evil and danger at the back entrance, and she heard distant voices. Quickly they hopped aboard a motorized cart and took an underground tunnel which they hoped lead to the city.

The passage was decorated with round windows that looked into reprocessing chambers. It was dimly lit by small gas lamps, but soon they entered a pitch black corridor. Dina felt strange beneath the sea floor.

"Quick. Light these matches," Joddar said, handing her a book. She struck a light and screamed when the mortorized cart headed for a stone wall. Seconds before crashing directly into the divider, Joddar swerved the cart to the left, and they began descending rapidly. Dina could feel goose bumps poke up on her skin from the chilly air that numbed her bones. Then Joddar pumped the brakes, and they gradually began to slow up and level off.

"Where are we headed?" Dina asked.

"The center of the earth," Joddar answered. Dina could see his gold teeth shimmering in the darkness of the cave. Soon they heard the sounds of large machinery and commanding voices giving orders.

Dina jumped out of the cart and tripped over a two foot stalagmite. Then she found a source of dripping water from above. She held her mouth open and let the cool liquid soothe her parched throat. Joddar held her hand in his and led her toward the voices.

"This is the stone tunnel Devon is carving to the center of the earth," Joddar said. "He uses the power source of eternity from the magical gems to speed up his project. The other planetary systems want the fuel he is seeking at the earth's core."

"You mean super petro?" Dina asked.

"Yes, then they will reward him with a special position in universal activities," Joddar said.

Slowly they crept up to the source of the sounds, hiding behind a large cave structure of calcite. The blue and brown mineral hung as draperies from the tunnel wall. "Their sophisticated equipment is also operated by a power source from the hard coal anthracite," Joddar whispered. He pointed to the short, smokeless flames visible from points carefully selected along the worksite. The slaves were moving at rapid, unhuman speed. They would operate the machinery, and run the digging devices of huge, powerful shovels into the earth's wall, delving deeper and deeper into its crust. Unexpectedly a worker would drop over only to be gathered in an open truck and toted away. Men and women worked side by side programmed to their labors.

"We need not get caught down here, or we'll surely be put to death," Joddar warned.

"Look over there," Dina said. She pointed to a large elevator shaft, and nearby, slaves were unloading bins of coal and other supplies. Cautiously the two crept toward the possible ride back up to the city where Sentra and Olgilvee would hopefully be found. Many of the guards had monstrous dogs on chains with links as thick as three inches. Most of the beasts were black or bronze, but suddenly the elevator shaft opened and out walked a guard with a grey wolf. It looked like Elkin, but she could not be sure.

"Let's make a run for it," Joddar said. "This may be our last chance."

With her laser gun ready for action, Dina followed closely behind Joddar, barely able to keep up. He was upon the guards in an instant, killing three of them swiftly. Dina lept into the elevator car behind Joddar and saw the door began to close. But back outside in the shadows, she recognized the grey wolf as Elkin. Their eyes met, and they locked in bondage.

"Come to me," she hollered.

The wolf lept furiously at his captor, ripping open his throat. Soon Elkin was squeezing through the small opening into the car. Then he lapped at Dina's face, and the elevator lifted them to the city above.

"Fortunately the trucks were traveling away from the shaft. Must have been the last load of the day," Joddar said. He gently brushed Dina's red hair out of her face, exposing her freckles. "You, strong woman, never give up, do you?" He winked.

"Dina." She heard a familiar female voice after the elevator door opened. Soon Olgilvee and Sentra were both hugging Dina.

"We escaped the sleeping chamber not long after you were taken away," Olgilvee said. Then he patted Elkin's soft fur.

"So good to see you, Great Aunt, and Elkin, too. Is this Joddar?"

"Yes. Please, Joddar, meet my grand niece Sentra."

He smiled and nodded. Then clearly, the man with the orange eyes spoke. "They're building a tunnel to the earth's center down below."

"Yes," Olgilvee said. "We heard them discussing some of their plans. They use the gems for a power source."

"What are they searching for at the earth's core?" Sentra asked.

"Petroleum," Joddar said. "A super kind which they also need to fuel their crafts for interstellar travel to another universe to the Andromeda X Galaxy. To get to their destination, the fuel will give them the power and protection to pass through the back hole in the center of the Milky Way Galaxy, through a wormhole, and out another black hole into the other universe. Then Devon will present the five jewels of power to an interstellar being who then will award him with authority."

Suddenly Elkin began barking. Olgilvee jumped back from a shiny purple spider, the size of a grapefruit, that scampered past his legs. Its small fangs were dripping with blood, and the insect splattered when he stomped on it. "Where did that godawful thing come from?"

"Look out," Joddar hollered. "Stay back, Elkin." Then a spider grabbed the alien into its fangs.

Dina looked down the corridor and saw five more of the deadly-looking creatures coming toward them.

"Go, my friends," Joddar told them "Your laser is useless against so many. There is nothing you can do for me now. God will be watching over you."

Dina screamed and watched the alien being dragged off by the powerful insects.

"They must be a species common to this area. They're dangerous for sure," Sentra said.

"I'm not taking any more chances," Dina said. "We need to get inside the exit tube in the slave chamber. That's our only way out now."

"But what about Amanda?" Olgilvee asked.

"And our three jewels she gave to Devon?" Dina finished.

Dina saw Sentra lift up her shirt, and there was the leather belt with the special pouch.

"I searched and discovered them in a power chamber after Olgilvee escaped and murdered our captors."

"Fast work, my dear," Olgilvee said.

"Great going, Sentra. Let's get out of here," Dina said, wiping sweat from her brow. Then they ran fast through the winding corridors with Elkin leading the way.

"Diving gear," Dina read. They approached the sign upon the door and entered. Quickly the three of them partially suited up. "Come on. The slave quarters are this way," Dina said, pointing toward another sign which read "Personnel Only."

Dina was quick to zap four guards with her laser. They all flopped over dead next to the limb-holding tanks. "Over here," she shouted. A large cylinder rose from the floor to the ceiling. It was encased in a type of clear glass, and a small door was bolted shut.

Dina opened it and entered the chamber with Elkin. She slipped on her mask, tank, and flippers and then suited-up Elkin, too. Slowly she cracked open another hatch. Forcefully the sea water swept in, and they exited into the cylinder. She waved at her friends who stood staring in amazement. Then she motioned with her hand for them to enter.

Soon they were all swimming their way up the cylinder, and Dina hoped the air supply of the double tank would hold out. Even Elkin was breathing evenly from his very own oxygen supply.

Suddenly she felt a current pushing her up at a faster speed. It increased until she felt herself shoot up into the air along with Elkin. Soon they splashed down in a calm sea right next to Olgilvee. Then Sentra jetted forth and crashed down, too. Their ship, the Empress, was rocking gently back and forth in the nearly still water. Dina felt herself cry on her swim for the ladder.

In minutes, on the early August eighth morning, the crew was once again back together on board ship with Feather. The gems were locked up in the safe, and they all longed for a hearty meal. Dina could see her ribs were poking through her dry skin more than usual. Her hair too lacked the shiny luster it once knew. A good meal, vitamins, and some rejuvenating hair and skin cream were in order, but first she needed to feed Feather, Elkin, and the weary crew. How and why the Empress was here in this exact spot never ceased to amaze her, but she considered it a blessing from God. They would worship the almighty with a feast this very night.

After eating, Olgilvee burped softly while seated near the radio equipment below deck. "It's all dead. No stations anywhere. We'll have to have these electronics checked out once we get to Buzzard's Bay."

"At Buzzard's Bay, in the oldest inn, is a white gem in a silver tin," Dina recited from memory.

"The marvelous fourth stone awaits us along with new dangers, too," Sentra said.

"Yes. Devon has a group of followers in that area. We must beware," Dina warned. Sentra gently patted Feather on the head, and the cat curled up in her lap like a doughnut. Softly Dina began to hum a hymn.

"Who wants to pray to our almighty God?" Dina asked. They gathered in a circle and held hands.

"How dare you destroy my plans."

A deep voice boomed, shaking the boat and making her ears ring and her heart race.

"Buzzard's Bay, you say? See you there, slut. I'll get my gems back," Devon hollered. Then Dina saw Devon standing in a mist of purplish fog. His green eyes glistened and penetrated the very depths of her soul, and they pierced her in the coldness of death. Then, as quickly as he came, he disappeared, leaving only a large, black, fuzzy scorpion where his feet once stood. Its tail curled up as it scampered under the table. Soon it reappeared, and Feather chased the poisonous prey into the open. Sentra quickly jabbed the scorpion with her long-handled fork, and it curled up and died quietly.

"Be gone forever," Olgilvee shouted. Sentra ran up to the deck to check the safety of their craft.

Devon must still have a power supply from the gems. Dina knew they would have to be strong to keep their edge, but she needed to know more of Devon's weaknesses, for she knew at the oldest inn he would be waiting. As for her grand niece Amanda, she may never see her again, but then stranger things had happened since they began their journey. Amanda had ways of showing up at the most inopportune times.

"Auntie."

Dina could hear Sentra call her from on deck. She ascended into the night, and the air was as still as an empty rocker. She felt a sense of awe upon gazing into the heavens where her grand niece was pointing. Small, purplish whisps of clouds ribboned the sky where the moon cast an eerie glow across the hemisphere. Soon a halo appeared around the waning gibbous moon, indicating moisture and an upcoming rain shower. Then the wind began to blow slowly, shaping the ribbons of clouds into symbols.

"Messages are appearing, Sentra, but what could it all mean? I must capture this scene on canvas." She returned below deck to get her paints and brushes.

By the time she returned, Sentra had set up a chair and easel for her great aunt. "Paint to your heart's desire." Sentra tapped Dina's shoulder and returned to the helm. With brush in hand, Dina began to paint. Shades of grape, black, and off-white began to fill the canvas before her. Soon a strange message became apparent and shapes materialized. Then the wind died as quickly as it had occurred, and Dina fell exhausted to the deck. She had worked at breakneck speed, inhuman to her, she knew. She flexed her aching fingers.

Quickly she lapsed into a dream state moments before she felt a hand lay her head upon her goose down pillow. Soon she saw her own body spinning like a top across a grassy beach. Water of crystal clear transparency lapped only inches from her feet where she sped along disoriented. She came to rest upon a seat of golden straw, and the easel was on the shoreline of a beautiful mountain lake. Swans swam gracefully by, and a pair of cardinals lit upon the beach to snatch up brown, damp seedlings. Carefully she stood up feeling light as a sheet of thin paper. Her bare feet carried her to the water's edge where she saw the reflection of her painting of the eerie, night sky. The mirrored image horrified her when the message became clear. The ribbons of clouds spelled out, "Death awaits those who find the gem of sin," she said aloud.

"Aunt. Wake up. You're dreaming of the sky you painted. You're safe in your very own bunk where I just brought you," Sentra said. Dina felt a sense of forboding and the Empress sway in the sea.

"How close are we to Buzzard's Bay?" she asked.

"We should dock by morning, nine a.m. if all goes well."

"You need a good night's sleep," Olgilvee said from his place next to her. Then Sentra left the room, and he drifted asleep. Dina lifted her head and spotted her lover snoring. His large, thick fingers were folded neatly on his lap, and a small amount of clear drool was dripping out from the edge of his wide mouth. Then Dina slipped off to sleep ever so silently.

She awoke to the sound of a bell and rubbed her eyes. Peering out the porthole, she saw they had docked. A large, wooden sign held by chains at each end swung from a pole that extended toward sea. "Stardist Town," it said in big, bold, carved letters filled with gold paint. She slipped on her red lace bra and red tank top. Her hips fit snuggly in her skin tight black jeans, which carressed her firm legs as she walked. Carefully she pulled the leather belt from the safe and checked the three gems in the pouch. Then she pulled it through her pant loops, fastening it tightly at her waist.

In her seventies, she felt fit and trim. The eternity of the Darrendon clan was worth the risk and stress placed on her emotionally and physically. The five gems would get them into the corridor of eternal life where they would all be reunited forever. Who knows what riches the vast universe would then hold for them, for they were good of heart. They were of a kind and loving nature, so much unlike Devon's clan of great evil and greed.

"Time for more exploring," she said, applying a quick splash of blush and some red lipstick. "Elkin, you come too," she said to her grey wolf. He jogged up to her side and sniffed at her outstretched hand. Sentra and Olgilvee must have gone for food she thought, and then she spied the lower refrigerator door flung open and empty. She quickly packed an overnight bag. "For safety," she said, hiding a small dagger beneath her shirt. "Devon is out there somewhere," she said. Dina perused the room again. "Ah, a note." She read the paper attached to the closed upper freezer door. "Gone to register at the oldest inn in Buzzard Bay. We'll be back soon." Dina noticed the phone book open to the inn section. She quickly found the phone number and dialed, but it was busy. She copied down the address of 410 Pinckney Ave and said good-by to Feather.

Once on deck the sound of New Englanders filled the air. Some were just leaving to fish out in Buzzard's Bay while others were walking into town to get a bite of breakfast. The smell of cod permeated the air with a salty breeze that blew a red curl into her mouth. Stopping at the end of the dock, a tanned and tall fisherman tweeked her hip as he brushed past. Elkin's ears pressed back, and he snarled protectively. "Now, boy, that's appreciated attention for a seventy year old, and quite harmless, too, I might add." Dina found herself winking at the grungy but firm fellow who turned and grinned at her.

Soon Elkin was sniffing at a wooden post where fish juice was dripping from a large catch hanging from a string. Dina carefully read the sign. "Settled in 1660 by the Tilver Family, Spanish merchants. They expanded the whaling industry in 1756 and built the warehouse before ye. By 1810, Stardist Town was the leading whaling port in the world." Dina sighed. "Oh those poor whales," she said. Then she spied a whalebone carved into a circle and hanging from the wooden sign. Quickly she thought of her friend Neptune, who had saved their lives in the Carolina peach plantation. How eerie she thought.

Walking farther, Dina shuddered at the dark iron statue of a tall, thin man. Elkin's hair stood on end, and he growled at the grotesque figure before them. "Lieutenant Oliver Tilver" the sign read. "Murderous whaling man and sorceror of Buzzard's Bay. Condemned to death and burned for the ax murder of a Pennsylvania petroleum king in 1848. T'was Tilver's sin," she read, gasping for air. In that statue was the Oliver from her childhood that had appeared as a ghostly apparation wanting to pick the meat off her bones. "So their last name is Tilver, from their Spanish father," she said aloud. She shivered, because she knew Devon and his followers were nearby. They congregate in areas where gems may be found Grandfather had told her. Danger was aloft.

CHAPTER TEN

After walking for one block, they arrived at Miles Clamshack and Bistro. Hungry for breakfast, Dina and Elkin settled in at a small outside table. The restaurant consisted of a long bar made of teak wood. Black stools, like polka dots, decorated the front, and waiters in silver leather pants and tops served the customers. Their table had a woven grey placemat on top, and a small vanilla candle burned from a center bowl. Quickly she gulped down the ice water and wafers, and the waiter left to communicate her order of a garlic egg and mushroom sandwich. Elkin happily munched on bread sticks at her feet.

Spying some brochures on the wall, Dina read one while she waited for the sweet smelling food. Not far away, she noticed a heavy-set man in a muscle shirt eating and staring at her. She could see numerous tattoos of naked women, and whiskey bottles adorning both arms, a scorpion tattoo on his neck, and a once large gash which was thickened with scar tissue crossed over his nose like a precarious lump. His yellow, pointed teeth showed between his thick lips, and he puffed on a big, brown cigar. The smoke curled up toward the ceiling and then hung like a musty blanket above their heads. Unconsciously she knew it was coating her perfumed hair. She read another brochure.

Although there were no pamphlets on the oldest inn, the street map to Cretch Whaling Museum clearly showed the inn stood on Pinckney Ave, one street over. She read on. The museum at 10 Whalebone Way, two streets over, was open to tourists daily for a small admission charge. It offered sightseers a look at logbooks, scrimshaws, and harpoons once used to capture the beasts. Dina thought again about Oliver Tilver and his unforgivable sin of murder. Because he was Devon's brother, he also had a strong longing to locate the powerful fourth gem. It would help Devon drill to the super petro, a fuel the dead petro king may have been forced to tell Oliver about before he was murdered. Dina would put the thought in the back of her mind, and maybe she could sort it out later. Quickly she gobbled down the sandwich the waiter served.

"Elkin, my boy. Let's get our room at the inn and check out some whaling artifacts at the museum. Perhaps we'll run into Sentra and Olgilvee on the way."

Elkin quickly stood up. A mustache of bread crumbs under his nose crumbled to the floor as the late morning sun shone its rays upon the pair. It was easy for Dina to notice the obese stranger who was following her. His reflection shown clearly in the large mug near the exit of the eatery. Perhaps he is one of Devon's spies, she thought, and then she recalled the scorpion left behind by her arch enemy. This obese oaf had the same black scorpion carefully tattooed on his neck. She hoped no harm would come to them, and she checked her leather belt pouch. The three gems were safe.

She walked down the cobblestone street for half a mile enjoying the beautiful white moonflowers that greeted her and Elkin. The passersby were friendly and colorful, and many of them had toasted skin from the summer sun. Towering elm trees lined the street, and chickadees sang merrily in the light of day that moved behind a small, puffy cloud. Many parallel parking spaces along the street were just now being used by shoppers who came into town for morning duties.

"Stop, thief," Dina heard a man order. She saw a tall, pale man running toward them. The robber quickly pushed past Dina, knocking her into a barrel-sized flowerpot filled with red geraniums, but Elkin snagged the man's leg with his sharp teeth. In moments, Elkin pulled the man down and bit softly into his throat until the guy muttered in agony.

"Don't kill me! Don't kill me!"

The boutique owner helped Dina to her feet. The handsome, bespeckled young man brushed the dirt from her arms, and she smiled and pointed. "Elkin's got your criminal." Quickly the two lunged on top of the crook just as a policeman walked up with handcuffs.

"Where's the golden egg, you thief," the owner said. Suddenly Elkin let go of the guy's throat and walked toward the gutter. In seconds, in his mouth he gently held a large, bright egg which he plopped down in the shopkeeper's outstretched hand.

"Thanks to you and your dog."

"He's a wolf," Dina said.

"Wolf. Dog. Whatever. He saved the day. I'm Jack. What's your name?" Dina reached out her hand and gazed into the man's lovely, soft, hazel eyes.

"Dina. And this is my companion, Elkin. We're exploring Stardist Town. It's such a lovely, quaint place. Have you been here long?"

"Born and bred here, ma'am. My parents also grew up here in the fishing industry." Dina attempted to straighten her hair, and then Jack took her by the arm. "You've saved me quit a large loss and helped capture a thief. I at least owe you something. Come with me to my shop where you can get cleaned up. I have an apartment upstairs with clean towels and soap."

"Oh, thank you," Dina said, feeling the creepiness of staring eyes. Across the street, trying to conceal his wideness behind a lamp post, was the tattooed man from the bistro.

"Here we are," Jack said. Dina saw sign cleaners busy working above the doorway. A cloth was drapped across the sign, and Dina was pulled toward the alley stairway. "This is my apartment," he said, pointing to a dark hardwood door.

"Hi Jack. New friend?" Jack smiled and waved at a policeman who walked by and touched Dina's arm. The sun's blushing makeup had done her good, she knew, and she acknowledged the refreshing gesture with a nod of her head.

"A friendlier approach from one of our locals," Jack said.

Dina grinned again, and then they entered the small, neat apartment where two leather couches sat upon new beige carpeting. Upon a glass coffee table stood a small calculator, a bottle of gin, and financial statements from a gift shop in Carlin, Massachusetts. Grandfather once told her he had acquaintances in that area she recalled.

"Bathroom's on the left," he said, pointing to the hallway. When she returned with Elkin, Jack had a sandwich and a cool drink waiting.

"I'll pass on the food, but the drink could do me good," she said.

"So where were you two going today. Maybe I could give you some directions around the city."

Dina thought it unwise to tell a stranger where they would be staying. "The Cretch Whaling Musuem was on our agenda." She noticed Jack wince.

"What special interest have you in this museum?"

"Oh, nothing really," she lied. "Just a necessary tourist attraction I'm afraid. Why? Do its walls hold something unusual?" A sudden knock at the door eased Jack's tension, and Dina and Elkin stood waiting.

Jack opened the door where Dina spied a shriveled up witch of a woman. She stood no more than four feet tall, and her back was decorated with a large, grotesque hump. Her huge, hook nose and tiny, red beady eyes were placed uncomfortably on her round, furrowed face. They looked each other over, and no introductions were given. Only silence ensued.

"We must be going. Nice to meet you Jack, and thank you for the drink."

"You've been a blessing to me today, my dear," he said. "Have fun in town."

Dina quickly shuffled past the old lady, but Elkin stopped to sniff the woman's dress. It was then that Dina noticed the scent of raw, bloody meat.

Once in the alley, they headed for the street front again. Dina gasped after she looked up. The sign cleaners had gone and the cloth was removed. "Tilver's Boutique," Dina read. They quickly scampered by. *Oliver's family, oh, no,* she thought.

Dina followed the map in her brochure towards the oldest inn and the museum. The inn was about a one-half-mile walk, but the weather was pleasing, and she felt good about having her wolf with her. After all, 410 Pinckney Avenue and 10 Whalebone Way could not be that far away.

Turning right on Pinkney Avenue, she began passing small, dark stores lit up only with candlelight. Peering into one window at number 408 near the open sign, she could see a glass cabinet filled with crystals of all colors and sizes. One particular piece of jewelry caught her eye, and she grasped at the good luck dragon which still hung about her neck. She had taken it off only once since the black artist in Grand Cayman had given it to her.

"Come on, Elkin," she said, looking down at the next storefront. "412 next door. What happened to 410, the oldest inn. How strange. Maybe the store clerk here at 408 can tell us something."

She pulled open the heavy, wooden door. The scent of rosemary incense filled the room so strongly that it made her eyes water. The store appeared to be empty and quiet except for the ticking of an old wooden clock which hung on the bare wall behind the counter. She felt wonder upon looking down at the pewter dragon earrings. They were beautifully crafted, made to create an illusion when worn by appearing to actually come through the ear.

"Anyone here?" Dina called. No one answered. Then suddenly the little door on the clock opened and out popped a tiny, fuzzy owl to announce the noon hour. Hand slightly trembling, she opened the sliding glass door to the jewelry case and took out the earrings. Looking into the mirror, she held them up to her ears. They looked wonderful with her necklace, as if they were meant to be paired. She put them on, admired them, and then set them back into the case.

Suddenly Elkin's ears lay back when they heard the soft tinkling of a door chime. Dina turned and walked toward the back entrance. At the source of the sound, only tall, purple ostrich feathers leaned forth, sprouting out of a large, dark brown basket.

"Hello. Is anyone here?" she said once again. Still, no one answered. The silence made her skin crawl.

Curiosity overcame her, pulling her onward with Elkin, out the back door and into a beautiful herb garden. The one-foot square paving stones beneath her feet were rooted with creeping thyme between each crevice. She walked on with Elkin who sniffed at mint and dill to the left of the path, and on the right Dina distinguised chives, parsley, and sweet woodruff. The entire garden was shaded by a towering oak tree whose arms stretched out to protect her crop. Then curls of smoke began to rise behind a small hedge where Dina noted an iron pot heaped and aflame with fragrant herbs.

"The sweet smelling smoke will rise to heaven and please the Gods," Dina read aloud from a small metal sign.

They walked toward the end of the symmetrical planting beds where Dina noticed what looked like a grand old house covered with green ivy. On a small, black mailbox she read 410 Pinkney Ave. At a closer look, she discovered a wall spilling rosemary, providing cascading blue color against dark bricks. The house had an eighteen-inch projecting overhang and octagon paned windows. Walking under an archway of vines, she spied a large, heavy door with a wooden plaque above it.

"Built in1639," she read aloud. Elkin sniffed at the doorstep.

"Come in." A creaky, deep voice echoed throughout the garden. Then the big, thick door slowly opened. Before her stood the four foot tall, beady-eyed woman she had seen at Jack Tilver's apartment. She stared a hole through Dina, and Elkin's hair stood on end. Dina sneezed softly into her hand.

"Bless you, and welcome to the oldest inn on Buzzard's Bay," she said. "We have just the room for you and your friend."

Quickly she handed Elkin a large leather chew toy she pulled from her apron pocket. The wolf snatched it out of her crooked fingers, walked over to the hearth, and lay down to happily gnaw on the snack. A beckoning, spiral staircase of intricately etched wood wound up three stories. Dina could not help but notice the superb collection of New England furniture and decorative objects that filled the spacious but comfortable living room. Many dark wooden-framed portraits adorned the walls, and the one over the mantel looked especially familiar. It drew an amazing resemblance to Jack Tilver. The soft, hazel eyes were accentuated and hardened by a deep scar over his left eyebrow. The man's thick lips proudly carried a dark mustache atop them, and his hair was a soft shade of brown. Could it be the home of Oliver Tilver, the murderous whaling man and sorcerer of Buzzard's Bay who was hanged? Devon's evil brother walks this house she knew, and she shuddered.

"Petroleum—," Dina whispered, stopping suddenly when the witchy woman interrupted her.

"Right this way," she said, her crooked finger trying to point upward to the stairs. "We have just the room for you, as it overlooks the pond. Of course, you'll have to share the bathroom with our two other guests. Come on." Dina, with Elkin by her side, followed the old woman and hoped the guests mentioned were Olgilvee and Sentra.

The wooden steps of the stairway, worn thin as wafers, creaked under foot on their ascension. The bannister, foreign in a slippery and cold way, stood steady beneath Dina's trembling hand. Once on the landing of the first floor, Elkin seemed to pick up a familiar scent, and his tail started wagging. Then suddenly he rushed ahead of the old lady, scampering to the second floor.

"Elkin." Dina could hear Olgilvee call her wolf by name. She suddenly relaxed when her two companions greeted her at the second-floor landing.

"You've met before," screeched the old woman admist the aromatic scent of dill that wafted up the steps. "The second door on the left is your room. I must go now, she snapped."

Within seconds she had vanished, and not even the sound of her footsteps could be heard. "Dill, the favorite herb of sorcerers who wish to cast their spells," Sentra said, leading Dina towards her own room. Quickly Dina explained to Sentra and Olgilvee about the disturbance with the thief and seeing the old hag of the inn at Jack Tilver's apartment above Tilver's Boutique. She would tell them more later.

"Sorry that happened to you," Oliglvee said. "We were just heading back to the Empress to retrieve you two. Glad you found our note. We had to ask at the gift shop for directions to 410 as no such address lines the street," Olgilvee said curiously. "A little set back."

"We know. So glad we're together." Dina hugged him hard.

Then Sentra flung open the door to Dina and Olgilvee's room and walked in, almost stepping into a colorful bouquet of dried flowers that greeted them. "Ah, scented with lavender," Sentra said. She pushed the short wicker basket aside, and they walked past. In the far corner, a queen size mattress sat on a low box spring above the dark, wooden floor. A patchwork quilt of maroon and brown covered the bed, and a lace canopy drooped over the top wooden frame. Next to the bed stood a small end table with a red kerosene lantern and long matchsticks. A large window rose eight feet high and five feet wide. The lace curtains were held back with gold cords, and the noonday sun streamed into the room lighting up tiny dust mites and particles that floated in the air.

"Look at that painting." Dina gasped, grabbing her "good luck" dragon necklace. Brilliant crystal eyes of the beast stared down at them all from atop the dresser where the dragon creature rested upon its black velvet canvas. The word "Death" was painted in red across the beast's chest. Dina felt light-headed and moved toward the window. She opened a top one and took a breath from the cooling air that blew in. Then she gazed at the pond below.

It was such a beautiful sight, and it reminded her of Fern Lake at her castle in New Foundland. She began to grow homesick and hoped their journey would soon be over. With the gems to sell and pay the creditors and The Book of Eternity, they were certain to make their way into the vault and down the corridor to immortality. And who knows what great wonders the vast universe would hold for all the Darrendons.

Soon, a large wooden canoe appeared from behind clumps of fir and spruce trees. A hulking figure was rowing slowly, and a pair of loons plunged straight down, attempting to catch their afternoon snack. The image of a large man with dark hair grew clearer as he grew closer. His flabby arms, which appeared to be dirty, were actually tattooed. The man from the bistro was down there in the pond. Shivers reverberated up and down her spine, and the thought of being captured by the grotesque male horrified her.

"That creep is down there," Dina warned

"What creep?" Olgilvee walked over to the window.

"See, in the pond, the stranger who's been following me." Sentra looked, too.

"Never seen him before, Dina." Sentra said.

Olgilvee leaned into Dina and carressed her waist. Then he spoke softly to her. "We'll keep an eye on him. Don't worry. You look a bit weary, too, my wife. Perhaps we could rest together this afternoon in the grand bed. I'll order up some food, and we'll dine in splendor."

Dina heard the door close softly behind Sentra. She imagined her grand niece would go exploring for the white gem in a silver tin. She then realized that if she switched the first letters around in the word silver tin, it would spell Tilver sin. She then recalled the painting of the sky where ribbons of clouds spelled the words, "Death awaits those who find the gem of sin," she recited. Then impending doom crept over her, and suddenly she remembered Knotty from her childhood who had given her an anecdote. "Sassafras berries, when crushed and rubbed on the skin, will ward off evils of silver and sin," she said aloud, rubbing her arm. She explained about the potion to Olgilvee and wondered where the berries could be found in the nearby woods.

"The gem is here. I know it," Dina said excitedly. "And this fourth one is known by Oliver Tilver for Devon and his followers congregate in areas where the gems are located. Remember when I told you about Tilver's Boutique?."

"Yes, the old hag and that fellow, Jack, were there. But just who is Oliver Tilver, and what does he have to do with Devon?" Olgilvee asked. He ran his long, thick fingers through his grey hair.

"He's Devon's brother, now an entity who once threatened to torture me as a child. Devon cast him into his stone statue, the one back at the dock. You see, Oliver was once a lieutenant, Tilver, whaling man and sorcerer of Buzzard's Bay."

"Yes, an evil one. And Jack must be a relative of his. We must beware," Olgilvee said. "And how did Oliver die?"

"He was hanged for the murder of a petroleum king."

"All for the love of whale oil," Olgilvee said. "This must have been after the whaling industry began to decline. Now I recall his statue back by the Empress."

"And what does your expertise tell you of whales?" Dina asked.

While studying whales during some oceanography course work, the whalers, I learned, fished out these waters for right whales. Then they moved to the Pacific and then the Arctic to hunt the right or bowhead again. The industry decline was later accelerated with the discovery of petroleum. This displaced whale oil as a lubricant for mechanisms and a source of lamplight. Whalers then had to move into manufacturing of cotton fabrics as a way to survive."

"Out of greed and a sense of loss from an age past, he murdered his adversary," Dina said. Quickly she recalled the spacecraft which had brought the alien body parts. The super slaves were digging for super petro. Dina told Olgilvee she believed Oliver Tilver forced information of the fuel's whereabouts from the petro king before Oliver murdered him.

"Money, too, I imagine, was a sore spot," Olgilvee said.

"Perhaps, but what was the extent of his sorcery? What evil actually grew from his magic?" Then Dina reminded Olgilvee that Devon and his wicked followers congregate in areas where the gems are located.

"The evil grows all over earth," Dina said.

"No place is safe," he said, picking up the phone. Soon Dina felt herself drift asleep on the soft bed.

The smell of food awakened her from her nap. She felt rather weak, and a slight cough had developed. "Some good grub, wife, and more rest today would do your body proud."

Olgilvee poured her some tea from a pine green pot. Dina recognized the hairy, gray-green leaves as horehound. "This herb was often used medicinally to treat a cough or cold," she explained to him. "The old witch is very observant," Dina said. She sipped the almost hot brew and remembered her tiny sneeze at the front door. "But why so nice? I hope this hasn't been poisoned."

Memories vented forth, and she recalled the herbal secrets from the old hermit of her childhood. In his own way, although now probably long dead, he was still aiding her with his wisdom.

Dina was amazed at the creative ways the old woman used her herbs. In the green, lettuce salad was the cucumber-like flavor of borage which legend says gives joyfulness, strength of heart, and courage to those who partake. The roasted chicken was sprinkled with crushed, green leaves of rosemary which sharpen the mind and prevent forgetfulness. And the caraway seeds in the rye bread would be sure to brighten her cheeks, she told Olgilvee, feeding him a buttered slice. "She's only making me healthy for a feast on my meat, bones, and blood," she figured. She pushed the plate aside.

"Now please, wife. Of course, we must be careful, but don't let it get to you."

NIGHT OF THE AUTUMNAL EQUINOX

After savoring the flavors of the Boston baked beans and old-fashioned rice pudding, Dina languished in Olgilvee's arms where he made love to her.

That night she dreamed about her grand nephew Steven. It had been a while since they communicated, but in her sleep they seemed to be reunited. He had docked his sailboat next to the Empress, and they sat on the pier and fished. He caught a rubber boot, and Dina pulled in a sea urchin.

When she awoke, Dina quietly looked for stationery, but the old dresser next to the bed had a drawer that would not budge. She tugged so hard that when it opened suddenly, she fell backward from her squatting position and cracked her head on the hardwood floor. Olgilvee turned and groaned but still slept. She noticed stationery and a pen had fallen at her feet. She read "Stardist Town's Oldest Inn" and quietly jotted down a letter to Steven, dating it August 10, 2001.

Dear Steven,

Much has happened since I wrote you last. I hope you are well and having luck with your sailing. Sentra, Olgilvee, and I are here in Stardist Town at the oldest inn, 410 Pinckey Ave, hidden behind 408, the jewelry shop. Our venture here will soon end with success, I hope. Then we can head back out to sea. I miss you so, dear one. As for Amanda, we lost her in a sea city because she became possessed by the evil force of Devon and his clan, old enemies of our family. She has unknowingly betrayed us. We wonder if she still lives. I hope to see her true self again. I pray for her soul, as you should too. We're all fine here, but there are strange goings on. Send me a postcard, and stop by if you're near. We'll only be here for as long as need be.

God bless you,

Love,
Aunt Dina xoxoxoxo

She mailed it quickly at a small postal shop.

The day progressed slowly as Dina hiked the immense property with Elkin, Sentra, and Olgilvee. The pond was filled with fish, and canoes were docked all around its shore. It seemed strange to her that such a lovely place had so few guests. Except for the sighting of the tattooed man, they were the only other people. The wildlife, however, was numerous, and they even spotted great horned owls in the shelter of an old maple tree. The birds swiveled their heads, their golden eyes staring unblinking at the strangers. On one of the back trails, they spied a raccoon family eating berries, and surprisingly one scampered up and sniffed at Olgilvee's ankle.

They soon followed Sentra down a widening path to a flowering field. Elkin chased butterflies who playfully flitted from flower to flower, sucking nectar. The path wound down across a bubbling brook where small colorful trout hid shyly among the grey, mossy rocks. The day was hot at nearly eighty-five degrees, and they all waded barefoot in the stream and drank from its crystal clear waters.

Soon Dina heard some noises in the distance. They put their sneakers back on and moved quickly down the remainder of the path, where it ended at a small, white hut nestled amid several towering spruce trees.

"You all stay here with Elkin," Dina said softly. Then she alone crept up to one of the high-hung windows.

"Kill the redhead, but save the young blond for us. She'll fit in nicely with our midnight Ritual," Jack Tilver said in a menacing tone.

However, Dina heard another strange voice, and she wanted to get a glimpse to whom it belonged. She pulled herself up so she could just barely peer into the window. Beneath his disguise, she recognized the hefty man with the tattoos, the one whom she spotted at the bistro.

"Will I do your bidding?" she heard the big man shout."

"Never. I'd like to bash you to pieces for what you've done to my daughter." Soon voices rang out, and she saw Tilver race out the cabin and run up the back hill.

"Let's be out of here," Dina yelled to the group. Then she lead them running in the opposite direction, Elkin barreling ahead of them.

Soon they were all inside their rooms at the inn. "Our adjoining rooms are being bolted from outside," Sentra said, watching four-inch bars roll across their windows.

"They have us prisoners now, but we shall escape," Olgilvee said angrily. Elkin began sniffing around while Olgilvee hurriedly checked for secret panels on the walls and floor hatches beneath the rugs.

Dina, moving out of his way, leaned back against the dresser, banging it into the wall. Suddenly the dragon painting fell down revealing a small opening behind it. Elkin began to wimper.

"Look," Dina said. She reached into the hole in the wall and pulled out a silver tin.

"At Buzzard's Bay in the oldest inn is a white gem in a silver tin," Sentra said.

"You're right. It's the diamond," Dina said. Then she pulled the gem out, the doors to the rooms opened, and the bars pulled back from the windows.

"Great Grandfather was so clever," Sentra said. "That old witch would have a fit if she knew she put us in such close contact with our desires."

"Ah, death awaits those who find the gem of sin," Dina reminded.

"Yes, maybe they want us to find it," Olgilvee said.

"Let's get back to the boat where we can put this natural beauty in the safe," Dina said, quickly stashing it in her leather pouch in her belt.

Soon they were all packed, but Dina felt fear like a growing flame rise in her when she saw the figure on the pond again. The hefty man with the tattoos was in his canoe, and he was watching their window. Elkin began to growl. "It's him," Sentra said. "The stalker." After she spoke, a single bullet shattered the glass window pane, grazed her cheek, and landed in the door behind her.

"Get down," Olgilvee shouted.

"Death awaits those who find the gem of sin," Dina said again.

"Yes. Someone out there shot at us," Olgilvee said.

"And maybe the gunman was the tattoed man who's been following me since early morning," Dina said. "He can't be trusted. Let's go."

Soon, Elkin was leading the way down the spiral staircase. The steps creaked and moaned on their approach to the first floor landing. The fragrant smell of rosemary incense was strong in the air that grew dark and thick as burnt pudding.

They kept descending, but it seemed like forever, because the first floor never appeared. They just kept climbing down and down as if into a bottomless pit.

"These stairs weren't near this long the day we checked in. Sections of the walls were moved," Olgilvee noticed. "Look, here is a crevass. They must be leading us into some kind of a trap below."

Soon the sound of chanting could be heard, and they felt and smelled the dankness of a cellar. Dina touched a small breeze upon stepping around an ancient, concrete wall. A man with long, flowing golden hair stood with his back to her. She could see he wore a floor-length black robe and was standing before an altar of stone. "Elkin, stay," she ordered the wolf.

"This is Friday night down here, the witches' sabbath," Sentra whispered to her aunt, creeping up behind her. "That must be Devon. On the islands he practiced voodoo for his power, but here, in the States, he's resorted to good old-fashioned witchcraft."

"I wonder how many followers he has?" Olgilvee said.

"Grandfather warned me he would occupy places near the vicinity of our gems. His soothsayer was right. I hope we're not captured and sacrificed," Dina said as she felt herself cringe.

Soon a woman with a purple veil appeared in the corner of the room. Before her stood a hundred gallon cauldron which bubbled forth with green froth. She carried a brown basket from which overflowed the poisonous herbs of goulda, mino, and morrow. "The bright, purple leaves of the goulda herbs, when eaten," Dina whispered, "will cause severe cramps and then sudden death. The spotted evergreen leaves of the mino herb will cause respiratory failure if ingested, but the silvery leaves of the morrow herb, just brushed against the lips, provoke the most disturbing and painful symptoms before death. The skin will first turn a mottled grey before big draining sores appear. Then the person's heart will seize. All these herbs she has put into the pot," Dina finished, letting Elkin nuzzle her hand.

Next she plopped in a goat head, frog tongue, cow's heart, and lamb lung. The smell of it all began to drift toward their hiding place, and Dina nearly vomited. "I certainly don't want to be a part of that stew."

"Look over there." Dina pointed to a dim area. "Who is that man?" She saw a dark figure crouching behind a rock near the cauldron. The women with the purple veil set her basket on the top of the rock. Then she turned, and her long veil tail knocked the basket off, spilling leftover morrow herb on the hidden stranger.

"Let's hope he brushes himself off," Olgilvee said.

"And let's get out of here," Sentra said, "for they must be expecting us. "You see the steps only lead to here. Let's try going back up. Maybe to the third floor. Perhaps we'll find a way out."

When the veiled woman appeared with a crystal vase filled with red blood, she began to chant, and her disguise fell to the floor.

"Goulda, mino, and morrow. Bring upon gem thieves great sorrow."

"Sentra, Olgilvee," Dina said excitedly. "It's Amanda since emerged from the underground sea city where we left the evil one."

The three of them shot up the stairs behind Elkin who bounded ahead to make safe the way. Large, grey rats like charging troops, scurried down from above. Soon their many pointy teeth bit into Dina's legs. She squeeled in pain, but Olgilvee got the worst of it, collapsing momentarily after one rather large rodent tore open his calf.

"Where are these coming from? Elkin! Kill! Kill!" he ordered.

Soon the wolf was chomping off rat heads and flinging them below. Then the stampede stopped, and they kept running up the stairway until exhaustion set in. Next Dina spotted the wooden door at the top of the steps.

"Come in. I've been waiting for you," a deep voice said.

A man dressed in the hide of a whale turned to greet them. "Oliver Tilver?" Dina said. Elkin stared and snarled as Olgilvee held the wolf back. Then Dina gazed at the soft, hazel eyes of the man she had peered at in the painting downstairs. "You must be ancient," she said. She brushed a red sprig of hair from her face, and Sentra grabbed her elbow to ease her trembling. "I saw your ghost when I was a girl," Dina continued. "You wanted to pick the flesh off my bones. Remember?"

"Ah, yes. My brother Devon spared you the torture and death, I see. Today I celebrate my two hundredth birthday, and I'm so glad you could all join me."

"But, sir, you were burned in 1848 for the murder of the petro king. Were you not fried to a crisp?" Dina questioned.

"Why yes, it must have seemed that way to those watching, but my sorcery set me free. Well, almost."

"Tell me of super petro," Dina said. Olgilvee and Sentra leaned in around her as Elkin grew more restless.

"Place the diamond upon this pedestal, red-haired woman," the creature said, ignoring her demand. "You know, the one you pulled from the silver tin. Oh, how I despise you." He held up his right arm, a piece of flesh missing.

"Be careful, Dina," Olgilvee warned. But she kept on.

"You smell of spring lilacs, my dear, old one. Still young at heart?" Dina said in an icy tone. She cringed when the walking, dead man placed a bony finger upon her cheek. His skin was transparent, and up close, she could see every vein pulsating with his fluid. "I'll bet beneath your hide, I could even see your cold heart pumping."

He immediately flung his whale skin to the ground, and Dina stared in disbelief. Tiny water moccasins crawled all over his body. Elkin began to growl.

"Heart?" he cried out. "I have no heart, you foolish woman. Now put the gem upon my pedestal, or you, too, shall be heartbroken."

Quickly Dina pulled the stone from her pouch and set it on the cool, rock surface.

"There's another who longs for this gem," shouted Sentra. She stood tall and unafraid.

"Are you aware of him? Your brother Devon?" Olgilvee asked.

"Ah, yes. He cast me into the stone statue, but I still beat him to the diamond. You see, my stepfather, Mitch the Magnificent and all offspring of Mother Gretchen, wife of Juan Tilver, have the right to eternity. I, too, am part of his brood." he said in his deep voice. "We are the rightful owners as the sorceress Sazran bestowed these stones on our family over a century ago. These gems belong to us."

He turned and walked to the pedestal. Dina, mustering up her courage, pounced on the man, knocking him to the floor. Suddenly Elkin rushed forth and gobbled up the ten tiny snakes that fell from his body. Then the wolf lunged at Oliver Tilver's throat and ripped it out, bringing forth his body fluid, and covering them with goo. "I can't die. I'm not human." Oliver stood up and grabbed the gem from the pedestal with both bony hands. Sentra and Olgilvee stood close to Dina with Elkin back by their side.

"Death awaits those who seek the gem of sin," Dina shouted. Then a new ghostly figure appeared, a man tall and grey-haired. Elkin stared in silence.

"Oliver Tilver," it said. "Now you must pay. You tortured me to death for the secret of deep-earth super petro for evil use. My children were left without a father." Suddenly the petro king threw a velvet bag at Tilver. Then Tilver began to shriek in terror, and his skin began melting off his bones. Soon all that was left were his two, soft, hazel eyes floating in a raw-smelling puddle of his remains.

The ghostly figure disappeared, and the gem was Dina's once again. Quickly she scooped it out of the mire. "But how do we get out of here? And what about Amanda?" Sentra said.

"That isn't your sister down there," Dina said.

"She's someone possessed," Olgilvee continued.

"Hello, everyone." Dina's mouth dropped open at the familiar sound of her grand nephew's voice. Elkin greeted him warmly. "It's me, Steven. Got your letter today and found this place from the address you gave me."

"Thank God, but don't move, Steven." Dina took her hanky and wipped leaves of morrow herb from his hair and top lip. "It was you in the cellar behind the rock," she said. "Let's just hope this plant didn't get absorbed through your skin."

"It can cause death," Olgilvee warned.

"Thank you. I was trying my best not to be seen in Amanda's evil presence."

"But how did you find us down here?" Sentra asked. Elkin stared curiously.

"Upstairs, while I was admiring their old English furniture, an old biddy crept up behind me. I saw her in the reflection of the glass hutch. She had a twelve-inch butcher knife poised at my spine," Steven said as he flinched.

"A murderess, too," cried out Olgilvee, slowly massaging Dina's shoulders.

"Well, I swung around and literally knocked her dead with a swift shove up of her long, crooked nose. What really urked me was when I looked up at Tilver's portrait. I had this overwhelming urge to take it off the wall," Steven went on.

"Did you find a passageway?" Sentra asked.

"Yes. Behind his portrait an entry led into the sabbath chambers below."

"And you were there when we came down the steps?" Sentra seemed certain.

"I was no less than six feet away from you, crouched down behind a large rock. After you all shot up the stairs, I found a granite boulder. I rolled the stone out, completely shutting off the room where Devon, the Tilvers, and the rest of his fifty followers were congregated."

"By closing off Devon and his clan in the basement vault, it shut off his power over the rest of the house?" Sentra asked.

"Yes, and now we should be able to walk out of the house on our own free will!" Dina said. "God bless you." She reached over and hugged Steven. Then Elkin nuzzled his outstretched hand.

"Come. We need to move the stairs." Dina pressed on the wall.

"Look here." Olgilvee pointed to a large metal lever protruding from behind the wooden door. "Sections of the wall were moved. Let's see if I'm right." He pulled on it, but it barely budged.

"I'll help you," Steven said. He grabbed the metal lever and pulled down with all his strength.

"Look." Dina pointed to the granite stairway that was shifting. Soon they walked into the third floor. Devon was no where in sight. They raced down the stairs, past the dead remains of the witch to freedom.

They ran to the dock and were soon sitting on Steven's sailboat eating lobsters and munching on breadsticks. Dina secured the gems in the safe, and Steven asked about the evil men at the oldest inn on Buzzard's Bay. Sentra and Olgilvee listened intently.

"You know they are one with Mitch the Magnificent through their mother, Gretchen," Dina said, "our families' enemies."

"And poor Amanda," Steven said. "She was possessed by some evil being, and she was doing all of Devon's bidding. She needs to be freed from evil if the chance ever arises, for only then could she join us in the year two thousand and one at midnight in the vault to eternity."

"And Devon seems to have a network of wicked ones," Dina said. "On Jamaica he had his followers, in South Carolina his plantation held his people, the undersea city was deadly, and now here in Stardist Town he's in cahoots with the walking dead relative Oliver Tilver and his clan. There's power in numbers." Dina suddenly noticed Elkin's fur stand on end. "Devon knows of the general location of the gems," she continued. "Grandfather said an evil soothsayer gave Devon this knowledge. He and his followers congregate in these areas." Suddenly Elkin began to howl.

"Who goes there?" Steven demanded in his deep voice after footsteps of a heavy person sounded in thuds and seemed to be approaching their boat.

"Spotlight," Olgilvee shouted to Sentra, who had just scampered below deck.

She ran back and turned on the big flashlight whose light shown upon the figure of the hefty, tattooed man running fast toward the end of the empty dock

"Sic em," Dina shouted.

The wolf lept down the wooden planks and lunged on top of the intruder. He ripped and tore at the man's pants, and the big guy hid his face, throat, and upper body with his massive limbs. He was so strong, he could stay standing up while Elkin clung to his buttocks. Then with a mighty blow to the wolf's mid-section, he had the beast off of him. Soon he ran out of sight, and Dina looked on just a few yards away to see glimpses of Elkin's bloodstained fur in the flickering light.

Much to everyone's surprise, the wolf dropped a grey-elskin wallet at Sentra's feet. "Good boy," Dina said. She gave him a gravy-dipped bone.

Inside the wallet was a one hundred dollar bill, a driver's license, credit cards, a photograph, and a phone number written on a piece of brown paper.

The driver's license bore the fat man's face with a large knotty scar on his nose. The yellow, pointed teeth and the scorpion tattoo on his neck were certainly those of the man from the bistro, the one behind the lamppost, the one who was at the inn, and the one who may have taken a shot at Sentra. His name was Brutus Barkwell, and he was six feet five inches tall and two hundred and eighty pounds.

"Who was he spying for," Dina wondered. She memorized the phone number on the crumpled piece of brown paper. Then she placed the wallet and its belongings in her pant's pocket. She knew she would call the number soon. Perhaps they would find on the other end the answer to the mystery of the tattooed man.

The two boats, the Empress and the Sea Serpent, were docked next to each other. Dina was overjoyed that her grand nephew, Steven, was among them.

He loved her so she knew, and he still cherished the Bold Rock beer bottle she had given to him as a boy. She only wished Amanda was well and here with them, too. Truly, early on, they were separated because of her tortured past of alcoholism, nasty men, and drug addiction. She was more susceptible to being bad. Was she now lost forever in the hands of wicked Devon?

To combat the current evil, Dina knew she needed to find the sassafras berries. She decided to take a hike and also paint with her water colors, for it was nighttime and all was quiet. Early morning they would set sail. But for now, Steven and Sentra slept silently on his craft while Olgilvee was snuggled up with Feather and Elkin on the Empress. It was during these quiet times, when the mere sound of a leaf falling could be heard, that she painted her best.

The faint, sweet breeze of the night was calling her, and she kissed the sleeping Olgilvee and the cat. Then she awakened Elkin. But she would be cautious, she knew, leaving a note on the nightstand. Quietly she grabbed her supplies, an easel, and a flashlight and left the boat with Elkin. The nature trail to the right of the end of the dock was well lit at eleven p.m. She caught a glimpse of elderly people taking night strolls for their health, and young lovers, hands embraced, turned down the path through the woods.

She slapped a small mosquito from her arm and walked up to the sign at the entrance. "Lost Sea Cove," she read to Elkin. Briskly, she and her wolf walked down the trail. The smell of salty water was in the air, and the dark canopy of red maple and gum trees glistened with its crystals. They sparkled in the bright lights like numerous stars which had strayed from their heavenly home. Every so often she saw a space between trees where thick clumps of sturdy grass, resembling spikes, grew along with the willowly goldenrods. Soon she came upon a large grouping of sassafras trees with their deeply carved bark, colored like brownish-red clay.

"Thank goodness, Knotty taught me of the sassafras," she said to Elkin. She recalled the old hermit of her childhood who had helped her survive when she became lost in the wilderness.

She knew the odor of its wood could fend off bedbugs, the oil of its bark was used as a fragrance for soaps and lotions, and that the roots could be used to make root beer.

"But what of its berries?" she said aloud. "The berries, when crushed and rubbed on the skin, will ward off evils of silver and sin. Elkin, let's gather these summer fruits, for perhaps they will help us get out of Stardist Town and into the Atlantic once again." Soon her sack was full.

The hoot off a small, brown, spotted Atlantic wood owl called in the distance on their approach to Lost Sea Cove. Than a large, slimy, red lizard with dark, raised bumps slithered up a maple tree. She could even hear the ribits of the green wood frogs as the water came into view. And in its midst, deep green seaweed floated aimlessly on its murky surface. She walked toward a bench that stood lonely and waiting around the cove's edge.

"Not a soul in sight," Dina said to Elkin. She rubbed his furry neck.

She soon set up her easel, and faced the water, by the bench amidst some cinnamon ferns. A dark, round shape in the distance caught her eye, but she passed it off as a large bird.

Then she sat quietly and painted the scene expertly as only the hands of an inherited talent could paint. The wild lily of the valley and clintonia became blurred when a vision appeared before her in the cove.

Up from the depths of the water rose a humpback whale. It was Neptune she was painting. Then he sank beneath the murky surface, moved its fluke upward, and rearranged the seaweed on top. Neptune moved the long strands until a message was clearly spelled out to her.

"The key to summoning me can be found at the whaling museum," she read aloud. Suddenly she heard bushes rustling in the distance where she saw the figure of a big man standing in the shadows. "Come, Elkin. We're not safe. Let's go."

Quickly, as the lights began to dim, Dina took her painting, berries, and Elkin back to the ship.

CHAPTER ELEVEN

It did not take long for everyone to give in to Dina's urgings to see the whaling museum where she believed a message would be found. Although she knew she was not completely convincing about the supernatural adventure at Lost Sea Cove, she was certain they were not too far from believing her. And Olgilvee was glad she found the sassafras berries.

Dina remembered not to wash the berries before storage so as not to wash off the thin, protective epidermal layer. Then she stored them in a cool dry place beneath the kitchen cabinet. The refrigerator would promote the growth of mold she knew as a result of surface condensation.

Olgilvee yawned and then sipped his morning coffee. "You know, Dina, it's a bit unusual to find humpbacks this far south in the summer. They're usually at the edges of the polar ice, feeding in groups."

"Then that makes this encounter at Lost Sea Cove even more important. He stayed behind to guide us."

"You saved her life when she was beached. She feels she owes you another one," laughed Sentra who entered the kitchen with Steven.

"And you owe us some supplies, Sentra," Steven said, guiding her back outside.

"Meet you at the end of the dock at nine thirty," Dina yelled.

Soon Sentra returned, and Dina felt secure knowing Steven would guard the ship while Sentra, Olgilvee, Elkin, and she were gone.

"Try catching some rays," she mentioned to Steven. She thought his skin had the same light grey hue of the silverspoon she used for breakfast.

Dina pulled out her street map of Stardist Town. Quickly she noted the Whalebone Way location of Cretch Whaling Museum, the one she and Elkin were headed for until they had the incident with the thief and the run in with Jack Tilver. Finally, they would be able to explore its contents, perhaps finding out about Neptune's message and why Tilver became irritated at the mere mention of the place.

The sun peaked out intermittantly from behind whispy clouds, warming them on their hike for one and a half miles to their destination. Fearing a possible visit by the tattooed man, Dina wore the gems enclosed in her leather belt in the expertly hidden pouch. Brutus Barkwell she thought to herself, and she went over the phone number in her mind. She stopped at a pay phone and dialed.

"Audio House, please leave your message at the tone," the deep male voice said. She hung up wondering if it was his place of business.

The walk through Stardist Town was anything but boring. They passed many small businesses, eateries, and flowering parks. The people too seemed generally friendly, smiling as they walked by.

"Ten Whalebone Way," Olgilvee shouted. A large, pink, brick, two-story building stood straight ahead, encassed by tall shrubbery on either side.

The line was short, and only a handful of people dotted the expansive interior of the museum. The curator, a tall, bony, dark-haired man with cheek dimples and a cane, greeted them warmly. He slowly handed them a directional guide of the museum's layout. It even included a small cinema with daily showings of sea movies. A wall mural of a humpback whale greeted them in the entryway. "Megaptera Novaeanglial," Olgilvee read in bold, black letters. "Translated that means large fin New Foundland."

"We have a Latin expert here," Sentra said. She brushed aside her long, golden hair, and the rose carving on her tooth stood out vividly as she grinned.

Dina stood back and studied the mural with utmost scrutiny. The mammal's long, white, knobby flippers were one third of its body length. The blowholes were situated behind its long, flat head which held two, tiny eyes. The dorsal fin was humped, and the flippers were scalloped, but it was the fluke that caught her eye. The tail markings, a whale's signature, looked similar to the one's she had seen in Neptune's tail.

"Elkin. Stay back."

She was startled when she heard Olgilvee reprimand her wolf for sniffing the mural. She could see a large kettle standing before them with a wooden sign above it: "This is a copper pot used to boil whale flesh to flense out blubber. This item was popularly used in Spitsbergen Bay," she read.

"The subcutaneous fat is called blubber. It holds in the whale's body temperature, because its body is unusually warmer than the water in which it lives," Olgilvee said. Then the old curator walked up.

"Perhaps you would be interested in this long whalebone, ladies. These skeletal remains were cut into stays which were used in corsets," the old guy said.

Dina felt a chill crawl up her spine, and she thought about the mass slaughter of these intelligent creatures, but where would she find Neptune's message? It certainly was not within the blubber kettle or whalebones.

They soon came upon a display of products made from whales. The first was a large bar of soap, a popular whale product of the seventeenth century. "This luxury item was made from the oil which was also used for lighting," the curator said. Elkin sniffed the soap.

Found in the next section were tools made of bone, slate, and flint of the earliest of whale hunters, prehistoric man. "How far back does whaling date?" Sentra asked the old curator. He leaned up against the glass case.

"A. D. one hundred, my dear. It was the Alaskian hunters of whom we first have records. Seems they got a taste of whale meat from one that beached itself. Later on, in the eleventh century, the Spanish Basque had hunting voyages in the North Atlantic which flourished by the fourteen hundreds. Then, the Greenland whales were killed off in Spitsbergen Bay. After ice fishing declined, whalers moved to the Pacific, fished out the bowheads, then actively picked up again here in the North Atlantic."

"Yes, and tell me the names of such brave whalers," Dina asked while sarcastically emphasizing the word "brave." Elkin nuzzled her hand.

"What whales did they hunt here?" Sentra asked.

"Pirates got in on the act. Many of them would kill these huge, migrating humpbacks and exchange them with merchants for valuable gems. Seems they'd be feeding on schooling fish and krill when these hunters would harpoon them until they died. The slow swimmers had no chance," the old curator said.

"A long agonizing death, I presume," Dina said. She felt herself wince and think of wicked Oliver, whaling man, who was also making their gem search a cruel ordeal.

"Yes, and many whales died by the hands of the thousands of men who hunted them," Olgilvee added. "Not far from here in New Bedford, Connecticut, in 1854, there were as many as three hundred and forty whaling ships."

"Is that so," Sentra said.

"Yes," Olgilvee said.

"And tell us of the great whale vessels," Dina demanded. Suddenly the old curator limbered off with Elkin in pursuit. "Stay Elkin," she said. The wolf returned.

Olgilvee ran his fingers through his hair and began. "The rigs were made of bark, and they had but one topsail. Many a crew member stood on large iron sheets near the masthead to watch for the whales. Two boilers were bricked up on the main deck, and two small houses stood nearby. The tiller had a special part on it to keep wary fishermen alert, and davits craned their necks high where whales were cut in."

Olgilvee folded his arms tightly and continued. "Many young boys would go aboard and sign for their 'lay'or ninety-fifth of all oil taken less medical and other expenses. Most of them had to sleep in the forecastle in the head of the boat. Quarters were cramped, and often the salty sea and nasty wind would blow in. The boy would be one of forty males who were skilled in sailing, harpooning, or cooking. Thick ropes were on board as well as lances, harpoons, and two smaller boats for whale chasing. When a whale watcher would see a whale blow, everyone was warned, small boats were flung overboard, and men and boys would jump in ready for the hunt. Quietly they'd sneak up on the peaceful, grazing beasts and then plunge harpoons into their flesh. The poor whales jumped, dove, and then thrashed until the water was churned into froth. Then a whale killer would thrust a lance into a struggling whale's side and twist it. Draining quickly of life's blood, the great gentle beast would soon turn and die."

Dina listened intently, and Sentra shifted from time to time, grimmacing at the recollection of the horror of such kills. "In detail, Olgilvee, what happened once they hauled them back?" Sentra asked. She ran her fingers through Elkin's grey fur.

"They cut the blubber off into sizes called 'Bible leaves' to better make oil with ease. And then, of course, practically every part of the whale was recycled into goods of various kinds."

"Gruesome," Dina said.

"Must have been highly prized and nearly depleted as a species due to their accessibility to whalers, who would find them concentrated near coasts," said Sentra.

"Yes, but the southern hemisphere humpbacks were offered protection in 1964," Olgilvee said.

"Has their population increased much since then?" Dina asked.

"Yes, wife. The species has increased in number, even though some are still allowed to be killed in western Greenland and the Lesser Antilles. I would estimate there to be five thousand humpbacks swimming the North Atlantic at this very moment."

"There used to be nearly one hundred thousand of these creatures before the great whaling expedition took place," Olgilvee said. He angrily eyed the harpoon.

When they approached the cinema door, Dina stopped to read the sign above. "This six foot harpoon is fired from a gun into the escaping whale. This sixty pound weapon consists of five barbs and a grenade head which is exploded inside the whale's body by a time fuse."

"Movie in one hour, folks," a tall, black man politely announced from the popcorn booth. Rows of empty popcorn boxes covered with decorative whales stood waiting to be filled. The hot, yellow butter was churning upward preparing itself before movie time. And the poppers made their music.

Dina stepped up and bought cool drinks for her friends who wandered off to the restrooms. Elkin, however, stayed by her side following her to a seat at a small table. Soon the poppers were hushed by a different sound of music. But who made it? She had never heard anything sound quite like it before.

"Dina, my wife. Are you enjoying the humpback whale songs?" Olgilvee grabbed a chair, turned it around, and sat down with his long legs wrapped around its base.

"I'm not surprised. It's a form of communication, right?"

"It's the sexual call of the adult male which can be heard for miles under water. He tries to get the attention of a ready female," Olgilvee said.

"It's so mournful. Has anyone ever deciphered its exact meaning?"

"It's quite complex."

"What about their sense of hearing?" Dina asked.

"Their tiny ears, about one-fourth of an inch long, are found behind the eye. The natural wax plug keeps water from entering the ear's chamber. And in the watery home they live in, sound carries better than it does in air."

"You'd think a structure so small wouldn't pick up much sound," Sentra said after emerging from the bathroom hallway. She took a seat next to Dina.

"Yes, but the nerve which communicates information to the brain is very large, making it possible for this mammal to hear sounds even lower or higher than humans can hear," Olgilvee said.

"Maybe the way to summon our friend Neptune would be found in a certain pitch, but where do we find the instrument to make this sound?" Dina said.

"That will be $4.00," Dina heard the concession man say.

"Make mine double butter, please." Dina heard the deep voice of the man on the Audio House recording.

She turned to see the fat man standing just three yards from their table. He was being obvious, and she did not feel fear. Elkin's ears pinned back, and his grey fur stood up like needles. Then he jogged over to sniff the man's dinghy blue jeans. His red muscle shirt showed lines of perspiration where it held taut over his flabby abdomen. Dina could even see the outline of his navel. Soon Brutus Barkwell ambled over to their table. Olgilvee stood up, his six foot four inch frame towering over the small, plaster stand. Sentra moved her chair back and looked defensively at the mass of man.

"So we finally meet," Dina said. She carefully scanned the close-up of Brutus's tattoos. The large, black scorpion was neatly imprinted on his thick manly neck and upper chest. The intricate outlines of its stinger pointed menacingly at her. Then she lifted her eyes to meet his eyes, which pierced her as if they knew of her inner workings.

"What do you want with us?" she asked. He pushed some popcorn into his mouth licking, his lips twice, then licking three of his thick, black encrusted fingertips.

"Ah, you can keep my wallet. And it isn't any of you I want. But maybe there's something I can do for you."

"In exchange for what, big guy?" Sentra asked. "Our lives, perhaps?"

"Nothing so simple, but I know why you came here to Cretch Whaling Museum."

"Oh really?" Dina said. Elkin began chewing on the man's worn, blue tennis shoe.

"First, tell us about yourself," Sentra demanded. "I need to know who we're talking to."

"Brutus Barkwell. I came from upstate, and I've been watching you not for anyone but for myself."

"Why?" Olgilvee asked. "What connection could you possibly have with us?"

"I, too, docked my boat here in Stardist Town. I stop here often to fish and enjoy the scenery. I noticed Dina take an interest in the tall statue of Oliver Tilver, so I followed her and the wolf."

"Yes, last we saw you, Elkin almost tore you to shreds. Earlier, I saw you at the Bistro and on the streets when you followed me. You were also in the canoe in the pond and in the woodland hut with Jack at the Oldest Inn. Something about your daughter. Evilness about our murders. What is the exact connection with Tilver?" Dina asked.

"Oliver's grandson, Jack. You know, the shopkeeper." Elkin began to growl.

"Yes, go on," said Dina, thinking over how very old that made Jack, who looked about fifty.

"He killed my only daughter four months ago. Ran over her with his car. Said she stepped off the curb, but I later found out he had just left his favorite tavern. He was drunk on gin at the time, but he paid off the officials. I hate the bastard."

"Revenge?" Sentra asked. She adjusted her beret.

"Yes. Candy-coated. You see I disguised myself and met Tilver at the oldest inn. I followed him to the cabin and pretended to be a killer-for-hire. He was plotting your murders and preparing to fish for the day. Then late the next evening, I just as easily followed Dina to Lost Sea Cove, and I, too, saw the vision. I also overheard your conversation at the inn about the gems you're searching for. They're the ones Tilver wants so badly."

"So how would you know how to find the message we seek?" Dina asked. She patted Elkin who stared intently at Brutus.

"My dear, as big, scary, and dumb as I seem, I'm really not the latter."

Olgilvee chuckled, crossed his arms, and stared at Brutus.

"I'm an audiologist," he said. "A marine audiologist."

Dina sat back in her chair and recalled the number she had dialed.

"I distinctly understand the hearing capabilities of the humpback whale, and I believe you're right, Dina."

"Hold it. You're trying to convince us of your goodness, but didn't you shoot at Sentra from the pond at the Oldest Inn?" Dina said.

"No. That was Jack Tilver, the sick bastard. He was shooting at me, and then he even threw a razor sharp boomerang at my head. Just bad aim, I guess. But he knows I'm out for revenge. And didn't you hear what I said? I think you're right."

"Right about what?"

"The way to summon your mammal friend is through a certain pitch."

"But how can that be found here at the museum?" Olgilvee asked.

Soon they were standing next to a gigantic tank the size of half a football field. Dina had not realized the grounds housed such an immense aquarium. "So this is what was out back behind the rows of tall shrubbery," she said.

Suddenly Brutus pulled a seashell up off the ground. It was the size of his large hand. He looked at everyone and grinned, showing off his yellow, pointed teeth. Then he blew, but no one could hear anything. Soon, it happened. A giant sheet of water soaked them from head to toe when the liquid cascaded over the side of the large tank. Elkin shook hard to release the moisture from his grey coat.

"A humpback," Dina shouted. The thirty foot beast's tail breached, slapping its thirty ton body into the water.

"Watch this," Brutus said. He quickly ran to the far end of the tank and once again blew into his shell. The humpback swam over, jumped out of the water, curved its body, and landed chin first. Dina could see its great nostrils close before it went under water. "The sound is inaudible to humans, because it's such a high pitch. This king conch shell releases up to 120 kc which is the upper limit a humpback whale can pick up."

"Oh, Barkwell. You're amazing," Sentra said. She squeezed the stinky guy's big arm.

Brutus took the conch and held it out to Dina.

"Take this shell, and use your belief that Neptune wants to help. You find those gems before the evil ones confiscate them. The vengence for my daughter's untimely death will fill my heart with joy."

Dina took the two pound orange, spiral shell and raised it to her lips. Then Brutus walked away. Suddenly she blew and blew until the whale came right up to the edge of the tank and stared at her through eyes as large as casaba melons. It was floating in the water with its tail down, and its eyes were just above the water's surface. Elkin jumped up on the side of the tank to get acquainted with the creature.

"It's spyhopping," Olgilvee cried out. "They're such amazing creatures. I wonder what it's thinking."

Suddenly the whale opened its mouth and emitted a sound louder than a locomotive. Elkin whined and covered his ears with his paws, and Dina's arm hairs stood on end. Then she lead the group back inside the museum toward the only exit.

Dina noticed the room's lights were dim, and the old curator and the black concession worker were gone. The only bright light was the one above the unopened door. "They must be showing a movie. Let's take our shell and get out of here," Dina said. "Gem number five awaits us."

The afternoon sun beat down brightly, urging Dina to put on her sunglasses. It would only be a one and one-half mile hike back to the Empress, and she wondered if their new friend, Brutus, would be leaving Stardist Town, too.

They clomped wearily down the wooden pier and saw Barkwell who bid farewell and hesitantly boarded his boat. Immediately he set sail. "Go through with it, and good luck," he said. Then his craft disappeared out to sea. Dina waved good-bye and went over his phone number in her mind.

It felt good to be back on board the Empress. Steven, still grey complected, hugged them all. Then Dina, Olgilvee, and Sentra leaned on the counter and explained the story of the shell and the tatooed man. "Sometimes it's hard to know a friend from an enemy," Steven said. He placed some papers and books on the kitchen table. "Hey, I'd like you people to meet Mr. Duponderon. He's a gem appraiser whom I met today through an ad I called."

A small man walked in from the hallway. Startled by the sudden presence of the stranger, Dina hesitated and then reached out a a hand. He grasped hers firmly and stared into her eyes. They were the same height and firmness of build. Then Mr. Duponderon adjusted his spectacles, shook the outstretched hands of Sentra and Olgilvee, and sat down at the table next to Steven. Elkin stared at him curiously.

"Do his references check out?" Sentra asked. She took a seat at the table, too.

"Yes. He's renowned on the east coast for his accurate appraisals. He owns Jules Jewelry store," Steven said.

"I assure you," the jeweler said, "my reputation is of the utmost grade, just like the jewels I sell." Olgilvee eyed him intently.

Allthough Sentra had some basic knowledge of gemology, which she picked up from an old boyfriend, it was minute compared to Mr. Duponderon's well-educated and official information.

"And how are we to know he'll keep his mouth shut," Olgilvee bent down and whispered to Steven.

Suddenly the door burst open and there stood Brutus Barkwell with a fourty-four magnum pointed directly at Mr. Duponderon's head. "There's only one way to assure silence," Barkwell said. "No Jack Tilver gonna get his hands on those beauties. You go on now, Mr. Duponderon, and explain the stories, authenticities, and values of each of the four gems. We shall listen with undivided attention. Just relax. You'll be okay."

The small man trembled for a minute and then stopped. Brutus lowered his weapon and took a seat in the corner. "I can't leave you people now, not just yet." He belched quietly.

Dina was not sure what to think of this unhired protector, but he was only trying to further their adventure. She decided Brutus was a welcome sight.

The little man reached into the jewel sack Steven set onto the table and pulled out the first stone Dina had found in Ft. Mariner. It was the ruby Sentra and she had located in the banyan tree. "I think it's about time," Dina said, "that we have an expert tell us the true nature of these gems and make their authenticity official." She stood close to Olgilvee, and they listened.

Everyone nodded at the small, bespeckled man who began to speak.

"This is a rare stone, indeed. It's bright red color is suggestive of Burma."

"Burma? But I thought Thai rubies were the finer stones," Sentra said to Mr. Duponderon. She ran a long finger across the gem the jeweler was holding.

"Since the mid sixties, due to decreased production in Burma and the negative holding power of communism, the Thai ruby, resembling the darker garnet, has become more acceptable and has also greatly increased in price. However, the lighter, brighter stones from Burma are of the finest quality in the world."

Dina watched carefully as he turned the stone over and over in his small, delicate hand. "Certain these are not synthetic, Mr. Duponderon?" she asked suspiciously.

"Of course, I need to rule out that this is not a hydrothermally grown corundum such as Kasham or Ramaura. But it seems to possess true pigeon-blood quality. There is the bright red shade of course, but not the slight mixture of purple."

"How do these stones form?" Steven asked, leaving his chair and leaning against the counter next to Olgilvee. Tightly he folded his arms.

"These grow naturally at famous mines in upper Burma. They're picked from the sides of hills where they formed in granular limestone. I'll fill in this colored stone certificate as we go along. First, this is a very large ruby, possibly ten carats. This is a fine size for international trading," the jeweler said. "Apparently and not unusual for corundum, it was probably cut and polished at the mine site. The proportion and finish I would rate a six. Rarely does one see a number larger than a four. The depth percentage is eighty-five percent with a brilliancy of ninety-eight percent for this fine and rare gem. This stone is a great investment. You see, with this near perfect brilliancy, the clarity also has a very high rating. I also give this stone a color rating of eight."

"It must be worth millions," Sentra said, realizing the extent of their wealth.

"I would estimate its worth at $250,000 per carat. Total value is $2,500,000."

"Great thunder," Olgilvee said in amazement.

Dina gasped, and Steven quickly put the stone into a small, velvet pouch along with the signed, colored, stone certificate and proof of authenticity and ownership. Elkin rolled over on the floor next to Feather.

Next, Steven pulled out the good-sized emerald which gleamed brightly in the ship's cabin. Mr. Duponderon's mouth hung open, and he tried to fathom the stone's magnificence. "No doubt, this one is from Muzo in Columbia, South America."

"Perhaps it once belonged to an Inca Indian," Sentra said.

"When the Spaniards conquered Peru, they took from them all their emeralds. Then they killed and tortured numerous Peruvians in search of the mine. But it wasn't until 1558 that they discovered Muso Mine. These stones are known for the quality of color and lack of flaws," Mr. Duponderon said.

"What makes the emerald mostly green over its faint yellow hint?" Dina asked him. She brushed a sprig of red hair from her face.

"It's due to the presence of a bit of chromium," he said. He cleaned his thick spectacles. "It is very unusual for a piece this large to have such strong green color and transparency. It's wholly unflawed. Such an exquisite gem I have never seen."

"Certain flaws are not inconspicuously hidden by its cut?" Olgilvee asked. He propped a foot on a chair and leaned forward.

"Certain I am, dear sir. This stone is perfect."

"Of better quality than an Oriental emerald?" Sentra asked.

"By far," the little brainy man said. He turned the stone over and over in the light. "This weighs an incredible fifty carats. I am simply amazed. This is definitely one of a kind."

"How do they grow?" Sentra asked. She poured the jeweler some herb tea.

"Gem beryl is formed in hollow areas that stem off the sides of volcanoes. As long as the physical elements and temperatures are right, the crystals form. This particular stone from the Muzo mine is actually referred to as a Muzo gem signifying its color of lime green with a faint hint of yellow."

"Weren't emeralds once thought to cure poor eyesight?" Dina asked. Mr. Duponderon proceeded to take off his glasses.

"By golly, the superstition proves to be fact." Quickly he tossed his thick glasses in the trash can.

"The magical powers of the gem come forth," Dina said, recalling what Grandfather had told her.

"Because of its perfection, I would price this stone at $25,000 per carat," he said. "Total gem value is $1,250,000."

"Wonderful," Olgilvee said.

"$3,750,000 so far," Sentra said. She rubbed her long hands together in anticipation.

"The eight million we owe the creditors to keep the castle are being whittled away," Steven said. He hugged his great aunt. We'll all pull together and get this job done," he said. Dina wiped a lone tear from her freckled cheek. "Only $4,250,000, and we'll be home free," Steven sighed. He placed the emerald and its signed, colored stone certificate and its certificate of ownership and authenticity in a velvet bag.

"Next please," the little man said, sipping down the tea. Suddenly Brutus Barkwell broke the silence.

"This calls for a brewski," he said. He pulled out a small glass bottle from his back pocket. Suddenly Brutus shouted after the faint sound of footsteps could be heard above. "Who goes there?" he said. Then Elkin barked. Armed and dangerous, Brutus crept up the steps. Soon a shot rang out. Injured, he fell backwards while blood gushed from a scalp wound. Within seconds, he was back up on deck shooting with Elkin by his side.

"What on earth is happening?" Olgilvee called out.

"Argh," the painful sound rang out and echoed in the late afternoon air. Suddenly Elkin howled.

"I got her in the shoulder blade," Brutus yelled from above. Then he returned below.

"Good job, my man," Olgilvee said, patting him on the shoulder.

"What did she look like?" Steven asked, his grey face turning pale.

"She was about five foot six, steely eyes, and dark hair," Brutus answered.

"Amanda has returned," Dina said. She called to Elkin and locked the hatch.

"Let's continue, hopefully uninterrupted," Mr. Duponderon said. He rubbed his bloodshot eyes. "My word," the little man said, his face turning a pale, ghostly white. "Am I not looking at the Star of India?" Quickly he weighed the sapphire and gasped aloud. "Six hundred carats. Nearly forty carats more than the largest one known to exist. No doubt this one is from the Hill of Precious Stone in Siam. They must have had quite a surprise when it washed down in the gem gravels from higher elevations. Even though it is not quite clear, due to the hollow cavities within, I would value this one at $2,000,000 at $3,333 plus per carot.

"Fantastic," Olgilvee said.

"The proportions, depth, brilliancy, and finish are all excellent," Mr. Douponderon continued. "Your total is $5,750,000 here in rare gems. How tempting this is for the robber."

"Not as long as I'm around," Brutus said. "The pirate descendants, that murdering hog Tilver and evil Devon won't come near these babies. This booty is for the Darrendons only." Brutus belched loudly in the afternoon, the excitement exhilerating and edging them to exhaustion.

"Let's continue," Dina said. She was anxious to find out the price of the fourth gem, the diamond she had found at the oldest inn in the silver tin behind the dragon painting.

"Next," Mr. Duponderon said impatiently. He grew nervous in Brutus's presence, his hands trembling. "I promise I won't utter a word to anyone about these magnificent stones. Please don't harm me when this is all over," the pale man said. Then he wiped a row of sweat from his brow. "And don't take me with you either." He gazed fearfully out the porthole toward sea.

"We're not such a bad lot to hang with," Sentra said. She popped a grape into her mouth and threw a dog bone to Elkin.

"Calm yourself," Olgilvee said as he placed a hand on the man's forearm.

"Of course you won't tell," Steven said. "Maybe we'll even give you a fine gift as a token of our appreciation."

"I agree," Dina said nodding her head. She wondered what frightened the little man so. What secret of the sea did he possess?

"Well let's have it," the jeweler said. "The diamond please." Sentra handed it over.

"Magnificent. A diamond from India, I am certain. Very little color makes this gem valuable. It ranges as a D color making it the whitest stone possible."

"How do these diamonds form?" Olgilvee asked.

"I know," Sentra piped up. "They form deep in the earth's crust. They need the right amount of pressure and temperature to grow in rock. It is composed of one element called carbon, and it is the hardest substance known to man."

"Atta lady," Mr. Duponderon said. He looked closely at the large stone. "They are actually igneous stones made in volcanoes rich in silica and olivine."

"The history of diamonds is quite fascinating so I hear," Steven said. "Care to elaborate?"

Sucking on a piece of peppermint candy, the little man leaned back in his chair. "It all started in Golconda, India. This was once the diamond distributing center of the world where the Hindus bragged of their splendor. From there the gems were shipped to Amsterdam, Holland where diamond cutting was invented. The mines of India have been so virtually exhausted from diggings that an Indian diamond is nonexistent these days. This diamond here is a rarity indeed. It is flawless and possesses the highest clarity range of any stone I've encountered. This sixty-five carat stone weighs even more than the Blue Hope diamond from Golconda, India. I would estimate its value at one million dollars. Quite a booty you've collected. $6,750,000 total so far."

"Truly awesome," Olgilvee said, throwing his arms into the air.

Brutus belched and grunted.

"The little man rubbed his red eyes, leaned back in his chair, and gently sipped from a glass of water. He seemed weary from the excitement of being able to appraise such magnificent pieces. He was thin and nervous, and he seemed to be easily intimidated.

Dina offered him a shrimp roll and filled his glass with berry punch spiked with a sedative. She felt bad, but it had to be done. In moments he dropped his head and fell into a deep sleep.

"What are we going to do with this fellow?" Olgilvee asked. He sat down next to the little guy."

"We certainly won't kill him," Dina said. She eyed Brutus menacingly. "He's a good man, and I will see that he is treated right."

"I wouldn't think of such a crime," the big man said. He flexed his upper chest and yawned at the late hour.

"We could take him with us," Sentra said, patting Elkin.

"But his family and friends will miss him" Dina said.

"We'll send them a note," Steven said while scratching his grey chin.

Quickly he reached through the jeweler's pockets and pulled out a brown leather wallet. A neat business card was tucked away inside. It contained his home address and phone number. Some pictures were stuck to it which Steven read "to my husband with love, your wife Starla." She was a proud looking brunette with a crooked-toothed smile. The second picture was that of a small child of about ten years. "With love, your daughter, Fauna," he read.

"We'll have him send them a note of a sudden business nature when he comes to," Steven said.

"And how long will that be?" Olgilvee asked.

"Yes. How strong was that brew anyway, Auntie?" Sentra said. Then she rose from the table and stretched out on the chaise lounge.

"Of course, not too strong," Dina said. She carressed the jeweler's forehead with a finger.

"Steven and I will put him in his lower bunk," Olgilvee said. They shuffled the jeweler to his cabin and returned.

"How's the weather outlook for our trip tomorrow morning?" Dina asked Sentra.

"Clear sailing as far as I can see, but I expect a good storm in a day or two. It should pass before we reach Jeffrey's Ledge. Lock the gems up," she said. She stood up from the chaise lounge and patted her brother's cheek, grey and a bit mottled.

Dina enjoyed watching the brother and sister interact with such love. Their relationship had always been a strong one. Now and again they would compete with sailing skills, but it was all in fun. Hate never entered into it.

But what about Amanda, their older sister, Dina wondered. She gazed out the porthole and remembered for a time such human evil had lurked in Amanda's heart. She had been so neglected of love as a child, she became filled with low self-esteem that hurt bad. Then anger developed inside her, and she even stalked her own family out of greed and selfishness. However, their love and trust on the early parts of the adventure had softened her inside. But now Dina knew Amanda was possessed. Yes, the torments of her past had broken her down, and she had become an easy target for the evil sorceress Sazran. There was probably little or no resistance as the spirit entered her. Long ago, when Grandfather Darrendon burned Sazran, once a good relative, at the stake, the evil sorceress had vowed vengence. Yet she hoped to return to good again someday. But still bad, Mitch the Magnificent and all the evildoers could summon her to do their bidding. The gems to eternity must not reach their hands, Dina knew. With the faithful crew of Sentra, Olgilvee, and Steven, victory would be theirs someday.

The gems already worked their magic. Mr. Duponderon's vision was restored one hundred percent by the emerald. She pondered the power yet to be unleashed. Then Olgilvee brought her to her senses.

"Wife, it's past midnight. You've been sitting here in the kitchen staring out that porthole for hours."

"Where are Steven and Brutus?" Dina asked. She wanted Olgilvee inside her.

"In Steven's craft, Dina. Brutus docked his boat across the way. Steven looked tired and wanted to turn in with Brutus as company for safety's sake. Dina sighed with relief and then listened to the little jeweler snoring soundly from his lower bunk in the other cabin. The ship gently rocked. "Sentra's sleeping, too," he continued, "in her hammock on deck with Elkin and Feather."

"We're all alone then." Dina led him into the cabin and then sat atop the dresser.

"I want you now," he said. In moments they climaxed in ecstasy beneath the last quarter moon that peered out from behind a cloud.

"Sweet sex washes the cobwebs from the mind," she said to Olgilvee. Then he carried her to their bed. Feather joined them and began to purr and bathe, and Dina felt herself drift off to sleep.

But soon she awoke with a jolt upon hearing the sound of crashing glass echo in the chamber. In moments, Olgilvee lept from their bed with rifle in hand. Dina followed.

"It came from above," she said through the sound snores of Mr. Duponderon. He still lay in his cabin curled under a blue blanket.

"Oh no. Sentra's up there," Olgilvee said fearfully.

They opened the hatch, and from outside a strange, purple light beamed down on them. Amidst it, Dina could see the outline of a figure in a purple cape. It turned ever so slowly, revealing a chalky white skeleton within.

"The sorceress has returned, but look. Who's that?" Dina asked.

A brunette stood next to Sazran, her back turned, waving a lantern back and forth. Out at sea someone in a large ship was returning the signal.

"It's Amanda. I just feel it in my bones," Dina said. Her heart raced furiously and her hands began to tremble.

"Is it Morse code or another kind of distinguishable interpretation?" Olgilvee asked.

"Not that I know of."

Soon from the ship at sea, two red flares shot up into the sky. Then a whooshing sound began. The waning crescent moon glowed through the hazy veil while Dina and Olgilvee watched in terror. Amanda's entire body burst into flames, and she slowly walked off the edge of the boat. Then a red glow zipped across the water until it reached the ship.

Sazran's purple cape dropped off, and she stood in human form, stark naked. Soon, she collapsed into a pool of purple goo. Then Olgilvee crept out to check her remains, but she suddenly rose in skeleton form once again and vanished into the air.

"Dina. Dina. What are you doing up here?" Sentra stood in her pink nightgown half-asleep by the hatch entrance.

"Where were you?" Dina asked.

"Down here, asleep in the top bunk with Elkin and Feather. I've been here for hours."

"We were very frightened," Dina said. "The sorceress and Amanda put on quite a show for us up here on deck. And there is a ship out there somewhere."

Dina looked out to sea and saw the ship vanish.

"You know, Sentra, we're glad you weren't up here," Olgilvee said.

"Maybe none of it was real," Sentra said. "The night can play funny tricks on people. Especially when the rings surround the moon. Remember, Auntie, the old hermit? Rings around the moon deliver in night a loon."

Dina was not sure if her grand niece was suddenly joking or beginning to doubt her sense of reality. Then Sentra broke out into laughter and climbed to the deck. Suddenly she slipped in the purple goo. "Yuck," she said. "Get this stuff off my night gown. Oh no! It's eating through to my skin." Quickly Olgilvee and Dina tore off Sentra's clothes.

"To the shower, now," Dina ordered her niece.

"Let's get this acidic mess off the deck." Olgilvee said. They swabbed until the wood came clean. Sentra slept soundly in her cabin with Elkin and Feather for comfort.

That night at two a.m. Dina could not stop thinking about the ship. Mr. Duponderon knew something she needed to find out. He did not want to be at sea, but why? She lay quietly in her cabin next to a sleeping Olgilvee, and then the door slowly opened, and Feather snuck in to cuddle up next to them. The door kept opening gradually until she could see into the other room. The small figure in the little bed began to move. Slowly the little man's head popped up from his pillow. He rose slowly and walked up the stairway. Dina followed close behind him to the upper deck.

"I know you're there behind me, Dina," he said. He sank into a chair. "Am I not your captive here at sea?" he said sadly.

"We're sorry, but we just couldn't let you go. Not with the knowledge you possess."

"About the gems?"

"And much more."

From the end of the dock she looked toward land. Only Steven's boat rocked quietly next to the Empress, and not a sole was in sight. Stardist Town was asleep under the spell of night. Quickly she shoved a note pad and pencil into the jeweler's hands. "Write. And make it convincing. Your family needs to know you're in good hands." she hesitated. "This is a business trip, of course. I will take good care of you." The little man wrote the note holding the pencil weakly in his delicate fingers. Dina would have Steven stamp it and drop it off in the mailbox early in the morning before they set sail.

The eerie, lonely sound of a foghorn echoed in the distance, and the little man began to tremble.

"Is it the night that frightens you so, or is it the sea?" she asked. "Tell me the secrets of the deep, blue waters, my little man."

He waited a moment and then spoke with seriousness. "It's out there. I can feel it inside. It makes my innards churn gnawingly. It makes my mind busy. It freezes me all over."

"What do you speak of?" she asked. She kneeled next to his chair, grasping onto the aluminum arm.

"There is a legend in this area about a Spanish ghostship. Hundreds of years ago a band of pirates siezed the ship called the Santo Dio. The treasure laden vessel from Spain was heading up toward New Foundland to sell their goods to an evil lot. Pirate Mitch the Magnificent slaughtered them all, except for two children, and took their mother, the Captain San Chez's red-haired daughter. The capture and killings took place near New Foundland. Of course, the mother's life was spared, too."

"I know of Mitch the Magnificent," Dina said. "It was my ancestor, Captain Darrendon, who confiscated the gems from him as he hung at the gallows. Then he sailed off with the booty, but his ship sank in the North Atlantic somewhere."

"Yes," Mr. Duponderon said. "And since that day the Spanish ghostship sails back and forth looking for its booty."

Dina recalled the story her grandfather had told her of finding the booty in their great ancestor's sunken ship. Then she felt a chill, and she remembered the bloated, dead man, and worst of all, the deaths of her mother and grandmother. "The jewels have magic to those who possess them," Dina said. "The sorceress Sazran cast a spell on the rare beauties."

"Sazran," he repeated.

"Yes. My ancient ancestor, once good, was burned to death for her doings with evil men. She was here tonight, and I believe she is now riding on the ghost ship out there." she pointed. "Somewhere out there."

Dina gave the jeweler some more spiked tea and then tucked him in bed, tying his hands and feet securely to the railing. She, too, must rest, for in the early morning hours they would set sail.

She lay down next to Olgilvee and Feather. The grey cat's soft purrs began to lull her to sleep along with the boat's gentle rocking, back and forth, on the Atlantic waters in Buzzard's Bay. Elkin entered the cabin, crawled beneath the bed, and then settled into a gentle snore. Dina was now deeply asleep.

Her dream took her quickly back in time, and she found herself sitting on the deck of a galleon, the Santo Dio. The long, narrow ship was a sailing man-of-war vessel: the blood stains on deck were given proof. On the full length of the broadside she spied many heavy guns. The keel, upon inspection, was one hundred and eighty feet long while the beam was not much shorter than sixty feet. The salty wind wipped at her ears, but she was able to raise her head upward and look at the five sails and three masts. They were worn yet in good shape.

Not a soul was in sight, and no sound but the ship rocking in the sea could be heard. Then a caw, caw sounded from a black crow sitting in the square-ended forecastle inside his own little basket. A small, silvery fish hung out of its mouth, and it chomped on the tiny head.

The sky was pale blue and cloudless, and the wind began to die down. Suddenly it became completely still, and Dina tied a red bandana, grabbed from an old wooden chest, about her pinkish neck. An old straw hat shaded her forehead and eyes from the sun's rays. She then realized the burlap sack dress she was wearing fit rather loosely, so she tied together three yellow bandanas and belted her thin waist. A tin filled with beef jerky stood open on a small, wooden table, and numerous flies gnawed into the meat. Several human skulls with mouths agape stood atop sticks peering out hauntingly from a huge, wooden barrel. A yellow basket filled with oranges, lemons, and grapefruits glistened in the daylight.

Suddenly a small, dark-haired boy of ten or twelve walked by carrying a wet, natural sponge from the sea. His brown eyes searched for spots of blood to clean, and he expertly swabbed the deck of all its murderous memories,

"Hey, boy," Dina called out. "What's your name?" She grabbed the child's skinny arm, but he didn't hear her, nor could he see her. "This is just a dream. Although it seems so real, I'm not really here. I'm in a time warp. You can't see me, but I can see you. I want to learn why I came here, little boy."

She followed him below deck where he curled up in a tiny hammock. From inside the pillow case, he pulled out a small book. "Mom? Read to me," he said.

Soon a beautiful woman appeared in a blue cotton blouse and a long, flowing brown silk skirt. She tossed her thick mane of red curls to her back and tied them neatly with a short blue ribbon. She sat quietly crossed-legged on the floor and gently rocked the little hammock and read from the tiny book.

"Oliver, I will read The Adventures of the Whalers," she said. She did so until the dark-haired boy fell asleep. Then when the woman set the book down, her silk blouse shifted, and Dina spied a magnificent green emerald the size of a half-dollar. It was carved into a perfect circle. The woman passed her hand over it three times when a blue blanket appeared with which she covered the sleeping child. She passed her hand over the gem twice, and a small pair of black booties appeared which she slipped over the boy's feet. Then she passed her hand over the gem once, it dissolved on her neck, and she disappeared.

Dina sipped some cool water taken with a ladle from a tin bucket in the corner of the room. The water dripped off her chin and down her burlap dress and splashed into a small puddle at her feet, but whose feet were those right next to hers? She looked up at a dark man standing before her, not seeing her, but gazing at the small child. He took his hand, bejeweled with exquisite rings, and stroked the boy's forehead as he slept. He wore a fine, cotton, black shirt which could not conceal the thick, black hair that curled up from his chest to his neck and down his back. Dina could smell a mixture of sweat and spice, and then he walked into another section of the living quarters.

She followed him into his chambers. He was the ship's navigational expert, she knew when she saw a ten by ten foot map of the world hanging on one wall with routes clearly marked with coal. An astronomical chart, used to determine his latitude, hung near his heavy rope hammock in the corner of his roomy quarters. Still another chart, near a thick, wooden table, showed various landmarks along the coast of North America, New Foundland, and even Europe. He sat down on a wooden chair and poured some rum into a mug. He belched, laughed, and tugged at his long beard as he became intoxicated. Then he called, "Gretchen. Come here now."

Then the boy's red-haired mother entered, naked and willing to please her husband.

They lay in each other's arms for half an hour absorbing the afterglow of lovemaking. "Another child for me," he said to the boy's red-haired mother.

"Yes, Juan my husband. We will make a sister this time for our sons. I do as you wish as it pleases me, too."

"Then take these five gems. Your father, proud and strong captain of this ship, gave them to me to give to you. They represent five children, the two we have with three more to grow." Gretchen accepted the stones he handed to her, and her eyes welled with tears.

"I will cherish these forever," she said. She set them on the wooden table and kissed his lips. Then they stood up and walked to the simmering pot in the far corner of the room. Into two big bowls she poured the seafood stew. Jumbo shrimp and fine, plump, white scallops along with mouth-sized lumps of lobster flesh and flounder plopped into their dishes A few green sprigs of parsley and some celery added color to the seafood treat. They sat and supped, and dipped and munched a large, hard crusted roll of bread she sliced and coated with oil.

Halfway through the meal, he wanted her again. They made love beneath the table and fell sound asleep from the intense passion.

Dina felt happiness for the deep love they shared. She also learned the true meaning of Gretchen's gift of gems from her father. She wept and thought of her love for Olgilvee. Slowly she walked out of the big man's quarters.

Once on deck she saw the ship's captain at the helm. Spanish Captain San Chez stood six feet tall and had black and grey curls cascading down from beneath his large straw hat. A purple cotton bandana was wrapped snugly around his neck. He was obviously the red-haired woman's father for he had the same color eyes and bone structure. One by one a crew of thirty dark complected men ran out on deck. Some were cleaning the guns while others oiled the wood and swabbed the deck.

Then the ship's bells sounded, and Dina saw the men split up at the first dogwatch to eat the late lunch of fruit and bread. After the meal, several young women entertained them at the table with dance and sex. Then they returned to work, and the women went below to freshen up for the second dogwatch.

The captain sailed the ship, but Dina noticed they stayed in the exact same spot. Only the sky changed. Cirrus clouds appeared, and then they thickened as lower clouds moved in. Slowly the winds increased in speed until even more clouds crept in from the west.

Then rain from the leaden blankets fell. The droplets were grape-sized and belted the ship and surrounding sea with great force, gravity pulling them down hard.

Although time on the ship seemed to progress, it was not in the same zone as the space beyond the galleon. In moments, busy work soon turned to chaos.

"Beware, it's Mitch the Magnificent," she heard Captain San Chez call out. Then quickly, men climbed on board from another ship. They slashed their way in on the unweary people, decapitating and delimbing the crew. His men were nearly completely slaughtered.

However, Captain San Chez killed many enemies before he was taken prisoner by Mitch the Magnificent.

"We fight a decent battle for power and weath," Captain San Chez said. "But your ways are devious. You have no right to call yourself Magnificent. Ha!"

"Yes I do Why look, it seems there is not much left of your crew," spoke Mitch.

"But please, I beg of you, spare my two grandsons and my daughter and her husband. My love to you, family," Captain San Chez yelled. Then Mitch raised his mighty sword and hacked the head from Captain San Chez's thick neck. The gory, bloody prize he quickly propped on the masthead.

Soon the red-haired woman was pulled from below deck, screaming and kicking. "You can't have me, too. I must mother my sons," she cried.

"We will spare your sons," Mitch assured her. "But I have special plans for you. Don't worry. We'll take good care of you. You're mine now, woman." Mitch quickly frisked her and scooped the gems from her pocket. "And the jewels are mine, too."

She bit clean through one of the men's fingers as they threw her overboard into their smaller craft. Then her husband, Juan, the father of her children, was brought forth and stabbed to death. Next, her sons appeared. One, a small, golden-haired boy, called himself Devon, and his brother, Oliver, was dark-haired. They fought the intruders piercing many hearts with the sharp tips of their blades. One tall girl with red hair, the spitting image of Mitch, put a saber to Oliver's throat. Then she pulled out another knife and cut a strip of flesh from his right arm and ate it. Oliver screamed in agony. Dina now understood the story behind his missing chunk of arm. It was the source of his anger he vented toward her. But it was Mitch's red-haired child he truly wanted to get even with years ago.

At the request of their grandfather, Captain San Chez, Mitch the Magnificent spared the young lives of Devon and Oliver yet slaughtered their own father. However, Mitch preserved their mother's life and was their stepfather now. Devon and Oliver fought for both the Spanish, their true family, and Mitch against the Darrendon clan. "So many enemies," Dina said.

Sickened by the sight, she stood near the forecastle and wept.

When the blood shed ceased, time repeated itself. Now Dina was standing alone on the ship adjusting her bandana. Not a soul was in sight, the sky was clear, and a salty wind nipped at her ears.

"Dina," Olgilvee said. She felt his strong arms around her. "Wake up, my wife. It's nearly noon. We've just set sail. You've slept in, along with Mr. Duponderon."

"Did Steven mail the jeweler's letter?"

"Yes, right before he left to meet his friends down the coast for the sailing regatta from Newport to Bermuda. He looked a bit grey, and I wondered if he should stay. Anyway, he left you this note. I found it on deck." Olgilvee handed her a sheet of paper. "By the way, Brutus stayed behind to help us out," he said. Then he went on deck.

Dina quickly opened it and read slowly.

Dear Auntie,

So much has happened these days; some knowledge has been gained and lives have been lost. Of course, it is all for the sake of the family name. Eternal life shall be ours one day.

I'm off to the Newport to Bermuda race. Sorry no personal goodby. Take it easy near Jeffrey's Ledge and the "graveyard of the Atlantic." My craft, the Sea Serpent, will carry me safely to my destination and probably win me the cup. God bless you. See you at sea.

Love, Steven xoxoxo

"How odd he did not see me before he left," Dina said. She drew the letter up to her nose and sniffed the faint scent of lemon and roses. She sniffed it again and thought it very familiar, a past familiarity which began to bring a feeling of dread. She needed more memories, pictures perhaps.

The little man lay sleeping soundly, his ankles still tied securely to the bed. She saw him roll over twice, and once he opened his eyes. Soon he began snoring, and then he closed his eyes tightly again. Everyone else was on deck, including Elkin and Feather.

Dina went back to her own cabin, glanced around the room and noticed the untidy bookcase at the foot of the bed. One large picture album was upside down and stuck out three inches farther than the other books. "Just what I need. Ah, memory revival time," she said aloud. She pulled it out, opened it, and lay on the bed paging through distant times.

Her childhood photographs with her mother and father brought tears to her eyes. One photo with Grandfather brought back memories of a fishing adventure they had at Fern Lake by the castle when she was a young woman. They had caught three-foot bass that day. Steven was pictured holding a 1901, Bold Rock beer bottle with an impression of a fisherman in its glass. It was a gift Dina had given him for catching his first bass. In the background peeking out from behind a large oak tree, was Big Barney, the creature who had saved her life when she was a girl. She knew she felt inside a closeness to the beast, but yet she felt frightened at the same time. There was Amanda with the beast, happy, for that instant, in the ignorance of fear. She was riding high on his shoulders. Then, taken a few years later, was another photo of Amanda on her birthday, posed with Dina's gift of perfume. She looked cheerfully at the camera, and in her hand, she held up the beautiful glass bottle.

Dina looked closely at the picture of her grand niece and made out the name of the perfume. "Lemon and Roses." Ah yes," she said. She held Steven's letter to her nose again. Suddenly it dawned on her, and a horror shook her very bones.

CHAPTER TWELVE

Dina prayed for Steven's safety and was nearly certain Amanda had him in her clutches. "We all need protection to leave Stardist Town," she said aloud. Then suddenly she saw a vision appear before her. It was a bearded man as skinny as a bean pole.

"Knotty," Dina cried out at the ghostly figure.

"You must use the sassafras berries, now, Dina, before the evil takes you, too. She reached out to grab the old man from her childhood, but he disappeared as quickly as he came. Quickly Dina ran to the kitchen and pulled the sack of sassafras berries from the cold, dark cabinet.

"When crushed and rubbed on the skin, will ward off evils of silver and sin," she said quoting Knotty the hermit. Soon she had everyone on the ship with a coating of the fruits she and Elkin had gathered at Lost Sea Cove.

She did not know what to do about Steven. But she would tell the others about her dream of the red-haired woman, the magical green emerald, and the meaning behind the gift of the five special gems. She could also explain to them about the mixed loyalties of the Tilver men. And she hoped the next and last gem on their list would have even more power than the one they had confiscated in

Jamaica, the one that had corrected Mr. Duponderon's vision. She thought hard about the final leg of their journey.

Sentra was sailing out of Buzzard Bay into Nantucket Sound, up the coast of Cape Cod, and around Provincetown Slope. So far, thanks to Knotty, nothing was holding them back. Up ahead, Jeffrey's Ledge was off of Cape June.

Soon the jeweler woke up. "Good afternoon, Mr. Duponderon," Dina said, watching the man rub sleep from his eyes. "We're now safely out to sea. I will untie you and let you walk freely. All weapons are secured, and keep in mind that Elkin will attack and kill on command."

"I'll behave myself. I'm just frightened, and if I might say so, I smell fish cooking."

Dina looked at the clock and noticed it was twelve thirty p.m., and her stomach began growling.

"Come on up. Time to eat," Olgilvee shouted down the hatch.

Dina ushered Mr. Duponderon on deck where Sentra, Olgilvee, and Brutus had grilled some Atlantic bluefish with basil leaves, butter, lemon juice, and salt. They sat down at the small, secured plastic table and ate heartily under the sun that beat down on their white umbrella. Not a cloud was in sight, and the winds were seven to ten knots, producing a gentle, constant breeze.

The little man looked out to sea, and his fingers brushed his blushing, sun colored cheek. "The daytime hours are easy compared to the night when the ghost ship comes out."

"Just relax, Mr. Duponderon," Sentra said. She stretched a long, golden brown leg out in front of her chair. "I have everything under control. Truth is we're heading past Jeffrey's Ledge for Sable Island and then on to New Foundland."

"Yah. Take it easy," Brutus said. He flipped open a beer. Olgilvee gently placed a hand on the jeweler's shoulder.

Then Mr. Duponderon vanished from his chair, and Dina spotted his delicate form poised at the front of the boat. He was pointing. "Ships," he said. "Look at all the sailing ships."

Sure enough, sailors were headed to Newport, Rhode Island for the race to Bermuda. At least one hundred sailing crafts were making their way toward the starting point. The Empress, too, sailed smoothly through the Atlantic, and Dina told everyone about her suspicions of Steven being held captive by Amanda. They would wait for a sign and pray. "He looked grey last time I saw him." Dina's voice trembled. "You don't think the morrow herb at Buzz...."

"Sh. Let's stay calm," Olgilvee said. He stood up and rubbed her down with sunscreen, and then he gave her a pedicure with pink nail polish. Last, he massaged her shoulders as she lay on her grass matt on deck. Dina drifted in and out of sleep and then woke to the whale sound of a jet engine.

She stood up and looked out to sea and saw them. Fifteen or so humpback whales surfaced with their mouths open, eating through a giant bubble cloud. Their fuzzy looking baleens were sifting out the good food, and the whales were then swallowing the delicate morsels of animal plankton and sandlance.

"Neptune," she called out to the massive creatures. But no one turned her way.

"Go get your shell," Brutus yelled. She quickly ran below deck and dug out the King Conch shell Brutus had given to her. Back on deck in seconds, she raised the pink tube to her red lips.

Hard she blew into the shell until a wave splashed on deck. Dina slipped on the water, bruising her knee and dropping the shell overboard. Within seconds, a whale flung the King Conch shell to her and stood spyhopping.

"He's back. It's Neptune," Dina said happily. The whale's tail appeared when it breached. The planet-shaped pattern was proudly displayed before the being disappeared back into the sea.

"Ah be durned," Brutus said. He crushed his empty beer can.

Mr. Duponderon looked at Dina in amazement, and she knew some explaining was at hand. Quickly she told him of whale kills, her encounter with the great mammal, and how they had saved each other's lives. "I'm certain he seeks revenge on the murderers of his ancestors," Dina said. She pulled a hair clip from her pocket. "And Brutus, you gave me the shell so I could help with that revenge." Brutus tipped his cap at her. Then in one firm tug, she twisted her hair on top of her head and fastened it securely. Upon seeing her bare, pure-white neck, Olgilvee walked up behind her and kissed the fuzzy softness.

"Let's go for a swim, wife." Dina didn't hesitate for the wind died down, and the sailboat barely moved at one knot. She put on her yellow tank suit, Olgilvee stripped down to green trunks, and they dove in. Sentra watched them carefully from the Empress, and Brutus announced their presence by snoring loudly from his lounge chair.

They could not have been far from Stellwagon Bank when Dina walked up on a sandbar. It protruded even further above the water the farther she walked upon it, and Dina found many habitated shells. Then Olgilvee and she lounged in the sun, their bodies turning pink as shrimp.

She prayed for Steven, her fine grand nephew, and she hoped he lived. Then suddenly something familiar washed up on the sandbar at her feet. It was an anitique, glass bottle that she had once given Steven as a child. It was his Bold Rock beer bottle from 1901, and it had an impression of a fisherman in its glass. Steven had always cherished the bottle, the one she had given to him on the night he caught his first bass at the castle lake in New Foundland. She remembered the picture she had recently looked at in her photo album. She also recalled how carefully she had shown him how to filet and cook the two-footer. Eagerly they had eaten it by a campfire beneath the stars that twinkled like stellar admirers from the sky. But how did the bottle happen to wash up here at her feet?

"Bold Rock beer bottle. Lemon and roses," she said aloud. "Where evil lurks, good can prevail. The winds, currents, and perhaps an unknown sea deliverer are on our side."

She sat up, picked it out of the sand, and pulled at the cork. It would not budge. "Olgilvee. Look at this."

He sat up and grasped and pulled at the cork until it opened with such force, he fell backwards. The note it contained had stayed completely dry, and she opened it carefully:

Aunt Dina or whoever finds this note be it friend.

I'm being held captive by Amanda. She forced me to write the previous letter before I set sail and she overpowered me. She wants the stones, or she'll have my life. She seems possessed with something evil. She may take me to Cape June on the coast. Help release me from the wicked one.

Steven.

xo

P.S. May I still be in one piece when you find me.

Dina felt the blood leave her face, and she gasped and lay back next to Olgilvee. She was right about the horror she felt at the dawning of the perfume discovery. "Lemon and roses," she said aloud. Then she showed the letter to Olgilvee.

The trip to Cape June, Massachusetts seemed fast. Sentra docked the Empress at the pier, on August 14th at 7 a.m., along with twenty other sailing vessels, including Steven's boat, the Sea Serpent. The entire crew had now learned of his capture. Elkin and Brutus would stay behind to keep an eye on Mr. Duponderon, the jewels, and The Book of Eternity. Dina bid farewell to Feather.

They asked everyone in sight if they had seen Steven, showing them a photo of him Dina kept in her wallet. None of them had, but then she passed around a picture of Amanda smoking a cigarette and holding a malt liquor.

"Why yes. I saw this woman a day ago," an elderly man said. He wore a blue ball cap set at an angle over his wrinkled forehead.

"Was she with anyone?" Sentra excitedly asked.

"Excuse me," a short, stout, middle aged, red-haired lady interrupted. "I know where this woman is."

"You do?" Olgilvee said. "And was this man with her?"

The woman grabbed the picture and studied it carefully.

"She was with someone all right, but he was wearing a large straw hat, sunglasses, and baggy clothing. He also had a mustache as black as night."

"Sounds like a disguise," Dina said, thinking deeply.

"Where are they?" Olgilvee asked. "It's very important that we find them as soon as possible." He handed the woman a one hundred dollar bill. She grabbed it quickly and then started running away down the sidewalk.

"Over there," the woman hollered. She pointed to a four-story, blue brick hotel.

The desk clerk had never seen the couple, and she called the guard to escort Dina and her friends out of the building. "We can't allow loiterers here," she hollered. Deliberately she was trying to embarrass them in front of the other partrons.

So Dina took the the next best action. She sent Sentra to get their binoculars.

"Coming to this park was a good idea," Olgilvee said. Then they sat behind a decorative, eight foot tall, six foot wide piece of granite at The Clearing, the town's public park.

Carefully Olgilvee scanned the balconies of the blue hotel where numerous people interacted. "An old gent having the maid in room 401. A woman eating salad in room 402. And, aha, there in room 403 is a man with his back turned toward me. He's a blond though and broad-shouldered."

Dina grabbed the binoculars and looked for herself. The man stood, turned, and looked directly her way. There was no mistaking he was Steven. Then a dark-haired man appeared, and a struggle ensued with Steven. Soon a brunette woman shoved the dark-haired stranger over the balcony.

"Oh no," Dina shouted. She saw him plunge four stories to his death. "The balcony is empty now," she cried. "They probably left before the police arrive."

Soon the sirens sounded, and the building was surrounded with uniformed men and detectives. Then the ambulance picked up the dead man and sped off.

Sentra grabbed the binoculars from Dina and scanned the parking lot. Then she saw Amanda drive off in a jeep with Steven in the back seat. "Let's get 'em," Sentra said.

Quickly she hot wired a nearby sports-car rental. Olgilvee took the cramped back seat, and Dina sat in front next to Sentra who zoomed up behind the jeep. Amanda turned around to see who was in the car, but Sentra picked a car with tinted windows, and they remained unknown.

"Stay back," Olgilvee said. Then Sentra slowed up.

Soon Dina heard shouting and saw Amanda bash Steven on the head with a crowbar.

"I hope she hasn't killed him," Dina said. The man in the back of the jeep slumped over.

Next, they drove up a winding, deserted forest road they had seen the jeep turn on. Sentra parked under an old, oak tree next to the jeep, skybound steam coming from under its hood.

"The path," Sentra said. She jumped out and played leader while Dina followed behind Olgilvee. They wound their way through the maze of dense forest.

"Help!" Sentra said. She suddenly shot upwards and dangled from a tree branch. She had stepped into a looped rope snare and hung upside down above the woods.

Quickly Olgilvee climbed the tree monkey-like and cut her down. "There's probably more booby traps. Let's be careful," he said.

Sentra rubbed the rope burns from her ankles. "Instead of following the trail, let's make a new path," she said.

Dina pulled a small machete from her backpack and began hacking. Soon a large, brown ratsnake, fur hanging from its mouth, crawled across her shoe, and in the distance she could hear a blue jay calling to its friends. The summer day was hot, and sweat dripped down her brow and into her eyes.

"I think I see a building up there," Sentra said. Olgilvee agreed.

Carefully they snuck up to a bin in a clearing, twenty feet in front of a log cabin, and looked in horror. Steven, his face grey and sad, was tied to a post in the middle of the compound, stark naked and bleeding from gashes on his face, ribs, and thighs. His lips were cracked and swollen, and he moaned in agony.

"Shut up, brother," Amanda shouted. Then she hosed him down.

The vile woman was raving mad. "Posession for sure," Dina said. They saw Amanda's eyes grow a brilliant green and sweat bead up like pimples on her brow. She ripped off her cotton T-shirt, and soon fur grew up pig-bristly upon her bare back. Then fangs appeared jutting out over her bottom lip, and she began dancing a strange kind of step. Her arms and legs flew out and about puppet-like as if she had lost control of them. Up and down she pranced around the post, occasionally tossing sand on Steven.

"Gems be mine. Forever mine. To carry into eternal time." She chanted over and over until Steven appeared to have blacked out.

"We must get him some medical attention," Dina said. A tear dripped down her cheek.

"I'll sneak up through the trees to the cabin. You stay here with Sentra," Olgilvee said. Then he took out a small gun from his pant's pocket.

"Please don't kill her," Sentra pleaded. "She's not herself. There is a good person in there somewhere."

Olgilvee nodded at the golden-haired young woman and then snuck off towards the log cabin. He slowly crept to the front door where a double-barreled shotgun propped it open. Behind him through the maple trees, Amanda kept dancing and running her fingers through her hair. Then she lay on the ground and rolled over in the dirt.

Suddenly a black rotweiller, the size of a small bull, came bounding out of the front door barking loudly. Olgilvee ran around the cabin, shooting into the air. Immediately Amanda ran to the front door, grabbed the shotgun, and raced to the back of the building. "Pepper. My Pepper," she squeeled. "I'll kill you if you harm my dog. Come out now."

Dina and Sentra ran up to untie Steven. They dragged him back into the woods amidst more shots that rang out, but this time they were shotgun blasts.

Suddenly they saw Amanda attempt to toss what looked like a grenade. It fell short, ricocheting off a tree, and then it bounced back into the cabin. Dina scrambled to cover and protect Steven when the explosion ripped the compound, blowing up the cabin. Several of the splinters of wood rained down like small, sharp toothpicks sticking in her arms and legs.

"Are you all right?" Olgilvee asked. He ran out of the woods and helped Dina to her feet.

"Come on," Sentra hollered from the handmade trail.

Olgilvee picked up Steven and carried him in his arms through the brush. The young man's breathing was shallow but steady. His color was grey with red-brown spots from the sun, and the gashes had ceased bleeding. They placed the wounded man into the back seat of the sports car and drove off, hoping Amanda would not follow.

"She's not dead, you know. I saw her dive into the brush after she threw the grenade," Olgilvee said. He mopped salty sweat from his face with an old torn T-shirt.

"Let's pray for the best," Sentra said. She tried to force water into her brother's parched throat.

At the Cape June Clinic, Dr. Helgadirt talked with Dina. He was a large, broad-boned man of fifty. He wore thick glasses and spoke with a lisp. "How fortunate this young man is to have been rescued. His wounds have been cleansed and one stitched.

He's dehydrated, but he'll make a full recovery. He's exhausted but conscious."

"Can we take him home," Dina said. She thought of the delay of hospital confinement.

"By all means. He needs bed rest, fluid, and nutritious food as soon as he is able. His IV feeding for dehydration will be done soon. May I suggest you stick around Cape June for a week? Bring him back in for a check up."

As much as Dina wanted to get on their way toward the Graveyard of the Atlantic to search for the fifth gem, she knew he was right.

After dropping the borrowed car off in the parking lot where they found it, they hailed a cab.

The three bedroom, third-floor rental unit was on the other end of town. Elkin, Brutus, and Mr. Duponderon would stay on ship with Feather where supplies were plentiful while Dina would help Sentra and Olgilvee tend to Steven at the apartment. Although he was alert, he was weak, grey-skinned, and bedridden. Although he could talk, he did not say much of anything except for requests for food, water, and bathroom facilities. Most of the time he would lay with his eyes open, staring out the window at the sea. Bob's Rental Beach Apartments were situated in a secluded cove. The ocean was only twenty feet away on the other side of the concrete sea wall where gulls dove and played while pelicans flew in groups searching for fish. The beach was private, so only hotel guests and maintainance people strolled the area. The full-sized scallop-shaped pool was warm as soup, and the lifeguard was tall, tan, and hot for Sentra. She ventured out in her golden thong, her firm buttocks gleaming with suntan oil.

Dina knew he was her new love interest, and her grand niece's time away left her alone with Olgilvee. In the kitchen they met while he carresseed her, and they soon swelled with passion. Steven was sound asleep in his room, the door was only slightly ajar, and the windows were locked securely.

After their love desires were met, they sipped on wine from fine, hand-blown goblets, but finally Steven called out. "Sweet shrimp Ramekins. I want to eat them soon." So Sentra sent Olgilvee to the small corner store near the apartment for the ingredients.

He returned in twenty minutes, and Sentra made the treats. Dina's mouth was watering for the prepared tray of delights she sprinkled lightly with parsley. Then she took them to Steven's bedside.

She helped prop him up with pillows, and watched him gorge on the scrumptious morsels that were saturated in lemon juice.

"The evil is in you, Steven. Just what did Amanda do to you?" Dina asked Her grand nephew stared at the sea in an unblinking gaze.

"Devon can't have the book. Amanda!. No! No! Take me to the church. Take me to the church," he uttered. Then he fell back to sleep.

"Oh no. Cookie book disguise uncovered," Dina said. She quickly phoned the dock manager.

Soon Brutus was on the phone. "Dina here. Everyone okay? Please check the safe now. I'll wait." After ten minutes, Brutus returned out of breath.

"Gems are safe, but The Book of Eternity is gone. No one I noticed entered or departed the ship, but there was a second when I thought I saw someone out of the corner of my eye. What now, Dina?"

"Just keep guard of the gems. I may find the book soon. Tell you later. Bye."

Then Sentra returned from the pool to check on her brother. Dina told her The Book of Eternity had been stolen and what a delirious Steven had said. Dina took the empty tray and covered the young man with a blanket. Then she picked up the phone book. There were three churches listed in Cape June: The Eternal Holy Mother of God Church on E. Main St., The Episcopal Church on Fourth Corner, and The Church at Freedom's Gate on Blackwich Blvd.

"Blackwich Boulevard," Dina said aloud. "Places of worship sometimes attract evil followers." Dina remembered Grandfather had warned her that Devon occupied different places in the world. She would beware.

"You're going to hunt down The Book of Eternity?" Sentra said. "Amanda too, who is presumed alive, may also show up at anytime. Perhaps Steven is part of it all now. Maybe he wants to lure you to a church for a trap."

Dina shuddered at the thought and hoped the week would pass quickly. In four days, on August 18th, Steven would go to Dr. Helgadirt for a check up. He was conscious, sometimes he appeared dazed, and he was still grey. He was under a spell of sorts, she knew, and she gripped the dragon charm that hung around her neck.

"Protect us, amulet," she said.

The next day on wednesday, Dina decided to personally check on Brutus and Mr. Duponderon at the ship and then take Elkin exploring on Cape June. Maybe a clue would turn up at one of the churches. She could even disguise herself. Sentra and Olgilvee warned her to be careful before she left them tending to Steven in the apartment. "Only go to the churches in populated areas," Olgilvee warned her. "Are you sure you don't want me to come along?"

"Yes. Elkin and I will be fine."

Back at the Empress, Brutus and his prisoner were playing gin rummy. "I won again," Mr. Duponderon shouted. Then Brutus handed over some pieces of coconut.

"I'm out of luck today," Brutus said. He chugged down a beer.

"Don't fret," Dina comforted. "At least the four gems are still ours tucked deep into the far right corner of the safe."

Elkin was sleeping soundly having just gobbled down an entire can of dog food. His leather, dog chew was stuck between his paws, and he cooed and jerked in a dream state. Dina stooped down and ran her fingers through the wolf's thick, grey fur. It woke instantly, jumped up, and licked her hand. Elkin was glad to see her.

"The wolf and I are going into town," she told Brutus. Feather meowed. Then she quickly explained Steven's condition, his delirious talk, and the fact they would not set sail until the end of the week on Saturday, August 18th.

"Be careful. And bring us back some coconuts," Brutus chuckled. Then he dealt Mr. Duponderon another hand.

The small, delicate man smiled tensly while his tiny fingers sorted through the cards. Somberly he looked out to sea as if the ghost ship would swoop up and grab him.

Dina and Elkin hurried to the road and asked directions. "Take a left at the next stop light," the street vendor said. "The Eternal Holy Mother of God Church is the second building on your right."

A concrete statue of Saint John greeted them as they walked up to the tiny red brick structure. Right inside, they spied its keeper. Bishop Borgony was a tired, old man who was hunched over and furrow-browed from years of listening intently to the problems of sinners. His small, puffy mouth he held just as to look like he was constantly whistling. He smelled of lemon incense, and his deep, grey cloak hung about him like a large, heavy sak. He also shuffled when he walked, and his arthritic hands trembled slightly.

He greeted Dina, then curtly reprimanded her. "No dogs in the house of God."

Dina led Elkin outside and told him to keep guard. She sat quietly in the Bishop's chambers and spoke slowly and distinctly. "How long have you been with the church, Bishop Borgony?"

"Some fifty odd years, dearie. Why do you ask?" He rubbed his left ear, and then he popped in a small hearing aid.

"Do you know of the Tilvers of Stardist Town?"

"Ah, the name conjures up images of scorpions and demons. I believe they are cultists. By the way, I do have a cousin, Magie Koons, who lives there. Did you happen to run into her? She's a nun at St. Mary's Cathedral."

"Bishop, time for counseling," a small dark-haired woman peeked in. Then he stood up. "God bless you in your search," he said quickly. The woman ushered Dina outside.

Dina, with another vote for Tilver's evilness, was getting weary in the lateness of the afternoon. They quickly left The Eternal Holy Mother of God Church and struck out for Fourth Corner. It was quite a hike following the signs that pointed towards the old church located at the end of town high on a hilltop. Stay in populated areas Olgilvee had warned her, but curiosity took hold. The tree-lined lane glistened with sunbeams where bluebirds and sparrows flitted here and there searching for food. Soon she came to a small, wooden sign nailed to a huge, old oak tree.

"The Episcopal Church," she read. "Three miles."

But what was that sound? Dina wondered. She could hear the faint whimpering of a small child, and soon Elkin was sniffing it out. Deep in the midst of a patch of brown-eyed Susans and purple thistle plants sat a tiny, red-haired girl. Her face was smudged with dirt and looked burned from the sun's rays. Her pink and white, flowered dress was wrinkled and tattered, and she was missing one white leather shoe.

Dina slowly walked up to the child and grabbed her in her arms scraping painfully against the thistle thorns. "Whose child are you?" she asked. The little girl began to cry. Dina wiped her eyes and nose with the corner of her shirt.

"Momma! Momma!"

"What's your name, girl?" Dina asked.

"Gretchen," she said. Dina immediately recalled the woman Gretchen on the Spanish ship. The captain's red-haired daughter was forever etched in her mind, the mother of Devon and Oliver Tilver.

"Here. Have some cheese." Dina watched the child gobble down a nice size chunk of baby swiss.

"More please," she said. She reached out her tiny hand. This time Dina gave her some apple and peanut butter slices.

Elkin lapped at the little girl's face until she began to giggle. Her two front teeth were missing amidst her round freckled mouth.

"Gretchen, how old are you?"

She held up six fingers and then began munching on her last piece of apple. Suddenly she jumped up and ran off into the forest.

"Wait. Wait, little one," Dina cried. Elkin ran in pursuit, but Dina tripped over a tree stump and twisted her left ankle. She grabbed a broken limb to use as a makeshift cane, gritted her teeth in pain, and hobbled along toward Elkin's wimpering.

The wolf was sniffing at a hole in the ground the size of a basketball.

"Oh no. Did she fall into the sinkhole?" Dina lowered herself into the upper cavity and cried into its darkness. "Gretchen. Gretchen? Are you okay?" She heard the small girl cry out in a weak and strained voice.

"Momma. Momma. Knee hurt. Help!"

With fear the hole could crash in and swallow them, Dina dug it out just enough so she could squeeze further inside, and Elkin followed her down the six foot drop. She plucked her flashlight out of its case on her waist and flicked it on. The Church at Freedom's Gate on Blackwich Boulevard the wooden sign read. It's arrow pointed straight ahead. Tiny, red beady eyes of rats glared back at her from the tunnel which descended into the earth and then seemed to rise six feet high. Its floors were brick, and lanterns were posted at various distances along the corridor.

Soon Dina spotted the girl and stooped down as the little one hugged her neck. She set her cane down on the ground and examined the girl's leg. A gash on her right knee oozed bright red blood. Dina spat on the wound, and Elkin licked it off. Then Dina quickly wrapped a strip of her shirt around it. The little girl stood on her own, Dina picked up her tree limb cane, and ordered Elkin.

"Go forth," she said. The wolf sniffed and pawed into the musty recesses. She and the girl walked slowly forward.

Soon the scent of rosemary incense began to hang heavy in the thick air. Then she heard it. The low voices of men and women resounded, chanting wickedly of power and evil.

Dina shivered wishing this was The Episcopal Church and not a church of the unholy. "Who is your father?" she asked the golden-haired girl, caressing her small, delicate cheek.

"Devon is his name. Mommy Sazran is dead."

So Devon and Sazran bore an evil child naming her after Devon's mother. Dina winced when she brushed into a hot lantern. Someone has been here recently, she knew, and she flashed her light around the tunnel. Pieces of flesh hung like strips of tattered cloth from the ceiling, some still dripping with blood. Then she stepped onto something brittle and hollow. The flashlight scanned the gruesome sight of skeletal remains, a boulevard in the center of their road.

"This is the chamber of death where they prepare human flesh for cannibalistic rituals," the girl said. Dina knew they too would be dead soon if they could not escape.

Quickly she reached back to grab the girl's arm, but she felt something sharp and moist. An adult alligator stood behind her with its mouth agape, and a human arm hung out of it. Suddenly it snapped at her, and she ran forward with Elkin. Not ten feet in front of her was Gretchen running, too. Then Dina saw her turn into a drooling hyena with large yellow fangs.

"Quick, Elkin. Take the left fork."

Soon they were splashing through ankle deep water which fast grew deeper and colder. Dina's flashlight batteries died, and they were swimming in pitch blackness amid floating debris which felt like bones. When Dina's foot grazed something tough and leathery, she knew the waters were infested with live alligators. For the moment, their bellies were full she realized when none tried to eat her. Within minutes, however, the water became shallow again, and soon they were on dry land. The little girl had lured them into this strange world. After all, the child was not human at all but some concoction of Devon and Sazran the sorceress.

There, twenty feet up a steep hill, was the oldest and most evil-looking church Dina had ever seen. It was lit up by gas lamps, and its pointed steeples resembled daggers in the night sky. Ominously, with hat and evil grin, stood the exact replica of the statue of Oliver Tilver.

"May I help you?" A hunchbacked old man with pale skin and eyes the color of violets greeted them as he rose from a concrete bench. "The church is closed to visitors after seven p.m., but perhaps I could give you a ride back to Cape June." He pointed to a horse-drawn carriage which stood still, its door swinging back and forth in the breeze. Dina felt goose pimples rise on her skin. Then Elkin's fur stood on end, and he growled deeply.

"No thank you, sir. You're too kind. We'll just head on back down the road," Dina said.

With that, the old guy sat back down and stared off into nowhere, his long, silver hair blowing in the breeze.

Dina walked away and hid behind a great oak with Elkin. Then they doubled back the moment she saw the old man had gone, for she had only blinked her eyes once, and he had vanished.

The old door was heavy and hard to pull, but she managed to get it open far enough to squeeze into the dark church. She flicked on a small night light on a round wooden table in the entryway.

On the wall was the painting of Oliver Tilver, but the soft, bown eyes she had seen before were now green. Someone was looking at them from behind the wall through Oliver's eyes. Quickly they walked into the reception area that led to the study.

Spying a large, locked glass case, she walked up and saw something which belonged to her that she had first seen in the castle in New Foundland in the secret room. It was The Book of Eternity, which had been on the Empress. Steven's clue was accurate. She tried to lift the case.

"Get back, bitch,"

She swung around to meet Devon eye to eye.

"Looking for this," he said. Dina could see him dangling a key from a green ribbon. Soon the key vanished in thin air.

"What good will that do you?" Dina asked. "You haven't a single gem. Without the creditors paid off on the autumnal equinox in the year two thousand and one, you will not have access to the vault of eternal life. The spell will not let you. You're a fool, Devon, a bloodthirsty one at that."

Suddenly Elkin lunged at Devon's throat, ripping out a small chunk of flesh and some cartilage. He stood moaning and clutching at his wound. Then the key reappeared, dangling from his fingers. Dina snatched it quickly. "Damn you," he said wretchedly. He stooped to the ground, gasping for air and trying to pry Elkin off his leg. Next, Dina unlocked the case, and the wind blew open every door and window in the church. Quickly, she grabbed the book and fled to the carriage. "Get in Elkin," Dina screamed in the darkness. The hunch-backed driver laughed hideously, and the velvet black horse lept into the air.

"Ya! Ya!" the driver ordered the horse. Suddenly they took off in a gallop.

"Stay away," Dina screamed upon seeing the driver crawl back from behind the reins. Soon he was strangling Dina, and Elkin bit him hard. Then he tried to gouge out her eyes with his long, stinky fingernails.

Suddenly Dina pulled out a metal carriage bar and drove it deep into the old man's side. He quickly flew off the moving carriage and crashed into the trees before landing in a neat pile by the side of the road. "Faster! Faster!" Dina called out. She climbed up behind the reins where Elkin lapped at the wind. She knew they could soon be in Cape June, but suddenly the road turned up again, and they were back at the church. Sitting on the bench was the little old man with the pale skin and eyes the color of violets.

"A twin, perhaps," she said aloud. But somehow, in the darkness, she had taken a wrong turn, or maybe the carriage was pulled this way again she knew. She let the horses get a breather.

Gradually the wind picked up until they could barely stand up. "We'll have to take refuge in the old church," she said. "But beware the evil Devon." Elkin began to wimper. Then they jumped down, Dina holding The Book of Eternity, and walked to the front door which opened easily. The fireplace in the sitting room had been lit, and the coal was burning brightly. Tea was steaming from a pot on a silver tray where two cups and saucers sat waiting to be filled. Dina knew they were not alone. Perhaps the bishop could not sleep.

Carefully and quietly she stepped into the sitting room and took a seat on the large, blue velvet sofa. The mantle clock ticked toward midnight, and she heard the howling wind outside. Her heart beat hard like a drum in her chest.

She poured some tea and sniffed it. It smelled herbal, but could it, too, be as poison as the juice of the arrow frog? Then Elkin lapped at the tea. "No, boy. No." But it was too late. Within minutes, her bodyguard wolf lay sleeping soundly on the floor. Dina held The Book of Eternity tightly in her lap. The night's music continued.

"Dare not open the book again for cursed be they who do so before the autumnal equinox in the year 2001," she heard a strange voice say. She wished Olgilvee and Sentra were with her.

Suddenly she heard the pitter-patter of rain and then bullet sounds of huge drops. The house was pummeled from above, the constant sound nearly putting her to sleep.

"Leave her there. Don't you see she's out of it?" Devon said coldly.

Dina was awake, but she dared not open her eyes. She felt someone adjust a blanket about her neck and then slip the book from her lap.

"The tea did the trick. You see we've outsmarted the old gal. Now if only we could get those gems," Devon said.

"Yes," a female cried out in a creaky voice. It conjured up images of craggy trees and the crone at Buzzard Bay, resurrected. "Or we could at least get her to tell us where the rest of the stones are located," she continued. "Ha. Ha. Argh. Now just to make her feel horrible when she awakens, let my shiny friend help keep her warm beneath the blanket." Dina heard a jar open.

Then she felt a horrible itch at the top of her pubic hair, but she dared not move. It grew painful similar to the sting of the black widow spider bite she received last year. Then she felt something crawl up her stomach, and cramps set in. Soon, her worst fears were confirmed when she peeked beneath the down blanket at her shirt. It was a black widow spider.

"Yow!" she screamed. Then everyone in the room scattered. She quickly threw off her blouse and shook the large female insect with the red-orange abdominal hour glass from her shirt. It crawled off opposite Elkin who lay still in a drug-induced sleep. Then Dina doubled over in anguish.

"She never drank the tea. Faker!" the female screamed.

"Lock her up in the bathroom until the poison's through her. We need her mind for later," Devon said.

"Should I call Dr. Bronner?" the hag asked.

"He's out of town. We'll let her tough it out."

Dina saw the light of the fireplace grow dim, and then she was shuffled into the bathroom and pushed onto the tile floor. Her head smacked into the faucet beneath the toilet, leaving a small gash.

The pain was excruciating, and Dina lay in a fetal position for what seemed like hours. Finally the hurt let up some, she filled the tub with warm water, stripped down, and took a bath. The lilac soap suds soothed her aching body, and she soaked from her neck down to her toes. She quickly shampooed her matted red hair and then lay back to think.

"How do I get out of here," she said aloud. She looked up, and the eye of a skylight winked at her from above.

She stepped from the tub, dried off, and quickly put her clothes back on. Then with ease, she tied towels together, attaching the metal towel bar to the end of her homemade rope. Carefully she threw the towels up through the glass skylight where the metal towel bar stuck securely in the opening.

Brushing some glass shards from her hair, she climbed up the towel rope and onto the roof. She grabbed hold of one of the needle-like steeples and began making her way to the rose trellis. But there was only one problem. She had to crawl past a large window, and she could see it was cracked open a foot. Soon, the sound of voices echoed within.

"Down, wolf, down."

She peeked in from the side and saw Elkin's blood-stained nose. The old hag was repeatedly beating her friend with a whip, and the bishop, his title engraved on his wooden headboard, was lounging naked behind her on the bed reading a paper and sipping brandy from a large snifter. The Book of Eternity sat on the dresser next to the bed.

Dina eyed the needle-like steeple and forced her body into it, splitting it off the main structure.

"Who goes there," she heard the bishop say. She saw the hag and him both standing near the window, one slightly in front of the other.

Dina quickly pulled the window open another two feet. Then she screamed and plunged at them with the steeple spear poised at their hearts. Through the both of them it went, and blood spurted like splattering paint over the walls and white carpeting.

"Let's go, Elkin," she shouted. She grabbed The Book of Eternity off the dresser.

Then they climbed down the trellis, jumped to the ground, and dashed into the cool night air. They fled down the lane where the night owls, like spectators, screeched, and bats darted in front of them. They felt like victims of a cruel game.

They ran through the woods and to the town of Cape June. Weary, they made their way back to the dock. The Empress rocked back and forth in the waters, and the waning crescent moon peered out from behind a dark cloud. Mr. Duponderon and Brutus were both sleeping in their cabin. Their cards still lay spewed across the table. Mr. Duponderon was tied securely to his lower bunk, and Feather, too, lay quietly curled atop Brutus's large stomach in the top bunk. The big man snored like a locomotive.

They would spend the night here in Cape June securely locking up The Book of Eternity. How it was stolen she did not know. The intruder Brutus said was merely a flash from the corner of his eye. Dina hoped Steven had made a full recovery, and of course, he was under the watchful care of Sentra and Olgilvee at the beach apartment. She was glad Steven gave her the idea to go the church.

Dina collapsed on her bed in the rocking ship, and she thought of gem number five and dreamed about a pegasus. The beautiful white stallion was flapping its wings into the galaxy past planets and stars. The comets were only an arm's length away, and star dust latched onto her hair and gleamed in the light.

Dina awakened at 8 a.m. to the smell of food and voices. Feeling refreshed, she went to the kitchen where she saw Olgilvee, Sentra, Brutus, and Steven sitting at the table. "So glad you're well enough to return to the Empress, Steven," she said. Quickly she told them of her adventure at the church and the return of The Book of Eternity.

"How brave of you. Pass the biscuits, please," Steven said. Dina buttered one for him and then threw Elkin a dog bone.

"Yes, and so determined, too," Sentra added.

"So glad you're safe, Dina," Olgilvee said. "Your grand nephew seems to be back to normal, but of course, we should keep a close eye on him over the next few days. After all, his skin is still grey and mottled more than it has ever been."

"You're right," Dina said.

"Sentra, you're quite a good cook," Steven praised.

"Please, the credit goes to Brutus," Olgilvee said. The big, barrel-chested pot-bellied man stood up and took a bow. His tattoos glistened festive-like, and he began to perspire in the kitchen heat.

"The pleasure was mine. Breakfast happens to be my favorite meal of the day."

"With beer for desert," Mr. Duponderon quipped as he entered the kitchen. He delicately lifted a small glass of orange juice to his thin lips.

In two days, Steven had his check-up and passed. Then Sentra made an announcement of their departure.

On August 18th, saturday afternoon, the Empress sailed serenely past the docked Sea Serpent and into the sea toward gem number five. Cumulus clouds hovered like mountains above them. The barometric pressure was thirty, and the winds were blowing up quite a breeze. Sentra's frog barometer was so simple but quite accurate. Sigmund was half in the water and half out of the water munching on a big fat fly.

While the others lounged in their cabins, Olgilvee and Dina were alone in the kitchen. He winked at her from across the table. She ran her toes upon his legs and noticed his heated stare. They left Elkin behind in the hallway and soon met in their room where Feather disappeared into an open cupboard. They quickly stripped, and then Olgilvee gently pushed Dina into the bed.

They made hot love, and then fell deeply asleep into each other's arms. Suddenly they were jolted from the bed. They made hot love, and then fell deeply asleep in each other's arms. Suddenly they were jolted from the bed.

Dina rubbed the walnut-sized lump on her head and sat up on the cabin floor. She felt dizzy, and her vision was blurred. She reached out for Olgilvee, his body stretched out beside her.

"Wake up, husband." He did not move. Then Feather crawled out from a cupboard, sat on his stomach, and began to purr. Olgilvee had a strong pulse, and Dina concluded he had been knocked unconscious. Quickly she placed a small pillow under his head and turned his face to one side. She bent down to kiss him and saw, beneath the bed, the remains of the conch. It lay shattered.

"Oh dear," she said aloud. She placed a cool cloth on his forehead. How the others were doing she could only guess, and she knew they could not have sailed too far from where they had left Cape June.

"Olgilvee! Olgilvee!" She kissed his lips, and he began to moan.

"What happened. My God I have a nasty headache."

"Stay still," she said. She kissed him again.

Soon he sat up, and Dina propped him up with pillows. Then she went up on deck with Feather to investigate. Sentra, Brutus, and Mr. Duponderon were all clinging to the side of the boat, a massive boulder beneath them. Elkin wimpered and paced before Dina who carefully checked out their craft. It was firmly wedged atop the rock and stood an inch above the water. "My instruments failed me," Sentra cried. "The boat has a gouge in it's hull. We'll have to patch it and sail back to land."

Soon Olgilvee appeared on deck rubbing his head. "Be careful," Dina said. She ran to his side.

"I'm fine, thank you. But what happened out here? Why the jolt?"

"Look for yourself," Sentra whined and pointed over the side. He thought seriously for a moment and then dove overboard to inspect the damage. He was able to repair it enough so they could get back to land with a minimal amount of water leakage, but how could they get the heavy craft off the boulder. Dina felt so bad about the destroyed conch, a gift from Brutus, that she dared not mention it yet. Apparently no one else thought of Neptune either.

Their appetites were high, and the spirits of the crew were a bit dull. So Dina and Olgilvee planned a treat for the disgruntled sailors. No pushing would budge the craft, and they knew they would have to rest and try again later. While Olgilvee readied his fishing pole, Dina hooked six whitefish out of the sea, just right for a fine meal.

Good food was a way to heal the spirits of the weary crew. They were stranded, and the situation would remain that way until help came along. After all, Sentra could radio for assistance, or they could wait until the water rose. "Who wants to swim to shore," Olgilvee shouted. He flexed his muscles.

"Fat chance," Brutus said. He smacked some lotion on his bulges.

Mr. Duponderon pulled a mouth organ out of his pocket and began to play. Dina clapped her hands as the delicate man hummed out some old favorites. "My father taught me the mouth harp, and my mother used to play a celestial harp professionally," he said.

"I never imagined you could have such a favorite pastime. You seem like the classical music type," Sentra said. The little jeweler laughed and then placed the instrument to his lips and belted out "Oh Susanna." Everyone applauded when he finished up the third verse.

"I had a glass harmonica as a kid," Sentra piped up.

"Yes," Mr. Duoponderon said. "Those were developed in the 18th century. Glasses with different amounts of water would sound off various notes. These sounds were achieved by rubbing moistened fingers around the glass."

"I struck mine with a spoon," Sentra said.

"With crushing results," Dina laughed. She could easily recall the cases of glasses the family went through that year.

"That isn't exactly what the early glass harmonicas were about, but close," Mr. Duponderon said.

"Both Beethovan and Mozart wrote music for this instrument," the jeweler said.

"Enough! Enough already," Brutus shouted. He slapped his knee hard. "More music! More music!" A strange, moody tune emerged from the little man who stopped playing and began to sing.

"Lost at sea, my friends and I. Captives of dark tea. We're stuck, oh my, but we're still alive. Save us God on high."

Everyone joined in, and soon the sun slipped behind some puffy cumulus clouds which were developing vertically, slowly filling the sky. "We've got some strong currents up there," Sentra said. She checked on Sigmund the frog who was sitting proudly, high atop his rock. Dina felt her frizzy hair, and the damp, salty air carressed her face. Mr. Duponderon kept playing and singing. Even Elkin howled along.

Then Dina saw the dark, fin-like objects protruding from the water. She squinted and then grabbed her binoculars. It was a group of humpback whales eating food admist their bubble cloud. One rather large male began slapping its tail on the water.

"The whales are back," Dina shouted. "One is lobtailing." Slowly the group came closer, and Mr. Duponderon kept playing his harmonica.

Then Dina saw the design on the tail of the large whale when it breached. The outline of the fifth planet was embedded in their friend's fin.

"Neptune! He's come to rescue us," she shouted. Elkin barked excitedly and lept into the air. It's the harmonica that summoned him, Brutus," Dina said excitedly. "We don't need the king conch, but so sorry it accidently broke," she squeezed out.

Brutus frowned and then smiled upon realizing the fact.

Soon she heard a big blast of sound, and Neptune came within four feet of the Empress. It's eyes were just above the surface of the water, and it looked directly at Dina. "Neptune. Our boat is stuck on this boulder. Please help us."

The creature let out a terrific blast and then sank back into the ocean depths. Soon his male friends formed a rowdy group. They clapped each other with their large flippers and then pushed each other with their noses. Then some females appeared, impressed with the goings on.

"It's unusual for this many whales to be this far south during the end of summertime," Olgilvee said. "They usually haven't migrated this far for feeding. They've even ventured awfully near the foul site."

"Foul site?" Dina said.

"We're only a few miles from the toxic, radioactive dump site."

"Stuff like PCB's and heavy metals?" Sentra asked.

"Yes, and the giant sewage outfall pipe is sending contaminated debris into these very waters," Olgilvee continued.

Dina was filled with worry about her creature friend, and she realized how vulnerable the whales were to man's past and present destructive forces. But the whales, as intelligent as they were, did not seem to be in any hurry.

Dina felt the Empress move a bit when Neptune and two of his friends pushed it with their noses.

"Good boy," Sentra shouted. She stood holding on to the boat with the rest of the crew, except for Mr. Duponderon. He had exited to his cabin after he took sight of the sea monster.

"Beware, tonight the ghost ship comes," Dina had heard him mutter and had seen him take his harmonica and flee the upper deck. Steven and Brutus had followed close behind him.

Soon the Empress was moved off the boulder, and Sentra began to sail it back to land. Then the whales spy hopped, Neptune breached, and Dina waved to him. "Thank you, dear one," she called out. Then the wind began to pick up speed. It had shifted to the southwest, and it seemed to push the boat toward land.

The barometer began to fall slowly at first, but within thirty minutes, the fall was more rapid. It was below thirty when the wind and rain began to reek havoc on their craft. Dina ordered all below deck, but Sentra and Olgilvee stayed behind to master the sails for best results. Elkin stood near Dina, and Feather crawled into a cupboard.

Below deck in the rocking ship, Mr. Duponderon told an ancient story. Dina listened intently while Steven and Brutus looked on.

"There once was a King and Queen who had a daughter named Andromeda."

"A galaxy is named in her honor," Dina said. She recalled the place, Andromeda X, Joddar had told her about. "It's where the great masters live beyond the black hole."

"Anyways," Mr. Duponderon continued, his voice beginning to tremble. "The young girl was very lovely, and her mother bragged about her until the Sea Nymphs grew jealous. These sea goddesses told Neptune, king of the sea, about the mortal woman whom they hated. He sent out a large whale who began eating the King's men until he sacrificed his daughter. The young woman was chained to a rock at sea, but when the whale came to eat her, a hero named Persues rescued her, and they rode off on his winged horse, Pegasus."

"What became of the whale?" Steven asked.

"He was supposedly slaughtered, but on one really knows."

"How sad," Brutus said.

"Tis only a myth, my dear man," Olgilvee piped up. He had snuck down from deck.

"Is it?" Mr. Duponderon said. "Perhaps our Neptune is really a killer who will one day turn on us. The ghost ship waits until dark. Then it comes out."

Soon Dina noticed Mr. Duponderon's eyes glaze over, and the little jeweler sat staring out the blackened porthole. Then his skin turned grey like Steven's skin.

Neptune would never betray them Dina knew. He had been her Pegasus, her savior. What was to be made of Mr. Duponderon's warning? Dina thought the little man had gone mad.

Twenty minutes passed with rain pelting the Empress. The wind rose to sixty-four miles per hour, and the rain gauge was five inches. Olgilvee, early on, had patched the boat very well as only a small amount of water leaked in. He had since returned to deck to aid Sentra.

They approached land north of Cape June, and Dina thought about the days behind them. Four gems were in their possession. She was forever grateful to Grandfather for leaving her the poem, the map to the jewels. It was forever embedded in her memory, and with these gems they could pay off the creditors and keep their castle home. Then on September 23rd, in the year two thousand and one with The Book of Eternity, they would find the vault hidden deep within the castle. Life would be theirs forever.

She bowed her head and prayed for God's protection. They were vulnerable to such great evils many mortals had never known.

The boat shook and rocked, and Sentra and Olgilvee attempted to steer it. Brutus fell asleep with Feather, Mr. Duponderon and Steven stared off in a daze, and Dina held Elkin and wept for the crew and for their very lives.

CHAPTER THIRTEEN

Dina awoke in the sun that shone through the porthole. In their cabins, Brutus snored soundly, and Mr. Duponderon and Steven lay sleeping in a fetal position, their skin grey toned. Quickly she went on deck. There she saw Sentra and Olgilvee huddled near the stern. Both deeply asleep, Dina went below and returned with a blanket. Gently she covered them. Elkin and Feather were sleeping next to them, but Feather awakened and ran below deck.

The boat had washed up on a long, quiet beach, and the anchor was stuck securely in the sand. Not a footprint was in sight. Dina awakened Elkin and they climbed out, wading through the water to the dry land. Fiddler crabs scurried by the hundreds, frightened by their approach. Sable and areca palms calmly guarded the front of the grey cliffs.

Then Dina spied an easel in the distance, and she walked toward it with Elkin bounding ahead. "Hi there. What lovely work you do," she said. Elkin sniffed him curiously as she walked up to the bearded man in the chair.

"Thank you, sailor."

"We were in the bad storm," Dina said.

"Yes, I saw you were here at daybreak, probably before you ever awakened."

"Where am I?" Dina asked. She pulled her stiff, red hair into a ponytail.

"Carlin, Massachusetts. We're an artist's community. Been here for centuries. Nearly everyone's ancestors here have been known in some way or another for their creative abilities."

"Yes, my artistic family have connections here, my Grandfather once told me. By the way, my name is Dina, and this is Elkin. What's yours?" she asked. The old guy pulled on his foot-long beard. His short, chubby arms and legs were bronzed from the sun, but his face looked fairly young. Dina assumed his large-brimmed straw hat and sunglasses were part of his daily garb.

"Gregory Darrendon."

Dina felt a strong curiosity upon realizing she might be talking to an unknown relative. Then she felt a chill and recalled Jack Tilver had a gift shop here.

"I, too, am a Darrendon."

"Really? From where?" He set down his paint brush and took off his sunglasses. His bright blue eyes were soft and loving.

"New Foundland."

"Up in Canada?"

"Yes. On the coast."

The old guy sat back in his chair and stared at Dina. "You know, you seem very like him."

"Like who? Grandfather you mean?"

Elkin sniffed at Gregory's brown bag. Then the old man grabbed it and opened it up. "Care for some peanut butter crackers? Hey, how about an orange?"

Dina quickly gouged into the fruit with her fingernails, the sweet juice oozing out. "So you know Grandfather, eh?" But Gregory did not respond. They remained silent, and Dina ate and observed her surroundings.

The day was a bit cooler and drier than the days before, and Dina realized time had gone by more quickly than she had thought. It was late August, and autumn was only five weeks away. In the distance, she could see some deciduous trees had begun to wear their new coats of colors, and the crisp breeze carressed her cheeks and blew at the old man's beard.

The chiseled cliff faces in the background were filled with various flowers. It was these beautiful plants the man was painting so carefully with his long-handled brush. The blue-green stalks of the rock samphire he accentuated with lime-green flowertops. Each petal of the delicate rock sea spurry was gracefully displayed, and the lavender squils stood proudly next to the vivid yellow beach violets. The pink thrifts, which resembled small popcorn balls, were home to a black and white spotted lady bug.

These hearty, wild plants clung strongly to the cliffs where they could survive the winter's cruel environment. Dina wondered if she too could bow her head in a safe harbor for refuge from the storms to come. Like the beautiful and delicate wild flowers, she too could survive.

"You even look a bit like him."

"Grandfather you mean?" she asked the old man again, iritation rising in her voice.

"Old man Darrendon, aritist extraordinaire."

Dina felt herself choke, and she knew the odds of meeting someone who knew her grandfather were slim but existent in these parts where he used to play. Elkin wimpered and nuzzled her hand. Then she spit up an orange slice and grabbed the man's plump arms. "I can believe you. You could have known my grandfather."

"Only for a few years. He spent many days here painting nudes on the beach, in the trees, and in the surf. He made big money at it, too." Elkin sniffed at his easel, and the old man tapped him on the head.

Dina would try to learn all she could from this stranger's point of view. Perhaps she would find some more help in her search for the remaining gem. "Is there a boat repairman in Carlin? The Empress has a hole in her hull."

"Yes, old man Rodney lives just inside Carlin. He'll fix it right and fast, too."

"Great. Take me to him. That is, if you can tear yourself away from such a lovely painting."

The old fellow chuckled and tugged on his beard again. Then he cleaned his brush and put his paints away.

"I must tell my friends," Dina said.

"Don't take too much time," Gregory said. "I need to get going." Then he sat and waved at Dina who disappeared toward the Empress with Elkin.

Sentra was showering while Olgilvee shaved, and Brutus and Mr. Duponderon were preparing breakfast. Olgilvee grabbed her when she stepped into the lower deck. "I met a man, Olgilvee, an artist who claims to have known Grandfather. Same last name, too."

"Oh come now. Are you sure he's not putting you on?"

"Yes. Grandfather used to live and paint in these parts. Relatives here you know. Let me show you. He may still be waiting out there by the cliffs. He also knows a man who will repair the Empress."

Dina led Olgilvee to Gregory's location outside, Elkin bounding ahead. They searched the area, found his footprints, but saw no one in sight.

"I think your new friend had better things to do," Olgilvee said.

"Yes, but maybe he'll be easy to track down," Steven said. He walked up from behind, pushing his blond hair away from his grey-colored face.

Dina turned around, and Elkin brushed up against her and licked her hand. She quickly kneeled down and squeezed the wolf's neck. "Well, we have to go into town anyway to bring someone here to repair the hull. Maybe we'll run into him along the way." Dina looked back at their footprints in the sand from their trail to the cliffs, and Steven rubbed the sleep from his eyes. She ran back quickly to their boat to tell the others of their planned hike.

"Be careful," Sentra called out to her. "The guys are down in the kitchen. We'll be fine." Dina waved good-bye to Feather and returned to the cliffs, the Empress becoming smaller in the distance.

"I left Sentra and Brutus in charge of Mr. Duponderon," she said. Then the four explorers, including Elkin, wandered off to the path that led between the cliffs. The autumn's ladies tresses were just developing their leaves around the flowering stems. In the breath of the wind, the greenish gold of the old man's beard plant blew back and forth grazing the legs of the passers-by. Gulls flew overhead, searching for delicate morsels of food, and the group trudged onward.

The path wound past some ancient wooden buildings. Elkin sniffed at various roadside debris. Then they heard the laughter of children when they came upon some tattered shacks in a poverty-stricken neighborhood. Many of its residents set up booths along the dirt road to sell crafts of wood carvings and carefully made, colorful afghans.

Dina stopped and purchased an especially attractive purple and green shell afghan, and she presented it to Steven. "To keep you warm in the coming months, my dear." She hoped his skin color would improve, and that the morrow herb was not responsible for his discoloration.

Steven wrapped his brawny arms around his great aunt and hugged her. Elkin nuzzled his legs.

The houses were becoming increasingly handsome the further they strolled into the heart of Carlin. It was a charming seaside town filled with the artwork of its locals. From oil paintings to water colors to acrylics, the streets were bustling with vendors selling their wares.

Dina searched for the old man up and down each street until they spied Rodney's Ship Building and Repairshop. Behind a large warehouse stood a grand sailboat. "All by my hands," said the emerging slim, sixtyish-looking fellow with blond hair the color of pine wood. "Name's Rodney. Glad to meet you." Elkin walked up carefully and sniffed the stranger.

"Same here," Dina said. Then she introduced the group. "Gregory Darrendon sent us."

"Ah, yes. We met a few times at art festivals."

"By the way, do you know where he lives or works?" Steven asked.

"Try Carlin's Art Museum in the center of town."

"Thank you," Dina said. "And I can see you're a wonderful ship's craftsman. Will you consider repairing our boat?" Rodney nodded, and they all walked back to the beach.

At the Empress, Rodney's gentle manner shown forth especially to Sentra. He estimated the boat's damage and asked for one week in which to get the lumber and repair it like new. Dina did not want to delay their trip but gave him a week for the necessary work. She would search for the bearded artist making good use of the time.

Dina and Olgilvee left the group at the Empress and walked back toward town, Elkin tagging along protectively. They found a small cafe on Elm St. where they ate a hearty lunch of oyster stew, breadsticks, and tuna melt sandwiches. There was exploring to do, and they started with Carlin's Art Museum in the town's hub. The old wooden structure stood near a water fountain filled with pennies from wishers.

Dina was glad Grandfather had mentioned Massachusetts to her, but why had he never stated the exact location of Carlin? Had he something to hide?

In the museum, the pine smell of rosemary incense filled the air. They thought they were the only ones inside until they heard creaking wood and saw someone walk down the stairway of the two-story structure. Elkin tilted his head to the side and listened intently.

"So we meet again."

Dina blushed, and Gregory grabbed her hand and shook it gently.

"You left the beach," Dina said.

"When my creativity wanes, I grow restless. I pack up and go home every morning after a few hours. I waited a while for you and your friends, and then I brushed in a small note on the rocks."

"I'm sorry. I did not see it," Dina touched his forearm.

"So you're the invisible relative," Olgilvee said.

"I'm curator here. Name's Gregory Darrendon."

Olgilvee shook his hand firmly and their eyes met. Olgilvee was on the defensive, and Dina could feel the tension. Elkin stood close to the pair.

"Right this way," Gregory said. "I'll show you our choice art work."

They strolled down the gallery, and Dina felt tears stream from her eyes when she witnessed rows upon rows of her grandfather's paintings. Some subjects were clothed models, but most were scantily clad or completely naked.

One particularly haunting painting caught her eye. It was Grandmother. Her wavy, auburn hair draped over her chest, covering her plump breasts. The green eyes twinkled back at her as if she had come alive.

"Tell me what you know of him?" Dina asked the curator. Quietly they followed the old man to a house outside the museum's back door.

The afternoon sun shone brightly through the window upon Dina where she sat with Olgilvee in Gregory's kitchen. Elkin sat quietly on the rug by the sink. "This was once your grandfather's house," Gregory said, standing near the window. "I bought it from him a week before he was murdered."

"How did it happen?" Dina asked, feeling shaken. She sipped on a glass of ice water.

"I found the old guy on the back porch. He was sprawled out in a pool of blood. His throat was slit from ear to ear. The thieves took some of his paintings and smashed his easel. He was too old to defend himself. Even I look over my shoulder. Will they come after me one day." Gregory looked down, and tears welled up in the corners of his eyes.

"Did the police ever find a clue as to who did him in?" Dina asked. Then she patted a tear from her own eye.

"They never found them, but the murderers did leave something behind."

"And what was that?" Olgilvee asked, crossing his arms.

"A drawing of a skull and crossbones."

"Pirates?" Dina asked.

"Like I said, no no one knows who did it. He had recently come back from some kind of boating trip."

Dina knew that trip was when Grandfather had hidden the jewels, written the poem, and somehow hidden the letter in the castle.

"All these material items were his. I haven't removed anything. I was very young back then, but your grandfather's presence in my life left me with an appreciation of art I'll never forget, and a name."

"You're not truly a Darrendon?" Dina asked.

"The old guy sort of took me in. I was a street person, an orphan. Of my real parents, I know nothing."

"But I thought for a minute you had the family's wonderful eyes." Dina felt wishful thinking had overwhelmed her when she had first met Gregory, but she was certain she felt her late grandfather's presence in the old man that stood before her.

"How old are you?" Olgilvee asked.

"110 years old today," Gregory answered. He tugged his beard. "A centenarian. I guess I have that Darrendon magic."

"This calls for a celebration," Dina shouted. "I'm going shopping. She rushed out the door with Elkin glad to be in fresh air to give her time to think.

The town grocery store was dotted with locals, and Dina made her way to the bakery. The glass enclosure was filled with different kinds of pies and cakes. She chose a yellow cake with chocolate frosting, large enough to feed the group. Then she filled the cart with applejuice, strawberries, and shrimp. At the checkout, she placed five boxes of birthday candles into her cart, paid the cashier, and marched on to the gift shop.

Elkin wagged his tail approvingly.

Streamers and cards she bought along with balloons and party hats, but picking out a present was difficult. There were shell crafts, figurines of glass, stationery, dried flower arrangements, plaques, and T-shirts. Finally one gift caught her eye. Behind the glass counter, she spied a sterling silver castle sitting atop a beautiful crystal. It was a lovely pendant which held much meaning for her. A woman wrapped it carefully, and Dina wondered if Gregory knew about the castle, the large debt, the entire search for the gems and their use to rid themselves of this debt. Did he know they needed to keep the castle in the family? Had he heard of The Book of Eternity? Could he provide her with clues to further them on their way? Then Dina thought of the dark side. Was he perhaps friends with Devon? Would he become possessed with Sazran and kill them? Only time would tell. She grabbed her dragon necklace the black woman in Grand Cayman had given her and made a prayer.

"Guide me, oh mighty God," she muttered, running her fingers through Elkin's grey fur. Then they dropped the goods off at Gregory's house. "I must gather our group back at the boat.," Dina said.

"Be careful and see you soon," Olgilvee rose from his chair and kissed his wife. Gregory nodded, and she ran off with Elkin by her side.

She told Sentra and everyone about Gregory Darrendon and the party. Quickly they secured Feather onboard. Dina took the four gems out of the safe where The Book of Eternity was still inside. Then Sentra secured the gems inside the leather belt she wore at her own waist. Soon Sentra, Steven, Brutus, and Mr. Duponderon followed Dina and Elkin back to Gregory's house.

At the party, everyone wanted to get to know the ancient man with the smooth face. Brutus ate half the cake and chugged down a six-pack of beer. He kept a very close watch on Mr. Duponderon, who was behaving very well, considering he was being held against his will. Elkin munched on a dog bone, and Steven enjoyed the biggest helping of shrimp. Everyone filled their plates high with the sweet seafood.

Dina kept filling Gregory's glass with wine until he was talking openly and slurring a bit, too.

"One time, Dina, your grandfather and I saw a ghost. She appeared on his boat at midnight on September 23rd, autumn. We had just finished catching about eight groupers when a pine scent of rosemary filled the air. Then a purple fog crept in off the water. She was beautiful, voluptuous, and young, and her skin was as soft and white as a magnolia flower. The name Sazran was engraved in her chest. 'Beware the gems of eternal life.' That's what she said before she disappeared back into the purple haze."

"The ghost ship waits in the dark," Mr. Duponderon said fearfully. Then Brutus took him down the basement and tried to calm the trembling jeweler. Elkin stood guard at the basement entrance.

Dina smiled when she lit the one hundred and ten candles. They were the kind you can not blow out with just one try. Then she shut the lights out. They sang happy birthday, and Gregory concentrated hard on a wish.

"Blow! Blow!" Sentra said. The old man made several attempts to extinguish the eternal flames, but nothing happened.

"What is going on here?" he laughed.

Finally, all the candles melted beneath their hot flames. Then the room was flung into pitch blackness. Soon the pine scent of rosemary wafted through the small house. Dina flipped on the light switch but to no avail. The room remained black as the creepy presence of evil thickened the air.

"The ghost ship partrols the coast. Soon you'll all be dead. Help!" Mr. Duponderon cried out from the basement. Elkin began to growl in a low tone.

"Matches," Gregory said. "There, in the dressser drawer near you, Dina." She pulled out a pack of wooden matches and lit a lantern and various candles in the room.

"Help me!" a horrified voice cried out.

"Be careful. It may be a trap," Olgilvee warned. Then Elkin barked and ran down the steps.

Olgilvee grabbed a candle and followed Dina who crept slowly into the basement. The smell of apple cider filled the air. Upon rubbing up against the mossy blocks of the wall, Dina called out. "Mr. Duponderon? Brutus?" No one answered. No one was there except for a bat the size of a coat hanger who hung upside down from the ceiling. She felt a breeze and heard the cellar doors banging open and shut. The night wind was playing with its toys.

Suddenly all the lights came back on, but Brutus and Mr. Duponderon were nowhere in sight. Then outside the cellar doors, Dina spied a tall, dark-haired, thin figure of a man with a goatee scamper off into the night. Elkin followed in hot pursuit. "Come back, Elkin," she ordered. "Halt, stranger," she hollered, but the man disappeared quickly.

"Who was that man?" Olgilvee asked, Elkin retreating to Dina's side.

"He may be one of Jack Tilver's creeps," Dina said.

"Let's hope our two friends are safe back at the ship?" Sentra said, appearing from the front of the house. She still had the gems strapped to her waist in the secret compartment of her leather belt. While Olgilvee, Steven, and Gregory searched the area, Elkin stood guard at the house. Then Dina and Sentra ran back to the Empress.

The boat rocked back and forth in the water. Rodney took some measurements. "Seen anyone here?" Dina asked.

"Anyone at all?" Sentra said.

"No one except for a mustachioed man who jogged down the beach an hour ago. I've been here since 6 p.m., and I've been alone on the boat. Why? What's wrong?" Rodney followed them into the night to search for the two men.

They could not find them, and after an extensive search, they returned to the Empress. Two policemen greeted them. They had accidently found the two bodies while chasing down a hit-and-run driver. The police traced their address to the Empress from a note Mr. Duponderon had in his pocket.

They were found in a swamp off the road, one half-mile from Gregory's house. The police said they were both shot in the head, holes as big as quarters. They were found laying face up in the muck, their eyes staring blankly at the distant sky.

"Your ghost ship came, little jeweler," Dina said sorrowfully. "So sorry, my little man."

Olgilvee and Steven, having left Gregory back at his house, returned to the ship, and they grieved over the disappearance and death of their two comrades. Dina identified the bodies and told the police where to reach Mr. Duponderon's family. Brutus's wallet, complete with identification, was in the law's possession, too. The search for the mustachioed man, a possible suspect, would continue.

Four days went by since they landed in Carlin. Dina felt she was beginning to know Gregory a bit. In three days they would be sailing for Sable Island to look for gem number five. Would she find any more information about Grandfather?

The next day, Dina checked the gems and The Book of Eternity and saw they were still secure in the safe. Olgilvee and Steven were going to get supplies, and Sentra said she would guard the boat. Then Dina took Elkin to a pet shop to buy him leather chew toys and dog food. On the way, she saw a delicate, little man in a brown shirt and beige slacks get out of a green jeep. She followed him into a gift shop in a dark, brick building.

"I could swear in choir practice that man is Mr. Duponderon," Dina said. Elkin raised his ears into a sharp point as they grew closer to the stranger. "A dead ringer."

"Did you bring the goods?" A bespeckled man with soft, brown eyes stood from behind the counter. Dina was looking between gifts at Jack Tilver, the creep from Stardist Town. Ah, this is his shop in Massachusetts she recalled. She remembered glancing at the financial statements on his coffee table in his apartment.

"Sorry about your brother, Mr. Duponderon," Jack continued. "When I heard he died, I had to notify you of possible connections with the Darrendons. They are an evil lot and probably just disposed of the jeweler after they got the information they needed."

"Thanks for the warning," the little man said. Then he pulled out an object. "For more information about Duponderon's activities, I have this for you. I hope it can help you with your family's pursuance of their dreams."

"Good. I want to put the Darrendons at every disadvantage possible!" A tall, thin, dark-haired man with a black goatee walked in from the shadows of the bathroom. Dina recognized him to be the man at Gregory's house the night of the killing. "And with Rock, here, and Otto's help," Jack Tilver continued, "we're bound to have success." The goateed man pulled aside his cotton jacket. Dina eyed the gun stuck in the front of Rock's pants. Elkin began to quiver.

Then Dina saw the little guy, no doubt the jeweler's identical twin brother, pass Jack Tilver a small black book. She could barely make out the engraving on the leather cover, but it looked like English words. Soon a musty odor filled the room, and Dina felt a tickle in her nose.

"That crew will never find the last gem without the knowledge this book holds," the little guy said. The two men shook hands, and then Dina sneezed.

"Who goes there?" Jack hollered. He looked her way, and then quickly she and Elkin slipped out the door into the street.

It was half past eleven, and she had a meeting with Gregory Darrendon. They ran quickly, hoping not to be followed by Tilver's henchmen. He showed up at the arts festival at the corner of Hope and Dove Streets. He was wearing his faded blue jeans, sneakers, and a red plaid shirt. His hat was tilted to the side, and he was eating a tuna sandwich while sitting and waiting on a park bench. The late August art festival was a grand event. Tourist's from every state showed up each year to buy the paintings and dine on seafood served at booths all around the park. Dina was especially fond of the lobster on a stick, and Elkin liked the pig's ear.

"You look vivacious this morning." Gregory stood to greet her and then offered her a seat next to him. "Where's your next stop?" the old man asked. He pulled on his beard and then patted Elkin.

"Past Jeffrey's Ledge to Sable Island for gem number five. Why do you ask?"

"Remember when you heard of Mr. Duponderon's death, and you said, 'your ghost ship came in'?"

Dina almost cried when she thought about the dead jeweler. "Yes. We had a supernatural experience with the ship called the Santa Dio of the dead Spanish pirates."

"It's true," Gregory said. "Your grandfather told me of this one night. He had caught pneumonia, and he thought he was going to die. He kept muttering, 'the Spaniards search the seas for their lost, red-haired woman and their booty. There is a black book of the ghost ship. Tell Dina she must read it for it tells ways to get past the ship's evil power force.' He recovered a few days later and made me take an oath never to reveal the secret, except to you."

Quickly she told Gregory about the incident at the gift shop with Tilver and what looked like Duponderon's twin. "Tilver looked right at me. He knows I know. I must have this book!" Dina cried out.

"But we need to be sure it is the same book your Grandfather told me about."

"You'll soon need it," Gregory continued, "for the ship will close in on you when you near your destination."

"How do we find its known last location?" Dina asked. "There is a way to help find out where the original book is by ruling out where it isn't."

"The original was buried with Samuel. It's in the oldest cemetary in Massachusetts."

They pulled up in Gregory's old pick-up truck. Dina could see the quaint Lutheran church standing quietly amid an oak forest. It seemed to cry out for attention. Its shutters stood open as if reaching out to passersby. Some of the stained-glass windows had been shattered, and small rodents and birds had made their homes inside the chapel. They entered, and then Dina saw an old bible still sitting on one of the pews, and a pastor's faded, white robe was hanging lonely on the back of an old wooden chair. Some vandals had written grafitti on the walls.

"No one keeps the place up," Dina said to Gregory. Elkin sniffed at the mildewed offering basket.

"At one time, these grounds were maintained by church members and their families. This entitled members to burial sites for their own with the only charges being for the opening of the grave. But one day a newer church opened a few miles from here, and this is what you see. Tall weeds, broken tombstones, and vandalism. The forgotton dead."

"Where's Grandfather's grave?" she asked.

"Come with me," Gregory said, the golden sun's rays cascading from the window carressing their faces.

They stood looking out the front, broken window, and Gregory lifted his pudgy arm and pointed to a small, grey, lopsided tombstone. "His stone lies directly between those two oak trees. That's the only way you can tell it's his. The engraving is worn off."

Elkin raced outside ahead of them and pawed at the stone. Then he started digging with his large paws while Dina picked some wildflowers. Gregory pulled his crowbar and shovel out from the back of his pick-up truck and let Dina dig, too.

"Six feet under, dearie, and by the way, you aren't superstitious are you?" The old man pulled on his grey beard and chuckled. Dina just kept digging deeper into the brown earth.

Finally, the shovel hit hard and penetrated the disintigrating wooden coffin. Then a warm breeze blew her red hair into tangles. "Aha," she cried out. Elkin jumped in and sniffed, whined, and clawed. Then Dina carved out just enough dirt around the base of the coffin for standing room. She carefully jammed in the crowbar and lifted the lid which soon came apart in pieces.

The skeleton inside stared at them, its clothes hanging loosely on its long, empty bones. "Right there in his hands I laid that black book," Gregory said. "It's gone now. Graverobbers probably."

They both instantly knew who had it. "Somehow Jack Tilver had found out about the book," Dina said. "Maybe he had the Duponderon twin dig it up, and he complied certainly out of vengence for her and their crew due to the death of his brother, the jeweler."

"I believe you are right," Gregory said. "You must confiscate that book before you leave for Sable Island. Its contents will help you get the protection you need to get the fifth gem and to make your way through the North Atlantic back to New Foundland."

Dina took one last look at Grandfather's remains, said a prayer, and then pieced together the lid and gently closed the coffin. The dirt hit hard, filling up the grave. The flowers she had picked, however, brightened up his resting place.

Suddenly Elkin spotted a rabbit and chased it into a nearby thicket. He reappeared with the fat, limp, white body in his jaws and laid it carefully at Dina's feet.

"Good boy. A sacrifice in the name of Grandfather, a feast of rabbit stew." She patted the wolf's head, flung the rabbit over her shoulder, and walked slowly with Gregory back to his old pick-up truck.

"My goodness. The tires have all been slashed," he hollered.

Dina bent down to inspect the damage. Long slits had been cut into each white wall. Then Elkin began sniffing some strange and large footprints that led off into the forest. Dina feared for their very lives, and then she heard a ping. She noticed the dent of a bullet on the truck's cab near her head. Then another bullet grazed her right elbow.

"Take cover! Everyone take cover," the old man said fearfully. He dashed behind a granite, moss-covered rock, and then Dina quickly followed, blood dripping from her wound.

"Stay Elkin!" Dina ordered the wolf. He snuggled up to her and licked the blood off her arm.

More gunfire pierced the silence and ricocheted off the rock.

"How are we going to get out of here? I have no gun with which to protect us," Dina said in despair.

Suddenly Gregory pulled something out from behind his shirt. It was so carefully concealed Dina had not noticed even an outline of the boomerang. Gregory flung it a short distance. Its razor sharp edge cut clean through a thick limb a short distance away. It returned precisely, and the second after he ducked, it landed neatly back into the tree behind his head.

Soon they saw the figure of a tall, thin, dark man with a black goatee run out from behind an oak tree. Once he got closer, the stranger began firing upon them again in madman fashion.

"He'll move in closer yet, and I'm gonna get him."

The old man took aim and waited patiently for the killer to emerge. Then suddenly the tall man lept out from behind the tree. Gregory let go of the boomerang. With perfect timing and aim, the razor sharp edge severed the killer's head, his body falling forward into some shrubs.

Soon the boomerang came back. Gregory ducked, and it settled, once again, into the tree behind his head. He dislodged it and cleaned it off with a leaf. Then Elkin raced out to sniff the dead man.

Sure enough the knife which was used to slit the tires was hanging from the dead man's belt. She recognized him as Rock, the man at Tilver's gift shop and the description of the man Rodney saw near the Empress. She also found the business cards of Brutus and Mr. Duponderon. "He must have killed them too," she sighed. Easily she recalled Rock's presence that night of their disappearance and murder. Dina took his gun and headed for Carlin. Gregory walked slowly beside her. Elkin took the lead, sniffing out the road ahead. The three-mile walk to town left them weary. The closest stop was Gregory's house, and that is where Dina decided to spend the afternoon.

The old man snored soundly from his bed. Dina poured herself a cup of herb tea and then sat at the table and stared out the window. The last minutes of sunlight were shining through a sun catcher, and Elkin slept soundly on the rug by the sink. She then recalled the tragic deaths of her mother and grandmother years ago on the beach. At that time she knew she had all the gems in her possession, just before her kidnapping and the days with Knotty the woodsman. Just before Grandfather found her in the wilderness and took the gems on a long trip to hide them, she knew how good she would feel once again to have them all back.

At 5:30 p.m. Gregory was sleeping so deeply that Dina decided not to disturb him. She left a note telling him she would be at the ship.

Dina and Elkin walked into the sunset, and soon the Empress came into sight. Sentra waved to her. "Where have you been, great auntie? I was just about to arrange a search party."

Dina explained she had only days in which to find The Black Book of the Ghost Ship. It was in the evil Jack Tilver's hands. The gift shop she was in the other day would be their starting point.

Sentra and Olgilvee agreed to keep watch of the ship's booty and Rodney's progress. Then Dina set off with Steven and Elkin.

They had disguised themselves as an old married couple. Dina wore long, white pants and a baggy shirt with a small knife stuck in her front pocket. The black wig and dark makeup made her look eighty years old, and the brown contact lenses hid her light-colored eyes. Steven wore green plaid pants, a black plaid shirt, and suspenders. His hair was colored grey like his skin, and he wore black-rimmed glasses. The little cane he hobbled on was made of wood and ivory. She even colored Elkin's coat with brown paint. Hopefully it would not rain and wash out their disguises.

The next morning before six a.m., they set out into the town of Carlin. The fog had not lifted, and the air was damp. They spotted a small park across from Tilver's gift shop. Steven waited on the park bench while Dina wandered over to the dark building to check out its backside. She found no rear entrance. Then she bought a Carlin newspaper from the curbside stand and shared it with Steven. They sat, watched, and waited for any signs of the demented man.

At seven a.m., Steven walked to a breakfast bar two stores down. For Aunt Dina, he brought back a bisquit filled with cheese, eggs, and sausage. Steven chomped down on a bacon and egg sandwich. Then the wolf stuck his nose into the cool air, sniffing out the goodies. Steven tossed him an egg yolk.

Then Dina noticed a light in the shop at seven forty-five a.m. Soon the building went black again. Since the one-story structure contained no rear entrance, she knew someone had been inside, in the dark. Steven glanced casually over top the sports section.

They waited until eight forty-five a.m. when a tiny hunchbacked woman came limping down the street. Dina quickly recognized her to be the witch she had met in Stardist Town and last seen at The Church at Freedom's Gate on Blackwich Blvd. The reborn hag took out a very large key and opened the front door of the shop. Soon a tiny light shown through the window, and the sign on the door was turned to read 'Open.'

"Let's wait ten more minutes to see if Jack Tilver shows up," Steven said. Dina nodded, and Elkin stood at attention. Time passed, he did not show, and they made their move. Perhaps he was already inside.

The familiar looking shop smelled of rosemary, and the mystical jewelry of silver, brass, and crystal filled the glass counters. A large, white whale bone with pegs hung on the wall as a hat rack. The old woman with the hook nose and beady red eyes spoke curtly. "May I help you?" she asked. Dina felt a shiver down her spine, and she hoped the disguise was convincing.

Suddenly Dina felt someone walk up behind her. She turned quickly. A man grabbed her arm and then her throat. Dina reached for her small knife, but it was flung from her hand. Then she heard Steven moan and saw him grab his head and slump to the floor. A few feet away, she could see Elkin's furry form stretched out on the wooden boards. A single dart protruded from his neck.

Then Dina felt the pinch of a needle. She felt herself go limp.

When Dina awakened, she felt her weight pull at her wrists from the shackles that cut into her pale flesh. The musty basement was crawling with fat, grey rats which scampered beneath her feet. At equal level, eight feet above the muddy floor on the opposite wall, hung Steven, but his eyes were closed. He was still unconscious from the viscious blow to the head. Dina could see a walnut-shaped knot pushing out from his brow. She did not see any sign of Elkin and hoped he was not injured. Then she spied black, furry spiders, with bodies the size of silver dollars, spinning their webs in the corners of the small room. And in the candlelight, dead center, was a barrel-sized black cauldron steaming up and boiling over on the red hot charcoals beneath it. A brown pile of onion skins, carrots, potato peels, and bones stood in one corner where many of the rats were gathered, feasting hungrily on the heap. Dina hoped the rats could not climb the slick, slime-covered wall from which they hung suspended in agony.

It could be hours, days or weeks before anyone would find them. Would they be tortured to death or killed quickly? Dina began to cry for the first time in a while. The salty tears she caught to dampen her parched mouth. What was crawling up her leg? God, it itched something fierce. Dare she look down or just close her eyes and hope it goes away?

She screamed at the pain she felt from something stinging her repeatedly. Then as quickly as it had crawled on, it crawled off. She heard its sticky legs let loose across the wall. She dared glance to the left, and to her horror, she saw one of the giant spiders scurry to its web, blood dripping from its fangs.

Minutes passed, and she realized she had not been poisoned by the insect. Perhaps it just wanted a drink, too. She felt gripped by terror, and then she saw one scamper onto Steven's chest. Within seconds, he opened his eyes and screamed out in agony. The spider was digging its fangs into his right breast. Then it jumped upon his grey-colored face and bit his forehead before scampering off into the darkness. Blood dripped down Steven's eyes as he called out to Dina.

"They've got us now. What are we to do?"

Suddenly the door opened and in walked Jack Tilver. He stood before them, stirring the cauldron, with a black book beneath his armpit. The rats, who had scurried when he entered, huddled in the corners.

"So you chose to snoop and get yourselves into trouble. Is that which you seek really worth your lives?"

Steven spat at him sending a yellow blob of mucous atop his hair.

Tilver quickly flicked the gooey mass off his head. "You dirty fool," he said. Then he flung some hot broth on Dina's young grand nephew.

Steven only winced, too proud to call out. Only now at this time of utter helplessness did Dina realize how strong Steven had become in his great agony. She knew he was planning an escape. He only looked beaten on the outside. "It won't be long before this fine soup is done," Tilver's voice crawled. "Its wonderful aroma is just now steaming upwards, and if you two behave yourselves, I'll let you have some. In the meantime, why don't you both take a nap? Those rats won't eat you. Don't fret."

Jack Tilver left the room, slamming the door behind him, and Dina felt a hatred grow in her like a gnawing hunger. This evil man, whose ancestor slaughtered innocent whales for profit, relative of evil Oliver and his brother Devon, was going to kill her, too. He would murder the entire Darrendon clan if that is what it would take for his kind to step into the vault and walk down the corridor into the universe of eternity. She must release herself from this danger. She shed tears of pain and loneliness until she heard the wimpering of Elkin.

Soon the door opened again after what seemed like hours. Steven had gone in and out of consciousness before her eyes, but now he was fully alert as a small boy walked in with Elkin by his side. "This dog is mine now, you know. Father gave him to me up there." He pointed to the ceiling. "He doesn't know we came down here. He doesn't even know I know this room exists."

The eight-year-old boy brushed his auburn hair out of his pale face and stared at Dina with brown eyes. "Are you a Tilver," she said. Then she hacked a dry, raspy cough.

"Never you mind who I am, lady. I'm telling you this dog is mine now."

"But that dog is not a dog. He's a wolf."

"And if you take that muzzle off, he'll rip your throat out," Steven said. The boy stepped back from Elkin, and his soft brown eyes grew large.

"A wolf? What's his name?"

"Just get the key to unlock these shackles," Steven said. "I'll tell you all about him. I'll even show you how to give him commands so he'll do your bidding."

"Oh come on. You're lying to me."

He led Elkin to the door and then turned once more when Dina spoke. "I know where his sterling silver collar is, boy," she lied.

"It even has the wolf's name on it. You know when he wears that special collar, he can perform amazing feats."

"Think about it," Steven said. "Come back later."

The boy left the room, slamming the door behind him just as Elkin's tail cleared the doorway.

After hours had passed, Dina heard chanting and smelled the piney aroma of rosemary filtering through the scent of stewed vegetables. The tones put Steven to sleep, but Dina stayed awake, watching the spiders spinning their sticky webs.

Soon the old witch entered the room to stir the broth. She set two bowls on the ground and poured a ladle full of soup into each one. Then she pulled out a long key.

"I'll unlock one of you at a time, and if you try to hurt me, those big spiders will attack you at my command."

Dina winced at the thought, and then she called out to Steven, telling him about the spiders. The sound of rats gnawing bones could be heard from the corners.

He acted weak and slightly off balance after the hag brought a ladder and unlocked first one wrist, then one leg, then the other two locks. He quickly climbed down, gobbled up the hot food burning his mouth, and asked for more. The witch also poured him a glass of water. He drank and then watched the small boy walk in quietly, coming in behind the old lady. With his one great push, she fell head first into the boiling pot. Her feet stuck straight up in the air and only kicked once in the cauldron that simmered over.

Steven grabbed the key she had dropped on the ground, resituated the ladder, and unlocked Dina. Her joints were so stiff that she crawled to the door and then stood up. Elkin ran up to her, and she took off his muzzle. Steven wrestled with the boy. "He's my wolf. The old witch was gonna cook him in that pot."

"So that's why you did her in," Steven said, wiping the crusty blood from his grey face.

"I'm gonna get my dad."

"Oh no you're not." Quickly Dina put her hand over the child's mouth, and they went into the hallway. "Which way out?" she asked.

"But we don't want to leave here without The Black Book of the Ghost Ship," Dina said in unison with Steven.

"Son," Steven said. "Where does you father keep his valuables?"

"If you tell us, we'll let you go," Dina said.

"And if I don't?"

"We'll lock you up in that room back there with the spiders and rats," Steven said. He pointed toward the dungeon and winked at Dina.

"Come with me," the boy said nervously.

The boy took them down the hallway to a third door. He opened it and went up the stairway into the gift shop. It was dark, and the clock struck one a.m. as they walked carefully behind the counter.

"His keys are gone," the small boy said with disappointment.

"Keys to what?" Dina asked. She munched on some mints from a small glass dish and gave one to Elkin.

"The safe in old Cranefield's barn. But I've opened it before with this." The boy pulled out a small metal object. "Dad doesn't know I stole Otto's safe opener?"

"Give it to me," Steven said, pulling the object from his hand.

"Perhaps your Dad's at the barn now. Let's go." Dina said. Elkin followed.

They stayed close behind the boy walking up a mile-high, rocky hill and then down into a valley. They traveled another mile until they came to the stream. "We need to follow this creek to the big rock. The barn will be just a half mile over the hill," he said. The boy closed his top button. The night was growing cold, and it was very dark and damp. The small flashlight from the store would have to do, but soon they would be down to matches. They trudged on.

"There it is," the boy said softly, pointing through the darkness to the faded, old barn. Steven pushed the creaky door open. Elkin trotted inside first, just as a tabby cat and two kittens ran out meowing, a rooster chasing them into a nearby pen.

"Why would you want to keep a safe in a hay mow?" Steven asked. He scratched his head through his thick, blond hair.

"That's exactly why. It's a most unusual place," Dina said, closing the door behind her. The boy stood still and stared numbly.

Suddenly the sounds of a car could be heard. Then bright headlights, like two moons, lit up the barn. "Quick. Let's hide in the hay," Steven said.

"Come, Elkin, and be quiet," Dina ordered Then she pushed the little boy forward.

To the upper deck of the barn they climbed. Dina moved bales of hay and stacked them high near the corner where they hid close to a sliding door. "Elkin, stay here," she said. Then they heard the car door slam. The sound of Jack Tilver's voice made Dina shiver, and then the sound of footsteps filled the barn.

"Next time, do a better job, Otto" he growled.

"So you sent the wrong guy. How was Rock to know the old man had a boomerang."

"And he nearly flubbed up the Duponderon-Barkwell murder, too. He thought Dina saw him at the scene of the crime. I'm ready to fire you, Otto." Dina could hear a horse winny, and then the men climbed the steps.

"What's so damn special about this book, boss?"

"The Black Book of the Ghost Ship tells how to outsmart the Spanish ghost ship in the Atlantic. You see, somewhere out there is one more gem. The Darrendons will go to retrieve the jewel, but they'll be killed by the ship of the dead because they won't know how to override its power. It's all right here. Give me the key, will you."

Dina held her hand tightly around the little boy's mouth lest he change his mind and cry out. They heard the closing clicks of the safe and the sounds of footsteps as the men descended. The slamming of the barn door caused the old structure to shudder, its sides heaving in a sardonic laugh.

"I want the red-haired one and her wolf, too, Otto."

Dina winced, and listened to them drive away. She uncovered the boy's mouth but held onto his arm. Quickly they made their way to the safe. The book was hidden not in the hay but in the grain room behind bags of wheat. Steven snapped on the special safe opening device and turned the dial. Four left, two right, and one left he turned it until it clicked. The safe opened easily, and the small flashlight quickly lit up the contents. Dina grabbed the book and put it under her shirt.

"Let's get out of here," she said. Elkin's ear's perked up at a sound coming from beneath a pile of hay. A small animal popped its head up. The short pointed ears and long nose were accentuated by the dark mask around its eyes.

"A raccoon. She must have a nest in here," the little boy said.

Suddenly the wild animal began to growl. It showed its fangs, and then foam dripped from its jaw. "He's rabid. Stay back," Dina warned. Elkin growled at the sick, furry beast approaching them. Its eyes glowed bright red, and then it weaved its aggitated body back and forth. It was slowly backing them into a corner of the grain room where there was no escape.

Dina released the boy and grabbed a pitchfork that was propped up on the wall. Savagely she jabbed at the creature. One prong nearly penetrated its abdomen, scraping along its black and grey coat. Then the creature lept into the air and came down on Steven's leg. He pulled on the back of its neck, trying not to let it sink its sharp fangs into his calf. Then Elkin grabbed ahold of one of its back legs and pulled some fur clean off. The coon let go of Steven and limped off squealing in the doorway. There it sat, all fifty pounds of him, staring at Dina in its agony. Slowly and carefully she poised the pitchfork and crept out to the poor creature. Steven, the boy, and Elkin hung closely by her side, the floorboards creaking with every step.

Then suddenly the floor gave away, and they fell through to the bull pen. Quickly, cattle scattered to the outdoors, bellowing in fear. Dina scrapped the manure from their twisted legs and then helped Steven up. Elkin, too, tried to clean off the goo from his thick coat. The raccoon floated lifeless in the watering trough, foam still oozing from its nostrils.

"Where's the boy?" Dina asked.

"He's run off, probably to get Tilver," Steven said.

The hike back to Carlin was tiring, and the deep night crept up on them like a dark blanket. The beach was calm, and the Empress floated serenely where she had been anchored. Dina's trip was successful, and The Black Book of the Ghost Ship was in her possession.

Olgilvee and Sentra hugged their old friends, and they boarded. Steven, grey-skinned and weary, was glad to lay down and rest after the rough road they had traveled. Elkin joined him. Then Dina carefully tucked away the black book beneath her mattress for later that night.

Rodney had nearly finished repairing the hull, and Olgilvee and Sentra had stocked up on supplies. Sentra even bought new clothes for Dina and some more sunblock. Most importantly, however, she had the object detection device repaired so another jolt with an unexpected rock would be nonexistant.

Dina had seen her young niece daily for three months, and her love for her only grew. The had saved each other's lives on numerous occassions, laughed together, cried together, and enjoyed the intimacies of relationships together. For a deeper meaning than she realized before, they were not only related, they were best friends, too. Sentra was not only Dina's protector but guardian of the ship and its booty. Surely Dina would share with her the contents of the black book.

As for Olgilvee, Dina was madly in love with him. They were man and wife. Over the months she had learned so much more about him. He was calm, yet he had his excitable moments. He would generally let her work out conflicts on her own. He, too, would comfort her with his lovemaking. With him she would share the contents of the black book, for if Sentra was ever killed or disabled, he would help steer the ship. His oceanography knowledge would be of great benefit throughout their adventure, and perhaps he too could walk into eternity with them.

Steven, still grey, was a bit damaged from his ordeal with Amanda. He suffered from nightmares, and he was not as sharp as she had hoped him to be, but within time he would make a full recovery. Because of his kindness and love for her, she trusted Steven with her very life. Tonight she would share the black book and its contents with all the crew. For tomorrow morning, they would set sail out past Jeffrey's Ledge in the deep North Atlantic.

During dinner, Dina pulled The Black Book of the Ghost Ship from her lap. She unzipped its cover and opened it carefully. The pages were slightly yellowed and a bit crisp, but the writing was legible.

'The Ghost Ship cometh,' she remembered Mr. Duponderon saying in his terrified voice. Dina turned to page one and began to read. "The curse of the Spanish Ghost Ship is upon all those who travel the waters of the North Atlantic in search of the gems of eternity. The ship travels by night and makes itself seen only when it senses danger, and then it can dissove into the very water around it only to reappear again in an unexpected spot. Its captain and the crew, all dead men, search for Gretchen, the red-haired daughter, and of course, the jewels the captain bestowed upon her. Pass the ship at midnight during the moons's glow, and your ship will explode into a fiery ball. Look upon the face of one of its crew members, and your flesh shall melt off like liquid wax melts down a burning candlestick. And when you near Sable Island to find the gem, beware the Ghost Ship sending a spirit to swipe your crew. A secret potion will reveal itself on the blank pages of this book when the witch makes her appearance. Proceed with caution, and good luck to all who venture in the Ghost Ship Territory.

Signed, Grandfather. With love to my darling Dina."

The very back page was blank, and she hoped it would soon reveal the secrets it contained. Everyone remained silent and deep in thought. Then they all went to their cabins. In the last second before she fell asleep, while thinking of her beloved Grandfather, Dina felt a tear running down her cheek, dampening her pillow.

CHAPTER FOURTEEN

Dina waved good-bye to Gregory on August 26th, a sunday. He sat on the beach by the rocks and painted on his easel. He tugged on his long, grey beard, waved back, and smiled. She knew she may never see the old guy again, but he seemed to have served his purpose.

"Good-by, Gregory," she hollered. Sentra, having just said her farewells to Rodney, sailed the Empress out to sea. Then Dina went below and locked securely in the safe and in her memory The Black Book of the Ghost Ship. Then she returned up top.

They sailed northeast to Jeffrey's Ledge in the day that held clear and breezy. The barometer was steady at thirty, and all hands were on deck.

While a pod of porpoises dove and played nearby, a flock of gulls swooped over the seas. Elkin watched curiously, and Feather kept her nose to the fishy breeze. Then Dina began thinking about her friend Neptune. The beast had saved their lives twice, and she felt forever indebted to the mammal. If vengeance was his mission by aiding the enemies of the evil pirate, then he would probably follow them through to the end. The signaling device Brutus had given to her was destroyed, and oh how she missed him, but she still had Mr. Duponderon's harmonica. If only she could play the mouth harp.

Quietly she excused herself and went below deck with Elkin and Feather. She put the cold metal to her lips and blew and tried to remember the tune Mr. Duponderon had played. "Lost at sea, my friends and I. Captives of dark tea. We're stuck, oh my, but we're still alive. Save us God on high." She thought it over and played the tune from memory, and Elkin howled along. Very much, she missed the delicate little man. After two renditions, she carefully placed the mouth harp beneath her mattress. Feather jumped off the bed and buried herself deep within an open cupboard, the independent soul.

Soon Dina and Elkin went up on deck, and she exercised with Olgilvee. Stretches were followed by deep knee bends, waist twists, sit ups, and leg lifts. Then they pumped some dumb bells. "Need to keep limber," Olgilvee said.

"Will anyone be afraid of the night?" Sentra asked. She looked out to sea toward Jeffrey's Ledge. Elkin, too, stared intently in the distance.

"As long as there are no ghost ships, I'm not bothered," Steven said. He casually munched a potato chip.

"Not yet, but don't take it lightly. We must heed Mr. Duponderon's warning and take Grandfather's advice. We'll be home one day soon." Dina said. Sentra nodded in agreement.

After several games of gin rummy, Dina sunbathed until she fell asleep. The afternoon passed by, and she woke up to the aroma of steaming lobster. She felt the encrouching evening darkness around her like a black coat. The moon, a waxing gibbous, had a halo of ice crystals around it. The barometer was beginning to fall, and Sentra announced rain early morning before daybreak.

Steven said grace, and then they began to eat on deck, filling themselves with dinner for the vast amounts of energy they needed each new day. "Look out there. See the red glowing light?" Steven alerted. He stared out to the waters in a daze. Elkin paced back and forth.

"Evil is near," Olgilvee said.

"Ah, yes. Don't look at the light, Steven. It's mesmerizing you." Dina turned the young man's grey-colored face away from the ocean. "Sentra, beware! There is a presence at sea," Dina called out. "Stay here, Elkin," she ordered. "Olgilvee, stand watch."

Then she led Steven to the cabin below. She sat him on his bed and brushed his thick, golden hair, and he stared at the wall in silence. Then she turned her back to get him a drink off the nightstand.

Suddenly something grabbed her from behind. It gripped her waist on either side and dug fingernails into her flesh. Dina wanted to scream, but she felt numb with terror. It pushed her face down to the floor and lay on top of her, the smell of rotted teeth pouring into her very nostrils. It pulled on her hair, twisting clumps out of the back of her head. It licked her ears and kissed her neck. Then it growled and moaned and uttered a language unfamiliar to her. She could not move a muscle or speak out for help. It wanted to possess her very being.

"It is you, my red-haired daughter."

Dina fainted in fear. Then she awakened again feeling the weight upon her disappear. She stood up and saw Steven was nowhere to be found. But the creature was on the bed and had his back turned toward Dina. He looked ancient. The sea captain's hat was dripping with green seaweed and kelp. He smelled of fish and salt water, and the flesh of his neck was deeply pitted and mottled bluegreen. His hair was thick and coarse, and he only wore a small, black bikini to cover his manhood.

"Where's Steven? Who are you?" she said. The creature slowly turned toward her. Dina shivered at the sight of The Spaniard who began to speak.

"Below is the garden of undersea beauty where you may be trapped for an eternity. No one would ever save you. Not even I." He rose, dripping flesh off his bones, and he soon disappeared out the cabin door.

Dina heard a long splash when the creature dove into the ocean depths. "Steven. Help me!" she cried out. Her grand nephew reappeared, sprawled out on the bed.

"You called for me, Aunt Dina?" he asked. He uncrossed his large arms and reached out to her.

"You were someone else. A dead man. The sea captain," Dina said. Her voice quaked.

"Nonsense. I've been asleep here all along."

"Quick, Dina," Sentra called from the upper deck. Then Dina raced to her side where she found Elkin pacing nervously.

"See out in the ocean, about three miles away," Olgilvee said, pointing. "A large Spanish galleon is sailing slowly by."

"Those red lights belong to the ghost ship," Sentra said.

"Probably home to the ghoul that just visited me," Dina's voice quivered.

"So that's what dove overboard They know we're here. I hope the creature does not return tonight," Sentra said. The soft glow of lanterns flashed back and forth at sea where the dead walked and waited in their lost world. Soon they all settled into bed hoping for a safe night.

In their cabin, Olgilvee carressed Dina into complete calm. Where evil lurks, life expectancy could be quickly altered she knew. Olgilvee would protect her. Elkin, too, stretched out by their bed.

At four a.m. she awoke to the sound of sobbing coming from Steven's room. Careful not to awaken Olgilvee, she rose to check out the unsuspected noise.

"Come, Elkin." The wolf followed. With flashlight in hand, she carefully opened the cabin door. Suddenly a strong force sucked only her inside. Standing on the bed glaring through steely blue eyes was Amanda, or at least the spirit of Amanda. She kept sobbing and wiping her tears with a dirty towel. Then she sat down on the bed, and Dina sat next to her. Elkin stared intently at the intruder.

"Why do you cry?" Dina asked.

"I'm crying for my soul, for my place in the family."

"For acceptance? For eternity?" Dina asked. She placed her arm around the waist of the creature. "What have you done to Steven?"

"The question is, what has he done to me?"

Suddenly the fiend began to glow a deep red. Then its body slowly turned to liquid, leaving a small puddle on the bed. But it soon dried leaving only a pinkish stain. Instantly Steven appeared, just like before, sprawled out on the bed oblivious to what had just taken place. Then Elkin walked in and sniffed the bedding.

Dina hoped the strange appearances would stop, but she knew they were in the spirit zone of the ghost ship and many phenomena would take place.

Everyone slept in, and Dina was the last to arise to greet the golden sun. The Empress was wet from an early morning shower that had cooled off the earth. The 75 degree weather felt comfortable with the decrease in humidity. Dina had not even heard the rain.

From on deck, far in the distance from where they had just traveled, she could see a sailboat. Throughout the day she and the crew kept an eye on it. The afternoon was quietly but surely closing on evening. The sun hung in the horizon like a large, golden chandelier of the near autumn sky. Sentra and Steven lounged peacefully, and Dina prepared the evening meal. It was one Olgilvee requested of abalone steaks, a favorite of her Grandfather.

She cooked and had a vision. She was in the castle playing with Barney, the beast who had saved her from perishing in the quicksand. She saw a portion of the castle wall move aside to reveal a long hallway. Then Barney disappeared down the corridor, and the wall closed again. Dina felt herself falling into the lake in the castle's backyard. She was floating among the lily pads with giant frogs whose eyes were rubies, emeralds, sapphires, diamonds and topazes. Then Barney rose beneath her and lifted her high above the water on his shoulders. Soon the dream faded, and she awoke. She rubbed her eyes and thought of her castle home in New Foundland. How she missed its immense structure and its subtle hominess. She only hoped the gardner and Big Barney watched over the estate in her absence.

"You cooked a fine dish, my wife," Olgilvee said from the table on deck. He wiped a stream of butter from his stong chin and tossed a tender piece of abalone to Feather.

"Grandfather taught me as a girl. We used to buy abalone at the New Foundland Seafood Market in the small town near our castle. We would ride our bikes down the gravel road, and then up the dirt path into the shop area. Sometimes we would stop and pick the wild flowers in the fields along the way."

"Did you have friends there?" Olgilvee asked.

"There was the creature." Dina pulled her red hair into a bun and put it atop her head under her yellow cap.

"A creature?" Olgilvee said in amazement. He placed a forkful of abalone in his mouth.

"Yes, Big Barney. He saved my life in the swamp when I was a young girl. Then he followed us back to the castle where Grandfather had taken me after the experience with the woodsman, Knotty. Sometime I could feel him watching me."

"You never actually saw him out there?"

"One time I caught him behind an oak tree. 'Grandfather, look,' I screamed. But by then he disappeared, and Grandfather and I were atop our bikes heading back into town."

"This beast, would he ever hurt you?" Olgilvee asked, looking deeply into her eyes.

"He seems to like fire, started one in the castle once. But I doubt he would harm anyone," she said. She held back a thought. "He certainly has the size and strength to be dangerous, but he just seems curious, not deadly."

"He must be very old by now."

"Probably ninety. He never really showed it. No wrinkles. No stiffness of the joints. No grey hair. Well, actually his head is bald, but I can recall his furry back."

Olgilvee finished up the meal, and then Dina served Sentra and Steven. She was glad she shared the fact of Barney's existence with Olgilvee, but she never told him about that one time they met. In the castle when she was searching for the map from Grandfather, the beast had followed her and then chased her. She could not be sure he would not harm her, but she felt protective of him.

It was destiny that she met Barney, for if he had not been there to save her life she would not be able to be on this quest in search of truth, fortune, and the eternal adventures of the Darrendons.

The night was quiet, but in the distance the strange sailboat still meandered. They had reached Jeffrey's Ledge where they threw anchor and cautiously kept a lookout for the stranger. The waxing gibbous moon hung in the starlight, and a slight breeze occasionally caught her hair and gave it a twist. Olgilvee lay on the hammock next to her on deck reading a book of poetry while Sentra and Steven snoozed soundly from below. Dina sipped on a cool glass of lemon-lime concoction, and Elkin chewed on a piece of fish skin. Even Feather was enjoying the night, clawing up her wooden scratch pole.

Then she heard the strange sound. "Hi, hi," she heard the small voice call out. Dina looked around but saw no one. Elkin ran to the side of the boat and barked.

"Olgilvee? Did you hear that?"

"Hear what, my wife?"

"Hi, hi. Hey you." She heard again the strange voice and flipped on her flashlight. "Elkin, shush," Dina said.

"My goodness, who is it?" Olgilvee said as he rose from the hammock.

Fifty feet from the boat, she could see a person's head bobbing up and down inside a black inner tube. The lips were white with salt, and they were cracked and bleeding. The hair was brown with thin crystals caked in it, and the skin was bright red and burned.

"Someone lost at sea, Olgilvee. Let's get him on board," Dina prompted.

The tube came near the boat, and Dina threw out the life vest. Two small hands grabbed onto it while Olgilvee slowly pulled it in. It looked exactly like Mr. Duponderon, the jeweler. In fact, they knew the man was the twin brother who had offered The Black Book of the Ghost Ship to Tilver.

She and Olgilvee lifted the nearly dead man on board, and Dina noticed he had only a right leg. The other appendage was an uneven, naked stump. Elkin licked the salt off the man's skin.

"Oh no. More enemies," the little man said. Then he lost consciousness. Dina noticed that the sailboat that seemed to be on the same course was still insight. Perhaps that boat out there was the poor man's dropoff sight.

"Stay up here, Elkin," Dina said, watching Feather scamper down the hatch.

Then Olgilvee carried the twin below deck where Dina sponged him off with fresh water. He began to moan and say, "drink, drink." Within minutes, Sentra and Steven were in the cabin helping out.

"Mr. Duponderon has risen from the dead?" Steven quipped.

"What happened to his leg?" Sentra asked. She washed the healed but jagged edge of protruding bone with the alcohol soaked sponge.

"He thinks we're his enemies. He thinks we killed his twin," Dina realized. Steven put some petroleum jelly on the little man's parched lips. Then they slowly began to move.

"Don't let the sharks have my leg," he begged. Then he began to shake violently. "I didn't take The Black Book of the Ghost Ship. Help! Help! Someone help me!"

Dina held the man's hand and squeezed it gently. He kept mumbling and trembling but to a lessor degree. "He's been severely traumatized and physically handicapped," Olgilvee said. "I supppose it was Jack Tilver."

"You're right," Dina said. "He went back to the safe in the old barn and found his precious book missing. He assumed Duponderon followed them, and reconfiscated the goods."

"The poor man," Sentra said so sadly.

"Who did this to you? Talk to me," Olgilvee demanded. He applied some aloe to the man's parched, red face.

"Tilver turned on me. I helped him, and he back stabbed me," the pitiful man revealed. "I still see his sails." He pointed out the porthole to the distant boat.

The jeweler's twin lapsed into a deep sleep, and Dina covered him lightly with a sheet. She carefully took out his wallet and noticed the driver's license was missing, but a small business card was folded in half: Duponderon's Jewelry Appraisal, North Square, Dumont, Florida.

"Why, they're both jewelers," she said. She put the card and the wallet on the dresser.

"Looks like we have ourselves another expert," Steven said. "And almost an exact replica of the first one."

At 5:30 a.m. the next day, the little man awakened. Olgilvee had carved him a wooden leg from one of the three remaining table legs. He could easily strap it to his stump. It was hollow, too, like Amanda's, and he had carved the name Mr. Duponderon on the bottom left foot. It sat in his cabin on the chair next to a new outfit of shorts, top, sandals and a wide-brimmed hat.

Dina peeked in and saw the little naked man sit up and rub his eyes. He grabbed the wooden leg and ran his hand upon its smooth surface. He strapped it on, stood up, and tried it out until he felt comfortable with his gate. Then he stopped and looked at himself in the full-length mirror. His body was thin, almost emaciated, and his ribs protruded from his sides on his five foot three inch frame. His right good leg had a three inch scar across its knee covered with thin, brown, curly hair. He lifted his long arms to reveal more soft curls of hair. Then he ran his delicate hands over the wooden leg. Slowly he turned around, twisting to see his backside. His tiny buttocks glistened white with small red patches of a saltwater rash upon them.

Dina could tell he liked his new leg. Quietly she kept peering in from the crack in the door where she saw him pull on his brown shorts and beige T-shirt. He looked at himself closely in the mirror on the dresser. Gently he applied a finger of jelly to his lips and carefully sprayed aloe upon his red face. The wide-brimmed hat he centered upon his head, his straggely hair sticking out from all sides. He frowned, picked up the scissors, took off the hat, and clipped his hair into a short do. Then he put the hat back on, admiring how perfectly it settled above his finely chiseled face.

"Breakfast, Mr. Duponderon?" Dina asked. She pushed the door aside. The startled man sat back on the bed and stared at her with brown eyes as big as small, dark moons.

"You've been spying on me?"

"Come up on deck. We'll chat and watch the sun rise. You know you're lucky to be alive," she said. Then he followed her upstairs.

"Yes, thanks to you. But how long will you keep me this way? Will you do to me what you did to my brother?"

"Your brother's death was at Tilver's command; however, there are strange forces at work here, ones we cannot explain. But thanks to The Black Book of the Ghost Ship we took from Tilver's safe, we shall be able to avoid them or at least deal with them," Dina said.

"So you're the thieves. Can't get my leg back for that one," Mr. Duponderon sounded bitter. Elkin wimpered and licked his elbow.

"Good morning. Please sit with us," Olgilvee said. Dina patted him on the back and seated him at the end of the table between Steven and Sentra.

"Have some warm milk and toast," Sentra said. She pushed the food in front of him, and he began to eat.

"Mr. Duponderon," Steven said. He tapped the little guy on the arm. "Good to see you up and about. You even tried out the new leg Olgilvee made for you." Olgilvee stared and smiled his way.

"You should talk about things that aren't right," the twin said. "Why do you look so grey?"

"It's a condition we've all grown accustom to," Dina said "We believe an herb caused Steven's discoloration."

"Go away. It may be contagious," the little man said fearfully. Dina buttered him a second piece of toast.

"Just relax, jeweler, I won't spit on you." Steven carefully leaned back in his chair.

"Grey face, just call me peg leg," the little man joked. Then he bit into a hard-boiled egg. Soon he began to cry onto the white tablecloth, dabbing the tears with a small napkin.

"Now, now," Olgilvee said, massaging his small shoulder.

"Here, have some more warm milk," Dina said, "then maybe you can tell us the past events that led to our meeting."

Dina gathered everyone to hear the tale. "Okay, Mr. Duponderon, or do you have a first name we may call you," Dina said.

"No. Please. Mr. Duponderon is fine. Now let's get started. After receiving the letter of my brother's business trip, I became suspicious. It wasn't like Jules to leave town so suddenly, especially with an international jewelry convention that week. He was looking forward to the Florida event. I worried terribly having no way to contact him. I even had a bout with an old ulcer due to the stress."

"You poor man," Olgilvee said. Elkin nuzzled his good leg.

Dina held his hand, and he went on. "Of course when I received news from the police, I was devasted. It was as if I knew something bad was going to happen to him."

"He didn't die alone. Brutus, another friend, was with him," Steven said.

"Oh, how comforting," Mr. Duponderon said sarcastically. Then he paused and sipped his warm milk.

"So how did you come to know Tilver?" Sentra asked.

"He contacted me after the police called. We met at a restaurant, and he told me he suspected foul play from the Darrendon clan. He explained to me he might help uncover the family's evil deeds if I could provide him with any information he needed about these waters and the Spanish galleon. It was Jack Tilver who told me where to find the The Black Book of the Ghost Ship." Dina's theory of the Duponderon's involvement was true. "Legend has it that a Spanish galleon haunts these very waters in search of their red-haired daughter and the priceless gems. Tilver says his soothsayer told him the book was buried with your grandfather, a book with secrets to avoid the wrath of the galleon. He said an outsider had to retrieve it or its pages would be blank. Later, after Tilver's instructions, I went to old man Darrendon's grave and dug up The Black Book of the Ghost Ship. Then I presented it to Tilver."

"Yes, at the gift shop," Dina recalled. She ran her fingers through Elkin's grey fur.

"You were completely convinced. Tilver is a slimy devil," Olgilvee said. "To be honest, we did keep your brother hostage for a while, but we were good to him. He provided us with information and appraisals of the jewels we found."

"And in return, we were going to reward him handsomely," Steven said. He munched on a muffin dipped in cream cheese and offered a bit to the little man who angrily pushed it away. Then Sentra took it from Steven and gobbled most of it down, throwing a small piece to Elkin.

"See? I was right. You kidnapped him, and he was killed. How selfish of you. Anyway, not long after the gift shop incident, I was taken by force from a shopping mall. Two big, stinking thugs threw me in the back of a van. I was bound and gagged and beaten about the head. They kept asking me what I did with that book, but of course, I had no answer for them. The next thing I knew, I was being dragged onto a boat. They kept saying they were going to track you down at sea. They wouldn't feed me or give me water. Then the horrible act took place."

Dina could feel him tremble, and his hands grew clammy and his voice began to quiver. "They put duct tape on my mouth, bound my hands and feet, and then cut a deep gash in my left leg so blood would drop freely into the water. It was daylight, too, and we were in a secluded cove. Soon the fins began to appear. Slowly they lowered me toward the water when suddenly a huge tiger shark lept up and bit off my left leg. I went numb and blacked out. I still couldn't tell them anything. One of them had poured alcohol over my severed, torn stump and sutured up the vessels so I wouldn't bleed to death. For hours on end they kept me below deck. Finally, on the fourth day after much healing of my leg, having your boat in view, they told me to swim for it. When they put me out to sea in that old inner tube, I was terrified."

"Complete disregard for your life," Olgilvee said. Sentra nodded in agreement.

"They just dumped you overboard?" Steven asked.

"Just like that. In that small tube I sat and floated forever with no water and no food."

"Then you heard us out here near Jeffrey's Ledge?" Dina asked.

"Thank goodness. I was about to perish in that salt water," the little man said. Dina hugged him, and he began to sob. "I miss him so much. For God's sake, it's like losing a part of myself. We dressed the same growing up, shared similar mannerisms, thought alike, and sometimes we'd say the exact same word at the exact same time. Tell me, why is all this so important to you?"

"It concerns our destiny. We're in a battle for an eternal existence in the universe," Dina said proudly. Elkin howled.

"My God that's complex," the little man said. Then he took one last sip of warm milk, closed his eyes, and put his head down on the table to sleep. Olgilvee patted his back, and Sentra went to the helm.

An hour passed in which Dina discussed plans with the crew to count the little man in. "He'll be useful to us. You'll see. He's grieving right now, but he'll get over it in time." Soon the man awakened "Shall we include you?" Dina asked Mr. Duponderon. Then he sat up.

"For what?"

"You keep your mouth shut, help us appraise the one last jewel we find, and we'll reward you greatly for your loyalty," Olgilvee said.

"Ah yes, the jewels," My Duponderon said.

"The Spanish galleon's booty, to be exact. We have one more gem to find," Dina said, feeling exhilerated.

Before the jeweler could say more, Dina had everyone form a circle and hold hands. "We are one. Loyal to the death," she said.

CHAPTER FIFTEEN

Mr. Duponderon slept the rest of the day, quietly ate again, and then returned to bed for the night. Dina was sure Mr. Duponderon would sleep until morning. The other crew members, too, retired to their cabins.

Relishing in their time alone, she and Olgilvee lay back on the mattress. He playfully kissed her ruby red lips. "I want you, my wife. You're sweet and ready. Give me some now." Then he grabbed Dina into his arms.

They finished satisfying their desires on the bedroom floor. Then Dina rolled over and spied a fuzzy, black scorpion hiding in the corner. It was the very harmful variety that can eject a neurotoxin. It reminded her of the one she had seen as a child crawling up Devon's arm, and the scorpion he had turned into on a previous night. Quickly she sprayed a deadly poison and watched it curl up and die.

She wondered how close Devon could be on their trail, and she feared for their lives. Tonight they would stay anchored at Jeffrey's Ledge and rest up for the trip out to Sable Island. The weather was calm, and the night was quiet.

But peace would not be theirs tonight. Dina awakened at 11:30 p.m. to feel something sitting on her neck. A part of it tickled her face with small movements, and she drew her hand upon it. The stinger of the killer insect was resting on her chin, and it was drinking from a small puddle of sweat between her breasts. She felt frozen beneath its sticky feet that moved a slight bit. She bolted upward and lept out of bed, throwing the blankets on top of Olgilvee.

"Dear God. What's gotten into you," he cried out.

"Scorpion in the sheets! Get out!" Dina shouted.

Her husband jumped out of bed, and they heard a crunch. Olgilvee accidently stomped on it and hollered and ran toward the bathroom.

Dina flicked on the lights and spotted smashed hair, guts, and a tail on the floor. Then Elkin pawed at the door, and she let him in. She reclosed the door tightly.

"Stay back, boy," she ordered the wolf upon noticing the scorpion still moved its head. She picked up the insect and flushed it down the commode. Luckily Olgilvee was not stung, but Dina began to worry if more scorpions would appear.

"Come to my arms, wife. The rest of the crew is unaffected. Listen to the silence." Dina allowed him to cradle her, and she began to grow calm. But a steady low sound became distinguishable, and it soon grew into growls.

"I hear something, and I don't think it's human," Dina whispered "Hear the growling sounds?"

"Yes, and it's not Elkin. He's right here," Olgilvee said, pointing to the end of the bed. "To the door, boy."

The wolf stood by the entrance where the growling grew nearer and more intense. Even Feather's hair stood on end as she sat in the far corner. Soon the pine smell of rosemary filled the air, and something stood just outside their door. "Quiet, boy. Stay," Olgilvee said. Elkin obeyed.

Then a hand reached underneath the door, gripping it and pushing inward. Dina could clearly see its long, bony, hairless fingers as pale as the milk she had drank last morning. And every vein on them pulsated with the rhythm of her very own heart beat.

She did notice something especially peculiar. This creepy hand had no thumb.

Quickly Olgilvee shoved a two-by-four board from the bed frame between the door and the casing. The entry could now only budge one-fourth of an inch, but it was enough to let the putrid stench of rotting monster flesh jab at them like tiny knives. Soon the fingers gripped so hard at the wooden door that finger impressions were made.

Suddenly the growling stopped, and the creature began to sniff. Then Elkin howled, sending it shuffling down the hall. Dina could hear it climb the steps to the upper deck. "It's the midnight hour," Olgilvee said, glancing at his watch.

"Yes," Dina said. "Pass the ship at midnight during the moon's glow and your ship will explode into a fiery ball. Danger is here."

Carefully they removed the two-by-four board, opened the door, and followed the sounds with Elkin sniffing out the way. Dina could see Sentra, Steven, and Mr. Duponderon sleeping soundly in their respective rooms as they passed by.

Once on deck, they saw Amanda in the darkness, facing the North Atlantic. Her brown hair was straggly and long, and her arms, drenched with seaweed, hung at her sides. Out in the distance, Dina could clearly see through the blackness the red lights of the ghost ship.

"She's come for us," Olgilvee said. Then white swords of lightning slashed at the night sky. Suddenly the creature of Amanda turned toward Dina, penetrating her with its steely grey eyes. She even held out a hand to Dina, one with four fingers.

"Come with me, Auntie. They wait for you, for us. You'll see."

"Elkin, stay," Olgilvee said. The wolf obeyed.

Then a white-haired creature, its face hidden behind its hair, walked out of the darkness, its creepy hands visible. Dina saw its four fingers on the right hand resembled the ones that appeared from under their cabin door. Soon Amanda began walking toward them, the white-haired creature in tow.

"Get them," Olgilvee ordered. Immediately Elkin lept up and gouged a piece of rotten flesh from the white-haired one's abdomen. Seawater poured out of it, and then it dove overboard along with the injured spirit of Amanda. A glow appeared to skim across the top of the water until the wretched beasts made contact with the ship. Then the red lights disappeared, and the ghost ship vanished.

"Thank God the dark clouds covered the waxing gibbous moon," Dina said. The night stood silent and unseeing.

Quickly Dina gathered up her cat, Feather, who had run up on deck to catch a glimpse of the creatures. Then along with Elkin, they went downstairs to the kitchen and lit a candle. "Sentra, Steven, and Mr. Duponderon are still sleeping quietly in their bunks," Olgilvee said. "They were not disturbed."

"Good," Dina said. They snacked on tuna crackers, and Olgilvee drank a shot of vodka.

"One sure way to settle my nerves while we stay awake a while longer in case we get another visitor," he said. Then he grabbed the candle. "And that book of yours may come in handy again." They walked to their cabin, secured Elkin and Feather in their room, and crawled into bed.

Soon their room brightened from the once hidden moon glow that seeped in through the porthole. Dina cringed and again recalled what The Black Book of the Ghost Ship said. "Pass the ship at midnight during the moon's glow, and your ship will explode into a fiery ball." But midnight had passed, at least for tonight. She looked at the clock, which read 12:30 a.m.

"Perhaps the night is ours now, Dina." Olgilvee gazed into her eyes. "Have I ever told you how much I adore you, my wife? You are what keeps me sane in all this madness. Forever I shall cherish our union."

He reached down and grabbed her hand and raised it to his thick lips. Gently he kissed each finger and then turned her hand over to run his thick tongue over the palm. Dina felt desire rise inside her. He took another shot of vodka and stared at her longingly.

"Tell me, Olgilvee, of your experiences. Ever spy such unusual seabound creatures like the one in today's encounter?" Dina asked. Olgilvee slowly sat up in bed.

"The creatures tonight were evil. Of the creatures in the sea, I have known only magnificent varieties of specimens programmed in the nature God gave them. Our loving God that is."

Suddenly the candle blew out, and a wiff of wax, mixed with the scent of smoke, filled the air. Then the moon's glow disappeared from their porthole.

"Who goes there?" Dina asked. Then she grabbed her dive knife. Olgilvee felt the table for matches and relit the candle.

"Evil revisits us, wife," he said. He pointed at two red, glowing eyes that stared back at them from the corner of the room. Elkin snarled.

"Down boy," Dina commanded.

"It's not human," Olgilvee said. Suddenly Dina raised her knife and threw it. A fierce groaning and moaning sound was heard, and the creature hit the floor.

Dina flipped on the light switch in the corner, but the room remained only candle lit. Whatever it was had a face covered with bristly, long, white hair, and the ears were pointed and hot. Two tiny red, beady eyes stared into space, and the nose was merely a hole in its face. The mouth was small with protruding sharp teeth, and it smelled like rotted fish. Elkin sniffed the corpse and winced.

Dina felt the creature's body and noticed the flesh was rippled and dry. She pushed it to the side with her foot and withdrew the dive knife from its chest. The red, sticky fluid left a puddle on the floor and a gooey mess on her blade. Then she felt the creature's hands. She pulled his arm over his body, and he, too, had no thumb. "Shh! There may be more where he came from," Dina said. "Our flashlight is not in here." She quietly reclosed the cabinet door.

"Come on," Olgilvee said. She quickly grabbed the candle. Elkin darted ahead of her out the door.

They crept out into the hallway just as another beady-eyed beast was dragging Mr. Duponderon up the steps. The little man's eyes were closed, and he was not putting up any struggle for his captors.

"Let's wait until he gets him upstairs," Dina whispered. "Stay here, Elkin."

Then she left Olgilvee in their cabin and went to check on Sentra and Steven. At Sentra's cabin door she heard the moaning of pained emotions. Two of the white-haired creatures were having their way with the young woman. One was beneath her, and one was above her, but she seemed to be drugged and submitting completely to their bad manners. Steven was present; however, he was not awake. They began to pant and sweat until they finished being rude. Then they pulled Steven from the room away from Sentra who lay in a pool of perspiration.

"Quick, Olgilvee. We've got to get up on deck. We're outnumbered down here," Dina said. "You too, Elkin." Olgilvee walked up the steps behind them to the outside.

The partial moon was shining on them at 3 a.m. when the intruders attempted to make an escape with their human cargo. They had a smaller boat tied to the Empress, and they were loading Mr. Duponderon and Steven onto it. Dina could even see three more of them in the boat. Then the creatures quickly tied the men and put duct tape on their mouths.

Dina, Olgilvee, and Elkin hid on deck behind the table and watched the intruders busily transporting Sentra to their boat.

"How can we stop them?" Dina asked Olgilvee. She tried to restrain Elkin.

"I don't know. Maybe we should let them go only to sneak up on them later."

"Are they men from the ghost ship?" Dina asked.

"Perhaps," Olgilvee said.

Dina looked out to sea, but saw no red lights. The ship had not made another appearance since Amanda's visit; however, she knew they were in dangerous territory. "Maybe Devon summoned even the inhuman," Dina said. "Looks like our trip to Sable Island will be postponed momentarily. We must keep advancing toward our goal."

"You're right," Olgilvee agreed. "Let's find out where these creatures' trail will lead us."

"It may be a trap," Dina warned.

"Maybe they believe their friend killed us," Olgilvee continued. Dina shivered in the night's warm air.

"And what did you do with the creature's corpse?"

"When you went to check on Sentra and Steven, I covered the dead body with the old cot. Put a big bedspread over it. They'll never see him. I was fast, wife. Now let's grab our spear guns, some drink and food, and get on our way."

"Yes," Dina said, "and of course, I'll hide the four gems in my leather pouch. Can't leave them behind, you know. The Book of Eternity and The Black Book of the Ghost Ship I'll strap to my back."

The waxing gibbous moon lit the night in which the boat with the ghoulish kidnappers and three human prizes sailed away. The Empress, now disanchored from Jeffrey's Ledge, floated softly in the small ripples of the water. The tide was high, and no stones protruded from the waters that washed slowly over the bird's empty perches. Dina sailed the boat, with Elkin and Olgilvee by her side.

Not far ahead, Dina could see a land mass surrounded by water on all sides.

"A small island I never knew existed," Olgilvee said in amazement. They watched from an angle the white-haired creatures that carried the three prisoners onto the small beach. One tall one tied the boat to a large oak tree and carried some supplies from it.

Then Dina heard sounds coming from the thick underbrush of the jungle, and she saw hundreds of monkeys flying through the air.

"The Kolobus simians," Olgilvee cried out. Quickly they anchored the Empress behind a large rock. "The island is full of them."

"What's a Kolobus?" Dina said.

"They're usually found in equatorial Africa in the ripe vegetation of the rain forests. If this island wouldn't be so overgrown, I'd say it would be impossible for them to survive here."

"How do you know about this species?" Dina asked. She rapidly armed herself.

"While exploring the oceans around Africa, I met a man, a zoologist, who was doing a study on the social behavior of the Kolobus monkeys. Some Africans were killing them for their silky fur coats and selling them abroad. He was trying to find a way to help the species avoid extinction."

Dina quickly secured Feather below deck, and Olgilvee threw anchor. Then he helped Dina off the boat, and Elkin lept onto shore. They stood silent behind an eight-foot high rock.

"Where did the name Kolobus originate?" Dina whispered to Olgilvee. Fiddler crabs meandered at their sandy feet and then scurried into awaiting holes.

"It's Greek for stunted. You see, the Kolobus monkeys have no thumbs." Dina felt a creepy chill overcome her as she remembered the four-fingered hands of the white-haired intruders. Then, of course, Amanda's hands, too, were now devoid of thumbs. Dina grew very quiet, and the slight breeze caught her red hair. She thought of the once soft, five-fingered hands of her grand niece.

"I know what you're thinking, my wife. I also noticed that digit missing on those creatures."

"But Amanda, too. What could it all mean?"

"It means we've stumbled upon some kind of part human, part Kolobus monkey tribe. Maybe these white-haired creatures are warriors for the Ghost Ship. Perhaps Amanda has just taken on their characteristics."

"Yes. Maybe they're all dead or alien beings."

"Shh. Someone's coming." Olgilvee slipped his hand over Dina's mouth as he spoke, and she could hear the sound of large feet crushing foilage in the woods.

"I know I saw a boat near the beach. Find the people and bring them to me." The gruff voice trailed off in the distance, and Dina could feel Olgilvee tremble.

"Come on," he said. "Let's track down our crew, Elkin." The wolf began to sniff the broken branches, and led them deep into the jungle. For late August, it seemed unusually warm, but how else could it be so thick and lush with food for creatures suited to another continent. How strange it all seemed.

"Sunrise will be here in one hour," Olgilvee said, looking at his waterproof watch.

"Look out!" Dina yelled. A jungle spider the size of a muskmelon jumped at Olgilvee. He fell backwards and became entangled in its web. Its fangs dug into his backpack, and Dina stabbed it in the stomach with her dive knife. Its juice dripped on the ground, and it curled up its legs around its body into a tiny ball.

Then Dina heard and saw the fluffy monkeys with thick plumes for tails playing overhead.

"I think I smell a campfire." Dina smoothed down her hair which had nearly been pulled out by a low-hanging limb.

Hiding behind trees, they spotted the clearing ahead. It was surrounded by gibbering simians, and there in the center sat Sentra, Steven, and Mr. Duponderon alit by a small flaming campfire.

"They're alive," Dina said relieved. Elkin wagged his tail, and they listened carefully to the white-haired creatures

"You have friends out there on the water, no?" The tall white-haired creature pulled Sentra to a standing position and slapped her violently across the face.

"No. No more friends. Only us," she said. A small stream of blood dropped from a cut on her forehead. She swipped it off with her finger.

"Come on, woman. Maybe the others who were with you still live. They'll come looking for you, won't they?"

Sentra was pushed back down, and then the short, white-haired creature spoke. "Our tribe cohabitates with the dead. We search for the gems to eternity, but the Ghost Ship kills many of our men. We search for The Black Book of the Ghost Ship to help us in our quest. Do you have such a book?"

"No. Don't know what you're talking about," Steven said. The short white-haired creature swatted Steven across the cheek with an oak branch, and the young man grabbed his face and winced in pain. His thick, blond hair fell forward and covered his damp face when he recoiled in humiliation.

"See? They're not one with the men of the Spanish galleon." Olgilvee said. He picked a tooth with a sliver of wood. "But do they congregate with Devon?"

"And, again, what about their missing thumbs?" Dina asked. "The creatures and Amanda have no thumbs."

"Transformation, perhaps? So much deception. We must be careful, for we're in a supernatural time zone of sorts." Elkin sat quietly and listened.

The Kolobus monkeys busied themselves eating green leaves, and the white-haired creatures gathered to talk. "My guess is that the white-haired ones are evolutionized Kolobus monkeys." Dina nodded her head in agreement, and they kept watching and saw their women talking in a group.

Soon the white-haired woman creatures brought food into the clearing. They put some meat and vegetables onto long pointed sticks and held them over the campfire. Within minutes, the crisp hot treats were served to the weary prisoners. They stared off while eating. Then they drank from hollow gourds a red concoction that dripped off their chins like blood. Elkin sniffed the air and licked his lips.

Soon the tall, white-haired creature brought out hand-woven blankets. Then Dina saw him bind the three prisoners and place a blanket upon each one of their sand encrusted bodies. Olgilvee looked at his watch. "That's odd. The sun should have risen one-half hour ago."

"Must be the land of night," Dina said. She looked out at the moon still glowing like a yellow cat's eye of doom.

"Put the blond one in my tent tonight," the tall white-haired creature ordered. He rubbed his swollen groin. Then quickly the short white-haired one forced Sentra off into the distance.

Soon the monkeys ran off into the jungle to sleep, and Dina began to worry deeply about Sentra's safety and what other animals they may run into in the next hours.

Crawling beneath a large bush, Dina and Olgilvee slipped off to sleep while Elkin stood guard. Suddenly Dina was jolted awake by a splash of wet liquid on her face. She wiped it off, looked up, and saw a giant red-plummed bird sitting on the limb. Then she heard the sound of an aircraft above Olgilvee's snoring.

"Olgilvee, I hear a plane."

"Could it be friend or foe?" he mumbled. Then he sat up, and Elkin began to pace nervously.

"And look!" Dina noticed. "They've moved Steven and Mr. Duponderon."

She did not know what became of the two, but sometime in the hours they slept, Steven and Mr. Duponderon had disappeared. She clutched at her leather belt with the gems, and the books were still intact on her back. She pondered how to save their friends. Then Dina insisted on freeing them alone and told Olgilvee and Elkin to wait quietly in the foilage. "One can be quiet," she said.

Carefully she snuck to the area with the tents and peaked inside one. Sentra, bound, lay silent and naked on the dirt floor while tiny beetles crawled across her body. The tall, white-haired creature was on his back sleeping next to her on a straw mattress, his four-fingered hands folded neatly across his chest. A stack of banana peels lay in a pile near his head. The long tail of the Kolobus monkeyman stretched out from behind him across the bed.

Dina took a stick and poked Sentra. Soon she woke up and opened her eyes. "It's me. Don't move. I'm going to get you out of here. Just listen."

Suddenly the tall, white-haired one rolled over away from them. His long tail humped up toward the ceiling, and he continued to sleep deeply.

"Our sailboat is down by the beach, hidden behind a rock about two miles from here. I want you to quietly crawl over to me. I'll clip the rope on your wrists and ankles, and we'll run into the woods."

Sentra was in pain, and her body was bruised from the rough hands of the white-haired one. She was soaked with perspiration, and her golden hair was tangled and stuck with twigs, bark, bugs, and sand. She slowly moved herself toward the opening in the tent. Then Dina, dive knife in hand, slit quickly throught the two-inch thick rope around Sentra's red, chaffed wrists and ankles.

Suddenly the white-haired creature rolled over again onto his other side facing Dina and her grand niece. His nose was covered with strips of dark fur all the way to the tip of it, where fluid was oozing outward. The nasal veins stood out like bold stripes.

"Hurry! That one looks sick," Dina said. Then the young woman crawled into the night. Soon they found Steven and Mr. Duponderon who both called out to them from behind a rock near the remains of the smoldering campfire. In a distant clearing, Dina spied a small plane overcome by Kolobus tribesman.

"Quick. Let's flee while they're distracted by the invader," she said pointing to the airplane.

They all took off in one fleeting motion. "Ouch," Mr. Duponderon hollered. Sharp leaves of the sandpaper plant cut into his flesh, but they kept scampering through the jungle. Soon Dina could hear the awakening calls of the Kolobus monkeys. Their presence had disturbed their sleep.

"Dina, Sentra," Olgivee hollered. Then Elkin took off running to greet them. But Dina tripped over a knotty tree trunk that blocked the path with its wooden leg. She wanted to scream out in pain, but she bit down on a branch instead. Her right ankle was sickly twisted to the left.

Sentra and Steven dragged her off into some dense underbrush after they heard the sound of limbs crunching rapidly in the distance. "It has suddenly grown quiet," Mr. Duponderon said. Olgilvee wrapped a hanky tightly around Dina's ankle. Then she broke the silence, wincing in pain.

"But listen. Now I hear the sound of water," Dina mumbled.

"Yes," Steven agreed. "And we must cross the barrier so the white-haired creatures lose our scent." Dina put her arm around Olgilvee's shoulders and grasped a tree limb cane beneath her right armpit. They trudged onward into the water, Elkin by Dina's side.

The stream was twelve-feet wide, and several alligators, like cement sidewalks, meandered on top of the water. Olgilvee rushed into the four-foot depths and cracked each reptile on the head. Quickly the alligators swam away, and soon Dina felt herself on dry land again.

"Let's hurry downstream," Sentra said anxiously. "I hear the commotion coming from the other side of the water." Dina grabbed at her leather belt knowing the books, too, were safe in the waterproof compartment on her back.

According to Olgilvee's watch, it should be noon, but the world remained lit only by the golden glow of the moon whenever a dark cloud blew off it. "Where are we?" Mr. Duponderon cried out No one had an answer.

Suddenly past feelings came back to haunt Dina, and she recalled the time in her youth when she was lost in the wooded swamp. Terror and extreme loneliness had gripped her then, but it was not quit so bad this time. Olgilvee and company were with her, suffering too. With sprained ankle, she knew she was slowing them down, but the pain was relieved some by the crutch. They found the old path they had traveled which quickly led them to the big rocks on the beach, but the boat was gone.

"How are we to find the Empress?" Dina said. She fell into a crumpled heap on the ground, and Elkin gently nuzzled her neck.

"We could always swim," Steven said. He gently stroked her ankle. "Or hijack that plane back there."

"You can be quite a jokester at times, young man." Dina said, standing up again.

"Look at these," Olgilvee said. He pointed to a pair of adult footprints. Elkin ran over, sniffed the indentions, and took off. Then they followed the wolf to an unknown direction in the dim light of the moon's glow.

"I'm over here," a familiar voice called out.

Soon they spotted a thick head of black hair, and Dina called out to their orange-eyed saviour.

"Joddar. What are you doing here?" Olgilvee asked. Elkin lapped at the alien's hand.

"I arrived here today by flight in one of Devon's aircraft I stole," Joddar said. "As soon as I landed here, I took cover. Then the plane was disabled by the Kolobus monkey men."

"So you were the pilot of that plane we saw." Dina hobbled over closer with the help of her crutch and Steven. Mr. Duponderon and Sentra looked in awe at the creature huddled inside a large palm leaf. On his left ear he had three silver hoops in the lobes, but the right ear was missing, and only a small hole pierced his head.

"Giant spider got my ear, but that's all," he said. He rubbed the bare spot with his hand and smiled, his golden teeth lighting up the night far more than the moon's glow.

"Where are we, Joddar? Why hasn't daylight come?" Dina asked. She stroked her friends's arm.

"Never daylight here. This is a shipping station invisible to all who don't know how to get past the dimensions of the space warp, but you sailed right into it. The time to enter this area must coincide with the tide's phase of the moon. Being in an exact time and place brought you here. I flew in to check on the progress of their launch. I hope to temporarily disable the rocket. Devon had this secret place charted on the map on his plane. Thought it might be on your route back home."

"Good thinking. Devon and his clan congregate in areas where the gems are located. You see, our last gem is on Sable Island very near this location. By the way, who are the white-haired people with no thumbs?" Dina asked.

"The monkeymen," Steven piped in. Mr. Duponderon folded his arms and stared curiously.

"The Kolobus tribe of this island is a weak and nearly extinct species of part humans," Joddar explained. "They work separate from Devon, but they too search for the gems to eternity. Sometimes they use the dead to assist them. A channel from the core of the earth, a gateway into the heavens, is located in this area."

"I know where you're talking about," Sentra said. "When we were in the tunnels under the sea, I believe Devon had several channels from the core outward."

"Yes," Joddar said. "And this will be one exit point out. But Devon needs the gem's energy source to carve through to the last barrier to the super pretroleum supply at the earth's core."

"This fuel will be used to get the craft to their destiny, to travel into another universe?" Dina asked.

"Yes," Joddar answered. "He will also give some super petro to the masters of Andromeda X Galaxy and also present them with the five gems of eternity."

"What then? A planetary position of sorts will be awarded?" Olgilvee said. He drew his thick fingers through his grey, dirty hair.

"Yes, my friend. He will become an evil ruler. We must be sure he doesn't get his hands on the gems, again," Joddar said in a serious tone. Dina pulled her hand to her leather belt, which was hidden beneath her blouse.

"They're safe. Don't worry," she assured him. Elkin wagged his tail.

Then Joddar stood up, rising six feet tall. "Come. Let's see how far they've advanced to lift off," he said. They traveled down a sandy path and then up a very steep hill. The brush became thick as briar, but they trudged onward. Then Elkin rushed off into the woods following a scent and returned shortly.

Dina could hear the sound of the Kolobus monkeys calling out from miles above. The tall trees were their playground where they swung from limb to limb, using their four fingers like hooks. Sometimes they would fall thirty feet onto another limb. One very acrobatic Kolobus simian turned in mid air after it spied an especially appetizing green branch.

Finally, after two hours of sweat and pain, Dina and the troop managed to get to the top of the hill. A gigantic opening resembling a gaping mouth greeted them. "This will be the point of exit for Devon's craft," Joddar said. He pointed down into the miles below them.

"How much farther do they have to go to get to their fuel source?" Olgilvee asked.

"I don't know. But they are nearing the end and the tunnels go miles deep," Joddar replied earnestly. "I want to remove their engine power transformer. Unfortunately, it will be a temporary delay only, I'm afraid."

"Better than no delay at all," Steven said. Mr. Duponderon nodded in agreement.

Suddenly Dina heard tree limbs crack and break under the weight of large, heavy feet. "The Kolobus tribe is approaching. We'd better take cover," she said with a chill in her voice.

Soon the white heads of the tribe encircled them, and the only way out was into the huge hole in the center of the island. "No volcanic activity here lately," Olgilvee said. He patted Dina's arm on their approach to the stairway. Elkin growled and pranced and then jetted ahead of them into the opening.

The stone steps were four-feet wide by four-feet long. "No pockets of magma for miles from this opening," Joddar said. "The further we descend, the warmer the temperature will be. The pressure will increase the melting point of magma."

Dina saw skeletons chained to the walls with spears still stuck in their bones. Then some rather large, white rats with eyes of purple scampered by her. But she kept climbing downward, the pain minimal because the crutch relieved the pressure on the ankle. Elkin stayed by her side.

Mr. Duponderon was being a good sport. He looked pale and thin, but he kept on with the rest of them. "Water please," he said weakly. Olgilvee handed him his canteen, a small, green, plastic pocket model.

"You ought to be glad I don't have vodka in there," Olgilvee said. He gently pulled it away from the jeweler's small, fine hands, water dripping from his lips.

"You're so much like your brother," Steven said. He patted the fragile man gently on the back.

"Now, Steven," Sentra said, "they both have fine, distinct and unique qualities, dead or alive."

"I agree. But tell me. Will your family soon miss you?" Steven asked. The little man coughed and then blew his nose on a corner of his shirt.

"Of course. I have a wife and son. But there are no signs of a search party."

"Don't fret," Steven said. "This place does not exist in present earth time, remember?"

"I don't even hear the Kolobus tribesmen in pursuit," Dina said.

"Maybe they took another route," Sentra said.

"Yes," Dina said. "It looks like there is a steep stair encasement on the other side."

"We must be careful in here," Dina said. She eyed the rocks that surrounded them. "We must take cover, for the Kolobus Tribe may sneak up on us."

The group descended into the air that grew hot and thick, and Dina's body was drenched in perspiration. She longed for a bath, but more than anything, she was getting hungry.

Suddenly a fat, pure white, four-legged herd of cattle-like creatures walked out of a rock chamber. They were eating a green substance that was growing out of the wall. "Stay, Elkin," Dina said. The wolf growled at the beasts.

Then Dina talked softly and walked up to them, but they scattered. Next, Steven bravely took a taste of the green mossy grass the cattle were eating from the walls. "Great stuff," he said. Joddar urged them all to sample the lettuce-like plant filled with protein.

"Sh! The Kolobus monkey men are coming," Sentra warned, peeking from behind a corner.

Suddenly one of the white-haired enemies snuck up behind Mr. Duponderon and tried to strangle him. Steven quickly slit his throat, and the jeweler ran.

"Quick. Let's be gone," Joddar said. He led the group down more steps and into another level. They were exhausted.

Soon the grating sounds of large machines could be heard chipping and breaking rock in the distance. More voices grew louder. "We must hide," Dina said. Elkin grew tense and began to wimper.

They entered a chamber, and Joddar climbed the wall and heaved himself onto a ledge. "Quick. Up here we hide," he said. Dina and the others followed close behind. She left her cane, feeling confident her ankle had healed sufficiently. But she was weary and knew they would have to travel even deeper into the exit point to find out how close to take off was Devon and his crew. Perhaps they would soon find his rocket, disable it, and then double back and find the Empress to set them free.

Upon the ledge, hidden back in the rocks she beheld magnificent webbed hammocks and a spider's lair. In a small tunnel she could see the eight-legged creature breathing and staring at them with its tremendous eyes. "Stay," she called to Elkin.

Voices and machinery grew louder, and they scrambled for cover. "We are in danger at both ends. Yow! Help me," Joddar screamed. He attempted to roll a heavy rock grate over the nest opening. Steven and Olgilvee pushed hard, too, until the opening was covered, and the giant spider was their prisoner. The great beast shuffled and screeched and then became tranquil and comfortable with the nest of babies she had with her. Soon the voices were right outside their chamber where they hid.

"Go ahead. Lay down," Joddar whispered. He stripped down and jumped onto one of the giant beds the hammock spider had woven. Steven quickly tried one out, too.

"Hopefully, we won't be found in here," Steven said. "When the sounds out there die down, we'll run for it."

"Good idea," Sentra said. She crawled into a blue hammock that hung low on the ledge.

"They aren't sticky to human flesh," she continued. Then she began swinging it back and forth like a cradle and singing to Mr. Duponderon who took refuge in one next to her own.

Dina snuggled up to Olgilvee in their blue hammock near the ceiling. Elkin lay quietly beneath them. No one would find them here she knew, and she drifted off. She awakened again to hear Kolobus Tribesmen rustling below, hunting and searching for them. She patted her leather belt and felt safe and secure with her booty of gems and books. Would the Empress be anchored near by when they returned up above? She placed her hand on her belt and prayed for their safety.

Then she thought of their arch enemy who had plans to use the gem's power source to get to the center of the earth for capture of the super petro. Their enemies' flight depended on the precious fuel. She could not allow the evil one to get control. Suddenly she heard strange grunting sounds coming from the sleeping ledge above.

"Come on. Let's go," shouted Joddar. The giant spider began pushing on the barricade to her home. Dina jumped up, and Elkin stood at attention.

Soon everyone was off the ledge and on the ground below. Then the spider heaved itself into the grate, pushing it over. Next, the huge beast crawled out suddenly. "Hurry! Or we'll be her breakfast," Joddar warned.

They climbed down the stone steps traveling deeper into the volcano.

"Sh! I hear in the distance the running of machinery," Olgilvee said. Even Elkin began growling and sniffing. Then Dina smelled the scent of fresh blood from the ground where tufts of long, white hair and pieces of flesh lay.

"Someone or something has ambushed the Kolobus Tribe," she said. She poised her dive knife while she approached the next corner.

"Ah, a bloody corpse," Sentra yelled.

Elkin ran up and sniffed the dead body of an elder Kolobus monkey man. Patches of his hair had been ripped out and his eyeballs were taken. Grotesquely, a one-inch hole in his chest was still seeping blood.

"They aren't more than an hour dead," Steven said, touching the blood with his fingertips. Quickly he grabbed up a spear.

"Maybe we should back track," Olgilvee said. Dina grew tense and began to feel vulnerable.

Suddenly they heard the footsteps of many men coming from above.

"What now?" Dina cried out.

CHAPTER SIXTEEN

"Here." Joddar pointed to a small dark opening. "Let's take this other tunnel upward."

Quickly they walked into the shaft and ascended, Mr. Duponderon trailing behind. Then they heard male voices. "Catch them, now! You forgot to close off the secret escape tunnel!"

"Look out, Dina," Olgilvee warned.

Then she felt four knobby fingers jab into her waist from a tall, thin Kolobus tribesman who gripped her firmly. "Hold it," he said. The other three held spears on the group. "Hand over the gems, or I'll sever you in two." Elkin growled loudly and then backed off when one thrust his spear at his face.

"You have no right to order us around," Steven shouted angrily.

"That's right," Sentra said, shaking a fist at them.

Then Dina began to tremble at the grey piercing eyes of her captor that penetrated her very soul. Mr. Duponderon placed a thin hand on her shoulder, and she spoke. "Devon's soldiers are coming in behind us," she said. "If we don't get out of here and disable the rocket, if we don't get up to the earth's surface in time, we'll all perish. Please here my truth." The tall, thin tribesman stepped aside and consulted with his monkey men. Angry voices rose forth. Then the voices quieted down, and the leader spoke again.

"But you'll owe us a future favor."

"Fine. Let's go," Dina said, grabbing Sentra's arm.

"Then we shall band as one. Come to the rocket room," the tall, thin tribesman said, flinging his white hair behind him. "We'll cut through the Titan cavern."

Dina knew the rocket was near when Olgilvee pointed out on the floor, titanium, a light-weight alloy often used in construction of space craft.

The entrance was narrower than the actual corridor, and Dina and Elkin squeezed in ahead of their group. Soon Joddar caught up to her, and the Kolobus tribesmen scurried onward. The shiny walls glistened with green flourescent beetles the size of large limes.

"Don't worry, Dina, those are edible," Joddar said. He grabbed one while passing and plopped it in his mouth. Then Joddar bounded ahead on his super-powered legs that took him past even the fastest of monkey men. The steps kept rising, and the air became less heavy. Dina could see Joddar's head bobbing up in the distance.

Soon they arrived at a platform, and for a moment, the group stopped, and a Kolobus tribesman cried out. "Let's listen for our enemies."

Quiet as sleeping children they were, and they heard what sounded like hundreds of men running through the tunnel.

"We haven't much time," Joddar said. He brushed his hand through his black and grey steaked hair. His orange eyes glowed like that of a cat in the darkest of night.

Suddenly a soldier walked out of a small opening that lay left of Joddar. He aimed his gun at Joddar's head, but Joddar was quicker and kicked out the man's entire chest with one punch of his foot. Blood and flesh flew into everyones's faces, and the soldier crumpled to the floor. Elkin ran up and sniffed the remains.

"There's the rocket room," Dina said. She caught up to the group, never losing sight or sound of her alien friend. "We must thwart their efforts to prepare the ship for travel."

"I need to disable it," Joddar said. Sentra nodded in agreement.

"But there must be many more of Devon's soldiers in there. We're outnumbered. If need be, though, we could just climb up the shaft steps, straight up and out of the top of the earth," Olgilvee said. "Do you all remember seeing the steep stair encasement from the gradually decling rock steps we were on?"

"Yes," Mr. Duponderon answered. Steven patted him on the back. "Dina pointed those stairs out when we were first descending."

"Even you will have the endurance to climb that flight," Steven said. He brushed the dirt from his blond hair and off his grey-toned flesh.

"Open her up," Sentra ordered a white-haired one. Elkin stared intently at the monkey man.

Then the Kolobus tribesman, one of twelve, slowly opened the heavy door to the rocket room. He pulled down the guard, slitting his throat, and then two more soldiers approached. Elkin darted inside snarling. Next, Joddar quickly kicked the two men to death with rapid thrusts of his feet.

Then they rounded a rock partition, and Dina could see the rocket made from titanium. It stood pointed, like an arrow, toward the heavens, and its tail fins were painted bright red. It also had numerous windows along the length of its sleek body. Steven ran his hand on the smooth sides, and Sentra flicked it with a fingernail.

"So Devon wants to blast off," Steven said.

"Seems sturdy enough," Sentra said.

"In such a magnificent structure," Mr. Duponderon said. He stared in amazement.

"Yes," Joddar agreed. He pulled a clipboard out from a wall pocket. "Flight schedules for take off. This day, Volcano One is scheduled for lift off in four hours. But of course, they have more than one rocket. The New Foundland Two take off is not yet scheduled."

"Devon and his followers congregate in my own backyard," Dina said, her voice trembling. Elkin nuzzled her hand.

"Let's try to disable this one for now," Joddar said. He tossed the clipboard to the ground.

"Let's hope he doesn't resort to using dianid for a power source. The world doesn't need any more disease," Olgilvee said in disgust. Mr. Dupondern nodded in agreement.

"You're right. I need to remove the engine power transformer now and smash its receiver. If they don't have another one, nothing will get that craft into flight. Come on, people," Joddar said. He motioned the tribesmen up the straight ladder. "You don't want to get trapped. Go on ahead. I'll catch up to you later. Remember, don't look down."

Behind the rocket, a few feet away, stood an eight-foot by eight-foot window. At least fifty soldiers stood and stared out with angry scowls at the intruders. Then the window was empty.

From the ladder, Dina saw Joddar enter the rocket and hurtle a soldier out from inside. Blood streamed forth from his slit throat. Soon Joddar ran out with a metal box in his hand. Swiftly he flung it to the ground shattering it into pieces.

"Hurry, Joddar," Dina shouted. Elkin barked nervously.

"It will only take them a few more minutes to emerge out from that observance sight," Olgilvee said. They looked down from the ladder.

Then Joddar ran in and up ahead of Dina, and she, too, started climbing straight up the inside of the dormant volcano beside Elkin. They were next in line behind twelve tribesmen and Joddar. Olgilvee, Mr. Duponderon, Sentra, and Steven brought up the rear.

Quickly they became enclosed in a rock tunnel. Dina felt safer because the bullets of the soldiers could not penetrate them through the walls, and they could not shoot up from below or down from above and kill them either. For even though the steps rose straight up, once inside the tunnel, they twisted and turned.

After climbing for what seemed like an hour, Dina felt her healed ankle ache. Her steps grew slower until the pain disappeared. Joddar was ten feet ahead of her, and she and Elkin tried desperately to catch up to him. Olgilvee came close to her and touched her gently to keep her spirits up. Steven and Sentra kept close to Mr. Duponderon.

Suddenly she heard a Kolobus tribesman holler out and crash down into the rocky and jagged sides of the tunnel. He brushed past Dina hurtling to the ground below, bumping into the unexpected turns and crushing his skull.

"Must have lost his grip," Olgilvee said sadly, breaking the silence. "Hold tight, Dina, lest that be you next time."

After hours of non-stop climbing, Dina saw a night sky up ahead. She heard the cheers of the eleven remaining Kolobus tribesmen and saw them jump on the green earth.

Dina had previously wondered what they would do to them once they reached the top, but in exhaustion, the Kolobus tribesmen collapsed and fell asleep. So did she fall into slumber in the darkness, sensing her group near her.

Soon she felt long tears of rain drain down her checks, awakening her. Then she looked around, and Elkin lapped at her toes and began chewing on one as if it were its toy.

"Hey, friend," Dina said. She pulled her leg up to her chest. But soon she noticed everyone else was still in a deep sleep within the shadows. Was it day or night she did not know. The rain kept falling, and the light never poked its arms out from behind the clouds.

Then she heard voices, and she shut her eyes and faked being asleep. Elkin, too, played opossum.

"We need to round up our human cargo for reprocessing. Do it while they're still out," Devon said. Dina felt someone put a foot on her chest and press down. "Save this one for my quarters. I have a bone to pick with her."

Dina could hear them walk away into the brush. She quickly felt the buckle of her leather belt which was secure. The secret pack, still strapped to her back, was cleverly hiding the books it contained.

She could hear Devon's soldiers in the distance fast approaching to take their human prisoners. Elkin lapped at the faces of their comrades, and Dina spoke. "We must escape to the Empress."

Soon the wolf had awakened their groggy group from the deep sleep. "Gas from the tunnel," Olgilvee said. "We're lucky to be alive." He shook his head and rubbed his eyes. Joddar awakened quickly and bolted upright. His orange eyes were the deepest shade Dina had ever seen them. They looked like two fireballs.

"We must find the Empress, Joddar. Run ahead and explore quickly. We'll catch up later," Dina said.

The black-haired alien dashed off into the distance. Then Steven and Sentra dragged Mr. Duponderon over to Dina. "He won't come to. He has a strong pulse, but he just won't wake up," Sentra said. She tickled his neck with a blade of grass. He did not respond.

"See his skin tone," Dina said, sounding concerned. "He looks grey, an even deeper shade than your own skin, Steven, since your interaction with the morrow herb at the oldest inn."

"Contagious, you think?" Steven said.

"Oh no," said Olgilvee, alarmed. "Let's hope not."

"Let's go. I'll carry him," Steven said. He flung the little man over his shoulder. "Hurry, soldiers are nearing."

Dina glanced at the sleeping bodies of the eleven Kolobus tribesmen and bade farewell. Their hands were curled up in hook fashion just like the little monkeys in the trees, and their white, silky hair flowed freely over the grass. She knew they had a need for help, and they banded together in that tunnel when the monkey men could have slaughtered them all. Why did they need the gems? Was their purpose to avoid eminent extinction? Were the lives of these few tribesmen worth another chance? Should they leave them here to be captured? You owe us a future favor, she remembered the leader tell her.

They soon approached the ledge of the volcano's top, and before they ran down the steep slope, Dina threw a lava rock clunking the tall, thin Kolobus tribesman on his white head. In seconds, he stood up and shouted leader-like to his friends to fight just as Devon's soldiers began to close in on the group.

Dina could see them in battle, in blood that flowed like a river, where soldiers fell wounded or dead. The Kolobus tribesmen were soon in the trees with thousands of monkeys who came in from the forests to help them defeat Devon's soldiers. "Come quietly. I've found the vessel," Joddar said. He bounded toward the beach. Elkin raced after him, and the rest of the group hurried forward.

The Empress floated easily in the ocean, its anchor holding it firmly to the shoreline. The sun suddenly reappeared, and they sailed away into the North Atlantic, but Joddar was not with them, for he had once again disappeared.

Soon Dina could see the heads of the Kolobus tribesmen, and they held their spears, shook them, and pranced a mighty dance. Then the island vanished.

Mr. Duponderon was not doing too well, but he was slowly gaining consciousness. Steven mopped the little man's brow with a cool cloth and put drops of water on his parched lips. Every once in a while he would moan in agony.

Steven, himself in the limbo of morrow herb sickness, felt an understanding for the delicate jeweler and saddened for the death of his twin. So much grief the man beared in such a short time. Dina also knew Steven felt a haunting sorrow for his sister, Amanda, and she wondered how long it would be before they ran into her again. Maybe she was with the Ghost Ship she thought, and she looked out the porthole into the brilliance of the day.

It was September, 1st, Saturday. They were safe out to sea, and Dina knew she could relax once again. Devon and his soldiers, for the time being, we're locked away on that island, fighting it out with the Kolobus Tribe, but Devon would be back for them she was certain.

Below deck, she quickly placed the two books and four gems in the ship's safe. Feather pushed open the cabin door, and Dina lifted the fat grey cat to her face and kissed her softness. She opened a can of tuna and let the hungry feline eat.

Contented with the meal, she bathed herself, licking longingly on the thick grey hairs. Dina watched and then began to fantasize about a feast for themselves of baked stuffed lobsters. She supplied the list of ingredients to Sentra and Olgilvee.

An hour passed in which the food was cooked. "Gin," Dina called out to Olgilvee. She set her cards on the table. Then the smell of the delicious dinner overwhelmed her. "Another hand, please." Elkin barked for her success.

Soon Mr. Duponderon entered the room and adjusted his wooden leg. Steven helped him sit on the bench at the kitchen table. "Nice to have you back," Dina said, feeling elated. She served him a steamy, hot rock lobster.

"My favorite," the little man confided. Then he put a forkful of the food to his lips and blew on it.

"The toxic gases in that tunnel got the best of you. You're fortunate to be alive," Olgilvee poured him a glass of white wine, and he sat down to his own meal.

"I'll pass on the alcohol. I still feel a little lightheaded," he said. He wiped his delicate fingers on the cloth napkin. "By the way, where are we going?"

"Sable Island off of Nova Scotia. About one hundred and ten miles southeast of Cape Canso," Sentra said. He washed down the last tender morsel with water. "Someone must sail the ship," she said. She scampered up to the deck.

"Aye-aye, captain," Olgilvee hollered.

"Why Sable Island? Isn't it a large sand bar?" Mr. Duponderon said.

"Yes. It's where our fifth gem should be found. I'm hoping for a large topaz I saw in my dreams," Dina said. She tapped Mr.

Duponderon on the hand with her fork. "You'll be able to appraise a magnificent, ancient topaz, won't you?"

"You'll never get that stone out of the Graveyard of the Atlantic," Mr. Duponderon said sternly.

"Oh so you know of this area?" Steven asked. He burped quietly.

"Just heard of it through sea tales," Mr. Duponderon answered.

"I know of Sable Island," Olgilvee said. "Visited years ago on an oceanography study program. It's about twenty miles long and a mile wide. It changes form, and at times the wind raises the sand elevations to nearly one hundred feet. It's gradually moving eastward due to the incoming sea on the west and the sand accumulation on the east."

"Is there vegetation?" Dina asked.

"Some grasses and hearty plants, but no trees," Olgilvee said.

"There must be over two hundred sunken ships out there," Mr. Duponderon said. He looked out the porthole, and his eyes filled with fear. "Beware the Ghost Ship cometh at night."

"You sound just like Jules. You're twin kept repeating that same line. Scared the bejebers out of me," Steven said, brushing a hand over his wet lips.

"Some people say the frequent storms and fogs have made the narrow strip of land invisible, but I say the wrecks were caused by the Ghost Ship," Mr. Duponderon said, sounding drowsy. He laid down his fork, stood up, and walked to his bunk. Within minutes, he was sleeping soundly.

"He's still messed up in the head from that toxic gas," Steven said. "He'll come around."

"Inside the Graveyard of the Atlantic, you'll find gem five in a bird's blue beak," Dina said.

"Say what?" Steven said, unbelieving. "A bird is keeper of a topaz?"

"Yes," Dina said. "Must be an ancient ceramic vessel."

"You know where to look?" Steven asked.

"We can't know. We just have to see what turns up. There are quite a few banks where the sand should be high. We'll dig deep."

"Glad you have all the confidence in the world," Steven said. Then he scratched a red patch on his right bicep. Let's hope it's only sunburn Dina thought, and she eyed the sore spot and remembered that morrow herb contamination causes huge draining sores.

"One has to have confidence, Steven, to find success," she said.

Olgilvee served strawberry parfaits topped with whipped cream to Dina and Steven. Then he took one up on deck for Sentra. Suddenly Olgilvee cried out, and Elkin started barking while bounding up the stairs.

"The sea is filled with dolphins," Olgilvee said. "There's a pod of them right here. Come, Dina."

Steven stayed below deck, and Dina raced towards Olgilvee. She watched twenty dolphins jump and play only fifteen feet from the boat. Then she remembered Neptune, the humpback whale who had saved their lives. The beautiful mammal had come to the sound of the king conch Brutus had given to her, but Jules Duponderon found it too would respond to the mournful tune he had played on his harmonica. How she missed the little jeweler and Brutus, but their presence had only enriched the adventure.

She decided to check on Mr. Duponderon in his bunk. Elkin followed. The little man was wide awake, and he was reading his Bible. "Need a bit of inner strength, huh?" Dina asked. She sat down next to him.

"I pray for us all, for tonight, when we reach Sable Island, hell shall break loose."

"But I know the secrets of The Black Book of the Ghost Ship, my man. We shall be triumphant."

Mr. Duponderon's eyes turned bloodshot and his hair looked more bristly than usual. Dina even noticed his skin was slowly turning a more ghastly shade of grey and becoming mottled.

"I can feel it, Dina. There is evil invading this ship at this very moment. Don't you fear for your very soul?"

Suddenly Mr. Duponderon grew cold as ice, and he began to shake furiously. Elkin sniffed his skin and wimpered.

"Steven," Dina called to the kitchen. "Come quickly."

Dina filled the bathtub with warm water, and they carefully submerged the tiny man. His skin was blue, and his heart beat ever so slowly. Where a tear had fallen from his eye, an icicle stood.

"It's in me. The evil is in me," he said. His eyes turned green mint, and his bloodless lips trembled.

Dina pressed some warm water to his mouth, but he shook so violently that it could not drip inwards. He began moaning painful sounds of deep agony, and then with one sudden shout, he fell silent in the water.

Olgilvee left Sentra on deck and ran down and helped Dina place him in the bed covers Steven had opened. She carefully dressed him in pajamas and then wrapped him up tightly in five blankets. "It's nearly 75 degrees in here. This is September 1st by my watch," Steven said.

Dina gasped and looked at the date setting on the ship's clock. The autumnal equinox was only 22 days away. September 23rd was fast approaching.

Dina took Mr. Duponderon's temperature and noticed it had risen slowly from freezing to 95 degrees F. She did not know a body could recover so quickly. "An internal freeze," she said. She touched her own warm skin. "Yes," she said aloud. She looked out the porthole. "The evil is here."

Within an hour, the winds began shifting and were now southeast to northeast. Sentra's frog was perched high upon his rock, and the barometer, at 30.10, began to fall rapidly. The puffy cumulus clouds that had developed vertically now began to grow darker, and the wind swept in, rapidly rising from six knots to fifty-five knots in less than an hour. They were in the midst of a gale, and Dina hoped the Empress would not be shattered into Sable Island.

She went on deck with Elkin where she could see Sentra at the helm. She was wearing her yellow hooded cape which helped shield her face from the stinging rain of the storm.

Suddenly lightning struck the mast of the boat, sending a streak of white through the darkness. The ship rocked in the waves which rose and swelled higher than twenty feet above the Empress. Feather jumped up on deck and ran frantically about, swishing her tail furiously. Acorn-sized pellets knicked Dina's flesh, and she held tight to the cabin railing. Soon Olgilvee was at her side holding on for dear life, and Sentra stuck it out at the helm. Visibility was only five feet to any side, and Dina feared the worst. She could hear Steven cry out from below. "Calm yourself, Mr. Duponderon. It's only a storm. We'll be okay."

"The Ghost Ship cometh," the jeweler hollered. The Empress kept tumbling in the mighty sea.

Suddenly, in the distance, Dina spied two red, glowing lights that seemed to sway back and forth. She could see the glow well when they were riding at the top of a wave. Then the pine scent of rosemary filled the air, and Dina noticed Sentra become stiff and thin as twine.

Slowly she turned from the helm to look dead straight at Dina. Enclosed in the yellow hood was the face of a skeleton. The sockets bulged with red pus-filled eyes that stared through her. Elkin howled at the creature. Feather hissed and arched her back, her hair standing straight up like needles.

"The witch is here," Dina cried out to Olgilvee. He pulled her and Elkin down into the cabin. "Sazran's possessed our Sentra. We must be near Sable Island." Soon Feather trotted downstairs, too.

Elkin lay on the floor curled up near the cupboards of the kitchen. His ears perked up and his eyes enlarged. Dina patted her wolf friend on the head and spoke. "The safe. I must see The Black Book of the Ghost Ship for the secret pages in the back I've never read. It's forbidden until a time such as this."

"When you meet the white witch in her waters in the Graveyard of the Dead, mix the secret potion well," she read from the books crispy yellow, back pages. "One frog leg, one sage leaf, three hairs of an old man, and one-fourth cup of menstrual blood. Mix over hot stove. When it boils, pour into coconut shell and drink it. Everyone of you it will protect from the evil of the sorceress."

Dina began by severing one tiny leg off the barometer frog. Into her boiling pot she plopped it. Then she added a sage leaf from her collection of spices. Next, she quickly plucked three grey hairs from Olgilvee's head. They curled up when they entered the hot water. Last, she squeezed blood from Sentra's tampons, easily producing over a fourth a cup of fluid.

She stirred and waited for it to boil. Suddenly hundreds of tiny, winged insects with glowing, yellow eyes encircled the pot. It sizzled over, producing a frothy, dark liquid which steamed up like acid.

Dina poured it and then sipped slowly from the coconut shell. She spit and choked and felt her whole body grow hot. Olgilvee drank his share, and then he took some to Steven and Mr. Duponderon. They, too, sipped and shuddered at the strength of the concoction.

Then they waited, and the pine scent of rosemary grew strong. "The sorceress uses that herb to sharpen her mind," Dina said. Soon they felt their eyes burn. Then low, deep growls of a creature from the depths of the earth shook their very senses.

Slowly a purple mist filled the bedroom of Mr. Duponderon, and Dina saw goose pimples protrude on her flesh. She held tight to Olgilvee's arm, and then the purple caped creature entered the room. Dina nearly gagged at the odor of rotted meat that replaced the smell of rosemary. "Don't look directly at her eyes lest your flesh melt like hot wax," Dina called out. The bones of the creature creaked and rattled on her walk toward them.

Across the beast's chest was carved the name Sazran. Dina could even see maggot infested lumps of tissue fall onto the floor at her feet, sending forth a tremendous unearthly stench.

"Look at me, bitch," Sazran the witch screamed in a raspy, deep voice. Dina could see her hair grow into long, dark tresses about her body, and soon the bones disappeared under plump, pink, ripe flesh. Even her nails grew on long, slender fingers. "The gems, give them to me. For they belong to Mitch the Magnificent of the high seas."

"You'll never have them, witch," Dina said sternly. "And look, look out to sea. The Ghost Ship waits for thee. The Spanish Captain will crush your bones into powder only to be blown away in the wind." Then the creature reached out and slit Dina's cheek with a long, pointed nail.

"I am your ancestor turned evil," Sazran cried. Then she pushed the cape off her shoulders.

"Lust for these white, ripe pomegranates, my love." The sorceress thrust her naked breasts beneath Olgilvee's nose.

"Don't look her in the eye," Dina cried out.

Her chest heaved in and out with each breath, and the pink nipples stood erect and seeped a white fluid. "Taste the sweet juices of eternal youth," she urged. Then her red pus-filled eyes turned a deep plum. Her breath smelled of sweet nectar, and she drooled saliva out from her pearl white teeth. She stuck out her long, pink tongue and ran it over Olgilvees' lips. Dina saw him shudder.

"Are you not destined to be good again?" Dina asked.

"Not just yet," the witch cackled.

"The Ghost Ship cometh," Mr. Duponderon said fearfully. He broke away from Steven and stumbled up the steps.

"Go after him," Dina ordered Steven. But then shrieks were heard, and death defying cries rattled the cabin.

"Ah, I smell the potion from The Black Book of the Ghost Ship. Damn you," Sazran screeched forth. She suddenly disappeared in a puff of purple smoke. Then the pine smell of rosemary returned and then began to fade. The ship began to rock more fiercely, and they rose to the top of a wave.

"Thank God we drank that brew," Olgilvee said.

"But dare we go up there?" Steven said carefully. "Maybe the brew's effects have worn off."

"You're right. We must be very careful," Dina said.

The moaning and groaning of someone in agony persisited, and Dina grabbed a gun. Quickly she snuck up the steps alone, Elkin growling a low, threatening sound. Carefully she peeked her head above deck, aiming the gun straight ahead. Steven crept up behind her.

There stood a gallows, and Mr. Duponderon was hanging and twisting from the end of a rope. In the distance, she could see the red, swaying lights of the Ghost Ship. She could hear the slow hum of a sea chant. The fiends were here trying to take hold of them, for they wanted not only the gems to eternity, but their very souls.

Soon Mr. Duponderon's neck grew chicken long, and he began to drool excessively. Then the rope broke, and he fell to the deck, his eyes blinking and his hands rubbing his throat. He began to choke and spit, and then when the lights at sea went out, his neck shrunk back to normal size.

"Looks like the secret potion still aids him somewhat after all," Dina said. Then she and Steven pulled Mr. Duponderon back down to his room.

The little jeweler lay in his bunk, staring at nothing and responding to no one. "Is he possessed?" Olgilvee cried out.

"Or possibly brain dead,?" Steven said. He placed some sauve on the rope burns about his chaffed adam's apple. Carefully he also put some sauve on his own red nodule on his right bicep. Dina could see it had swelled up.

"Who sails the ship?" Dina asked.

"It seems to be rocking less. Maybe the storm has passed. Sentra, talk to me now." Soon her grand niece appeared in the cabin. "Thank God you're okay."

"Yes, auntie. Don't fret. I've been keeping us right on course. The gale force winds have died down, and night is upon us. Soon we'll be anchored at Sable Island." Dina knew Sentra knew not of her sudden possession by Sazran. The witch had come and gone using Sentra as a vehicle, the only one who had not sipped the protective brew.

Dina and Olgilvee retired for the evening. She leaned back on the bed and fell asleep in Olgilvee's arms.

The next morning she woke up to the sound of seagulls and called out, but no one answered. She was alone on board, except for Feather. The Empress was anchored, and the gems were locked in the ship's safe. Quickly she slipped on her bikini, visor, and thongs, waved good-bye to the cat, and went exploring. The ocean water felt comforting, and she waded inland. The sun was brushing the yellow sands with its golden tongue, and Dina's toes slipped into the soothing grit. Sea oats swayed in the breeze where thousands of fiddler crabs scuttled about, some poising their pincer in defiance. A vast assortment of sea cucumbers scattered the area, and the water quietly washed in rearranging them. Dina touched a green one with her toe, and it hardened quickly.

She pulled the visor down above her light eyes and could see across the islands width, which measured just one mile. Not a ship was in sight, and for the moment, she seemed to have the place all to herself. "I must find the bird's blue beak," she said aloud. She trudged forward.

But were those Elkin's tracks in the sand? They resembled wolf paw prints, and Dina followed them. She traveled one mile up and down slopes, stopping every few feet to dig into the sand, searching for gem number five. The 70 degree sunlight beat down on her with rapidly increasing intensity, and a blue crab bit her toe. Where were her friends? Maybe they were digging on the other side of the island.

Recalling Oliglvee's description of this place, she was not surprised to find so much vegetation. Green plants grew carpet thick in some spots, and many even beared small, pink flowers. There were, however, no trees to be found.

Approaching a large sand dune, she decided to climb to the top, which rose one hundred feet, and take a look around the length of the island. There, sitting directly north, she spied a hut made of driftwood and thatched with braided plants, but still there was no sight of humans or animals.

She trudged another mile to it and sat down on a bench made from sand. One of their own pitchers stood, full of drinking water, on a small sand table, its sides sweating profusely. She drank. She sat. She waited and watched and studied the structure before her. Then regaining her strength she carefully opened the door to the twenty by thirty-five foot hut. A rather large home for such a small island, she thought and stared in at the empty room.

Whoever built this place had moved out long ago, she knew, spying some cobwebs creeping up the walls. "Hello? Someone must be here. Thank you for the water."

"Ahoy, my friend."

Dina looked up and saw Steven walking over a distant sand peak. "Did you get our note? You were so deeply asleep we didn't want to bother you," he said apologetically.

Soon Olgilvee, Sentra, and Mr. Duponderon walked up, too. Then Elkin pounced over to her.

"You must have swam over here," she said, noticing the smooth sand along the straight beach line.

"Yes. In fact, we caught rides on some sea turtles," Sentra said. She pulled her orange cap down over her eyes and squinted at her.

"Well, what did you discover?" Dina asked.

"No people. Only an empty hut. Island's desolate. No man or beast," Olgilvee said. Then he dove into the water.

Dina stared at the flock of gulls who were lunging into the sea near him for some fish. The gray and white birds held silvery fingers in their mouths, and they settled on land to eat their catch.

Soon Olgilvee returned and lay on the beach next to Dina. She caressed his chest with her hand, Sentra and Steven gathered shells, and Mr. Duponderon floated in the ocean. The day was long and quiet, and soon Dina fell asleep along with Olgilvee and Elkin by her side.

Suddenly Dina felt something poke her back from beneath the sand. "Olgilvee, dig here with me. Come on." They shoveled sand with their hands. Soon Dina pulled out a three-foot-long, white ceramic bird with a blue beak.

"We've got it, everyone. Gem number five, our last one inside this bird," Dina hollered. She held up the topaz for all to see.

Back on board, everyone gathered around the table, and the little jeweler shared his expertise. "Wish Jules was doing this instead of me," he said. His tiny fingers turned the gem over and over. "The flat surface here indicates it was once broken away from a rock cavity. The topaz is formed in the last stages in the crystallizations of igneous rocks. This deep yellow stone is found only in the Trek Mines of Siberia. It is such an unusually deep shade of yellow. I've never seen a forty carot topaz look so perfect." The little man set down his tools and leaned back in his chair. "Valued at two million dollars according to its rarity, age, color, and shape."

Dina gazed at the gem once more before placing it in the ship's safe. "Great," she said. "$8,750,000 in Grandfather's gems. These will bring in enough money to pay the creditors and keep our castle. Thank you, Mr. Duponderon. Your help is appreciated."

"Now to get these valuables back to New Foundland," Olgilvee said.

"And find a jeweler to sell them," Sentra said.

The night arrived quickly, and the crew prepared to set sail. The sky, lit by the full moon, remained clear, and the water was as gentle as a bathtub's.

They decided to dine quickly on the beach while Sentra cleaned the Empress, deck and all, of dirt and debris. Dina carried lanterns onto the sand, aiding the moonlight so Olgilvee could build a campfire. Soon sparks like orange glitter flew up into the night sky to join the constellations. "Who wants to tell a supernatural story?" Steven asked.

"We shouldn't arouse the evil forces within this territory, for tonight is our night of thankfulness," Dina cautioned her friends.

"It's just all in fun," Steven said. He popped open a beer.

"You know The Black Book of the Ghost Ship warns that the ship makes itself seen when it senses danger. Perhaps it will find us threatening," Dina said, sounding optimistic.

"Let's just hope it's too late for them. The last gem is ours. We just need to sail safely back to New Foundland," Steven said.

"But we are actually in the most danger now of losing the five gems all at once to evil," Dina warned.

"Let's pray for peace and protection tonight, now, before we sail. Everyone join hands," Sentra said, appearing from the Empress. The campfire crackled, and they sat down around it and spoke to the creator.

"Oh mighty God on high. Walk with us on our journey. Lead us on the safe path. Guard us from evil. For our friends who've gone before us, take them to the sacred place at the end of the road to the vault to eternity. Protect our loved ones and our booty. Cast a web around the Ship of the Dead. Amen."

A sheet of black, silvery pre-aluminum clouds blew in, suddenly covering the moon and the blanket of stars. They passed the water jug around, and drank, and rejoiced, feeling protected by God's spirit. But out on the distant sands, Dina could see the glow of red balls, two at a time. Slowly night creatures began to encircle the group. From the land and from the water, red eyes dominated ghostly figures of dead men.

The campfire cast an orange light upon the twenty ghouls. Turbans covered their flesh-chipped heads, pieces of skin hung from their bones, and pitted knee caps creaked with each step. Dina covered her nose from the stench of rotted meat that permeated the air. The ghouls had chains which hung heavy from each wrist. They moaned an agonizing noise, and the pain of the shackles at their ankles bit into their very bone. The emotional pain of being undead and searching for something mere mortals have control of was unbearable. They walked in a large circle around Dina and her friends. Soon Mr. Duponderon's eyes glazed over, and he began to moan too. Suddenly he stood up and walked with the ghouls

"Elkin, no!" Dina shouted. The wolf snarled.

"Don't look at them, or they'll take you in," Steven hollered. He reached out and grabbed the jeweler by the arm and drew him back toward the campfire. "Wake up. You're drifting away from us."

Steven slapped the little man across the face, leaving his grey flesh red and swollen. A maniacle laugh echoed from Mr. Duponderon who then cackled and danced around the flames. Then he took off his shoes and walked through the hot coals.

Steven wrestled him to the ground and sat on him, holding him still. The little man grew calm while the ghouls kept walking and emitting their dreadful moans. Silver streaks lit the sky through the aluminum-colored clouds. Then tiny raindrops fell upon the campfire making it smoke upwards to the heavens. Soon the little man began to rise, with Steven sitting atop him. Dina gasped, and Olgilvee tried to hold onto the man's legs, but he kept rising.

"Steven. Jump off of him," Sentra called out. But he seemed oblivious.

Ten, fifteen, then twenty feet into the sky they ascended. The ghouls began to chant, and the rain fell hard like pebbles. Soon Mr. Duponderon and Steven were out of sight, and the night seemed to close in on them.

"The potion weaknened. The spirits have swiped part of our crew. But it will still protect them from being fully possessed. You'll see," Dina assured them.

Suddenly the fire went out, and Dina stood still holding hands with Sentra and Olgilvee. "We'll find them," Dina said. Then Elkin howled at the night sky.

"Look, the creatures are returning to their graves," Sentra said. A long flash of light pierced the sky.

Sand doors lifted up on the island, and the dead men walked into their very own tombs. "Don't call this the Graveyard of the Atlantic for nothing," Olgilvee realized.

"Count on that brew to help Steven and Mr. Duponderon," Sentra said, sighing.

"And pray to God. Let's get back to the ship now before it's too late," Dina said.

Once on board, out in the distance Dina could see red glowing lights swaying back and forth. Slowly they came near. Then a red streak of light shot across the top of the water headed directly for the Empress.

"Quick, Let's get below," Olgilvee ordered. Dina locked the hatch, and Sentra and Olgilvee sat at the kitchen table. Elkin lay on the floor, his ears perked and his fur standing on end.

"Feather, Feather," Dina called to her grey cat but saw nothing. "Are you in here?" She opened the cupboard door and peeked inside with her flashlight. Sure enough, Feather was curled up in a ball in the corner with something sticking out of both ends of its mouth.

A closer look revealed the head and tail of a scorpion. Its long, black hairs poked outward like small, sharp needles. It curled its tail up attempting to sting Feather, but she bit clean through it. Then she lept out of the small space.

Suddenly tiny baby scorpions burst out upon the floor of the cabin. They scampered everywhere around Feather who caught some and munched on the newborn nasties. Dina hollered when she felt a painful stinging sensation on her arm. Then she felt the legs of a scorpion crawl into her thick hair.

"Help me, Olgilvee," she screamed. Then another black one climbed up her leg, and her arm began to feel numb and swell.

"My God, they're coming out of all the cabinets," Sentra said. She violently smashed them with the bottom of a pan.

Then three of the unusually large insects roamed into Elkin's fur and stung him hard. The wolf rolled over on the floor attempting to rid himself of the predators. Soon his muscles began to twitch, and he sneezed. "Look at poor Elkin. Mucus is flowing from his nose," Dina cried out.

"Feather. Help me," Dina screamed. She crawled atop the kitchen table. Soon Olgilvee and Sentra joined her above the scorpions that crawled over the floor, filling it in like pieces to a puzzle.

Then the cat hissed, snarled, and pointed her tail. The insects began to climb on top of each other forming a large pyramid. Next, they began fighting and stinging each other to death. One by one they curled up on the floor until every last scorpion was dead.

The Empress began to shake. "It feels as if we're being pulled out to sea," Sentra said, fear rising in her voice. "The boat is moving forward."

Dina looked out the porthole and saw small, red glowing embers of the campfire disappear in the distance. "This is the stroke of midnight," Olgilvee said. The increasing chill in the air began to grow colder. "Thank God the full moon's glow is still hidden by clouds."

Dina pulled some sweaters out of a chest on the floor, and the ship began to rock and sway in the open seas. "Something has a hold of us," Sentra called out. She lit a rose-colored candle with her shaking hand.

CHAPTER SEVENTEEN

"Can you hear their song," Dina said. She rubbed her ears and listened to the mournful chant echo from outside the hatch. Then the pine smell of rosemary, the fragrant shrubby mint, began to fill the room, and the chant grew in intensity. The sound became so annoying, Elkin howled.

In seconds, the cabin walls, like a chest, moved inward and creaked loudly. Then they moved out until Dina thought its lungs would burst. Next, a voice boomed forth from outside. "Gretchen, the red-haired one. Your father wants you on deck. Wear your jewels to bedazzle the crewmen, for they are about to mutiny. Woman, come to me."

Dina clutched herself, and the walls continued to breathe. "Be careful, Great Aunt," Sentra warned, holding tight to Dina's arm.

"Maybe we could trick them with some of Sentra's costume jewelry," Olgilvee said. He walked to the porthole. "My God. Look at that magnificent ship."

Out in the water, the great Spanish vessel appeared with its ten sails erected fully. A lion stood as the figurehead, its eyes glowing as if it were actually alive. Lanterns hung from the wooden railing all around the ship, and two more shown on either side of the flagstaff.

Tied securely to the mainmast was the naked body of a giant man. He stood three feet above the heads of the ghoulish soldiers. His black hair hung long, like curled ribbons, onto his furry chest which was pierced by the broken bones of his ribs. His throat displayed a deep gash which oozed with a flowing liquid that flamed blood red in the night.

Dina looked closely at a male prisoner shackled on deck, and she saw it was the face of a Darrendon. "Oh no, my great grandfather," she cried out. Tears streamed down her cheeks. "It's him. He was once a pirate who gathered the jewels from Mitch the Magnificent as he hung helplessly on the gallows."

"They are trying to upset you," Olgilvee said. "Stay calm, my wife."

Suddenly Dina shuddered when she saw the ship's captain with the magnificent hands pull out prisoner Darrendon's heart, leaving a gaping hole in his chest. "How disgusting," Dina cried out. Then the captain calmly took a knife and sliced a piece of the organ and ate it in front of the other prisoners who looked on in horror. Then the man's head dropped to one side, and he sank to the deck. The chanting grew louder.

The ship was one hundred and fifty feet long, and it had many gun-ports along its sides. "Come, Gretchen. We need you now to adorn your body with jewels. Only you can bedazzle my crew. Hurry. Our boat is waiting," the captain called out.

"Tell them you'll be there soon," Olgilvee said. "Maybe they'll quiet down for a while so we can have some time to think."

Dina put on her wetsuit, to protect her from the cold waters and donned Sentra's phony gems. She knew Olgilvee was right. "I'm coming," she announced. She would make the thieves think they could have what they wanted. She began singing softly, and Sentra and Olgilvee sat in silence and prayer.

Bravely she climbed the stairs to the deck, clutching her false jewels that hung on a silver strand around her neck. Olgilvee and Sentra bid her farewell, and she opened the hatch.

Quickly she was whisked away in a cloud of vapor. Next she found herself inside a small boat with an unsightly skeleton crew. The bony figures rowed into the night to the Ghost Ship of the dead that came so near she thought she could touch it. Soon the chanting started again. Dina took out a small harmonica and played and sang the sad song of rescue, and the dead men kept rowing.

Then she heard a loud sound, like a jet eingine. The waters began to grow rough as a saw blade, and the salty brew splashed into the boat. Suddenly a whale breached forward, spinning in the air and landing on its back. The fifty tons of body sent a tremendous splash, knocking one bony guard overboard, his hand still clinging ghoulishly to the oar.

"Neptune. Save me from a fate worse then death itself," Dina cried out into the blackness. Soon she could see the fluke with the tell-tale design of her friend. He disappeared into the water until they came even closer to the ancient vessel. More small boats emerged to usher them in, and Neptune came up underneath one and flipped it over quickly.

Dina readied herself for a dip in the cold North Atlantic waters, and she said a prayer. In succession, more boats were overturned, and the skeletons floated like seaweed riding up and down on the waves, their rotted flesh falling off into the deep.

Soon fins appeared, and Dina feared the worst upon seeing a small boat pull up with a knife-wielding sailor. Dina kicked the blade out of his bony fingers and knocked the remaining ghoul out of her boat with her own oar. But the oar went overboard too, along with the other one which had broken off. She was fearfully floating closer and closer to the ghost ship.

Suddenly something grabbed her from behind, and she was quickly pulled into the water. Gasping and choking for air, she felt herself lose consciousness.

Upon waking, she felt small bumps beneath her and a sharp wind sweeping across her body. She opened her eyes and could not move from the air pressure. She was riding on top of Neptune's head, and he was taking her away from the ship. With magnificent speed, they glided, ski-like, on top of the water. Dina, exhausted and nearly in tears, fell asleep.

She had a horrific dream about Steven. He was being held prisoner in a small room made of wood. His hands and feet were shackled, and large red-eyed rats were crawling over him. Some nibbled at his flesh at times causing him to cry out in agony. "Help me," she heard him say. His grey face was swollen and bruised, and his lips were cracked. They bled when he talked. Dina kept hearing her grand nephew cry for help. Suddenly she awoke and ordered Neptune to take her back to the Empress for supplies.

Out at sea, Dina saw the red lights swaying back and forth in the darkness.

"Help me. Please!"

She was certain it was Steven calling out, and she hoped Mr. Duponderon was safe with him. She knew she must rescue them or they would be lost forever. Quietly she crept on board the Empress, and Olgilvee and Sentra helped her pack supplies. Neptune waited.

Wrapping her hair up in a gold bandana, she armed herself with a dive knife, a gun, snacks, and water. Carefully she stepped back onto her whale. Feeling certain she did not want to endanger the rest, she bid farewell alone. "Elkin, sure you want to go?" The wolf lept into her arms, and they slowly traveled upon Neptune in the cold water toward the ship of the dead.

The lantern lights became larger, and the pine smell of rosemary permeated the air when they grew near the ancient vessel. All ten sails were raised, and they barely moved in the small wind. Spying a long, thick rope hanging from the side of the ship, Dina straddled it and climbed up into the vessel. She lowered a large basket over the side which Elkin jumped into, and slowly she pulled him to the top of the boat. "Wait here, Neptune," she said. The whale sank into the ocean depths just enough to stay hidden.

Standing in the bulkhead, she could hear the sound of something licking its lips. She looked to the front of the ship at the figurehead of the lion whose eyes opened and glowed golden in the darkness. His tongue reached out and lapped over its jaw, and saliva drooled down to the sea below. Elkin's ears lay back, and he growled at the beast.

Slipping up over an edge, they stood next to the foremast. The ship was quiet, and no one was in sight. She walked toward the hatch and opened it carefully. A whiff of rosemary escaped from within, and the pine scent drifted into the night sky.

"Help me! Help me!" Dina heard Steven cry out.

At least he was somewhere here she knew, and she climbed down below to the bottom of the ship in the storage bin. Enormous rats scurried across bags of wheat and corn to hide in the shadows. Elkin sniffed at one sack which was moving across the floor. He tore at the burlap, and a three-foot rat emerged and bit him on the end of the nose. Blood oozed out, and Elkin whimpered and rubbed at the wound with his paw. Then the rodent turned on Dina. It rushed at her, tearing into the calf of her right leg. She screamed, drew her dive knife, and gouged it eyes out. Then she pierced its heart, and blood squirted forth. Soon eight baby rats scurried out of the sack and ran into the corner.

Dina spied a small bottle of whisky. She opened it and poured the strong liquid over her wounds. One was so deep, she would need to stitch it. She wrapped an old rag above the deep gouge, and she and Elkin wandered back upstairs to search for the sleeping quarters. She needed a needle and thread badly. She had to keep looking for Steven and Mr. Duponderon.

At the mizzenmast she found another hatch. It led directly to the passenger's quarters. She opened a small wooden door, entered, and sat at a square desk. Carefully she lit the silver lantern and opened the drawer. Elkin eagerly sniffed its contents. Four tiny spools of thread and a needle carved from a whale's tooth were inside. The tiny etchings on the needle led Dina to identify the piece as scrimshaw, the folk art of the whalers. When boredom and lonliness set in, they would use their creative abilities to combat the bad feelings.

Dina poured some more whiskey over the wound on her right calf and winced in pain. "It's okay, boy," she said. Elkin nuzzled her. Then she stitched the gap shut with eight tight pulls of the needle. She wrapped a doily around her lower right leg and tied it with two pieces of cord. Then she raised the whiskey bottle to her lips and took a long, hard swig. It burned all the way down, settling in her stomach like a lead button. She looked around the room and found more scrimshaw including an intricate clock case, fancy corset stays, a cane head made into a serpent, and a jewelry box. A small jacknife and an awl lay on the table by the single, wooden bed.

Dina turned a picture frame around and gasped at the painting of Oliver Tilver and a young, dark-haired woman. She remembered how Tilver had melted into a puddle of goo at the oldest inn in Buzzard Bay. Quickly Dina recalled how Devon's evil brother had been a whaling man using cruel techniques to torture and kill the beasts years ago. Had he not wanted to torture her as a child. No wonder Neptune was so intent on revenge.

"Evil runs in families," she said to Elkin. She recalled it was Mitch the Magnificent, Devon's stepfather, who was the pirate who took the gems from the Spanish and kidnapped Devon's mother, the captain's red-haired daughter. Perhaps the dead Tilver was here on the ship with the ghouls. Devon must have gained knowledge of superpetro from Oliver Tilver, his brother, who had years earlier been hanged for killing the petro king, forcing him before his murder to reveal the secret whereabouts of the fuel. It was an inherited secret she knew, and she patted Elkin who lay at her feet.

Where could Steven and Mr. Duponderon be found she wondered. Dina rose from the desk and sat on the bed. In the nightstand's drawer she found a small jewelry box. Inside were tiny pieces of whalebone carved into beads. One was painted yellow, one blue, one green, one white, and one red. The colorful balls, like her jewels, lay quietly in their secret place. Dina sipped some more whisky and lay back on the down-filled mattress. A musty odor welled up when dust particles, like a powder finish, settled onto her face.

She felt herself drift asleep into a dream perhaps of the person who had once placed their head on the same pillow.

The cedar boat traveled at five knots, and the giant humpback whale swam along the surface of the sea. The dark-haired man named Oliver dove his harpoon deep into the flesh of the whale when they rowed up beside it. In pain the great beast cried out and swam fast with their boat in tow. Blood flowed out from the hole around the harpoon which stuck out from the whale's flank.

Suddenly the beast took a dive, and the rope line was running out fast. Just as it began to pull tight, only seconds before their small boat could yank under, the mammal came toward the surface. When the boat's bow touched the whale, Oliver dove a wide lance into the beast's lungs. However, it did not die quickly but flapped its fluke onto the water several times. Then it rolled over and over, spewing its blood into the water making it a rose-colored soup. Rowing up to it again, Oliver thrust another lance into its side. The whale cried out in agony and jerked in its death struggle.

Although the beast was still alive, it was immobilized. Oliver and his crew tied it to the boat with its tail forward and towed it to the large ship. The greasy chore of butchering the whale made Dina vomit.

While it was still breathing, they cut into it with huge blades and blubber hooks. Slowly it was hoisted into the air where the whale wrenched two times and sighed once again in agony. Thick strips of blubber were pulled off and chopped into large "horse pieces" which were then cut into "bible leaves" for pot boiling.

Dina cringed when she saw them slice off the whale's head and hack up its brains. Even the eyeballs were gouged out and thrown around the ship in a game of toss.

After Dina awakened from her dream, she heard the chant of the dead. Sounds of shuffling feet scuffed from above, and soon Elkin was lapping at her chin, helping her struggle to clear her groggy mind. Where were Steven and Mr. Duponderon? She had to continue searching she knew, and she rose from the bed.

She peaked out the door and saw no one, but the chanting grew louder. Then she heard the sounds of agonizing groans. The hatch she was to climb out of moved and rattled, and she knew that exit was out of the question.

Another stairway led down into the captain's quarters. His cabin included a fireplace, an oak table and chairs, a fancy etched mahogany cabinet, and a double bed with a goose-down mattress. However, Dina could not take here eyes off the portrait above the fireplace. There staring back at her, was the beautiful Gretchen, the captain's daughter. Her head was topped with wavy redness, and her large, green eyes were surrounded by long, dark lashes. The cleft in her chin was deep, and the touch of high cheekbones spoke of elegance.

Suddenly the lantern on the nightstand came on all by itself, and Dina felt a chill in the room. Elkin whimpered in the eeriness. Then faintly she could see the outline of a large, dark man. His tall hat was tipped to one side, and his arms were outstretched. He stood over six feet, and black hair curled up out of his white shirt.

"Gretchen, come to me," he said. Dina saw the spirit walk toward her, and she fled to the far side of the cabin. "Gretchen, let me clasp your necklace for you."

Dina leaned back into the wall and felt a metal hook poke her into the right shoulder blade. She pulled on it and flung open a small door which went to the cannon room. "Help me!" she heard.

She opened a tiny metal hatch and walked into a small dungeon. Elkin sniffed the strangeness of the place and stood close to Dina. Ahead of them, several rooms were situated down one long hallway. Some shackles still had the bones of their victims in their grasp. "Steven?" she called out. Then she walked toward the last barred cell. It was locked.

Thin and gaunt, her grand nephew lay huddled in the corner on the bare, wooden floor. Elkin began to wimper and paw at the bars. Then a large rat scampered out from the cell. "They took us captive, Mr. Duponderon and me. They took him away not more than an hour ago. Upstairs."

Then he started coughing, and Dina reached through the bars and felt his head with the back of her hand. He was burning with fever, his grey skin looked mottled, and red swollen nodules stood out on his arms. Dina picked the lock with a metal pin and walked into the cell. Elkin lapped at his face and tore at his shirt, and Dina gave him a sip of whisky and some cheese crackers. Soon Steven regained his strength.

"We must find the jeweler and get out of here," she said. She helped him rise and led him to the upper deck.

All was quiet. Dina could not even hear the sound of a chant, the scuffling of feet, or the hum of the wind. She pulled Steven toward the mainmast where she spied Mr. Duponderon tied to it. His eyes stared straight ahead at a twenty gallon pot that bubbled and steamed before him. Sharp butcher knives lay on a wooden table along with spices and vegetables. Elkin sniffed the air and moaned.

"The dead don't need to eat," Steven said, putting his fingers to his lips. Soon many ghouls came out from the shadows.

"Stay, Elkin," Dina ordered. The creatures then gathered hands, chanted, and danced in the darkness. Lumps of rotted flesh fell off their bones with each step they took.

Dina could see that Mr. Duponderon was tied securely. There was a rope around his neck, one around his wrists, one around his waist and hips, and one tied his ankles together. She ran her finger along the blade of her dive knife and slowly crept out while the creatures were busy.

"Mr. Duponderon. It's me, Dina. I've come to save you."

"Huh? What? They're going to eat me. They're a bunch of cannibals."

Her knife sliced easily through the ropes. "Neptune is waiting. Follow me."

They snuck quietly to the basket. Just as she began to lower Elkin to the whale's back, one of the creatures came down on Dina's head with a wooden stake. Elkin knocked him over and jumped at his throat. In seconds the wolf ripped off his head. Then more came over, but some of the ghouls just stared off and pointed.

Soon she saw the outline of the captain walking toward them, the man from downstairs. The other creatures made a circle around him as he grew near. "Gretchen. Come to me. Let me put more jewels around your slender, white neck." He grasped her bandana and pulled it off, allowing Dina's red hair to flow freely in waves down her chest. Suddenly Dina tore the false jewels from her neck and threw them at the captain. "These are not stones of the ancients," he roared. "These are not my powerful gems. You are not my Gretchen. Ghouls, kill the intruder," the captain hollered. His face grew red and hot and lit on fire.

"Neptune," Dina hollered. Suddenly the whale surfaced. "Quick. Onto the whale's back," she ordered. She lowered Elkin first, and then Steven and Mr. Duponderon followed.

Just as she was sliding down the rope, someone cut it from above, and she landed with a thud on top of Steven. Spears flew in every direction, and Neptune took them away. Dina could see the red lights from the lanterns swaying back and forth, and she thought she saw the captain waving, but then the ship disappeared. Neptune, their savior once again, deposited them at the Empress and returned to his pod.

The weather was on their side; however, Mr. Duponderon was weary and Steven's rash and nodules concerned Dina. She wished them both a good rest. As the wind was with them, they sailed to Dina's homeland of New Foundland. She missed her castle, the gardens, and the solitude, but mostly she missed the nearness of her heritage. "Let's hope we don't run into any nasty fog or icebergs on our way home," Sentra said, sailing the Empress. "If trouble becomes ours, Joddar or Neptune will rescue us."

"Thank God for them," Dina said. "They've shortened our journey."

"Yes, we're almost home, but first we must stop quickly at the Grand Banks for some fishing," Olgilvee said. "We're about out of food."

"What do you know about the Grand Banks?" Dina said. She pulled Olgilvee's hair just enough so he would say ouch.

"The fishing's fantastic, even though the weather can be quite bad. Won't take us long to catch our dinner. In the 1400s Bristol fisherman used to catch mass quantities of Cod there. By the 16th century the French, Spanish, and Portuguese were going there to fish, too. The beaches of New Foundland would be filled with fisherman driving out their catches. Many of their large fishing schooners measured one hundred and seventy-five feet in length and weighed two hundred tons. They were very sturdy vessels with long strong masts. The only trouble was in the cramped sleeping quarters where crewmembers were merely sardines in a can. I hear it's great fishing the Grand Banks."

Below deck, they all went for lunch. Olgilvee lit the candles which scented the kitchen with vanilla. A sparse meal was served, and it was only one p.m. Their last trek was ahead of them, and they would strengthen their bodies and spirits for the trial to come.

"To our health and future," Dina said. She patted Elkin and Feather brushed up against her legs.

"To a safe and easy sailing," Sentra said. They clicked glasses, and Mr. Duponderon broke into prayer.

"May the soft waters guide us to the land of our destiny. May our lives be spared from the savage seas. May God walk before us, behind us, and to our sides. Amen." Then the jeweler disappeared to his cabin.

"And amen," Steven said again. His grey face stretched into a yawn.

Then Dina played soft classical music on the stereo and casually supped with her comrades. Soon the symphony was interrupted by a weather report. Stormy skies and rough seas were ahead of them, and temperatures were dropping to thirty degrees.

"Prepare for the worst," Olgilvee said. He filled his glass with more wine. "Everyone get out warm stuff: sweaters, jackets, scarves, mittens, earmuffs, and boots," he continued. "We're in for some bone-chilling weather." Sentra then donned warmer clothing and disappeared to the deck.

Later, Dina could feel the need for extra blankets on their bed. She put on the quilt and snuggled close to Olgilvee. The space heater, too, kept the room nice and warm, and they drifted in and out of sleep. Even Feather and Elkin lay on the bed with them, and they sailed in the cold North Atlantic.

"Anyone for hot chocolate," Sentra called out toward the cabins. Carefully she rolled her tray down the hallway. The Steaming mugs of the sweet brew scented the air, and the winds outside blew in the nasty cold spell. Even Sentra had added mittens and a scarf. "It's getting nippy up there," she said. She nudged Olgilvee with her tray.

"What time is it?" Dina asked.

"Three a.m. by my watch," Sentra answered quietly. "I slept only an hour and then manned our course again. We're heading toward the Labrador current. The fog is as thick as a wool blanket. There are warnings all over the radios. My radar picked up a freighter about twenty miles due north." She turned and headed back up to the deck.

"We're definitely in the shipping routes now," Olgilvee said. He sipped the warm brew.

"Winter in September, too," piped up Steven. He stood in their bedroom doorway sipping slowly from his mug.

Suddenly the boat halted, and hot chocolate flew everywhere. Dina could hear Mr. Duponderon holler, and she followed Steven and Olgilvee to his cabin to see what was wrong. Elkin rushed forward barking loudly.

In the glow of her flashlight, the little jeweler lay on the floor with a broken mug handle still in his grasp. Steven began laughing uncomfortably, and Dina and Olgilvee helped Mr. Duponderon to his feet. Then they guided him back to bed. Steven slipped into a deep sleep curled up on the floor.

"We've hit an iceberg," Sentra announced from the deck. Then Dina, Olgilvee, and Elkin ran up to her in the frigid air. Dina gasped at the vision before her in the glow of the wide spotlight. Giant sheets of white-colored ice stretched out highway-like for what seemed like miles.

"Hopefully the wind will veer and open up a channel for us," Olgilvee said. The Empress bobbed back and forth on the cold waters.

Suddenly Dina smelled the pine scent of rosemary, and a thick, purple fog moved into the light. Soon they saw a skeleton cloaked in a long, dark robe. It began to fill in with soft, white flesh. The nails grew long and pointed, and dark hair grew out of the skull. The wind began to howl and blow puffs of snow into the fog.

Sazran the sorceress stood before them on the ice sheet with her arms outstretched. "Elkin," she called. "Come to me."

The wolf perked its ears up, and its white fur stood on end. Before Dina could hold him back, her companion's eyes became glazed, and it lept over the side of the boat onto the frozen water.

"No, Elkin. Come back," Dina shouted to her pet. But the wolf ran across the ice and disappeared behind a group of jagged chunks.

"No. No. Dina, don't go out there," Olgilvee shouted. He and Sentra held tight to her arm, but she had to rescue her lifelong companion from Sazran. The ice was slippery and cold, and she glided twenty feet across the silvery lake. The frigid air nipped at her nose, and she poised her flashlight on the dark corners. Cautiously she followed Elkin's pawprints around a tall boulder. Where there was a gaping hole in the ice, sea otters splashed and played. The water was warmer than the air making steam rise high into the night sky. She touched the water with a naked finger and was surprised at its temperature as warm as the gulf stream.

Then suddenly she heard a whirring sound from the heavens. An oblong spacecraft with glowing purple lights was slowly descending to the top of a giant ice mound at fifty feet above her head. Dina knew the ice was stationary, deeply rooted possibly four hundred feet below.

The red-hot glare from the engines slowly died out, and the craft landed nose up on the glacier. Soon the large door slid open and a tall, black-haired person emerged. Dina immediately recognized Joddar with his three earlobes and orange glowing eyes. Sentra snuck up behind her and startled her so, she shook for a second.

"Look, Sentra. It's Joddar. What on earth is he doing?" Dina asked, approaching their alien friend. "Maybe he can free our Elkin from the clutches of Sazran."

Then she heard the sound of an object emerging from water. The warm center of the glacier bobbed atop it a round dome. To Dina's relief, Elkin ran out from behind a block of ice and stood motionless at the tip of the opening. Then the dome's hood began to rise. Soon cargoes were shuffled from Joddar'spacecraft toward the dome. The men in silver uniforms were careful with the large crates until one tripped on an ice stalagmite. He dropped a crate, flew across the ice, and landed in the steaming water. He shriveled and sank.

"But look," Dina said to Sentra. The crate had been jarred open and out poured several human limbs of various sizes and shapes. They appeared to be in a frozen state. "This is another exchange site for alien body parts, but what's in that barrel being transported from the dome?" Dina asked.

"Some kind of pay probably," Sentra said. Soon Elkin disappeared below the water into a long tubelike structure. "Let's get a closer look at the spacecraft, and beware another appearance by Sazran."

They skated across the ice and up to the rear entrance of the ship. The purple lights were still blinking, and the back door was open.

"Come in, my friends." Dina heard Joddar call out. Then Elkin emerged from the exit end of the tube to greet them. Joddar handed Dina a plate of peculiar looking objects. The gold platter shimmered beneath the unusual treats. "Go on. Try one," Joddar said. He patted Elkin on the head. Then Dina bit a yellow, gooey blob that melted in her mouth. It tasted of lemon and was sweet, but soon after she ate it, her fingernails glowed yellow.

"Vitamin fortified space snacks," Joddar said.

"Why are you here?" Dina asked. She saw soldiers in silver uniforms filing by outside. "Have you turned evil?"

"No. Our band of reprocessed people are fighting the likes of Devon. We live on a planet not far from earth's galaxy. He uses our people for his own gain until we are devoid of substance. His efforts are for his evilness."

"What are you exchanging with the dome?" Sentra asked.

"Defective body parts. We've found a chamber below leading into Devon's underground city. We can't allow him to get to the center of the earth."

"The super petro is there?" Dina asked.

Yes," Joddar continued, "but if he takes too much of it, the earth will die inside. All beings here, all life will be destroyed, and the earth will crumble into rocks. The pebbles of this planet shall hurtle into space like aimless bullets."

"But I thought he needed the power of the gems to get beyond chambers next to the fuel source," Dina said.

"He does, but he can also use another source to give him energy called Dianid," Joddar said. Dina quickly remembered Olgilvee's comments of the fatal substance. "This source will emit toxins, lower immune systems, and further diseases. He strives only to please the high masters. If he gets ahold of those five gems, he will not only use them as a power source, but he wishes to present them to the keepers of the universal authority. He wishes to rule into eternity beyond the realm of the Milky Way."

Dina shuddered and bit into a red tube-like candy.

"Frozen polar bear arteries, my dear," Joddar said.

"Yuck," Sentra said, looking disgusted.

Dina puked up the red stuff which landed in Elkin's grey fur. He gingerly licked up the remains.

"With ineffecient workers partly composed of defective body parts, the process will be stifled," Joddar said. He smiled and combed a hand through his dark hair. "I do have quite a prize out there, however." He pointed to a stairway outside. "Go on up and have a look."

"Elkin, stay," Dina ordered. Then she and Sentra walked around the large spacecraft, climbing the spiral staircase to the enclosed top. Dina looked out one of the small, round windows and gasped at the sight in a large, glass portion of the ice sheet. A purple fog was slowly fading, and Dina could see Sazran the sorceress encased in agony and complete frustration. Her eyes were bulging, and bright red fluid dripped from the corners. Her long hair stood out from her head for three straight inches. On each strand, grinding into her skull, was a tiny spike with barbs on it. Intermittently the barbs poked into her skull and into the very recesses of her brain. From her open, parched, thick lips, yellow drainage slipped forth and ran down her chin, seering tiny holes in her flesh. Her arms at the wrists and her legs at the ankles were shackled to thick wooden posts.

"Sazran the sorceress. They've captured you. Now you can do no harm," cried out Dina. "Maybe now we can straighten you back to being a good member of our family again."

"Found our prisoner I see," Joddar said. Dina jumped two feet into the air, clinking her head on the top of the rocket.

"How did you do it?" Sentra asked Joddar. She rubbed Dina's sore spot which protruded like a small walnut.

"We set a trap. We put out bait she couldn't resist. Look for yourself."

Grey mountains of beasts rolled, meandered, and mated on the sand around her feet. Their gigantic, grey, stubby trunks poked up out of the water in the mote that surrounded the beach. And oh how the sorceress moaned, and her tongue lashed out to lick up the yellow drainage.

"She can't resist eating the flesh of the elephant seal. It's an insatiable craving the witch has," Joddar said. He turned up the sound chamber.

Dina covered her ears from the deafening noise. The beasts moaned, groaned, gurgled, and barked like hyenas. It sounded like a riot when many of the elephant seals went to battle. They smashed chests and attempted to grab the trunks of the other beasts in their jaws. Chunks of flesh flew, and the gnashing of teeth could be heard. One male placed his trunk into his mouth and made the sound of a resonance chamber. The three ton mammals, measuring nearly twenty feet, fell in battle and rolled over on the young, crushing many to death. The squeals were sickening.

"I've seen enough," Dina said. She descended the stairway leaving Sentra behind.

"Sad to see one of your own go down with evil in her blood, Dina. I'll be in the rocket. Stop in if you need me," Joddar said. He stroked Dina's arm and quickly disappeared. Elkin stayed close to Dina's side.

The moon, a waning gibbous, glowed brightly in the night sky upon them as they perched atop a chunk of ice. In the distance, Dina could see the Empress moving slightly back and forth at the edge of the iceberg.

Olgilvee was signaling her with a white flashing light. She knew Sentra, her grand niece, was still in the top of the rocket watching the sorceress. "Come, Elkin."

She glided across the ice on her boots, and Elkin slid hard and heavy on his stomach. Olgilvee was just leaving the Empress when she glided up. "So worried, wife. I see you've found Elkin." The wolf licked his outstretched hand.

"Yes," Dina said. "And Joddar has captured Sazran."

"Good news here, but bad news back at the Empress. We're having a little trouble with Mr. Duponderon."

"What's wrong?"

"Seems he tried to jump overboard. He talks nonsense, and his eyes are glazed. Steven has him tied up below deck."

"Oh no! Does he seem possessed?" Dina asked. She adjusted her scarf.

"He keeps muttering the name of Sazran," Olgilvee said.

"Perhaps Sazran is still able to use sorcery to manipulate Mr. Duponderon to do her bidding," Dina said.

"No doubt, but we have to gather everyone together and hope a channel clears through this ice so we can be on our way to New Foundland," Olgilvee said, patting Elkin.

"Yes, I know. It's crucial we cash the the gems in to pay off the creditors."

"Look out you two!" Sentra unexpectedly called out from behind them. Soon Dina heard a loud cracking sound while water rushed in beneath them and the Empress tripping Olgilvee.

"Quick! The ice is splitting," Dina hollered. Slowly she could see them become separated from their path to the Empress as the huge sheet of ice drifted away. There was finally a good thirty feet to their vessel through bone-chilling waters. "Hold on, Steven and Mr. Duponderon," Dina said. "We'll get back to you." Sentra carefully helped Olgilvee to his feet, and Elkin licked off his wet knees.

They began searching the grounds for a watercraft. Dina, needing help, summoned Joddar from the rocket. He showed them to a tiny building in back where Dina found a rubber raft. In ten minutes, Sentra had it blown to its full capacity. They all climbed in, but soon the stop came out of the plugged hole, and they jetted all around the ice sheet nearly falling into the giant, steaming water hole.

Sentra blew it up again. Then they bid good-bye and safety to Joddar.

"I will be traveling to New Foundland ahead of you," he said, "to try to disable Devon's rocket."

"God be with you," Dina said. Then they floated off toward the Empress. Dina hoped Joddar could do in Devon before he succeeded in his evil project. She prayed a deep prayer, and a net-like fog set in. If it were not for the hazy glow of the moon, they may have steered in the wrong direction.

Soon the raft was crashing into the sheet of ice where fifty feet across stood the Empress, proud but battered. Elkin lept out first, and the others followed.

Quickly Dina found Mr. Duponderon on board and placed a cool damp cloth on his forehead. Then she gently caressed his hand. "He's been like this since two days ago," Steven said, his grey face still flushed with rash. "I'm afraid we may lose him."

"God bless the poor soul," Olgilvee said. Elkin stood by, staring intently.

Then tears began to stream down Steven's cheeks as he came to grips with the nearness to death of his friend. Dina lifted the little jeweler's shirt and found strange, swollen red nodules on his chest. Some broke off in her hand, leaving an open hole in his flesh.

"Just like the ones on your arms," she said. She pulled up Steven's shirt, and he also had several bumps on his chest.

"Yes! I have it, too. I now believe the morrow herb poisoned me at Buzzard Bay, and poor Mr. Duponderon caught it from me," Steven said. Then Dina felt her grand nephew's head for signs of fever. She noticed a slight one and remembered Steven's progressive symptoms through the weeks.

"What makes a person susceptible to this sickness?" Dina asked. "No one else has caught it. I'm not so sure a quarantine is necessary. But we all better be careful of you sick ones. Do you have any other symptoms, Steven?"

"None I'm aware of," he said. He opened a can of beer. "I might end up getting worse like Mr. Duponderon." The little jeweler muttered incoherently, and his glazed eyes stared dead-like. The night grew even more dark and deep after the moon eased in behind a black cloud. The Empress began to rock in the wind that picked up, and the waters grew rough. The ice moved back and forth until a small channel began to emerge.

Soon Sentra sailed the vessel into the new path hoping it would not be crushed by icebergs. Then Dina heard the sound of rocket engines and saw Joddar's craft shoot into space.

"God be with you," she shouted. His light, like a comet's tail, breezed through the dark sky.

Mr. Duponderon's condition gradually grew more severe, but Steven showed no new symptoms of the illness. The nodules were now appearing on the jeweler's face and hands. Even his eyeballs contained the strange growths.

It was when his flesh became back to back with oozing blisters that Dina began to pray over him. The areas of raw meat soon became infected, and the ship's flies fed off of him and laid eggs. Dina spent hours picking the fat maggots from his flesh, and he gazed unknowingly. He became thin and dehydrated, and one night he began to speak. "Jules. I see you. Come hold my hand." The room filled with the faint, pine scent of rosemary, and the little jeweler drifted away forever amid the rainy night.

The next day was bright and cloudless, and Dina held a rite for their dead crew member.

"I don't think any magic potion would have saved him. He wanted to be with his twin," Dina said.

Steven placed his body in a burlap bag along with a concrete block, and they threw him over the side. The icy North Atlantic greeted him warmly, and he sank to the depths of the salty sea. "Go meet your brother," Olgilvee said.

Everyone tipped their goblets of wine, and Dina sprinkled some olive oil into the ocean for good fortune. Steven wept openly.

"Thanks for your expertise, buddy," Steven said sorrowfully. "So sorry it was forced upon you." He threw his glass overboard, and Dina watched Sentra sail down the channel. She was careful to guide the boat and to use and set the sails just so they would not crash into the floating chunks of ice.

In the distance, Dina saw large ships traveling on their routes. She hoped and prayed for clear weather, and she hugged Sentra's grey cat, Feather, "We're heading home. It's been such a long journey. New Foundland, here we come." Elkin sniffed the air and howled at the unknown.

CHAPTER EIGHTEEN

Days passed quickly, and Steven grew healthy again. He and Olgilvee fished often. Then on a Sunday at two a.m. Dina could hear Sentra shouting. "Everyone up now. Fire! Fire!" Out in the ocean, not too far from the Grand Banks, a ten story mass of orange flames rose from the water. The point of one oil tanker stuck straight up in the air and was sinking fast.

"A ship crash. Two oil tankers," Dina said.

"My god, the wall of fire extends all the way to the beach," Olgilvee pointed.

"There's no way through to the castle on High Cliff," Sentra said. "Let's head for the next beach."

"I'm with ya," Steven said.

The receptionist at the Gerten Town Inn was cold as the night itself. Her tall, thin body was topped with a brown bun and decorated with a gaudy, gold bow. Her white blouse was buttoned all the way up, and she looked as if she would die of suffocation at any moment. "Rooms 98 and 99, third floor. Double beds, refrigerator. Check out at 11 a.m.," she whined.

First Sentra and Steven settled into room 98. Then quietly, in room 99, Olgilvee unpacked their overnight bag and settled Elkin onto a blanket in the corner by the door. "We'll be safe for the time being. The evil can wait," he said. Dina checked her gem and book stash.

"Everything is here, thank God," she said. "I only hope Feather will be safe back on the Empress secured in our cabin." She stretched her arms into the air and yawned. "Oh, how a long, hot bath would do me good."

"Me, too," Olgilvee said. Dina was first to climb in. The lavender gel filled the tub with luxurious bubbles, and she lay back resting her head on the blue tile wall. Her red strands of hair fell into the soapy water like a seafan.

"Yes, Olgilvee. Run the sponge down my legs."

Her gray-haired husband took the louffa pad in his big hand, kneeled down next to her, and washed each toe. Then he slid the sponge up her ankles and along her calves. Then he carefully buffed her face, leaving her complexion glowing and smooth as peach skin.

She turned around in the tub, and he took off all of his clothing. Then he slid into the tub to make love to Dina.

Dinner was served late for all of them, each in their own rooms, for a fifty dollar tip. The cook, who lived behind the kitchen, had to get up just for their desires.

The t-bone steaks, baked potatoes, and succatash were delicious. The meat was doused with brown sauce, and the potatoes were drenched in butter and sour cream. Halfway through the meal, they heard chanting, and soon the pine scent of rosemary filled the air.

Elkin began to growl, pant, and whine. Gently, Olgilvee tapped the wolf on the head to calm him. Then he taped The Book of Eternity and The Black Book of the Ghost Ship to Dina's back.

"It's Devon. He's followed us here," Dina said. She lit a small, red candle on the table. "He wants the powerful stones." She pulled up her shirt to check the clasp on her leather belt. The gems were worth at least $8,750,000.

"We need to cash these in, but hopefully it won't be hard to find buyers," Sentra said, entering the room through the adjoining door. "The creditors must be paid within days on the autumnal equinox, September 23rd, or we'll lose our castle home."

"Yes," Dina said. "We should find a jeweler here and sell the gems."

"I'm sure many wealthy people from all over the world will be interested by the magnificence of these perfect stones," Olgilvee said.

"For sure," Steven agreed. He walked into their room and sat down at their table.

"But what about Devon?" Sentra asked Dina.

"We must destroy him. It's only a matter of time before he'll run out of patience and resort to dianid for his power source."

Sentra poured a glass of whisky and drank it down rapidly. "Yes. Perhaps we can beat him at his own game." Steven popped open a beer, its foam sudsing over the side of the can.

Then the chanting grew louder, and their outside door began to shimmy. Soon Dina heard footsteps in the hallway. At first it sounded like one person, but soon the outside seemed crowded with people. Elkin growled a low and threatening sound.

Dina opened the shutter and looked down onto the deserted street. The moon glowed brighty on the Empress which rocked gently at the dock. "I will pray our Feather will stay safe in her heated cabin on board," she said.

"Amen to that," Olgilvee agreed. Dina bowed her head in prayer.

Then in the distance she could see a herd of animals, with heads of bears and bodies of dogs, coming toward the inn. Then the entire building began to shudder, and Dina saw the earth crack open in the center of town. "It's the rocket exit point Joddar learned about in the logbook back at the volcano," she said. Then many stores and homes began to collapse into the gap that grew bigger.

"Devon must be ready to launch," Steven said. "I'll bet Joddar is planning his next move."

"But they need our gems to complete their plans. I hope they don't use dianid," Dina cried "What do we do now?"

The doorknob began to turn, and Dina and Olgilvee pushed a dresser in front of it. Elkin grew increasingly tense, and suddenly their window shattered needles of glass into the carpeting.

The crevice grew until a round hole with a six hundred foot diameter stood in front of them like an open mouth ready to spew forth its contents.

"We're going out this window. It's our only chance for escape," Dina grasped. "We could make it to the Empress in no time."

"But where will we sail? The oil spill is still burning," Sentra warned. They could see flashes of light outside.

"Why don't we leave the boat and jump start a car. We could drive through the back roads. Probably take us an hour," Steven said. "I'll just call the sailing service and give them the address to the castle. They'll tow the Empress, Feather and all, to High Cliff for a decent fee," Steven quickly made the call. The boat delivery would be made in a few hours.

One by one, they shimmied down a sheet rope three stories to the ground below. Before Steven descended, he lowered Elkin. Just then the bedroom door was broken in and the dresser shoved aside. Steven slid so fast down the sheet he had burns on both thighs.

Dina ran through Gerten Town leading the group to a crowded restaurant with a parking lot filled with cars. Steven picked a black sedan rental and jump started it in seconds. They all piled inside.

Dina could see the small town disappear behind them on their drive away. But the large hole stood black and dangerous under the moon's lamp. Then suddenly a car revved up behind them. Dina could see both the brilliant glowing eyes of Devon, the driver, and Jack Tilver sitting next to him. They were pointing guns at them outside their windows.

Steven squeeled around the corner and flew down the winding, country road. The early September snow began to fall again, and the car slid on sheets of ice. The men shot at Dina, grazing the side of her face causing blood to trickle forth.

Suddenly she heard a loud crash and saw the car behind them had slid off the road and slammed into a telephone pole. Liquid was pouring from the broken gas tank.

"Stop, now Steven," Dina ordered.

"Easy now. These roads are slick," Steven said. He gradually slowed up and pulled to the side of the road. Then they all piled out and ran up to see the damage.

"Let me die, bitch, and you'll never see Amanda again," Devon muttered to Dina. Her protective nature for her grand niece overwhelmed her, and soon her immediate wish for Devon's nonexistence slowly faded. Elkin sniffed at the puddle of gas and pawed at the ground. Then Jack Tilver moaned from his passenger's seat, windshield glass splinters sticking from his face.

"You saved me from being tortured when I was a child," she called out. Now she felt his controlling force and pity for his vast evilness. "If we don't get them out, they could burn to death if and when that gas ignites," Dina said.

"Don't want to take any chances losing Amanda forever either," Olgilvee said. Then he placed a hand on Dina's shoulder. "Who knows what these creeps have up their wicked asses."

Quickly they pulled the two men from the crumpled heap of metal. Just as they reached a safe distance, the car burst into flames. Dina put her hand over the gaping wound in Devon's bleeding thigh. Both men were now unconscious, but soon Jack Tilver began to mumble.

"We need the gems, Devon. Time's running out."

"We can't leave them here, and we certainly can't take them into the hopsital. Their mumblings may lead the police to our gems," Sentra said.

Olgilvee and Steven carefully lifted the two men onto blankets in the back seat of the sedan. Then they sped down the road toward Ramea Island, 300 miles away.

Dr. Dory took Olgilvee's wad of one hundred dollar bills and laid his stethoscope on Devon's chest. He checked each man thoroughly and then stitched up Devon's gaping wound. Carefully he set Jack's broken arm and ankle, and then he handed Dina a bottle of antibiotics. "Your two friends here are very fortunate. This one fellow has lost a lot blood. He'll be very weak for a few days, but they should both recover completely as long as infection doesn't set in. Keep the wound clean and dry. They need plenty of fluids, too."

"Thank you, Dr. Dory," Dina said. She shook the small man's pudgy hand and noticed his eyes looked curious behind his thick, black glasses.

Olgilvee and Steven tied up the two groggy men and put them back into the sedan. Then they drove on down the winding country roads, far away from the small town medical clinic at Gerkin's Way.

The moving car lulled Dina to sleep as she slipped into a dream. She was in the castle garden lying in the flower bed.

"We're home," she shouted when she opened her eyes. She exited the car quickly and ran to the front door.

Icicles hung like clear stalagtites from the damp bricks above her head. The sun, just rising, began to melt the ice sticks. Soon a small drop of water hit her forehead and slid down it, splashing the clean and perfectly straight welcome mat at her feet. She looked up at the detailed nine-inch face of the brass door knocker. It stared down at her, and she reached up and gripped the large iron ring in its teeth. It felt familiar, but she did not knock. Instead, she pressed in the tab on the large brass handle, but the heavy, carved wood door would not budge. Quickly, she walked into the snow-caked shrubberies and came out with a silver key. It fit perfectly in the lock, and the door eased open. The smell of burning logs warmly greeted her.

"We're finally here inside the castle," Sentra said. She took the key from Dina's hand and hung it in the hardwood case on the wall. Dina stood on the navy-colored, braided rug, and Elkin walked in quietly and lay at her feet. She saw no signs of Big Barney, but on the small, Parisian console, beneath the circular antique entry mirror, she spied a sheet of white paper. She read it carefully.

Dina,

It's all over the countryside that you're returning home to High Cliff. I've kept the place just as you would have wanted me to. The fireplaces are lit, and food is on the table. I've retired to my quarters for the evening. All was quiet while you were gone.

I'm sure this old place missed you as I know I did.

Dean, the gardner.

They all helped carry the two men upstairs to a back bedroom where they were each placed upon the double bed. Dina left Sentra and Elkin in charge, and Olgilvee bound their prisoners to the frame. Steven offered to serve the food, and Dina returned to her room to dispose of the gems.

She opened the door, and the fire greeted her. The crackling logs sent glowing embers into the chimney. Then she lay across the queen-sized, four poster bed on her chenille comforter.

In minutes she left the bed and locked the bedroom door with the rose carving. Next, she took off the leather belt around her waist and stripped off all her clothes. Then she grabbed a scissors from the nightstand and snipped through the top of the tape which bound the books to her back. To keep their castle and pay the jeweler's appraisal fee, the $8,750,000 from the gem sales would be due in a few days. Then, on the night of the autumnal equinox, they would walk into eternity.

She opened up the leather pouch and dumped out the five jewels. Next, she picked up the phone.

"Markem's Jewelry Store, please, on Oberdeen Drive," she said. Quickly she jotted down the address number and then fell asleep with her arm wrapped around her prizes.

Dina awakened to a cold room. The window had edged open and snow was blowing in from outside. She quickly lit the candle on her nightstand upon seeing the last flicker of light in the fireplace die.

The gems were cutting into her elbow, and she calmly picked them out. Carefully she wrapped them in her blue silk scarf and stuffed them and the two books beneath her mattress. Then she donned her robe and proceeded to close the window.

Suddenly she heard creaking floorboards. Then the brass doorknob began to turn She ran to the door and secured the top bar. Soon someone called out.

"No door can hold me back from what is rightly mine!" the sorceress Sazran said.

The wind blew in a big clump of wet snow, but Dina left the window ajar knowing it may be her escape route. The ice had frozen on the rim, and it stuck that way, allowing the chilly night breeze to continue seeping into her chamber. The thick, flannel robe felt warm over her cold, bumpy flesh.

"Open the door, Dina Darrendon, or I will break it down!"

Dina believed Devon had summoned the witch out from Joddar's encasement. Soon the pine scent of rosemary crept in from beneath the door. She looked down at her feet where long pointed fingernails reached under the door. They disappeared leaving deep marks imbedded in the wood.

Soon the door began to shake, the creature attempting to frighten Dina. She felt herself tremble violently. Then she bravely pounded on the door with her fists. When she stopped, it grew quiet until she heard the floorboards creak. Then silence prevailed once again.

"Dina. You okay?" She heard the reassuring voice of her husband and smelled food. "Let me in. I've secured our prisoners, and Sentra and Steven are keeping watch. Let me in!"

Dina quickly unlocked the door. She screamed in terror at the skeleton that stood before her. It held out both hands, and walked toward her. The smell of rotted flesh made her choke, and lumps of it fell to the floor.

Quickly Dina grabbed the books and the gems from beneath the mattress while keeping an eye on the ghoul. She grabbed her belt and tape and forced the window open just a little more so she could slip through to the icy ledge. She slid down the slope of the roof and flew fifty feet through the air. She then landed in a snow drift which cushioned her fall. Carefully she placed the gems back into the secret pouch and strapped on the belt. With the tape, she secured the books beneath her breasts.

In the distance, she could see the chimney smoking in the gardner's quarters. She ran like a rabbit and glanced back once and saw the ghoul staring at her from the tower room.

In a flurry, she burst into Dean's kitchen. Then something grabbed her from behind and lifted her into the air. The smell of rotted teeth made her gag as she turned to face her captor. Before her stood Big Barney, the castle beast. His long, thick tongue scraped over his few brown teeth as he began to speak. "I remember you. The fire. I'm sorry. I-"

"It's okay. I remember you saved my life in the quagmire when I was a young girl."

"Our Knotty the woodsman, he died. I bury him."

"Please, put me down," Dina said, pleading and feeling the beginnings of a tear.

Slowly he let Dina's feet touch the ground and let go of the back of her robe.

Dina looked through the window and saw the ghoul approaching. Then it turned into the beautiful sorceress, Sazran. Her long, dark hair flew like a silk sheet in the wind, and she ran toward the gardener's quarters. "She'll kill me. You must help me, Barney."

Dina hid inside the pantry and heard the two meet. She peeked through the tiny crack in the door, and saw Barney break the sorceress in half. She howled wickedly before he tore off her head and flung it into the flaming fireplace.

"God bless you, Barney," Dina said. She ran out to hug the beast. "She's gone forever, I hope."

His now furrowed face showed the wear of over a hundred years of existence. "Let's make a snowman, Dina. Come on."

Dina felt him pick her up, and they strolled out into the cold air. He plopped her on top of the snow-covered picnic table and began to roll a snowball. "I love you," he told Dina. "I waited for you to come back home."

Dina felt warmth from the beast who expressed his possessive nature. Then he sat down next to her and hugged her tightly about the waist.

"Ouch! Careful," Dina said. She hoped he would stay sweet, and no further aggression would arise.

"Dina!" She could hear Steven call her, and soon he was trudging towards her from behind the wood shed. "Thank God you are all right. Get away from her, beast" he said to Big Barney. Then he raised his rifle.

"He's gentle," Dina called. But her words were of no comfort to the beast.

"I go now," Big Barney said. He stood up and bounded off through the snow.

"No. Not there," Dina shouted. It was too late. The sound of cracking ice, like breaking china, destroyed the winter morning, and Barney plunged into the frigid lake. "We must save him." Dina ran to the supply shed and grabbed a rope. Quickly she tied one end to a monstrous oak tree.

"I'm sorry. It's all my fault," Steven said woefully. "He just looks so scary."

"Then help me save him."

"Hold on!" Steven called out to Big Barney, but Dina could see the three hundred pound man struggling. Each time he would grab onto the edge of the ice sheet, it would break off and he would plunge deeper into the castle's cold second lake. Gradually he turned a shade of blue like the September sky.

"Grab this rope," Steven said. He threw it with a large rock tied to the end of it just in reach of the big man. When he went to grab the lifeline, he screamed out in pain.

Clinging to the left side of his face was the head of Amanda.

"My God. So she reappears," Dina said. "We save the likes of Devon and Jack Tilver to protect our own, and Amanda returns again in evil form."

Her teeth clung desperately to his fleshy cheek, and he howled in agony. While trying to dislodge the creature, he sunk into the lake. Amanda, too, disappeared. Dina could see blood spew up and begin to freeze along with the water.

"I think we've lost him forever," Dina said. Soon his body bobbed up to the surface, and she could see the left cheek of his massive face was ripped away.

"He's dead. Let's get back inside," Steven said.

"But we can't be sure."

"Come on," Steven said. He grabbed Dina's arm and pulled her toward safety.

Sentra quietly guarded the two sick men while sitting near the doorway. Elkin sat by her feet staring intently at the prisoners. Her semi-automatic rifle was loaded and aimed directly at her silent captors. She propped her long legs upon a wooden stool and snuggled into the leather chair. Her golden braid hung down at her side and touched the floor. Feather batted it with her paw and then jumped up onto her lap and began to bathe. The Empress must have been delivered by the sailing service she knew by the presence of the cat.

"How are the men?" Dina asked. She walked over and patted Elkin. "Glad to see you've been delivered safely," she said to Feather, petting her grey fur.

Sentra, startled, nearly dropped the rifle, and Steven put a hand on her shoulder

"Where were you two?"

"Well, the sorceress had made an appearance disquised as Olgilvee," Dina said, wondering where the real Olgilvee was hiding. "Barney believed he destroyed the sorceress to protect me."

"Then we ran into Amanda at the lake," Steven said. "In evil possession, we think she killed Big Barney in the frigid water. Then, she disappeared."

"Oh no! What's next?" Sentra asked. "Are the jewels safe?"

"Yes, of course." Dina ran her fingers along the leather belt around her waist. Then she felt for the books which were stuck beneath her breasts. The tape was still stuck to her flesh, but only one book remained secured. "The Black Book of the Ghost Ship is here," she said, pulling it out. "But The Book of Eternity is gone. Oh, no," she said, realizing someone had snatched it. She slipped the remaining book back beneath her breasts, and the two men moaned and fell asleep again.

Back in her bedroom, Dina noticed the red light on the answering machine blinking. Quickly she checked the message. The creditors were waiting for their cash, and if they did not receive it, they would have their way with her property.

The next day, September, 6th, Dina and Elkin went over the bridges into town, leaving Steven and Sentra behind. She stopped the rental car at the jewelry shop in Ramea Island at a small, brown brick building near the center of town. Mr. Markem was an old friend of the family. He used to dine with her grandfather, and he had sold him many fine jewels. Dina informed him she had only about seventeen days to come up with the money. Many investors were contacted, and soon deals were made. Mr. Markem never saw such expensive, perfect gems, and of course, Dina did not let the stones out of her sight. But sometimes the hand is quicker than the eye. So to be certain they were not swapped, she marked each gem with an invisible code of ink that was only detectable under her blue light.

Elkin sniffed at the jeweler's thin legs, and then he sat back down by Dina's feet. Dina pulled the scarf tightly around her head, and the jeweler requested up to an hour of waiting before he could have the funds available from the sale, $8,750,000. He was pleased with the thought of his $250,000 broker's fee.

After the appraisal fee, Dina would be left with eight million five hundred thousand dollars. The castle would remain in her ownership until their earthly departure when the gates to eternity would open. Then she would not have to forfeit the property to unknown sources, for she would give the estate to the community for tourism revenue.

Suddenly she heard scratching at the door, and Elkin began to growl. She peered out the front store window and sat back down, the sight horrifying her. Four bear-headed dogs were standing there licking their chops. Behind them stood a red-haired fiendish looking man dangling a string of bloody intestines, a treat for his pets.

"Who's there?" Mr. Markem asked. He pushed aside his black, greasy hair and lit a fat cigar. Some ashes fell on his expensive, silk suit, making a small hole. "Damn it! Second jacket this week."

"Is there another way out of here?" Dina asked. She noticed there were no back doors or windows.

"Afraid of robbers? I have my gun right here." Mr. Markem pulled out a 44 magnum and laid it on the table. The scratching stopped, and then the phone rang. He picked it up. "Sounds good," he said into the receiver. He hung up the phone. "Dina, I already have access to the money." He stood up and carefully put the gems in a safe behind a mirror. Then he wrote out a check for $ 8,500,000 and handed it to her. "Pretty fast, huh?"

"Of course this is good," Dina said, staring at the check. Elkin snarled at the man.

"Now, Dina, I'm a loyal friend. Did I cheat your grandfather when he sold me the four million dollar diamond?" he said. His fat fingers fidgeted with his phone pad. Dina quickly glanced down at his desk and noticed Jack Tilver's boutique phone number standing out boldly in black ink.

Dina ripped up the check, pulled the 44 magnum on Mr. Markem, and ordered him to give back the gems.

"I have since learned what fools you Darrendons are. Here take them, bitch, but you won't get to keep them for long," he said angrily. Then he pulled the jewelry back out of the safe.

"We'll see about that," she said. "Elkin, guard this menace." The wolf stood at attention. Then she ordered Mr. Markem to lay face down on the floor. Quickly she checked the stones under her blue light, safely tucked them away in the leather belt, and then strapped them back to her body. "You'll make a nice morning snack, I'm sure, when they find you do not have my gems," she said. He, too, was part of Devon's pack. Within minutes, the beasts would burst into the room.

She threw up the carpet and found a trap door. "Come on, Elkin. Let's get." She closed the hatch just before the front door came crashing down.

Through the underground exit they crawled until Dina saw a streetlight. The steel jaws of the cold morning air nipped at her cheeks when they ran out into the snow. Elkin stayed by her side, the white flakes falling upon them. Her car was gone, and she needed to take cover.

Up ahead stood an old church where Dina and Elkin decided to take refuge. No one was inside, and she kneeled and prayed at the alter until the heated air warmed their bones.

They walked through the streets of the small town until she found another jeweler. He too was amazed at the rarity of the stones. Together Mr. Jerome and Dina walked to the bank where she cashed his check for $8,500,000. Same appraisal values and same broker's fee. He had made it all so easy. Immediately she desposited the amount into her account, and money orders were expressed mailed to the creditors.

She wept on Elkin's fur where she kneeled near the forest at the edge of town. Soon she knew Olgilvee would come looking for them. She felt different about life for the months that had passed had aged her. She learned that she could push herself to the point of mental and physical collapse. She had strengths she never imagined, and the trials had increased her stamina. Certainly she knew what a person had to endure to cling to life itself, for foul creatures of the earth could destroy a human's spirit. The good spirits, however, had brought Joddar and Neptune, to aid her and her comrades.

Suddenly in the distance she could hear the crunch of tree limbs. Then Elkin took off toward the sound. "Be careful, boy," she called out. Then she began to jog toward town when something raced out of the woods and galloped behind her. She saw the bear-headed dogs gain on her, and she raced toward a restaurant. Suddenly one pulled on her pant leg and dragged her down to the cold ground. The beast stood on top of her and tried to bit into the back of her neck.

Then Elkin bounded out from the woods where he had been following their scent. He jumped upon the beast and ripped into its side causing blood to pour out from a deep gash.

Dina ran into the restaurant, and Elkin raced after her. They sat alone at a small table. No other customers were in the place except for an old man who leaned on the bar sipping a beer. A stout, middle-aged waitress with fuzzy hair brought them some water and a basket of crackers. "What would you like?" she asked. The barlights above her blinked like flashing big eyes.

"Ginger ale."

Dina took out a quarter and went to the pay phone in the corner by the restroom. "Olgilvee," she said into the receiver. Dina could only hear a deep growling sound on the other end. "Hello! Hello!"

She felt her heart race upon realizing a horror. She jumped from her seat and left the restaurant with Elkin. Stopping at Ron's Rental, she borrowed some snow skis and hurried home.

Back at the castle she propped the skiis up near the back door by the garden. The September sky was full of early falling snow in the evening that drew nigh. The outside light flashed on, and the back door creaked open. Elkin picked up a scent and ran in toward the chair facing the fireplace. He sniffed and howled, and the chair began to rock. Soon the fireplace lit, and the flames lapped into the mouth of the chimney. Then the pine smell of rosemary filled the room. The floorboards upstairs began to creak, and next, the sound of chanting echoed throughout the castle.

Dina armed herself with a rifle and called out to Olgilvee. She turned toward the kitchen and saw the outline of her husband in the doorway. "Devon and Jack overpowered Sentra. She's fine, but they are free," he said. "We must kill them, then fight for entry into the vault to eternity."

"But what about the rocket?" Dina asked. She looked back out the window. Suddenly she heard an explosion and saw a brilliant flash of light in the night sky. Elkin howled. Then through the window in the kitchen, she could see a massive ship, from the direction of Gerten Town, lift off into the heavens. She knew inside herself Joddar had tried to intervene in the rockets accension. Perhaps he was still trying to find a way to destroy the craft.

"Good question." The voice Dina now heard, suddenly sounded different. She froze. "His crew is escaping toward the outer galaxy," he continued. Elkin growled. "You got your money, but I gave them the gems, the power source they neeeded to reach the super petro down in the earth's core."

Dina slowly turned her head from the window. Olgilvee had vanished, and in his place stood Mr. Jerome, the jeweler to whom she sold the gems. His black, curly hair stood straight up, and it glistened in the firelight. His bulky frame was intimidating, and he walked toward Dina. She aimed the rifle at his heart, and he stopped dead in his tracks. "We hope you got all the super petro you need, because you are not getting anymore. I'll see to that," Dina said. "Devon and Jack will never survive in these castle walls."

"Not as long as we are here!" a woman called out.

Dina was surprised to see Sentra standing next to her. Her gold braid hung down her back, and she steadily aimed a crossbow at Mr. Jerome's head.

"And what about the power source of dianid?" Sentra asked the evil jeweler. "Soon, when you've used up the super petro for the masters and to ship slave parts to other galaxies, you will use this nasty fuel and destroy immune systems on the planet earth. Death with no rhyme or reason will occur, and disease will run rampant, destroying the human race."

Sentra pulled back and let the arrow fly. It pierced Mr. Jerome's head between the eyes, and he fell backwards with a thud. Elkin rushed forward and sniffed the dead man. Crystals from the jolted chandelier above rained down on them. Then Olgilvee appeared dazed from the hall closet, and in moments, the dead jeweler vanished.

The chanting grew in intensity, and the ghouls marched upstairs in the hallway.

"Olgilvee, can you hear them," Dina called out. But he, too, vanished, and where he had stood, Big Barney's dirty footprints littered the floor. "He survived the lake incident, Sentra."

"Yes, and he has Steven," Sentra cried out. "Listen."

"Dina, help me," a male voice pleaded.

Dina could hear Steven call out her name, and she walked toward the sound into the pantry. A small elevator stood in the rear, and she pressed the tower button. She climbed in along with Elkin and Sentra. Then they rose three stories to the highest point of the castle, and the door opened quickly in the attic room. In the dimness, Dina saw wooden chests scattered across the floor, and even a closed closet lined part of one wall. But Big Barney's wardrobe was strewn everywhere, except for one orderly corner. Dina walked into it and lit the cinnamon candle on the floor. Its light revealed a five-foot-high wooden stand upon which stood a glass case.

"Ah, there is our lost book," Dina said, glancing at The Book of Eternity sitting inside. Elkin walked up and sniffed it.

"And its case is sealed tight," Sentra said, her efforts to open it, fruitless.

"Barney is keeping this safe for us," Dina believed. "God bless the brave soul. He was the one who took this book from me, probably when he hugged me about the waist before the lake incident."

She placed her hand upon the case and said a prayer. Then lightning flashed outside. Elkin wimpered.

"Help! Help me!" Steven cried again.

Elkin tore over to a rather large chest in the opposite corner of the room. Sentra followed and quickly opened it. From inside, Steven popped up with hands and feet, tied securely with rope. "Thank goodness you found me," he said wearily. "A man wrestled me down and put me in here. I think he was actually trying to protect me from the ghouls."

"Could it have been Dean the gardener?" Sentra asked. Elkin pawed at his ropes, and Dina untied him.

"Whoever it was snuck in behind me." Sentra began searching the room, and flung open the closet door.

"Oh God! Look!" Sentra shouted in disgust. Elkin began to whimper nervously.

Inside on a hanger, Dean the gardener dangled, like a sack of shoes, from the back of his jacket. The handle of a rake stuck out of his chest. His mouth was wide open as if death took him by surprise, and blood was still dripping from it. "Who or what could do such a thing?" Sentra slammed the door shut.

"My poor friend," Dina expressed sadly. "We have to quickly kill Devon and Jack. We will leave the safety of Amanda's soul to God. No more intimidation. They may use dianid. They must not escape into eternity, especially with those jewels. We must not allow the evil power to reign in the universe," Dina said. "For we want to present the gems to the high masters of good."

Suddenly the elevator door shut, and the car descended. Dina ordered Elkin to stand guard by it. In five minutes, the elevator ascended and opened. Immediately, Elkin howled and pawed the floor.

"What is it, boy?" Dina asked, fear in her voice. The car was empty or seemed to be empty until the room began to fill with a purple mist, and a headless figure stood before them. The skeleton's arms reached out, and scattered chunks of its rotted flesh fell to the floor. The stench was overpowering, and Dina covered her mouth with clothing. The others followed suit, except for Elkin who stood back and growled.

"You'll never win this game," Sazran the Sorceress said. Her head appeared and bones filled in with pink, smooth skin. Soon her fingernails grew into long points. "Eternity is ours. You don't even possess the gems anymore. You fools!"

Lightning cracked outside, and the castle walls shook. Elkin wimpered and ran into the corner after the sorceress jabbed at him with a finger. "We'll need to keep you occupied until well after midnight on the night of the autumnal equinox," the witch said. She heckled a hellish sound.

Suddenly she disappeared in a puff of purple mist, and the elevator door closed. Soon it opened again emitting four ghouls.

Two of them grabbed Sentra who squirmed and hollered. Quickly they tied her up and put her face down on the wooden floor. Dina and Steven stood frozen in their tracks, but Elkin lept at the ghouls. He was knocked hard to the ground.

"You okay, boy?" Dina called out to her wolf. He lay stunned from the blow.

"Shut up," a dark ghoul ordered. Then Dina and Steven were bound and placed face down on the floor next to Sentra.

"You'll all be in the reprocessing chambers very soon," the palest ghoul said. "You can help us drill for more super petro."

Dina felt lonely and cold upon the metal floor in the back of the delivery truck. She only hoped The Book of Eternity back in the attic would be theirs again soon. "Ouch," she hollered after another rut in the road sent her head crashing into the side. She heard Steven and Sentra moan and felt the vehicle barrel down the winding trail.

Dina knew their lives as humans would soon be over if she did not act. It was then that she noticed a screen between herself and the driver, a ghoulish-looking brute with sallow skin and black eyes. "Elkin. Gnaw my ropes," she whispered. Quickly the wolf went to work. Dina pulled the ropes away from her wrists and then from her feet. Then she came upon a plan unlike any plan she tried before. She would have to be brave, unthinking. She whispered her idea to Sentra and Steven.

"Be careful, Dina," Steven mumbled. Sentra only stared in speechless amazement.

"Hey you! Driver!" Dina pulled her shirt apart and pressed her breasts through the screen. Then she licked the metal wires with her tongue. "Want to have some fun?"

"How'd you get untied, woman?" The black-haired ghoulish thug turned to gaze at her ample breasts. Then he reached his fingers through the screen and fondled her eagerly. She licked his hand. Suddenly he pulled his shirt back and produced a gun.

"No! No!" she cried out. The van driver turned and fired tranquilizer darts into Elkin, Steven, and Sentra.

"Just putting them to sleep for awhile, bitch. Now let's get it on. I've been without for months."

Dina knew she had to get him out of the van so she could lock him outside and drive back to the castle. So she removed the underwire from her right bra cup and plunged it deeply into the driver's jugular vein. His thick hairy neck bled goo rapidly. He stopped the van, opened the door and stepped outside, falling like a lead weight into the snow. Quickly Dina jammed the screen back and crawled into the driver's seat. She slammed the driver's door to keep out the ghoul.

"Bitch!" he shouted. He stood up and pounded on the passenger's window. "You'll have to run me over if you want to steal the van," he shouted. He walked and stood in front of the hood. "You will never escape us."

She revved up the engine and drove over him, flattening the driver ghoul into pulp. She looked back and saw him dissolve into a pile of goo. Then she drove fast and furious to the castle with Steven, Sentra, and Elkin sleeping in the back of the van. She hoped Olgilvee was okay, and that the evil ones had not made off with The Book of Eternity.

Then suddenly up ahead in the road, she spied a large, dark figure. Dina tried to stop the van in time, hitting the brakes and swerving. But it was too late. They slid around and smashed into a massive tree that blocked the road. She got out and tried to move the heavy, wooden obstacle, but it would not budge. She pushed hard and then went into the back of the van to awaken Steven and Sentra for further strength.

"Quick! I'll explain later. Just help me now," she said to the groggy pair. Elkin, too, woke up, and he lapped at her face. Once outside she saw the path in front of the truck was cleared of the tree, and in the lonely road stood an old friend.

"Joddar!" Dina said, noticing his transportation, an old car, parked back in the trees. Elkin ran up to greet him.

"Thank God," Sentra said, flinging her arms towards the heavens.

"My God," Steven cried out. Then they all ran over and grabbed him by the arm. His orange eyes glowed underneath the thick strands of jet black hair.

"I told you I would fly to New Foundland to disable their rocket," Joddar said. "I tried to stop them, but this time I could not get past the guards to retrieve the energy power transformer. I did, however, swipe some fuses from the electrical system. I saw the rocket launch at Gerten Town, but God willing, it will not make its destination. Just missed you at the castle and headed back to one of their local reprocessing chambers hoping to rescue you."

"Good thinking, Joddar," Dina said. "A ghoul was taking us there, but we outsmarted him."

"Great! I'm so glad I found you," Joddar said. "We have to get back to the castle now, Dina, for time will skip ahead."

"How?" Dina asked. Elkin stared intently, his head cocked to one side.

"Tonight it is past midnight, Friday, September, 7th," Joddar said. "In the next few days before the autumnal equinox, if the lightning strikes in multiples of two and then hits the castle walls, time for those within shall slip days ahead quickly to September 23rd," he said, his eyes appearing to brighten.

"Let's go," Steven said, pulling Sentra to the van.

They all jumped in and headed home. Dina drove fast, rounded a curve, slid over a sheet of ice, and missed hitting an oncoming car. Then upon seeing a bullmoose cross her path, she slammed on the brakes swerving the van full circle on the road. The snow began falling faster, and soon they reached the castle gate. Two, four, and six flashes zigzagged from the sky and into the brick home. They hopped out and entered the front door.

The calendars all read the year 2001 on September 23rd, a sunday with a waxing crescent moon. Joddar was right. Time had slipped days ahead inside the estate. The fires were lit, and the chandeliers sparkled star-like in the living room. Suddenly the glass cases of lepodoptera shattered, and the butterflies came to life, flitting around freely. The rare species lit on tabletops, chairs, sofas, and unlit candles, leaving the room ablaze with color.

"Stay Elkin," Dina ordered. The wolf curiously watched a lavendar-colored Grenitz butterfly.

Easily Dina could see Big Barney's wet footprints in a path going up the stairs. "I wonder if he has Olgilvee in his lair," she said. She remembered the tower room.

Then the chanting sounded loudly, and skeletons came down the stairs, pieces of their rotting flesh dropping to the floor. When one reached the bottom step, Joddar wacked off its head with a swift kick. "You may be right about Olgilvee. Let's go," he shouted.

A heap of bones lay before them, the last skeleton sprawled in a heap at their feet. Quickly they scampered up the steps. Soon they were on the third floor at the tower room where Dina lit a wall sconce so they could see. The tiny, magenta carpeted space had no aroma of the one-time fire. In the corner lay Barney's winter jacket. Elkin pulled it across the room allowing its yards of material to uncover the trap door. Dina fiercely yanked open the hatch.

Then suddenly she lost her balance and hurtled backwards onto the carpeted floor. "You okay?" Olgilvee asked. He peeked out of the hole and held a hand out to Dina. She grabbed him and kissed him, and he pulled her inside. Then Joddar, Sentra, Elkin, and Steven descended into the opening.

"Barney brought me here. I've been waiting for you all," Olgilvee said in the semi-darkness.

Then Dina lit a match. The small table in front of her stood proudly with a crimson candle in the center. She lit it, and its flame shot into the air illuminating all but the far corner.

Carefully Dina walked into the darkness. In the matchlight she saw a giant of a man sitting at the small desk. He held Feather in his arms, and the weight of his body made the seat of the chair sag down, almost touching the floor. Joddar nodded a hello, and Barney stared intently at the orange-eyed alien.

"Big Barney, precious one. Thank God, you didn't drown in the icy lake. You did, however, take my book from my chest and put it in the castle attic." Dina said. She smiled while he turned to greet her. His flesh was pitted, and his tongue stuck out of the left corner of his mouth where his cheek had been ripped away. Its three eyes stared warmly at her, and the protruding fur from its large nose moved in and out with each breath. Elkin pawed at its feet as he shuffled them beneath the desk.

"Yes, look on the table. It's the The Book of Eternity I brought from the attic," he said. Dina could see the book lay open to a blank page.

"The map to the vault should appear here," Dina said. Suddenly a purple mist filled the room, and the singed sorceress materialized.

"Scat, cat," she said. Feather lept into the far corner, hissing. Elkin snarled at the sorceress. Then Sazran forced Big Barney to kneel down, and she ran her long, slender fingers across his bald head.

"Ha! I was resurrected from the flames to see that Jack and Devon receive the information about the map. Soon the invisible letters will appear," Sazran said. She gazed deeply upon Barney.

Dina looked at the blank page where words began to appear. "The time is soon," Dina said. Then she made out the first set of instructions to find the hidden vault. She began shaking, and the sorceress spoke first.

"The vault is at the bottom of Fern Lake," she read "A large opening is in the lakes's center, and it's lid must be twisted off to enter."

"But what will stop the waters from flowing in?" Sentra asked.

"Magic, bitch" cried out the sorceress. She thumped Barney on top of the head. Suddenly his skull split open, and gems fell to the floor. "Go ahead. Pick them up, Dina," the sorceress screeched. "After all, wasn't it you who traveled the great seas to find these beauties." Dina reached out to grab a brilliant ruby, but it singed her fingers.

"Ouch!" she hollered. She stuck the red tips into her mouth. Elkin whimpered and nuzzled her in her pain.

"Your cruelness runs deep," Joddar said. He jump kicked Sazran's face, missing it by inches.

"Ha! Ha!" laughed the sorceress. "Now I must tell Devon and Jack the secret of the pages I just read." She disappeared in a puff of purple smoke, and Steven tried to grab her throat.

Then Barney stood up and rubbed the now healed top of his head. Dina saw the gems had all turned into pieces of worthless gravel.

The map was nearly completed, Dina could see, and she ripped the page right out of the book and secured it beneath her breasts. Soon the trap door above slammed shut.

"There's no going back," Olgilvee said.

"You're right. The ghouls are everywhere in the castle," Dina said, "and worst of all, Devon and Jack are in charge again. However, we still have a chance to save ourselves."

"What do we do now?" Joddar asked. He turned toward Big Barney who began crouching down in the small room.

"Lake Fern is frozen." Dina said. "We can't crack the ice ourselves. It's too thick. And we'll surely die in the cold water. Tell me, Barney, do you know how we can get to the vault of eternity?"

Barney groaned loudly and beat his chest. "Jump on board!"

The broad-shouldered beast knelt down, and Dina noticed handles made of human flesh protruding on his back. Soon Joddar, holding Feather, Sentra, Olgilvee, Steven, Elkin, and she were straddling the beast and clinging to him. Big Barney's body grew hot and red like a heater.

Then he bowed his head and rammed a body-sized hole through the wall. With his teeth, he grabbed The Book of Eternity, and they galloped down an unknown hallway of the castle.

Soon Barney took them down over an edge. Next, they thumped hard on Fern Lake's icy surface and skidded across into its center.

"Hold tight," Barney said. Then he jumped up and came down with front arms aimed like a pick, making a hole in the ice. The quick dive to the bottom of the lake was frightening and cold, but his body heat kept them alive. Dina's entire life flashed before her eyes until Barney opened the vault lid. Quickly they entered the underground chamber.

Dina gasped for air, and her flesh felt relief from the frigid water. They all hopped off Barney's back, and Steven and Sentra rubbed Olgilvee's near frozen arms. Then Elkin lapped at his wet fur, and Joddar with Feather, wandered off down a corridor. Soon the scent of lilacs and lavender filled the air, and they heard someone calling out to Dina.

"Dina. Come this way. It's Grandfather." She stood up and started running toward a white mist with Elkin following closely.

"No! Don't go," Olgilvee shouted. Suddenly the white mist turned into a jagged lightning bolt, scaring Dina and the wolf back to their friends. Hot sparks flew off of it, and it shimmied into a wall before them, disappearing as quickly as it had appeared.

"Devon's tricks!" Steven shouted in disgust. "Beware!"

"But where is the vault to eternity? And Barney's gone," Dina said. She called to him and he answered, but he sounded very far away. "He's in there," she said, pointing to a crevice in the rocky walls.

"Might be a trap," Steven warned. But suddenly more lightening bolts pierced the room they were in, forcing them into the crevice Barney had entered. Dina quickly found it led to a room with a throne where Devon sat with his bear-dogs on either side. Right behind him stood a large vault with a silver gate. Elkin pointed his nose to the heavens and howled greatly.

"The vault to eternity," Dina whispered to Olgilvee. Even Barney was right inside. And after they all entered, the crack sealed shut behind them.

"We got you now," Devon said with sadistic pleasure. He rose, and his brilliant green eyes glared coldly at Dina. "Ha! Ha! I have everything I need. The gems are mine, and the map route to the vault, thanks to Sazran, brought me here. Even my rocket was launched. And thanks to you, I was able to use the power source from the gems to penetrate the largest vein of super petro known to exist in the Milky Way Galaxy. The great masters pay greatly for such fuel, all of which we'll sell to them. And more alien body parts are being shipped in for the reprocessing plant. Soon every one of you will become my slave."

"But what of the dianid?" Dina asked.

"Yes," Devon said, his voice dropping to a hush. "It will be such a pity to resort to its use for fuel. But once we walk through the vault of eternity, what else can we use to pull our final flight to the great masters? It's a shame the world's people shall die of incurable diseases."

"You are evil, and you shall not conquer," Dina shouted.

"Amen to that," Steven said. Barney grunted.

"Kill him, Elkin," Olgilvee ordered. "He has no control over our Amanda now, no control over the lives of earth's people."

"Yes. No more intimidation," Sentra said. Elkin lunged at Devon's throat, but soon the bear-dogs and the guards were upon the wolf. They tied him up in a small bundle and left him on the floor.

"Barney! Do something." Dina stroked the beast's hairy arm, and he bent down and pressed a kiss upon her cheek. "They must die," she whispered into his tufted ear. Then Jack entered the room, and Dina looked at her watch. In one hour it would be one a.m. in the year two thousand and one on September 23rd, the autumnal equinox. The silver gate before them would soon fling open widely and welcome them.

"You can't have your way," Jack shouted. He pointed at Dina, Olgilvee, Steven, and Sentra. Barney huddled around them.

"Ah, yes we shall conquer," Dina said. "For we learned much from our long journey. We teased death, and it nearly took us. We met our enemy eye to eye and truimphed. We possess great bravery and warrior skills we never knew existed. The same people we met and fought for died painfully, but never will they be forgotten. Supernatural powers too, both good and bad, had their way with us. But with the help of our good spirits and comrades, including our part human friend, Joddar, and the whale, Neptune, we triumphed over the bad force.

And now, after all the hunting and fighting and winning," Dina continued, "we are not about to give up the final trophy. Beyond the gate awaits Grandfather, Mother, Grandmother, all the family we have lost on our journey. Perhaps even Amanda will make it within the gates."

"Yes," Sentra joined in. "The universe will be ours to rule and bring goodness into its vast domain. No, not now at the final hour will we give up."

Quietly Dina whispered to Olgilvee, Steven, and Sentra to stand guard with Barney, and then she slid into the darkness down the corridor where Joddar and Feather were hiding. "We must find a way to overcome the slaves and soldiers in the chamber," she said to Joddar, his orange eyes glowing.

"Yes. Let's summon the sorceress," he said.

Dina and Joddar sat down, and she lit a small candle she found on the floor. They clasped hands and called to Sazran. "Out of darkness come to us. We wait to meet you, the evil one," they repeated, first Joddar and then Dina.

Soon the purple mist, pine-scented with rosemary, filled the space above the candle flame, and the great caped skeleton of Sazran appeared. Her feted odor of rotted flesh puked the air making Dina gag and Feather retreat behind a rock. In the outer room, she could see Olgilvee, Steven, Sentra, and Barney guarding the entrance to the corridor. Devon was busy talking with Jack and his soldiers, and time was ticking away. The silver vault gate stood still, waiting to rise to the occasion.

Soon Sazran began to speak, and a rotted tooth fell from her mouth onto Dina's lap. Quickly Joddar kicked the skeleton's head off, and it rolled into the wall. The squeeling of pigs came from her throat, and the decapitated body danced in its purple cape. But soon the cape was alive with flames from Dina who held the candle to it. Then Joddar thrust a stick into the open mouth of the skeleton head, and it bit down hard. He flung the skull into the burning heap of cape and bones, and Dina cried out.

"Never return as evil again. Your wicked ways are dead forever!"

She knew the sorceress was attempting to become whole for her once burned head reappeared in full form, but the entire body was just a pile of ashes.

"I want to be good again, Dina," her voice sounded sweetly. "I want to be back into my family, the Darrendons."

"Once you vowed to return to goodness," Dina cried out. "Then return to full form and help save us Darrendons. Clear our way to the gate to eternity." Joddar and Dina watched Sazran grow into a good beauty.

"I will defend thee," she hollered. Then she quickly found a blade shoved beneath a rock. It glistened on its razor sharp side. Soon Joddar ordered Dina to whimper until they heard the howling bear-dog talk. In minutes, the beasts came sniffing around the corner. Quietly Sazran sliced off their heads one by one. Blood grew three inches deep, and it spilled like water from their wounds upon the concrete floor. But more started seeping in from the rocks, and Dina was now waist deep in the sticky flood. Feather, who had climbed high upon a rock, was hissing, back arched. Then they trudged back down the corridor into the room with the gate to eternity.

Soldiers cried out, and Devon shouted, "Man the canoes!" Soon boats were brought forth in the blood that rose deeper. Sentra swipped one of the canoes and rescued Joddar, Dina, and Feather. Steven, Olgilvee, Big Barney, and Elkin, now free, had their own canoe, and they were battling many soldiers. Quickly Joddar tipped an enemy's canoe over, spilling three of its crew into the blood lake. Sazran pressed their heads into the sticky fluid until they drowned.

Dina dove into the lake, blade in hand, and came up behind Devon's canoe. She quickly cut off his golden braid and jabbed him in the gut. He turned and glared at her and grabbed the hole in his stomach. Then Sazran bit his head off and swallowed it whole. Soon Jack swam towards Dina with his knife and cut a small streak in her forehead. Then she slashed out quickly with her blade nearly cutting his head off. His body began to sink. Then Sazran held him down until he drowned in the red lake.

Suddenly a grating sound was heard, and the gate to eternity slowly opened. The blood turned clear and disappeared into a land of whiteness where brilliant-colored flowers and ivy covered the landscape. "Behold such beauty," Olgilvee cried out. Their canoes were now on dry land, and they all climbed out. A tall, wooden book case stood before them containing The Black Book of the Ghost Ship and The Book of Eternity. Each were embossed in gold.

Then Dina spied a large globe upon a brass table. She grabbed her dragon charm and looked into the sphere. She could see Devon's rocket explode and burn and his soldiers disolve into flames. Even Jack Tilver, his skeleton father Oliver, and the hag burned in a blaze of heat. Then a vision of a ship appeared in the globe.

"The Spaniards of the Ghost Ship are at peace now. They have their Gretchen, the crew, and another set of jewels to keep them happy. Maybe brothers Devon and Oliver will be returned to them in goodly form," Grandfather said. He appeared with outstretched arms.

"And Mitch the Magnificent?" Dina asked, running towards him.

"He is dead forever, my granddaughter."

"The power of the gems is in the hands of God," Joddar said, his gold tooth glistening. Dina grabbed her grandfather and hugged him. Then her precious mother and grandmother walked out to embrace her, too. Even Amanda stood there in a flowing white robe, smiling greatly. Then Grandfather presented Dina with the bag of gems and spoke.

"Our Sazran is good again. It was she who confiscated these gems from Devon's rocket before it exploded. Her last supernatural powers were used to help her own kind. She is with the good masters now. And you, Dina, are to present the gems to them," he said.

Soon a rocket appeared behind a white mist, and they all entered. Expertly the alien, Joddar, jetted them off, steering the spacecraft toward a strong gravitational force. "They're waiting for your arrival, Dina. Mission complete. The good shall inherit greatness," Grandfather said. Mother and Grandmother nodded in agreement. Then Big Barney patted Elkin who howled into the vastness of space.

They had all been forever changed by the experience Dina knew. They zoomed toward the eerie and spiritual symphonic sounds of the black hole in the center of the Milky Way Galaxy. It would take them through a passageway called wormhole that connected to another blackhole into another universe. And in this other universe, Andromeda X Galaxy awaited them.

"Look straight ahead," Dina called out in awe.

She could clearly see Christ with his arms outstretched to greet them.

"Our Lord appears amidst the colorful molecular gas clouds. HOME AT LAST," she voiced gleefully.

Elkin, Feather, and friends surveyed the outer space for the strong x-ray source at the event horizon.

In the Beginning God created the
heaven and the earth.

Genesis 1:1

KJV

ABOUT THE AUTHOR

Mary Graves, an Idealist and Gemini, loves life and spiritual knowledge. Creative writing has been her bliss for many moons. Night of the Autumnal Equinox is her first novel.

With a second novel awaiting her return and a third novel in the works, she continues to exercise her right-brain talents. Her handcrafted poetry book, Ethereal Wanderings, fascinated many fans. She prays to Jesus Christ daily for guidance and harmony in this chaotic world.

www.ingramcontent.com/pod-product-compliance
Lightning Source LLC
LaVergne TN
LVHW061538070526
838199LV00077B/6827